DIGGING

TWO

GRAVES

By

Linda Rainier

Copyright

This is a work of fiction. Names, characters, places, and incidents either are the product of the author's imagination or are used fictitiously. Any resemblance to actual persons, living or dead, events, or locales is entirely coincidental.

First paperback edition January 2021

Cover Photography by Ken Irons

ISBN: 978-0-9600229-4-6 (Paperback)
ISBN: 978-0-9600229-3-9 (Hard Bound)

ISBN: 978-0-9600229-5-3 (EBook)

Table of Contents

Chapter 1

Before you embark on a journey of revenge, dig two graves~ Confucius

A warm glow of fading sunlight glimmers in deep-red hues as it stretches across the length of Emma's floor. The late-winter air is still crisp despite the old radiator vents struggling to heat her small apartment. Freezing rain layers the outside world, causing street lights to dance and twinkle on the road and car windows below. Emma can feel the cold seeping through the thin pane of glass as she clasps her arms against the cold. The cool feel of her copper armbands is a constant reminder of all they have been through.

A soft beeping draws her attention away from both the scene outside and her pointless thoughts. Striding over she presses the button to silence the alarm and turn off the oven. With a pair of oven mitts, she removes the baking dish from the oven, and the aromatic fragrance of roasted chicken and fennel tickles her nose. As the dish cools, she sets a plate and utensils on the table.

Three weeks after their encounter with Thanatos, her physical wounds have healed, yet she still has a lingering unsettled feeling. The god of death remains locked in the darkest hole in Tartarus, along with the Gyges that aided him. His attempt to awaken the powers of the Fury was successful, but he failed to resurrect the original three and control them.

Both Mei Li and Olivia continue about their business as though nothing has changed. Each time she brings up the subjects of her and David or the future, the two women busily brush the topic aside. After all she has endured, part of her still hopes for a chance to live once again.

A strange restlessness pulses inside her, but she shakes it off. Walking to the refrigerator, Emma pours water into her glass and the ice swirls and clinks in the silence.

The glass slips from her hand, shattering on the floor, and a wrenching pain tears at her insides. Doubling over, she gasps for breath

as an itching distress slithers under her skin.
Every thought and impulse screeches at her to
leave. With shaking arms Emma pulls on a
heavy sweatshirt and steps out into her
hallway.

The corridor is empty save for Mrs. Van
Buren, who lives in the last apartment down
the hall. Carrying a worn shopping bag, she
smiles softly as she shuffles past Emma. Her
shoes squeak delicately, and a thin layer of
moisture clings to her Burberry coat.

Emma quickly travels the length of the hall
and punches the button on the elevator. A
ghastly layer of ants seems to scurry along her
skin; the sensation, clogs the air in her throat.
Inhaling a thick breath, she fights the urge to
claw at her arms and face. The white-painted
doors of the elevator open and Emma pushes
inside.

She leans against the metal wall and struggles
to regain her senses, pitted against the rising
tide of panic. All around her, the polished
nickel walls reflect her blurry and distorted
image. Mercifully, the discomfort begins to
fade, but the needling urge to press forward is
still there and in that moment, she realizes she

has no idea where she needs to go. The coffin-like walls now feel as though they are squeezing in from all sides, and a thin bead of sweat trickles down her back. Her heart thunders in her chest as she inhales the seemingly inadequate air.

As desperation and terror wash through her, she touches the nearest wall, opening a portal. The destination is unknown yet her every instinct is screaming to escape. The wall ripples like a fluid mass of molten metal, though Emma knows there is no danger from the heat. Beyond the mirrored surface, the darkened tunnel awaits and the inky blackness engulfs her as she leaps into the passage. Once through the doorway, the air is stagnant and heavy, but this is a sensation she's familiar with. Just outside her reach are the barriers holding this space, guiding her towards her destination.

Emma stumbles out of the portal and the warm night air blankets her skin. A full moon peeks through the densely layered canopy of trees overhead as lush moss and grass cushion her feet. This place is far from her apartment back in Boston. It is either somewhere on the other side of the planet or someplace in between worlds.

A low whistle draws her eye to a cluster of bushes. Aidan's form slips effortlessly out from the darkness of shadows. His thickly curved black horns catch the dim moonlight. Emma's hammering heart steadies as she cautiously approaches him. Advancing forward the discomfort of her insides begins to wane with each shaky step.

"What is going on, Aidan?" she asks, scanning the woods around them.

"I had to summon you. I need your help." His tone is sharp, and a nervous energy swirls around him. "Olivia is here as well. Come with me and I'll explain along the way." He beckons her to follow and his pace quickens. Emma is forced to jog several steps to catch up with him.

"Where is Olivia?" Emma scans the tree line but can't make out anything.

"She rushed ahead. I tried to make her wait, but she didn't want to."

"You let her go off on her own?" Emma snaps through clenched teeth.

"Excuse me, but I've seen that woman fight. I'm not getting bludgeoned to death because you might be worried." Gaping at him, Emma struggles to find fault in his logic. Seemingly satisfied, Aidan turns with a nod, heading briskly into the woods. For several seconds they trot along in silence. The moss-topped ground gives under her feet as thick branches claw at her cheeks and clothes. The densely overgrown thicket seems so isolated from man.

"Do you mind telling me something? Your calling me here–is that what caused the pain?" Emma asks as she shoos away a buzzing gnat.

"I'm sorry. I didn't realize it would cause discomfort," he states sheepishly. "If I had more time, I would have found another way of contacting you."

"How do you even know how to do that?" Emma's mind races, never rationalizing that it could be possible for someone to know how.

"My family is very old. Our lineage dates back to nearly the beginning of time and some of the oral traditions are still maintained. But that is of no importance right now. My friend Marshall is a centaur and has been placed under arrest in a mock trial. They are accusing him of murder and treason, but he is innocent." Aidan holds a thick branch aside, letting Emma by.

"Tell me what happened."

"The centaurs are nearly as old as the satyrs. It is said that our family lines are closely tied to one another. Marshall and I have been friends since we were children, but he is more like a brother to me. Even as we went on separate paths, we maintained an unbreakable bond. I entered the succession to be the head of my family; Marshall became a steward to the Binici clan. Their two families had decided to merge through marriage and the Binici's eldest son, Philip, would marry Marshall's sister, Rosalind. As an act of good faith, Marshall would act as Philip's right hand and steward for the two years leading up to the ceremony."

"How did Marshall feel about this arrangement?" Emma asks, sucking in deep breaths as she fights to keep up.

"Philip was a good man and Marshall trusted that he would be a good husband to Rosalind. Each side of the family insisted that everything was in accordance with a very traditional wedding. It even included the 'taking' of the bride."

"What do you mean taking?" Emma's gaze narrows as she studies him.

"It is now only a symbolic gesture, but the roots of the practice date back millennia. The groom and his best man will sneak the bride away the night before the wedding. In her place the groom's family would leave a great many gifts."

"Rosalind was a participant?" Emma arches her brow.

"Yes. It was actually Rosalind who suggested their union in the first place. But when Marshall, Phillip and Phillip's brother, Craven, arrived to collect the bride they were ambushed with only Marshall and Craven surviving. Now Craven says Marshall killed them both."

In the far distance she can just make out the faint glow of a campfire. As Emma approaches, a loud argument slashes through the silent forest. Just outside the circumference of fire glow, Aidan slows their pace and Emma observes from the darkness.

About twenty or so centaurs encircle a large fire pit; its flames dance and roar as embers skitter up into the night sky. Their gaze is focused on some kind of happenings in the center. As they shift and move, Emma sees Marshall kneeling and shackled. Another massive centaur paces angrily around the first, pointing a meaty finger as his tail flicks rapidly back and forth.

"These are all lies." The chained man shrieks in anger; his metal shackles clank loudly as he struggles. The crowd, in a near frenzy, breaks into an uproar of screams and bellows.

Another part of the crowd breaks and Emma spies a familiar face; Olivia watches from inside the circle. Her features are stern as she observes the scene playing out before her.

The thunderous dispute covers any sounds as Emma strides slowly into the circle, followed by Aidan. She walks through the ring of men and their collective voices die down to an eerie silence. Her breath hitches as every eye turns, regarding her with suspicion. Emma's heart thunders wildly in her chest as the subtle chirping of crickets fills the night around them. Olivia's gaze settles over her and a potent hum of energy dances along her skin.

"Emma, my sister; we are glad you have joined us. The centaurs have asked that we oversee their dispute." Olivia nods to Emma, beckoning her to stand at her side. She advances gingerly, striding warily across the soft sand around the bonfire.

"We have not asked you here," snarls the monstrous centaur standing before them. "We centaurs handle our own affairs; we neither want nor need your meddling." A solid mane of jet-black hair falls down his back in a tightly woven braid. His woven tresses swoosh wildly with his exaggerated movements, whipping the dark pelt of his lower horse half. Thick bands of dark tattoos mark his muscular upper body. The vast light

being thrown from the fire obscures a clear
view of many of the men standing on the
perimeter. Yet Emma can distinguish some of
the varying hues of the centaurs. From pinto
pattern to palomino, the lustrous horsehide
shines by the firelight. Five centaurs stand
within the circle but apart from the remaining
crowd. Heavy black robes are draped from
their shoulders and cascade down their backs.
Their demeanor and bearing are that of the
quintessential judges, observing everything
that is said around them.

"We were called here, were we not?" Olivia
asks calmly, her steady gaze moving
throughout the crowd.

"Our goal in being here is to find truth, is it
not, Craven?" a silver-haired centaur asks the
larger, hulking one. His wise eyes return to
study Emma and Olivia. "My name is
Demetrius. I am curious as to why you believe
you are needed here?"

"Our duty is to seek justice for others. It is an
obligation that cannot be subverted," Emma
explains formally as she arches an eyebrow at
them.

"Being summoned by the satyr provides you with no authority here. He is not one of us," Craven spits as he throws out his arm, pointing sharply at Aidan. Emma glances over the fire and spots him standing next to the kneeling centaur.

"Nevertheless, we have been summoned and we are now honor-bound to see that fairness is served. Even if we wanted, we cannot leave until we are released from our obligation, and primordial law places you under the jurisdiction of the Fury." Olivia studies the crowd with an unwavering gaze. Emma's insides knot and turn as she senses the vast range of emotion rolling off of the crowd; the underlying tension only feeds into her anxiety. Olivia's shortly cropped platinum hair blazes a warm-red glow from the fire, and she appears as composed as ever.

Craven glares at them with cold, inhuman eyes. A small muscle ticks rhythmically in his neck, as his hooves stomp the ground restlessly. "Very well. But understand this; I strongly object to your kind being here. And if it comes to light that an undue bias sways your judgment falsely, I will hold the Fury personally responsible.”

The crowd snorts and grunts in approval as Craven circles the fire until he stands before them again. His chest puffs as he feeds off of the dangerous energy of the mob surrounding them.

“Your objections are duly noted.” The corners of Olivia’s mouth lift faintly; her gaze never leaves Craven. “Shall we begin?” she asks properly. Craven studies the group silently for several seconds before turning to face the chained centaur.

“Marshall, you stand as charged. A tribunal of your clansmen is here to judge your guilt. You betrayed your clan; you murdered your chieftain and his bride. How do you answer to these charges?” Craven’s voice booms through the spacious night.

“I am being falsely accused,” Marshall shouts through gritted teeth. His chestnut-hued hair and chest are matted with dried blood and earth. A thin stream of blood flows from a circular wound on his shoulder. Emma notes the fresh cuts and bruises that actively seep

and mar his skin. Less noticeable are several
deep-brown bruises that seem several days
old.

"How can you dispute the eyewitness
account?" Craven rebuts coldly. The malice in
his bearing sets Emma's senses racing. A
steady hum of impending violence beats
throughout the crowd of men.

"Your lies alone place the guilt on me. You
would have my brethren believe that I did
these things in order to hide the fact that it
was you–you who killed Philip and his bride."
Marshall fights as he stares pointedly at the
men holding him. A cut on his lip has
reopened, dribbling fresh blood down his
chin.

"Come now, Marshall. Why would I kill my
own brother? Why would I kill his betrothed,
Rosalind? Yet it is well known that you have
stood against Philip on many occasions."
Craven gestures to the group of men for
concurrence as a few nod and voice approval.
"None amongst us was more loyal and
devoted to Philip than I. My duty and place
have always been at his right side." Craven

stares down at Marshall, a tiny smirk gracing his cruel features as he basks in the moment.

"This clan is my family; Philip was my blood, and I loved Rosalind–she was my sister. You killed him to take everything that was his. He was no longer blinded to your treachery, and he chose me as his second, not you. When I disagreed with Philip, I brought my concerns before him. I did not slither within the shadows as you do." Marshall screams as he strains against his bonds, trying to stand but held firmly to the ground. "Every man who stands here knows me. They know I would gladly give my life for my clan."

Marshall cranes his neck, studying each of the men watching. "You all know me. I have failed in my duty to protect Philip and Rosalind, but I didn't betray them. I didn't kill them." The soul-wrenching plea in his tone crushes Emma's soul as she watches him implores them for his life and his honor.

"Enough." Craven's voice booms. "The clan deserves justice, and we demand a judgment." His stare settles on the five judges.

The judges glance between themselves. Demetrius stands at the end, his hooves thumping the earth softly as he moves. "Such serious claims require some contemplation. We should retire for the night. In the morn, with clearer eyes, we will see the truth of it." The tribunal and crowd begin to recede as several centaurs gather up Marshall to lead him away.

"No," Craven roars to the throngs and all heads turn to face him. Trotting towards Marshall, he wrestles the lead of the restraints from the guards. With a forceful yank, Marshall staggers to the ground. "Philip was our chieftain. He was loved and honored by all of us. Above this, he was my brother. Retribution for his murder will not be forestalled. The clan will judge this murdering pig this evening, or I will exact vengeance myself." Craven's chest heaves solidly as he clasps the chains with white-knuckled fists.

"Brother Craven, it is unwise to make such decisions rashly. What will one more evening gain or lose us?" Demetrius asks. Emma notes that the ivory Centaur's soothing tone has little effect on Craven.

"Perhaps we could help?" Emma steadies her voice as the crowd of men turn their equine eyes to her.

"We do not need your help!" Craven bellows, spittle frothing at his mouth.

"It seems that you do," Emma states calmly. She looks past Craven to the five judges. "There has been a grievous crime committed and you wish to make an appropriate judgment. I suggest that we judge Marshall and show to all what has happened. From there you will have all that is needed to make a fair judgment."

"They are allied with the satyr. How can we trust these witches? They will lie on his behalf," Craven shouts as he yanks again on the lead holding Marshall.

"Our purpose is simply to seek justice, and I do not have the ability to augment the visions during a judgment. Nothing I can say will force you to trust me; that is your decision to make." Emma meets the gaze of each adjudicator, measuring her words carefully.

"The satyr helped them. We cannot know that their so-called 'visions' will be true." Craven glowers at them in disgust.

"Magistrates, bear in mind that we aided the satyr first; his actions following were only a repayment for a previous kindness." Olivia steps forward, closing the distance between herself and Craven. "Your options are simple: Allow us to do our duty and come to a just resolution, or ponder the events and never really know if your decision was the correct one." Olivia crosses her arms and she patiently studies the judges.

"Very well. Show us." Demetrius whispers as the judges move back into the circle.

"This is an outrage," Craven barks, jerking Marshall to his feet.

"Silence, Craven." Demetrius holds up a hand to still the enraged centaur. "We will hear what they have to say; the end judgment is still ours to make." Craven's face is shadowed in darkness, but he holds his tongue. All eyes once again shift to Emma and Olivia.

"Show them, Emma." Olivia's voice rings out over the crowd and Emma's stomach wriggles. Never before had she tried to show others the visions of judgment; she doesn't even know if it is possible. "As Emma speaks, look deeply into the flames," Olivia commands as she gestures for Emma to approach. The crowd focuses intently on the dancing fire.

"I know you will pretend to judge Marshall so you can change the events they see." Craven's form pulses a force of pure loathing as he stares down at Emma.

"I won't be judging Marshall. I'll be judging you, and the evidence of the crime will come directly from you." Emma extends her hand to Craven. Arching her eyebrow, she applies her most pleasant, trustworthy smile. "Now, if you would be so kind, please take my hand." Dumbfounded, Craven's gaze flashes between Emma's hand and the judges. Finally, he squares his broad shoulders and clasps Emma's hand in a crushing grip. Olivia's hand settles on Emma's shoulder as the steady thrum of power starts to pulse from Olivia and into her, intermingling with her own energy. From her peripheral vision Emma watches Olivia's free hand rising, pointing to the raging bonfire.

"Look into the flames," Olivia calls out. "It is here that you will see what lies in this man's heart." The bright orange and yellow flames dance madly as a viscous black smoke bellows from the base of the fire. When the onyx vapor intermingles with the inferno, the flames grow dim, taking on an eerie darkness.

Emma reaches outward, pushing her mind through the concrete barrier of Craven's mind. There is a constant pressure as his will battles hers. Slowly, she peels away the layers of his defense and a murky image develops in her mind and is mirrored against the dark fog of the fire.

Tree branches part as Philip leads them through the brush path. Marshall walks alongside him as the two talk quietly. The soft clop of the fatted calf's steps echo as it is pulled along behind them. They enter a clearing, and nestled along a copse of trees is a collection of several stone farmhouses. A simple horse fence surrounds the structures, and the stark-white moon glow cascades over small food plots in front of the houses. Coming around to the main house they quietly tie off the calf at a hitching rail by the door.

The house is a simple stone-carved dwelling but is proportionately larger to accommodate the inhabitants. Marshall gently raps on the front door. Within seconds it is answered by a striking young woman. Her colorings are much the same as Marshall's. She peers out cautiously at first with large doe eyes, but when she spies Philip she smiles warmly, rushing outside to him. She drops a small shoulder bag on the ground and takes Philip's extended hands.

"Everything is prepared," Philip whispers as he kisses her forehead softly.

"Good. My family will be at the glade come morning to witness the ceremony. By this time tomorrow you and I shall be husband and wife." Wrapping her arms around him, she nuzzles his chest. Philip reaches down to collect her bag. Their gazes never part from each other.

"Before we go, I'd like to be the first to congratulate the two of you. Your happiness warms my heart and I have a special gift I'd like to give you both," Craven announces as he trots towards them.

Without pause Craven grabs a leather satchel that is tied by his withers. As he opens and reaches into the bag an uncharacteristic smirk lifts at his lips. With lightning speed his arm flies up and it seems they have no time to react when they see the gun. Craven fires the unfamiliar weapon blindly; Philip grabs Rosalind, trying to shield her as they dart for the door. Several shots explode through his back, but he pushes Rosalind forward towards the door. Marshall lies unconscious as two rounds find their mark, hitting Rosalind and sending her crashing to the ground. She lands just across the threshold.

Calmly, Craven approaches the couple and shoots them both two more times. Standing over Marshall, he measures his aim, pulls the trigger and is met with only an empty click.

Craven howls as he rips his mind from Emma's intrusion. He pushes away, sending her stumbling backward. Stomping forward, he rears up as if to trample her. Emma scurries and barely avoids his crashing hooves as thick puffs of dirt fly up around her.

"Lies. All of it is lies." Several centaurs rush forward, grabbing and subduing Craven's arms. "I told you these women could not be trusted. They made you see things that are not true." He struggles wildly against the men holding him.

"No, we believe they have shown us the truth." Demetrius studies Craven coldly. "Craven Binici, you have been found guilty of the murders of Philip and Rosalind. We will determine a suitable punishment for such a crime." With a nod, Craven is hauled off through the woods, his howls echoing through the night sky. The crowd watches the scene, and finally Demetrius turns back to them. "We thank you for your assistance in this unpleasant matter." With no other words the judges turn around, walking from the firelight. The host of centaurs quickly disperses, melting into the darkened brush.

Emma and Olivia find Aidan kneeling next to Marshall. With a small key he releases the shackles and pulls the wounded centaur up.

Aidan quietly reassures the man, then stands before them.

"Thank you for this." Aidan's tone is genuine as he pulls something small from his front pocket. Extending his arm, he offers a small copper coin. It's crudely molded and heavily tarnished; three serpents are entwined on its surface.

"What is this?" Emma cautiously studies the metal in his hand.

"It is the payment for justice. As you receive this coin it severs the bond of my calling. You both will be able to go." Reaching up slowly Emma takes the coin from Aidan. The metal feels warm in her hand, and as she closes her fingers around it a soothing pulse flows through her. Opening her fingers to inspect the coin again, she is surprised to see that it has disappeared. Aidan turns back to Marshall, helping him stand.

"Hey Aidan," Olivia calls out, and he turns to face her. "If you are a smart man, you'll keep the method of calling us to yourself." Aidan nods as he and Marshall walk away.

For several seconds Emma studies her empty palm and Olivia watches the dying fire. The night air feels cooler than before.

"I guess we are on our own to get out of here," Olivia huffs as she walks up to Emma.

"It is sad that Craven's desire for power would lead him to kill. Blessings in life can be so far and few between. He threw away all that really mattered for something so superficial," Emma muses quietly, feeling a profound sympathy for Philip, Rosalind, and their needless deaths.

"It's like Romeo and Juliet. Unfortunately, it is not an uncommon occurrence." Olivia speaks coolly as she studies the landscape.

"I would like to believe that it is part of our duty to make the world a better place, but too often it seems we are too late to save anyone." A shiver runs through Emma as she mulls over their purpose.

"We are unfortunately at the tail end of the process. We are brought in only after the crime is committed. Hopefully, our presence can deter someone. Perhaps that is our true purpose." Olivia gestures towards a path leading into the woods; a high mountain range looms in the distance.

"So, what does that mean for us?" Emma asks.

"What do you mean?" Olivia responds over her shoulder.

"I mean that if it is our destiny to be forever trapped in a cesspool of violence and evil, is there any chance for humanity or us to find happiness?"

They approach the sheer cliff wall of the abutting mountain. Moonlight streams into the opening, highlighting small bushes and shrubs. Olivia gently swipes her hands over the cool stone surface. The stone material shifts and sways, becoming a swirling liquid portal.

"The happiness and safety of humanity is what we work toward. As for us, I think that ship sailed a long time ago." Olivia watches as the edges of the gateway solidify.

"If that's the case, shouldn't we take happiness where we can?" Emma argues, fighting the growing sense of frustration.

"Emma. I know what you are asking, and we've talked about this before. We are on our own out here." Olivia raises a hand to point to their surroundings, but Emma knew she wasn't just referring to their current setting. "When the original Fury succumbed to love, it destroyed them. We can't let that happen to us." Even in the dim light Emma can see the real sympathy gleaming in Olivia's eyes, but it doesn't help.

"But the original three weren't human; we are." Emma states pointedly, and she steps closer.

"We were human, but not anymore. You and Mei Li are my life, and my purpose is seeing that we survive. I couldn't stand it if I lost any of that. And I know David is a good man, even with what he has become." Olivia holds up her hand before Emma can interrupt. "I know that what he is, is not by his choosing. I'm only asking that you wait until we know more before doing anything. David is patient and I know he understands," Olivia pleads softly.

"It's been almost a month with no new answers." Emma fails to keep the irritation from lighting her tone.

"Yes. But you have an eternity. A couple of months is very little time in comparison. We will talk about this some more at a later date." Olivia smiles weakly before stepping through the portal. Staring at the gateway, Emma breathes deeply, fighting to quell the upsurge of emotion before she also steps through the gate. Quietly, she prays her dinner is still salvageable.

Chapter 2

Hunger gnaws at Emma's insides and she fumbles with the lock to her apartment door. It feels as if she's been gone for several hours. Opening the door, she is greeted by the subtle aroma of roasted vegetables. The dim lights hang above her meager dining table, flickering softly. A lone dinner setting is still waiting for her; the apartment is dark and quiet. All is how she left it.

A barely audible thump sounds from within the apartment, setting her nerves on edge. Immediately, an overwhelming sense that she's not alone washes over her. She scans the small space, searching for the origin of the sound. A second bump echoes; this time she realizes that it is coming from behind the closed door of her bedroom.

Emma's pulse races as she scurries over to the front door, retrieving the baseball bat she has stowed there. Several of her neighbors had their apartments burglarized last year, and while she doesn't have much in the way of valuables, she'd prefer not killing a human over a stupid low-end television. There is a certain level of uncontrolled messiness that arises when the human police get involved. Unfortunately, more times than not it leads to too many questions Emma can't answer. So far, the bat has served its purpose, in that it scared off a few idiots who are too dense to leave well enough alone.

Choking up on the bat, she silently tiptoes towards her bedroom door. The clamorous pounding of her heart nearly overwhelms the foreign noises. The fumbling and bumping sounds emanating from the confined space are sporadic and muffled. Stretching out a shaking hand, she clasps the doorknob lightly. In the void of silence, she can almost hear the metal scraping against metal as the latch releases. As she pushes the door open, its progress is hampered by the thick bedroom carpet, yet she is allowed a scanty view of the darkened room. A soft shaft of light from the streetlamp cascades into the area, illuminating the bed. Studying the room's darkened corners, she can see no hidden intruder.

Edging over the threshold she reaches out
with all of her senses. Emma strains her ears
to hear any subtle indications of a burglar.
Pushing her aura outward, she can quickly
determine that the presence is not a human.
The air is heavy with a powerful familiarity,
but she cannot judge its source. Emma jumps
and inhales sharply as a solid thud echoes
within her closet. The pointed staccato sound
is followed by a muffled noise; almost like
talking, though she can't make out the words.
Her insides leap and twirl as she inches
towards the closet door. She vigorously rubs
the sweat from her hands on her jeans, then
readjusts her grip on the bat. Her fingertips
graze the cool metal of the knob; her heart
stutters as all sound from within ceases.

In a smooth motion she flings the door open
while swinging the bat downward in an arc.
Just the slightest breath of hesitation stops the
bat before it collides with David's upturned
forearm. His eyes are unyielding and cold for
the briefest moment until a recognition settles
over him. Emma allows the bat to fall limply
in her hand as she wrangles in the terror and
rage frothing just below the surface.

"David. What are you doing here and why are you in my closet?" Emma chokes out. The coarse adrenaline is still pumping through her, clenching at her throat. David's nostrils flare as he inhales deeply. He is obviously attempting to battle his own response. They both know the fight-or-flight reaction is not easily dissipated.

"I came by to surprise you, but I heard something. And I thought the noise was coming from in here. The door closed behind me and wouldn't open." He gruffly runs a hand through his hair as he steps cautiously from the closet.

"Well, you definitely surprised me." Emma studies him briefly before exhaling noisily and setting the bat down. "Do you want something to drink? I may have some really old beer left in the refrigerator." Her hands fidget mindlessly, but Emma knows it is not from the recent scare. She has missed him, and seeing him standing there in her bedroom causes an excited warmth to flow through her.

With an unearthly grace he glides across the room, closing the gap between them. Carefully, he pulls her against his chest. She instantly relaxes in his hold, wrapping her arms around his broad back. For several seconds she enjoys the simple feel and smell of him, allowing herself to be lost in the wash of his being. She gently touches his chestnut-colored hair, feeling grounded by the uncomplicated contact. Even his scent calms her with its soothing warmth. As he pulls back slightly, she lifts her eyes to meet his gaze. His fingers brush her chin and cheek while he kisses her temple, then the corner of her mouth.

"I missed you," he whispers softly against her skin.

"I missed you too," Emma breathes back as her heart rate quickens.

"I'm sorry I was away for so long." His voice rumbles softly in his solid chest. The coolness of his skin presses through his shirt into her palms. To look at him, one would have never guessed that he was a vampire. Aside from the silver tint to his eyes, the man standing before her is radiating life.

"I understand Bastian can be strict when it comes to education. How goes your training anyway?" Emma asks, tenderly rubbing the nape of his neck.

"Bastian is strict, but not the worst I've seen. A lot of the training is learning diplomatic nonsense and how to control unruly temptations." David smirks, causing a flash of fang to peek out from his lips.

"Unruly? You?" Emma feigns astonishment but can't seem to hide her own smile.

"He has taught me a great deal, but I know that it will take some time before I really know what I am." His expression is somber, and Emma lightly touches his cheek.

"I often feel like there is a part of me I don't really understand or know. Like this deep well of churning emotion that threatens to rip me apart. I always feel the need to keep myself in check, always guarded against myself."

Emma studies him gently and nods. She can sense his uncertainty.

"You and I are in a state of transition. Things will be difficult, but we will see this through. In the end I know you, and you know me, and that's all that matters. Come on, my dinner's getting cold. Do you want anything?" Emma asks, tugging him towards the door.

Her breath hitches at the hunger she can see in his eyes. David's gaze refocuses as he pulls himself back from his own thoughts. A glimmer flashes in his eyes and he returns his normally charming, yet slightly naughty, smile.

"I'm alright for now," he replies as he follows her into the kitchen.

"When was the last time you fed?" Emma inquires, opening the refrigerator, retrieving a cold beer, and flicking off the cap.

"It's been a few nights." He nods and takes the offered beer but doesn't drink.

"Should you be going that long? I mean, you are just newly turned; one would think you would need to feed more often." Emma sits down in front of her plate, cutting into the piece of chicken.

"I don't really like the idea of feeding off of some stranger," David remarks with a shrug. He pulls out the chair across from her and sits as well.

"Aren't those who come to Bastian's house volunteers?" Emma asks.

"Yes. But there is something that's just…" He stammers, searching for the right words. "It's just not right for me." David stares down at his hands. He begins to pick away at the label from the cold beer bottle.

"I understand." Emma nods as she takes a large bite of chicken. "For some, the feeding can be a very bonding and intimate experience; for others, not so much."

"Do you mind if I ask what it was like for you, with the vampire that killed you?" David probes as he shifts nervously in his seat.

Emma sets down her fork, pondering his question.

"I didn't mean to upset you." He quickly reassures her with a raised hand.

"The question doesn't bother me. But honestly I've just never thought about it before," she responds with a dry smile, and David relaxes visibly. He lifts the beer to his mouth before its distasteful nature seems to make him lower it again.

"His name was Victor. When he killed me, I didn't really feel anything, just terrified and so lost. Later, I despised him, so I think that probably barred me from forming any sort of bond. But I can see the draw to it. There is this overwhelming sense of being wanted. It's not about the sexual or even the emotional, just the pure want. In that moment, I was no longer me. I became a part of everything and nothing all at the same time." Emma shrugs to herself, picking back up her fork. "As a Fury, that's the problem with coming across your killer; all that strength you've convinced yourself is there just seems to seep away."

"That's why you blame yourself for Alec's death, because you couldn't save him." David's eyes soften under the dim light. Emma nods to David as well as herself.

"He was a good man and he deserved better than that." Emma forces another bite of the now-cold chicken. As she chews, she stares out the large bay window. Reflected lights dance from the frost clinging to the hand railing of her fire escape. The night seems so quiet and peaceful. "He taught me a lot about fighting and surviving—how to use a sword and how to navigate the political battlegrounds of the Fury. He was a nobleman by birth, but even his title couldn't protect him from being ostracized by his own people." David tilts his head curiously at her. "He had six fingers on each of his hands. In his time, it was viewed that people born as such were touched by magic," Emma explains, wiggling her fingers at David.

"He seems like an interesting man. But I don't think he would want you to carry around the burden of his death." David watches her carefully as if trying to gauge her response.

"I guess you are right. It is still difficult, knowing that I could have done something if it had been anyone else." Emma sighs loudly. She stands, taking her plate and fork to the sink. Her hands tremble uncontrollably, and she struggles to rinse off the dish. David's arms wrap around her waist as he pulls her closely into him. She rotates in his hold, wrapping her arms around his neck. Emma lays her cheek on his chest, hugging him tightly to her. It would be nice to stay like this forever.

"Sorry to bring up bad memories." His voice hums in her ear. The subtle scent of his soap hangs around her.

"Memories are just memories; good or bad, they can't hurt me." Emma lifts her gaze, staring contently into his comfortingly familiar face. David lowers his head, his lips a breath away from hers.

"We can make some good memories together." David's breath is feather-soft as his lips brush her skin. The unassuming touch fans a deep-seated fire within her, quickening her pulse. Instinctively, she pulls him closer, clutching at his shoulders. He lifts her upward and with a single hand secures her face as his mouth seeks out hers. Emma flushes with the growing heat, kissing him equally with her own intense need. His free hand roams, stroking and squeezing her hips and ass. A fevered pitch builds within Emma and her heart pounds wildly as David picks her up. He carries her forward with ease, setting her down on the countertop.

Instinctively, Emma wraps her legs around his hips and her back arches as his tongue grazes the sensitive skin of her neck. Pressing into her, David's hand roams upward along her stomach, sliding underneath her shirt as he nuzzles and licks her neck and ears. His breath sears her skin, raising goose bumps along her flesh. David's fingers gently play at the hem of her lace bra and a jolting quiver races through her. With a smooth motion he draws the fabric aside, pulling the undergarment down and exposing her flesh to the cool air. Her hands snake through his hair, clinging to him, his mouth covers the mound of her breast. A throaty moan escapes her when he sucks and nibbles at the taunt flesh. Her body sags and bucks; he moves to the other breast, taking it into his mouth. She eagerly whispers his name while his fiery tongue laps and teases at her skin.

Her fingers claw and yank at his shirt, trying to pull it over his head. David straightens for a moment, breaking the contact to discard the shirt on the floor. His eyes are dark with a sensual need that mirrors her own. Coming back to her, his mouth engulfs hers again, fueling the raging ache within. David kisses a trail along her chin and down the line of her throat. Her pulse beats savagely against his mouth. A sharply familiar pain resonates

through Emma's body, and her addled mind
snaps into focus, understanding instantly the
cause—fangs.

Panic floods her already-overworked system
and she pushes him away. Caught off guard,
David stumbles backward, knocking into the
table. The flimsy furniture skitters across the
floor. Emma hops down from the counter
instinctively; her hand shoots up to her neck
and it comes back with specks of blood. She
can't manage her breathing and her legs
threaten to give out. Visibly trembling, David
shakes his head as he struggles to collect
himself. Inhaling deeply, he lifts his gaze to
her, his hands raised plaintively.

"Emma, I didn't mean to…" His voice is
strained as his own terror sets in.

"I can't give you that. Ask me for anything
and I'll do it—but not that." Emma's breath
comes in coarse gasps as a scorching emotion
constricts her throat.

"I would never hurt you." His eyes are
desperate. It is a sight that further slashes at
Emma's heart. David's gaze flickers toward

the window seconds before the thunderous crash hits their ears.

It is the sound of something solid landing squarely on the cold metal of her fire escape platform. They turn quickly, rushing to the window. The corners of the glass pane are frosted, but Emma can see a body lying on the lattice. The unconscious woman's long red hair is draped over her face, obscuring her features. She isn't wearing any winter clothes, clad only in a t-shirt and shorts. Emma's heart drops as she sees the woman's arm draped over a swollen belly.

"She's pregnant; we have to help her." Emma's throat is gravelly as she reaches for the latch of her window. David's hand on her halts her action and his stare pierces out into the night.

"It may be a trap," David says cautiously as he presses himself into the glass, trying to see the floors above and below her. "I'll go get her."

"Just hurry," Emma urges as she inhales deeply, trying to slow her rapid pulse.

David unlatches the window and lifts the glass. Arctic air sweeps in, swirling around them. David hunches over the prone woman and briefly surveys the area before scooping her into his arms. Carefully, he maneuvers himself back into the apartment. He brings her over to the sofa as Emma closes and locks the window. Glancing out, she notes that all of the adjoining apartment windows are dark and there is no one visible on the street below.

There is an uncanny stillness to the girl, who is perhaps no older than thirty. Emma can sense that she is dead, yet it has to have happened recently as her body is still limp despite the frigid temperatures outside. Emma kneels down next to her and checks for a pulse but finds none.

The mother's skin is cool but not cold and while she is pale, her flesh is not waxy.

Emma makes contact and can sense life there within. Reaching outward with her mind, she searches for any sign that the woman could still be alive.

Restless images scatter across her vision. Fragmented memories slip away as the remnants of the soul fade. Emma can only pull away the reflections of a shuddering darkness teeming with blood and suffering. Searching for a wound, she scrambles to try and heal the woman's form, yet there seems to be nothing holding onto this girl.

As the remnants dissolve, Emma is left within the hollowness of the corpse, and her heart breaks for the loss of this unknown woman. Her features are pleasant and soft and if she were alive, she could be considered lovely. As Emma withdraws her senses, she is suddenly halted by something that is still there. While it is weak, the tiny heartbeat is barely detectable and Emma pulls back.

"The baby is still alive," Emma says, tension squeezing her throat.

"Can we get her to a hospital?"

"I don't think there is enough time." Cold sweat trickles down Emma's back as she wipes more perspiration from her forehead.

"What can we do? We can't let them die."
David states firmly. His eyes dart quickly back
and forth between Emma and the body.

"Help me lift her onto the floor; we have to
remove the baby." Emma's voice breaks as
she stands and her whole-body trembles; she's
only seen this done once before.

"What?" David wheezes, his already-pale skin
losing more color.

"We don't have time–please help me." David
nods, but there is an uncertainty in his eyes.
Lifting the dead woman, they set her down
with an unnecessary delicacy. "Go into the
bathroom; I need the first aid kit and clean
towels."

David leaps up, crossing the small living room
and running into the bathroom. Emma
hurries into the kitchen and starts a pot of
water. She rummages through some drawers
until she finds a small pair of scissors.
Unlacing her shoes, she places the shoestrings
and the scissors in the boiling water.

He emerges from the bathroom as she grabs a
large knife. It is the sharpest one she has and,

hopefully, it will work. David stands near the sofa clutching the towels to his chest. Emma drapes some of the towels on either side of the woman.

"Are you going to be able to do this?" David asks as Emma spots his trembling hands.

"I have to." Emma's mouth is arid, with a tongue that feels thick and lifeless. Kneeling down, she lifts up the t-shirt, exposing the spherical belly. The dead woman's stomach flexes and bows from the hidden pressure underneath. Inhaling deeply and trying to calm her rattled nerves, Emma pulls on the latex gloves with quaking hands.

With a clean slice she opens the abdomen. Dabbing away the blood, she slices again into the uterus, and her vision struggles as she works. Gently, she eases a hand into the cavity, feeling for anything. Groping around inside, her fingers brush against something warm and firm. She quickly realizes it is a tiny arm and, pushing farther in, she follows the appendage until she has a firm grasp.

Slowly, she eases the baby out, securing the head and praying her hold won't slip. She cleans the child with the towels, wiping the gore from his tiny body. Emma snips the sterile shoelace in half and ties off the umbilical cord. With shaking hands, she scissors through the thick cord as it fights her every snip. The diminutive infant gazes at her with startling blue eyes as she cradles him in her arms. After several seconds, Emma allows herself to breathe and David reaches out, softly touching the boy's head.

"I'll call Bastian. He'll help with the mother and see that she's taken care of properly," David whispers as he studies the infant. "But what do we do with him?" He lifts a brow.

"Mei Li will know what to do." Emma watches as his tiny hands open and close. How long had it been since she held a baby?

Chapter 3

An ominous darkness shrouds the lone party in an eerie heaviness, and the intricate network of tunnels stretches out for miles. For Bray the task should have been simple enough–enter Tartarus, find Moss, and kill him. While the three wolves with him had volunteered, he would have come by himself. There was no need for the rest of them to risk their lives for his vengeance.

Unfortunately, the stubborn pack would not abide him going out alone. As head of the clan, it is his duty to seek retribution for his father's death; it is his and his alone. But as determined as he had been in his convictions, they had argued that Jackson was not just Bray's father but their family as well. Their greatest strength and weakness is that they are too overly protective sometimes. Isaac is an incredible tracker, probably the best in the pack, and despite Bray having covered his tracks, they still followed him to the underground entrance. The others, Chase and Martin, were just stubborn mules too loyal

and dumb to take no for an answer. Even
when ordered to go home, they flat-out
refused.

Now they are aimlessly wandering the
claustrophobic mines, buried miles under the
earth. With the moon and sky out of sight it
has become increasingly harder to judge the
distance they have traveled. The heavy stench
of decay clings on every surface, making it
impossible to discern any useful scents. They
walk cautiously in silence, listening for any
stray sounds from the gnarled stone walls of
the cavern, which are adorned with semi-
absorbed skeletons. A gruesome collage of
human body parts juts from the marble
barriers.

The air warms as they spot a dim torch
burning down at the far end of the corridor. A
small trickle of sweat glides down Bray's
cheek as an unyielding awareness clenches at
his guts. The solid-oaken door looms
forbearingly as they approach. Even from the
impressive distance Bray can discern a thick
layer of dirt covering it. The number thirteen
is gouged deeply into the masonry over the
door.

"Is this the right place?" Isaac asks, his golden gaze flickering vigilantly about the cave. "This place smells wrong. It could be a trap, and I don't trust anything about it." His bronzed skin appears to glow under the dim light.

"Yes, this is the place, and I imagine everywhere in this place smells wrong," Bray states calmly as he approaches the door. He schools his features, slowing his pulse so his men won't sense his underlying tension. He had to call in every favor and even threaten others so he could get here. But how well can you trust people like this?

Inhaling sharply, he knocks on the door. The petrified wood barely resonates sound. The seconds tick by while they wait breathlessly. The door slowly creaks open as Bray is about to knock again, and a tall man holds the door ajar, eyeing them suspiciously. His square face is covered with a thick black beard. He'd seem just a kid save for his piercingly cold onyx eyes.

"What do you want?" the doorman asks gruffly. Bray catches sight of an iron pipe clasped in the man's off hand.

"I'm looking for Jasper," Bray replies, keeping his voice low but firm.

"What do you want with him?" he inquires with an unnerving grin. He allows the door to swing open as he crosses his arms over his chest, displaying the pipe now tucked under his arms.

"I was told he could help me with a problem." Bray trains his gaze on the man.

"Jasper doesn't help anybody for free. Were you told that as well?" His mouth cracks open in an arrogant smile, obviously amused by his own humor. Bray notes that one of his front teeth is missing. "There's a pretty big risk in helping outsiders. If someone discovers that you were allowed in here, my life would be worth shit." The guard's petulant expression is quickly becoming exasperating.

"Of course not, and as we both know, fair trade is the way of the world. Are you Jasper?" Bray asks, trying to speed the process along. He removes a small, wrapped chocolate bar from his coat pocket as Jasper nods, never taking his eyes off of the wrapped

confection. "I assume this will be adequate."
Bray holds up the candy for inspection.

"Damn straight. We are not allowed the
simple pleasures down here. That right
there"–he points at the candy bar– "is worth
its weight in gold." Jasper timidly takes the
offered chocolate.

"A candy bar? You are risking your life for
candy?" Isaac asks incredulously, his
handsome features twisted in bewilderment.

"Yes." Jasper answers firmly. "I wasn't there
the night Thanatos was defeated, but I am still
stuck down here in this hell-hole, guarding the
ones that were involved, and guess what?
Guard duty down here is for eternity. Up in
the Hallow you can have food, but down here
it just rots away. Now as long as you keep
your word about why you are here, killing
Moss, and no one else, and I get to keep this."
he holds up the chocolate–"I'll help you."

"All I want is Moss. I have made it clear that
no others are to be harmed," Bray assures
him.

Jasper nods as he removes the wrapping of the nougat-filled bar. With a long inhale, he smells it before taking a huge bite. An awkward silence surrounds them as they watch this odd man chewing his treat.

"Why is it that they don't allow you food down here?" Bray asks as he battles to control his growing agitation.

"It ain't that they don't allow it." Jasper's lips smack as he gnaws off another piece. "It's this place. Like I said, it's different from either the Hallow or Erebus, and something in the air turns food to dust." Jasper places the remaining piece of chocolate in the flat of his palm and leans so that just his hand crosses the threshold and the chocolate instantly turns white and ashy. Jasper upturns his hand, allowing the bit to fall to the ground and rubbing the dust away; he looks back to the men. "Answer your question? Ok, let's go. I don't have all night."

Silently, the small troop of men passes over the threshold into a narrow stone corridor. Fluted light sconces dot the walls, traveling on for an impossible distance. Jasper leads the way as they are forced to walk nearly single file. After traveling for several hundred yards, the passageway bends sharply, transforming into a limestone stairway heading downward.

"If you weren't involved with Thanatos and his men, then why are you in here?" Isaac asks from over Bray's shoulder. His voice is a solid whisper, traveling through the space without being overly audible.

"I was involved with Thanatos; all of the Gyges were. My job was to guard Erebus, while others had different jobs. I just didn't know about his plans to take over the Fury, and me and a couple of the others weren't there that night, so we are guarding down here instead. I think they knew we weren't involved but couldn't have us running around the free world with no one holding us under their thumb. So, they wrap up a lesser punishment and make it seem like a reward." Jasper calls over his shoulder with a crass laughter. Just as Bray is about to shush them Jasper waves an impatient hand at him. "Don't worry about being quiet here. No one ever comes to these parts of the caverns and I'll tell you all when you need to shut up." Jasper chuckles awkwardly.

"Things may have turned out a lot worse if Thanatos had won," Bray remarks as he notes the lingering heaviness in the air. The spacing between the torches is becoming greater. There is no longer a sense that they are underground, but somewhere deeper, farther from the light. This is no place to exist, he thought to himself, wishing to be out of here as soon as possible.

"I didn't really give a rat's ass either way. My life wasn't getting any better regardless of which one of them won." Jasper halts and turns around to face them. His black eyes glow with a bitterness against the flickering flame light. "If I hadn't been laid up in the hospital, I'd have been the first in line to watch them all beat the piss out of each other. Cause anyplace is better than this shithole."

"Why were you in the hospital?" Bray inquires, his worries suddenly set alive. Anger and emotion plume from Jasper, but he can't sense that he is a danger, at least for now.

"I got in a fight at some dive bar and two or three guys jumped me. A bunch of punk-ass human kids, so I couldn't rightly kill them, but I should have." Jasper points at his missing tooth. "Broke my jaw and knocked out a tooth. Come on, enough chitchat–it's getting late." He turns and starts descending the stairs again.

Bray can taste the deceit in his words, but who knows what it really means. It's not like he's stupid enough to trust Jasper completely; the man may sell out his own mother for some jelly beans. But as long as he doesn't do anything moronic like trying to stop them, then he'll live to enjoy his candy.

He nods to the wolves flanking him and they follow in silence. The stairway ends at another closed door. Old rotted wood that is held together with thick iron bands. Bars at eye level reveal nothing but inky blackness, and a heavy layer of cold air sweeps through the portal from the other side.

"From here on out you say nothing, got it?" Jasper points to them. "Through this door is a long hallway. You'll follow it until you come to an intersection, go to the right. Follow that and you'll come to another door. This leads to the holding cells. Moss's cell is all the way in the back." He hands over a large brass ring with a single skeleton key hanging on it. "You'll need this to open the cubicle doors."

"Wait–you're not coming with us?" Isaac nearly shouts.

"No. Once you leave this room you are on your own. If I see you in there, I will treat you as intruders and if you try to kill more than just Moss, I will kill you." Jasper's features harden as he eyes each one of them.

"I understand. Thank you for your help." Bray nods.

"Don't thank me; just kill Moss and get out. That dude is one sick fuck. Let me just tell you, you meet all kinds down here, and there is something seriously wrong with him. Oh, and there is a door at the end of all the cells. Don't open it." He slightly leans toward them. "No. Matter. What." Before Bray can question him, Jasper nods toward the doorway as he steps to the side.

Stepping through the entryway, the group fans out, searching for any hidden threat. A chill settles over Bray's skin as the ambient temperature around them drastically drops compared to the previous rooms. The rank stench of decay clings to the air in a thick vapor. This has been the dwelling place of death for more than a millennium. The knowledge sparks a nagging fear that slinks around inside his gut. Above ground, he can always detect an underlying presence of life, yet it is as if this place is a vacuum where nothing living can survive. Never has there been a more apt description of Hell. Though in the far distance he can sense the faint trace of lifeforms.

The masonry walls are black as midnight and a viscous fluid oozes from them. Square alcoves carved into the stone hold dimly glowing tallow candles, and Bray can feel a delicate draft that wafts about them, yet it seems to have no effect on the flames. Any stray noise is swallowed by the oppressive environment, which may work in their favor by covering up any sound of their approach. Even the beating of his heart is muted against the rising malice around them.

Quickly, they span the length of the corridor, reaching the intersection. Isaac crouches as he presses himself flat against the wall, and with a swift motion, he steals a look around the corner. Scanning the area, he motions everyone forward with a backward-stretched hand. They all stack up in a line behind Isaac as they move in unison towards the metal door. The group breaks off into pairs, each standing against the wall in order to be clear of danger should someone or something come through the entry.

Bray steadies his hands as he slides the key in the hole. They had run through the plan several times on the trek here; everyone knows what they need to do. *To be brave and to protect the honor of his family is the greatest respect he can give to his father's memory*, Bray reminds himself. The rusted tumblers creak and click as they align. As the lock releases, the door slowly swings open under its own weight. Bending low, the men file into the room.

An uncanny ease washes over him as he surveys the area. Two columns of cells line the walls on either side of the cavern. Each unit is barred on three sides with the fourth wall comprised of solid granite. A single path leading to the far wall stretches out ahead, and the hallway is empty of guards. Each recessed cell is engulfed in utter blackness save for a miniscule amount of torch light that extends into the space. Aside from a random cough, the chamber is deathly silent. Bray battles the weakness of his nerves as the breadth of air pushes down on him.

With a keen awareness they travel the length of the line. Their eyes shift back and forth into each cell as they search out any avenue for an impending attack. Their shoes pat almost silently across the dirt floor. Bray's heart races as they flank each side of the last cells—two identical units, both shrouded in shadows. Damn, Jasper never said which one it was. Bray curses to himself.

"If you are looking to surprise him, you failed," a disembodied voice chimes from the cell to their left. Bray's gaze shifts to the sound as a figure steps forward, barely touched by the glow of light. Even after only one meeting, Bray instantly recognizes Thanatos. Black shoulder-length hair and brown eyes that look almost black as well under the dim light. Despite the confines of his cell, Thanatos exudes a startling level of power. Bray senses no evil or malice coming from the god of death, nor does he feel at ease around him either. Thanatos is neither good nor is he evil. Simply, he seems a force of nature, an earthquake that kills without care or joy. The group moves as they press towards the center of the narrow hallway, not wanting to be in close proximity to the prisoner.

 "He has known you were coming for a while now." Thanatos's tone is cool as he studies them, his hands lightly gripping the bars.

"How?" Isaac whispers. He licks his lips nervously.

"As soon as you entered Tartarus, we all became aware of your presence." Thanatos leans forward, his cheeks pressing nonchalantly against the iron rods.

The door next to them flies open as two shadowy figures leap outward at them. The beings are devoid of any distinguishable characteristics. Slender forms with smooth charcoal-colored skin stretched taut. Long clawed hands hang at their sides as they seem to study the group from eyeless faces. A soft series of clicks come from them, almost akin to a growl. Their forms flicker between solid and transparent. Bray's bowels clench as the faceless blink and dart forward, spanning the short distance between them.

The wolves pair off, taking on their own monstrosity as a team. Bray and Isaac dodge the faceless as it snakes towards them, and they attempt to circle around it in the cramped space. The four wolves shift instantly, clothes and skin ripping away as their own fur and claws rise to the surface. With their increased strength, they'd all stand a better chance against their foes, but their larger size could prove a hindrance in the small corridor. It can't be helped, Bray realizes as he narrowly moves out of the way from a downward slash of razor-sharp fingernails.

Leaping back, he slams into Thanatos's cell. The imprisoned man steps away from the bars but continues to watch them with a keen interest. Isaac drives into the faceless, wrapping his arms around it as it lurches toward Bray. An unholy shriek bellows from the thing as it struggles in Isaac's hold. Its claws rip and gouge into the wolf's skin, causing fresh streaks of blood to well up and soak through the fur. Bray rushes forward, grabbing the flaying beast as he bites at its neck. The skin is incredibly tough and he has to gnaw at the flesh, whipping his head back and forth, before the tissue gives way. His mouth and snout are awash with the beast's acrid, foul blood. Even as his stomach rolls, he persists, tearing the flesh away in large chunks.

The faceless sputters and gasps as it slumps to the ground. Bray looks up to see Chase lying lifeless near the still-open doorway. A gaping hole in his chest sloshes out blood in a heavy flow. Martin's bulky form is hefted into the air and slammed into Moss's cell. The iron screeches and buckles as the door clatters off of its hinge. Martin's head lists to the side as the faceless he is fighting stalks towards him. Long-fingered claws glint with blood under the low light. Moss appears through the broken cell gate, jumping over Martin's prone form and only glancing at them briefly as he bolts toward the door. The irresistible urge to give chase nearly wins over Bray, but he focuses his attention back to Martin and their opponent. Bray and Isaac leap in unison towards the faceless as it tracks towards

Martin. It turns quickly, catching Isaac midair and tossing him down the corridor with one hand. Isaac's thick body bounces and skitters to a halt.

The predator launches itself toward Bray, its shoulder catching him squarely in the stomach. His air is forced out in a painful whoosh, but he holds on, landing a sharp elbow between his adversary's shoulder blades. Bray slashes at its rough, leathery skin, yet this one is sturdier and much stronger than the last one. His sharp claws skitter along its flesh, barely marring the surface. Even his sharp teeth and powerful jaw struggle to find purchase on the monster's shoulder and neck. The faceless bellows as it lifts Bray effortlessly into the air with one hand clamped around his throat. Bray is pushed away as the claws of his feet dig weakly into the ground; his back and head slam into a stone wall. Relying on instinct alone, Bray manages to snatch the monster's downward strike with his clawed hand. His muscles strain as he battles his opponent, its curved nails inching closer to his face. Bray tries to focus all of his power into his arms, knowing that this stalemate won't last forever. His gaze is torn from the formless mask of its face to the jagged talons of its hand. The nails elongate from their curved shape, straightening into needle-thin daggers. The tips begin steadily moving towards his eyes, and the world blurs around him.

"Hold." The one-word command echoes through the confined space. The nails slow to a halt as they graze Bray's eyelashes. The faceless stands stone-still. Bray chances a look toward the voice and glimpses a regal woman of Asian descent standing in the open doorway. He recognizes Mei Li from the night of the ritual when they captured Thanatos. She watches them sternly, hands clasped firmly in front of her as the pretty blonde, Olivia, stands beside her. Both women exude a mysterious calm, and they seem to glide rather than walk. "Release," Mei Li orders, striding into the chamber. A small bronze talisman, around her neck gleams brightly with a blood-red ruby embedded in the center that catches the light. The faceless clicks and chirps wildly at her approach. Was it talking? For a second Bray wonders if the faceless will obey. But its grasp slackens and it backs away. Its eyeless gaze never leaves Bray and it glides back through the doorway where it came from; everyone watches the darkened doorway in silence.

"I would ask what you were thinking by coming down here, but it is obvious you weren't thinking at all," Mei Li snaps at him fiercely. "You risked your life and the lives of others. For what? Revenge?" Her stare lasers him where he stands.

Bray's body shakes and pulses as he reclaims his human form. Fur retracts as his mass shrinks to a proportionate size. Bones crack and pop, fusing back into smaller joints. When he was younger the pain was excruciating but with time he has become accustomed to the transition. As his body stills, he stands before the small group naked and appearing completely human once again.

He smirks to himself when Olivia's complexion shifts to a deep shade of red and she becomes aware of his state of nakedness. Diverting her gaze elsewhere she trots quickly over to Isaac and Martin to tend to them. If this Fury can heal as well as Emma, his men will be just fine. Even from this distance he can tell their wounds are only superficial.

Chase was a good man; unfortunately, no amount of magic can help him and Bray mourns his lost friend.

Mei Li glides towards him, handing him a blanket. "To keep the chill at bay," she adds with a slight smile.

"I am well aware of what I was trying to do here and what was at risk," Bray answers, his tone somber as he returns his gaze to Mei Li and wraps the scratchy cloth around his waist. "I take full responsibility for any damage caused this evening. My people were here only at my request."

"You are their leader and they just followed you into hell without question. Now one of them is dead and a prisoner has been allowed to escape. Resolving this issue will not be easy," Mei Li fumes with a dark expression, her arms folded across her chest. Her thick black hair is woven into an elaborate bun that catches the dim light.

"He killed my father, so I will hunt him down and kill him," Bray barks mulishly.

"You will go and find Moss and you will kill him, and bring his body back here, as proof. But you will not risk the lives of your people," Mei Li addresses him coldly.

"Mei Li, I don't think it would serve well to have him going after Moss alone. The wolf's death will benefit no one," Olivia interrupts as she steps up, standing next to Mei Li.

"He will not be going alone. You will accompany him. You are an exceptional tracker, so finding Moss should be no problem for you. Also, you have bested Moss in combat before. Bray and his pack will get the retribution they seek, and we will get confirmation that Moss is no longer a risk," Mei Li explains. Olivia opens her mouth to argue but is silenced by Mei Li's uplifted hand. "We must not allow our pride to stand in the way of the correct course and I believe this decision is the correct one."

Olivia's expression sours as she glances over at Bray and he inhales deeply. Isn't this an interesting turn of events?

Chapter 4

Mei Li hadn't sounded thrilled when she received a phone call so late at night but she came as soon as Emma had a chance to explain the situation with the newborn, arriving well before the vampires that were sent by Bastian.

When Emma opens the door for her, Mei Li sweeps into the living room. Her burgundy silk gown sweeps quietly over the wooden floors and her thick black hair pulled back into a neat bun. Wasting no time, Mei Li gently lifts the baby and examines him. Emma watches morosely while the deceased mother is cleaned, wrapped up, and carried away. The vampire crew diligently scrubs her floor, removing any visible signs of blood. David surveys the scene in silence while chancing only a brief glance her way while the vampires finish up and file out of the room. In the presence of others, they often kept their interactions to a minimum. David's gaze lingers for a brief second before he nods curtly and steps out into the hall, closing the door behind him.

Once they are alone Emma looks on anxiously as Mei Li inspects the child cradled in her arms. After several minutes Mei Li's gaze lifts toward Emma. An untold level of emotion vibrates and flows from the ancient mother. Emma's skin prickles, and her nerves are set on edge.

"Well, he isn't human, not completely anyway." Mei Li's voice is a soft whisper, her delicate brow creasing.

"What else is he?" Emma asks, in her own hushed tone.

"I'm not sure. I sense no evil or malice from him. But it is as if there is some blank space within him—one that is yet to be filled. Some species do not exhibit their supernatural side until a certain age. Perhaps that is the case with this small one." The baby boy sleeps soundly in Mei Li's arms. His tiny hands open and close as his mouth suckles the air softly in his slumber. "And you say he was born this evening?" she muses, sounding curious.

"Yes. I had to remove him once I determined that his mother was dead." A cold chill runs along Emma's spine, recalling the emergency cesarean. Nervously, she wipes her sweaty palms on the legs of her jeans. She had already washed her hands three times before Mei Li arrived, but they still feel tacky from the wet blood.

"It's odd. He just seems older than a premature birth or even a newborn, for that matter," Mei Li points out as she softly touches his cheeks. Both their eyes settle back upon the infant; judging an age at this point is nearly impossible, yet even to Emma, the child appears different from a mere hour ago. His cheeks are flushed with a warm hue and despite the dim light they look full and healthy.

"For now I will return with him to the Hallow. He will be safe there until we can determine his lineage and what to do with him." Mei Li gathers some additional towels to wrap him in. As she reaches the door, she turns to face Emma once more. "Get some rest while you can and come to my room tomorrow evening. Hopefully, we will know more by then." With a nod, Mei Li leaves, shutting the door behind her.

A jumpy energy works its way through Emma and she plucks an apple from her counter. Sleep won't come easy tonight. The skin of the sweet fruit snaps when she bites into the flesh. Why was the mother brought here, of all places? Or did she find her way here on her own? Emma's gaze falls on the fire escape outside her window. Taking another bite, a thin stream of apple juice runs down her arm. Finishing up, she discards the core and washes her hands yet again.

The wooden window frame yelps in protest as she pushes it open. The pre-dawn air chills, wrapping around her, and Emma steps out, shutting the window behind her. A steel rail encloses the confined space while the grated floor and similar base of the upper levels allow easy access for the wind and rain. Much of the city still lies in the dormant state of nocturnal sleep. Only a few cars travel the darkened streets, their headlights beaming a measured light before them.

Under the low light Emma strains her eyes, searching for anything that could be of use. At first the space appears barren as her gaze sweeps across the area, but she spots a bit of fabric stuck in the grate where it meets the stairs that lead up to the next level. With a slight tremble in her hand she reaches out, grasping what turns out to be a cord. Despite the meager light she can see the blood smeared across the rope's surface. As Emma shifts her feet to stand, a glint of light catches her eye. An object reflects back the amber glow of the streetlamps. Emma eases her fingers into the small gap of the grate, trying to maneuver the shining bit of metal. After fumbling for several seconds, she pulls the silver coin free. The small disc glistens in her hand while she inspects it. It's the same size as a quarter, but its markings are foreign to her. The polished bit of silver hums with an underlying current of energy and she quickly stuffs it into her pocket. Standing up, Emma sighs deeply, pulling the surrounding frigid air into her lungs.

Emma drops to her knees, a scorching agony ripping through her. The sweet flavors of apple and bile flood her mouth. Somewhere deep within her mind, just below an audible level, she hears a mild chanting. The words are too low to make out clearly, but they echo and resonate within her core, pushing her into action. It is an unmistakable demand, compelling her to leave with the same urgency she had felt when Aidan called on them to help with the centaurs.

Once again, she has no idea where she should go, but the pull is intense. Spasms wrack her body so fiercely that her knees bounce along the grate. Pushing to her feet, she clamors noisily back through the window and into her apartment. Any thought of ignoring the sensation is cast away when she doubles over, heaving, and the apple comes back up. Crossing the room, Emma stumbles and searches for a clear wall to open a doorway. Her pulse races, and she fights to restrain the rising panic, feeling as if every nerve within her has been splayed open, exposed to a raging sandstorm. Raw emotions boil and swell to the surface and Emma chokes back an irrational sob. *I need to get out of here.* The singular thought pulses through her mind. A powerful force inside her pushes her feet into motion. Marching forward Emma swipes her hand over the smooth wood of her front door, opening the portal. She inhales a ragged breath, stepping through and into the blue-black depths.

She gasps loudly, emerges through the undulating gateway, desperately pulling air into her lungs. Emma bends over weakly, resting her hands on her knees, steadying her haggard breath. Blood continues to pound through her neck, but the pain has lessened. She slowly lifts her gaze to take in her surroundings.

The large bay window frames a bulbous moon that illuminates a wave-lapped shoreline. Palm trees sway softly against the coastal breeze and the sky is bathed in the muted shades of indigo and blue, signaling the impending sunrise. The studio apartment is open, with several plush couches lining the far walls. Under the pale moonglow, subtle hues of gold and silver stand out against the stark-white room. Gold thread and beadwork shimmer across the surface of the sofas and throw pillows. Ornate metalwork decorates the otherwise-barren white walls. Even the tile floor seems to have flecks of reflective metal woven throughout it. Turning around, she spies a spacious kitchen which is shrouded in shadows behind her. A lone door stands next to a stainless-steel refrigerator.

Pivoting, Emma continues to assess her environment. A gilded harp sits semi-concealed within an obscured corner of the room. A fifty-gallon fish tank is mounted in the wall; tiny bubbles of air rise and swirl around something in the water. Emma cautiously walks towards the aquarium, her gaze flicking about the room. The dark shape sways gently in the middle of the tank. She runs her hand along the top rim of the tank until she finds a light switch. Harsh fluorescent light illuminates the tank and surrounding area. She squints and as her eyes adjust, they focus on a pelt floating in the water. The seal coat swells softly under the water as its dappled surface reflects the light.

"He makes sure I can see it all of the time," a male voice echoes behind her. Emma turns sharply towards the sound. For the first time, she spots a bare foot resting on the floor as it sticks out from around the side of a couch. Sidestepping, Emma eases her way around, peering into the corner, and her breath catches at the sight of the beautiful man sitting before her. Taupe-colored hair falls elegantly about his face, barely grazing his shoulders, and his eyes are the color of sun-kissed rum. Though his face is not ruggedly handsome, it can only be described as simply stunning. His facial features are a nearly perfect compilation of hard and soft lines. The man sits lazily on a plush mat, his back leaning against the wall. He rests an arm lightly on one raised knee, and an iron collar is latched securely around his neck.

"I'm guessing that is yours?" Emma gestures to the fish tank. His intense gaze never wavers from her, yet he nods. "Selkie?" she asks, trying to work some moisture back into her mouth, and he nods again. His outward demeanor is cool, almost disinterested, yet a subtle level of fretful energy crackles the air about him. "Where is Olivia?" Her eyes sweep across the open room again, but she can't sense Olivia anywhere near here.

"I don't know who Olivia is," he replies, reaching into his front pocket and withdrawing a shiny piece of metal. Emma instantly recognizes the ancient coin. "Aidan said I just needed to say the words and you would come to help." He idly rolls the coin in his fingers, his thumb rubbing the raised serpents.

"If Aidan gave you that coin, why didn't he help you? For all I know I may not even be able to aid you," Emma counters. She reaches outward again with her power but senses only the two of them.

"The reputation of the Fury is well known, and I know you can help me. As for Aidan, no one would blame him for not wanting to take on my problem." His head cocks slightly to the side as he speaks.

"Alright, let's start from the beginning. Who are you and what exactly do you want help with?" Emma asks, crossing her arms over her chest, making no attempt at hiding the frustration in her tone. A prickle of annoyance needles its way along her spine as she glares at him. *So much for Aidan keeping this to himself.*

"My name is Bryan. And as you so astutely deduced, I am a selkie. My home has always been in the sea; its depths offer boundless freedom and wonders." Bryan looks longingly out the bay window to the shoreline. "But on occasion I will shed my skin to walk the dry land. I find the human species to be fascinating, unlike anything I've encountered under the waves. It was from my exposure to the humans that I discovered my talent for harp playing. Creating beautiful sounds that will draw others to me." A chaste smile graces his lips.

"I'm sorry, but are you going to get to the point any time soon?" Emma asks tersely. While fatigue frays her nerves, she still contends with a strong feeling of empathy for him.

"Yes, of course." He nods. "On my last excursion to the shore I slipped off my pelt and hid it under a large rock. Then in the early morning hours I returned to find that my skin was gone; you see, it had been stolen. It was shortly after that I found out it was taken by a troll named Luther. As you may know, if a selkie's pelt is stolen they are prisoners of the individual who possesses it. I can only go home to the sea if I get it back." Bryan's voice breaks under the strain.

"So, what does this Luther want from you?" Emma's gaze flicks over to the skin floating in the fish tank, then to the harp standing in the corner.

"Trolls are affected strongly by sound and music. I am guessing he heard me playing and decided to add me to his collection of treasures," Bryan replies brusquely, thick anger in his voice. "I cannot force him to return it to me, nor can I go home without it—hence the reason for calling on you. It seems we have a fair trade; I need my pelt back and you need this coin to be on your way." The coin reflects under the dim light. Bryan winces as he leans back to replace the coin in his pocket. As the natural light level rises, Emma can make out the patchwork of bruises that litter the skin of his arms and chest.

"You think I can beat up a troll to get your pelt back?" Emma nearly laughs as her mind races and she tries to come up with a solution that doesn't involve being pummeled by a crazed troll. "Couldn't I just smash the tank and give you the skin? Seems the simplest answer."

"That should work." Bryan nods and stares intensely at the tank. With a strained grunt he pulls himself to his feet.

Emma steadies her nerves as she walks stiff-legged towards the wall. Although the task is easy enough, her body seems to be fighting her as she moves. The tingle of irritation from before has bloomed into a near-hysterical panic. Studying the wall and tank, Emma tries to sense any trap or spell placed on the area. Stretching out with her power, she can only sense a weak sentry hex. There appears to be no reason why such a flimsy enchantment should cause such a physical reaction.

Emma's knees quake as a boom of energy pulses from behind her. She whips around to face the kitchen and the exterior door. Although the space is empty, the well of staggering power ripples through her in massive waves. An echoing rumble of footfalls shakes the ground, resonating in the air around Emma. The white-pine door is thrown open, slamming into the refrigerator as a mountainous man strides in. His hulking, sinewy frame fills the constricted space. With a relaxed swagger he closes the distance between them until he is effectively blocking the exit. His platinum hair is shaved close and is nearly white under the low light. The thick, bushy set of eyebrows that hood his iridescent-green eyes and bulbous facial features are telltale signs that he is a troll.

"What do we have here?" his thickly accented voice growls at them; deep-set, penetrating eyes glare at them. "You are either here to take what's mine or… you're a gift." His gaze travels across Emma's body, making her skin crawl. "Is that it? Did someone send you as a gift for Luther?" he asks.

Emma, in turn, studies Luther, trying to figure out the best way to handle him. He could pounce at the slightest sign of weakness. Her insides shake and churn, knowing that trolls are most often better left alone.

"I am no gift. I am a Fury, and I am here to retrieve this selkie's pelt so he can return to the ocean." Despite her best efforts, Emma's voice trembles. Trolls can be troublesome opponents as they have incredible regeneration abilities and the use of magic. They may not be the brightest foes, but they are physically imposing.

"Now, why would I give you one of my treasures when I worked so hard to get them, especially my pretty songbird here?" Luther asks as he points to Bryan.

"Worked hard?" Emma mocks with the slightest of derision.

"I'm smarter and stronger than the rest; can't blame me if someone else is stupid." He smiles widely, exposing a large gap in his front teeth.

"I imagine the reason you have all this stuff is through thievery and deception," Emma states calmly with an arched eyebrow.

His eyes shift to a stern ferocity. "No, not true. I outsmarted them all." He nods as he taps his temple with a meaty finger. "Most will underestimate me. It makes them dumb, so I get what I want."

"Well, I've always heard that trolls aren't smart. But what do I know? There's really no way to see if you are as intelligent as you say." Emma's tone drips with condescension. She knows that she'll have to play this out right so she and Bryan can get out of here alive.

"I can prove it." Luther's chest puffs with indignation.

"Alright, perhaps a simple riddle can prove how smart you are." Emma tilts her head thoughtfully as she sneaks a glance towards Bryan. Standing stone-still, he studies them both with wide eyes.

"What do you wager? If I answer right, then what do I get? Maybe I get you?" He leers at her as he licks his lips with a slick tongue.

Emma swallows a disgusted groan. What could she bet that was not herself? Her mind goes to the coin she found on her balcony.

"No, I have something that is worth far more," Emma answers as she pulls the coin from her pocket. His eyes widen faintly as the silver glints, catching the light.

"One bit of silver?" Luther asks with a snort. "That's not worth the selkie."

"Are you sure?" Emma counters, rolling the coin in her fingers. "It's very old. I doubt there are any like it in the world. Can't you sense the magic it holds?" Luther's stare is locked onto the coin.

"Fine. Ask your riddle. If I guess wrong then the selkie gets his skin and can go. But if I am right then I get the silver–and you." He smirks as he crosses his thick arms over his chest.

"I am not part of the wager," she states rigidly, holding her ground.

"Then no deal. It's the only terms I'll accept," Luther shoots back stubbornly.

Emma silently curses to herself, more than anything wishing Olivia was here. Olivia was always better at negotiations.

"Very well, but I need a moment to think," Emma sighs.

Luther nods with a grin and Emma leans against the arm of a sofa as her mind races. She is pulled back from her thoughts by an audible click. The end table and wall lights turn on automatically. The room dims as the glass of the bay window blurs and darkens, blocking the light from the rising sun.

"Alright, are you ready?" She inhales deeply as she observes Luther, while he rolls his head, producing several loud cracks. Luther nods slowly as he focuses his attention on her.

"You walk into a public restroom–inside are four urinals and two stalls. There are two men in the stalls and two men washing their hands at the sink," Emma explains as she holds up two fingers. "The two washing their hands leave as another man enters. His name is Chet. He's a sales analyst from Seattle, coming into town for a business convention. So, he stands there talking to you about his four kids, Travis, Lilly, Joseph, and June. He talks about his work while the two men in the stalls finally leave after washing their hands." Emma watches Luther's eyes dashing back and forth as he tries to keep track of everything. "After Chet uses a urinal he washes up and leaves. How many people are left in the bathroom?" Emma tilts her head, allowing a subtle smirk to lift her lips as she spies Luther's perplexed expression. His fingers flick slightly as he works through the numbers. "I can repeat it if you need," she offers.

"No. I have it," Luther barks, as he gnaws at the dry skin of his fingers. "Four minus two, plus one, minus three." He mumbles to himself, his eyes narrowing as he scrutinizes her.

"Do you have an answer?" Emma presses as she silently prays that this works. "How many people are left in the bathroom?"

"None, everyone left," Luther answers with a sneer, seemingly proud of himself.

"Are you sure?" Emma asks, trying her best to appear nervous, knowing the answer is wrong. She needs him to feel confident in it, though.

The cocky smile spreads wider across his face as he nods. "Yeah."

"Wrong," she answers coldly.

"No, it's right," he argues, shaking his head. His ugly face contorts in a mask of confusion.

"Your answer is wrong. Everyone else left–that is correct–but I never said that you left. The answer is one because you are still there," Emma explains. "Now, if you don't mind, I'd like the pelt and the key to Bryan's chains." She keeps her features neutral as she extends a hand.

Luther breathes deeply as his fists clench. Finally blowing out a lungful of air, he reaches into his jacket pocket, retrieving a small key ring. With a lift of his brow, he jingles the keys as he swaggers towards Bryan, but his demeanor radiates a tightly leashed rage.

The space between Bryan, the harp, the sofa, and Emma is narrow, and as Luther nears, Emma sidesteps out of the way. Luther crouches down and clutches the collar around Bryan's neck, yanking it to expose the lock. Her instincts scream for her to give him a greater berth, but she needs to stay close should he try to hurt Bryan. In a flash of movement, Luther launches at her and at once closes the distance between them. His huge mass crashes into her and they tumble backward. Emma's spine smacks the floor hard and forces her to scramble backward, but he follows, giving her no space to move. Her pulse races, and blood careens through her veins. She slams into the display case behind them. Emma only distantly recognizes the sounds of breaking glass and the warble of metal on wood, a fierce bloodlust lighting Luther's eyes. Capturing his wrists as he reaches for her throat, she is struggling to hold him at bay when a heavy brass orb falls from the shelf above, landing inches from her head.

Clinging onto his right wrist, she swings a leg over his head, resting across his chest. Pushing with both legs she forces him onto his back with a solid thud and she arches her hips, applying pressure to his elbow joint. Luther struggles and roars in pain as the cartilage snaps under the pressure. Emma releases the useless appendage and scurries backward, using the display case to stand as Luther claws at her feet with one hand. The tendons and joint of the other arm mend and repair themselves with the sound of wet pops and cracks. Emma stretches, grabbing the brass orb.

"You can't hurt me with that. What do you think you're gonna do?" Luther laughs moving toward her, his fist raised to strike.

"This," Emma shouts, heaving the ball at the bay window. The orb contacts the open panel and sends glass cascading down with sunlight streaming into the room. The sun's rays flow over Luther, his skin petrifies and turns to solid grey stone. Within seconds, he is completely frozen and lifeless.

Emma gasps for air as she struggles to her feet, wanting to scream in frustration. With trembling legs, she searches the floor for the dropped key ring. Under a bit of rubble, she finds it and walks over to Bryan, unlocking his chains. With great effort he stands, rubbing his wrists and neck. Emma lifts the lid to the aquarium and retrieves the pelt. She notes how soft the flesh is as she hands Bryan the skin and he clutches it tightly to his chest.

"Thank you." Bryan's voice trembles as he passes her his coin. "I am in your debt."

"You can repay me by keeping this to yourself. Are you well enough to make it out of here on your own?" Emma asks as she watches him closely.

"Yeah, I'm good. The ocean is there." He answers, tilting his head towards the shore. He turns and gingerly makes his way down to the waterline. She watches silently as he strips and pulls the pelt over his form. Within seconds the bull seal that is Bryan flops into the waves, disappearing from sight. With heavy arms Emma opens a portal back to her apartment. Her room is fairly dark, and she collapses into the bed, falling into a numbing sleep.

Chapter 5

Going to the Hallow to meet up with Mei Li should have been a simple matter of opening a gateway in her apartment. But this morning, Emma finds that she really needs a hot coffee, something warm to melt away the persistent chill that has nestled in her bones. She hasn't gone shopping in several weeks and her cupboards haven't been this empty since she moved into the apartment.

Stepping outside her building Emma is jolted by the bitter cold of the morning air. With this being early spring, the sunrises are still uncomfortably chilly despite the warm-up in the afternoons. The winter still clings fiercely to the area but there are subtle signs of the changing seasons.

Emma pushes open the single glass door and the bellowing waves of heat and fragrant aromatics envelop her. The coffee shop hums with activity. Some patrons come and go while others sit quietly reading newspapers. The line to the counter moves quickly as baristas mix and steam orders of varying complexity with exceptional speed. For a moment she feels ridiculous ordering a simple hot coffee regular after the young girl behind the counter asks what she would like. Within minutes she has the steaming cardboard cup in her hands and is stepping out into the crisp morning air yet again.

Emma measures her steps on the icy sidewalk and wraps her worn sweat jacket more snugly around herself as she tries and fails to keep out the biting wind. She shivers violently, which only adds to the mounting ache that has settled into her bones. The sun barely clears the tree line but when Emma crosses into a patch of sunshine, the chill is temporarily pushed away. With too little sleep, her thinking is slow and foggy, and she is lacking the focus needed to process simple tasks. Cautiously sipping the scalding coffee, Emma rolls the events of the last two nights over in her mind. The oddity of it all saps the remaining energy from her as she feels her pace slackening.

There is a slow-rising tension that needles at the edge of her senses, almost imperceptible.

The weeks since the events with Thanatos have been so quiet–almost boring. Now, suddenly within days, something seems to be brewing.

It is still early in the day, but the bustle of the town is starting to pick up its pace. A steady flow of traffic lines the roads as people make their way to their places of work. An errant horn sounds out in the predawn air. In the distance, Emma watches as two motorists yell back and forth at each other from their open car windows. The sidewalks are dotted with walkers clothed in thickly padded winter wear, plumes of vaporous breath wafting over their heads.

Another shout rings out, echoing and bouncing along the street. A young woman dashes from a convenience store door, trailed closely by an employee. The girl's light-red hair swooshes and flies wildly as she runs, clutching several small items to her chest. As she darts across the street, she is momentarily stalled by a passing car, which allows her pursuer to gain ground. Just as his hand nears, mere inches from her coat sleeve, the world around them halts. Like a rippling sound wave, the pulse of power emanates from the escapee. All others seem oblivious to the wave even as it envelops them and they are locked in a frozen paralysis while the girl continues to run.

As she turns down a nearby alley, the haze of confusion drops and the people on the sidewalks resume their hurried pace. The shopkeeper stands mystified in the center of the road, his gaze darting around as he tries to determine where the shoplifter has gone. A nagging curiosity tugs Emma down the street, turning to follow where the fleeing woman went.

The beams of sunlight bend at odd angles across the silent alleyway. Wooden planter boxes attached to window sills are spotlighted as a single shaft of light breaks through the surrounding darkness. Petrified plants peer out over the rim of the worn boxes. The length of the alley is cloaked in vast layers of shadows, while small bits of debris and clumps of snow dot the walkway. With measured steps Emma enters the space between the two brick buildings, cautiously scanning the dimly lit recesses. Her throat tightens as a faint white noise floods her straining ears. A steady flutter of power bounces along the length of the narrow pathway, washing over her skin. *What is she doing here?*

Emma picks up the sound of a low whispering coming from behind a dumpster. Even though the words are partially obscured by the residual energy flowing around them, the diminutive sound that tickles Emma's ears ripple the sensation down her spine. Inching forward, she peers into the blackened space beside the dumpster. The young woman from the convenience store is crouching and holding a small tin can of cat food. She watches without a sound as the girl scoops out some of the canned meat onto a discarded lid. A small orange and white kitten slinks out from the shadows, edging forward watchfully, its large, green eyes flittering about.

"I found him here in the alley and I don't think he has a mother to care for him," the woman says, never looking in Emma's direction. The kitten gazes upward, studying Emma briefly before greedily devouring the presented food.

"So that's why you stole the food?" Emma inquires as she watches the zealous kitten gorge itself. In the emptiness of the alley Emma can detect the diminutive chirps and mews of delight. An uncanny aura of light energy radiates from the girl. She is definitely not human, but Emma can't quite place what she is. If the pulse of her power were malevolent it would be thicker, almost stifling to be around. This girl's nature is potent, ancient but not evil.

"He was hungry and in need, so I got him some nutrients," she answers blankly as she softly pets the cat's head. A loud purring rolls from its tiny form as it licks the lid of all the lingering food.

"Why not just take him to a shelter or at least buy him some food?" Emma asks.

"I have no money and have never had a need for it. In a shelter, he would be lost among the millions there, simply another stray left to the predation of others." Emma notes the sadness in her tone. The girl stands, turning, her almond-shaped, reddish-brown eyes staring back at Emma. Even within the cold darkness of the alley, her hair catches the light and

warms the space around them, reminding
Emma of summer wheat bathed in the late-
day sun. A striking purple stone sways as it
peeks from the layers of her coat, and the lilac
color glows brightly despite the folds of cloth.
"He chose me to protect him; he has honored
me with his trust, so I will now devote myself
to him. To dedicate one's existence to others
is a great reward. To see their happiness and
achievements attained, even over your own,
can provide a sense of meaning and purpose.
Perhaps our purpose today is to save Logan."
She gestures to the kitten, which is now
licking and cleaning himself.

"Logan?" Emma asks as she studies the infant
animal with such an adult name. "What is
your name?"

"My name is Nina, and Logan means one who
lives in a hollow." Nina scoops the kitten
from the ground, holding him closely. "Tell
me, Emma, is there someone in your life to
whom you have dedicated yourself? The one
who is of extreme importance to you, that you
will give everything to see them succeed?"
There is a light, almost playfulness to her tone
that interchanges with a startling wisdom.

"How do you know my name?" Emma strains, her insides fluttering under the scrutiny of Nina's deliberate gaze. There is an underlying sense of feral strength hidden under the woman's gentle façade. It is not as potently violent as a wolf's, but deadly just the same. Nuzzling Logan, Nina sidesteps Emma as she stands in the center of the alleyway.

"It was very nice meeting you, Emma. I look forward to seeing you again." Nina dips her head in a small nod and turns, making her way out of the alley.

Emma stands dumbfounded for several seconds, watching the young girl leave. Something deep inside her warns her to be cautious, but there is something so familiar about this woman, Nina. Emma can sense no evil at her core, yet there is something unsettling about her nature. Inhaling sharply, Emma pushes aside those thoughts for another time. Quickly glancing around Emma ensures that the alleyway is clear of any onlookers before she opens a portal and steps through.

Emma crosses the threshold onto the stone-paved floor and into the Hallow. As a general rule, no one is allowed to open a gateway directly into the main assembly room, which might disturb a meeting or trial in progress. This particular corridor has always been the least used, so it is the area Emma opts for more often. It is amazing how some habits are so hard to break, even in light of all that has happened here. The network of hallways is vacant and undisturbed. The deep layers of blood and bodies have been swept and cleaned away, but the slightest hint of death still lingers in the air. Even from within the copper-fueled haze of that night Emma can recall the pure violence–limbs hacked away and blood soaking into the earthen floors. The lives of those she considered her sisters snuffed out. Before Thanatos's attack and attempted coup, these halls would have been bustling with other Fury and their Gyges, coming and going from one duty to another. Too many had lost their lives on that day, all for the power-hungry aspirations of one man.

Sara's death has still left her feeling painfully alone and empty, a heartrending wound that may never heal. Sadly, even after all of the death that Emma has seen, part of her still hopes to see Sara skipping down the hall toward her.

Approaching the huge double doors of the assembly room Emma can hear voices echoing throughout the vast area. The tumblers of the door handle creak and moan loudly when she turns the knob, opening the door. Mother Mei Li and Bastian are standing on the dais and Emma walks into the room.

The great hall is empty save for the two of them. Emma quietly makes her way up to the first row of bench seats, silently surveying the couple as they acknowledge her approach and Bastian dips his head a little when she nears.

"Emma, we were just discussing you." Mei Li nods as well. Her posture is composed, almost rigidly ceremonial. "Bastian has asked for our aid in the coming weeks."

"What exactly is he asking for?" Emma inquires. Her insides instinctively clench; Bastian has proven himself a worthy ally but can she completely trust him?

"Oh, it's nothing too difficult. A European dignitary of great importance will be coming to the area to oversee some peace talks, and Bastian's clan is to host as an intermediary party. He has asked that we help with maintaining the peace, that is all." A small smile graces Mei Li's lips as she explains.

"Do you expect that there will be trouble?" Emma counters, a gnawing uneasiness growing within her.

"It's nothing more than normal. I'm sure it will be boring, to say the least," Mei Li assures her. "Though our situation has changed slightly, we will still maintain our primary purpose." An unspoken tension simmers between them. On several occasions, Emma has tried to broach the subject of her place within the group and a life with David. But each time Mother Mei Li has shut her down, outright refusing to discuss the matter.

"I guess you are right," Emma nods, attempting a tiny smile. "How is the infant?" Emma changes the subject before her mouth causes trouble.

"He's doing quite well, good color and seems to be growing steadily." Mei Li's eyebrows furrow as she taps her lower lip in thought.

"Do we know yet what he is?" Emma finds it impossible to gauge Mei Li's troubled expression.

"Not as of yet, except that he is partially human. I will need to study him further. We also still need to discover who his mother was and why she was killed; we have found nothing out about her. She doesn't match any missing persons, and has no identification, apparently no past or even fingerprints. I fear we will need to broaden our search to find out more." Mei Li thoughtfully toys with a bronze medallion hanging from her neck, rubbing the bright ruby set in its center.

"I can always take him in if the need should arise." Bastian offers softly, his blue eyes reflecting a soft kindness, contrasting his vampiric nature. His dark, hooded features exude the frigid malice of a capable predator.

"I'm certain he will be safe with us for now," Mei Li answers demurely. The wooden doors at the far end of the hall swing open, crashing into the stone walls.

All three turn and gaze sternly; at the white-haired man storming toward them. Two of his goons flank him and they make their way through the assembly area. Poe rides their heels, glaring at them.

"My apologies, they refused to wait and were starting a ruckus out in the hallway," Poe barks through gritted teeth. His short-cropped black hair and eyes reflect the dim torchlight. Emma is amazed that the scars that had marred his skin have not returned. Although her ability to heal wounds is her strongest trait, she had some doubts that she would be able to keep the scars at bay. Holy silver can cause deep-set and permanent wounds in a vampire. Bastian had requested that she try and heal Poe to alleviate a debt owed and thankfully, it seems to have worked, so there may not be a need to see if he would keep his word.

"As I have told you before, Calder, there is nothing more I can do for you," Mei Li addresses the intruders coldly. Mei Li isn't a queen among them, but she is a Mother, a title of equal importance.

"What do you mean there is nothing you can do?" Calder's face crinkles as he sneers at them. Streaked grey and white hair is shorn closely to his head and thin-rimmed glasses frame a set of malice-filled black eyes. "You are the only reason I am even here in this shit hole!" Calder's face twists in vile disdain as he plants bony fists on his hips. His partners cross their arms over swollen chests in unison and Emma is certain it is a well-practiced mannerism. The skin along Emma's arms prickles at the pure wickedness that plumes from the trio and she steels herself against the urge to rub the stink of it away.

Emma's vision flickers as she studies them, and the subtle hum of white noise washes over her. Obsidian darkness pulsates as it steals her sight for a millisecond before it returns. In the background the scene before her shifts and morphs. Mei Li and Bastian remain constant in their location, seemingly frozen against the perceived chaos around them. Emma's heart thuds wildly as the shutter effect clicks by, playing out with Calder's men, causing a delicate thrum of rage to quicken in her veins. The scene stalls with one man bent over–his fingers, a sickly purple color and his wrist skewed at an odd angle. His partner is collapsed on the floor, clutching his throat. With a raspy inhale, the vision slips away and the overpowering fog rolls off, revealing the hall and everyone as they were. Shaking her head, Emma calms her breathing, scanning the room. Adrenaline pumps through her as the heady emotion claws for release.

"We have not asked you to come here," Mei Li counters; her eyes are cold and unmoving. Her gaze flashes, settling on Emma momentarily before returning to Calder.

"What would you have me do? Sit by, while you have all of my businesses shut down?" Calder spits as he furiously jabs a finger at them. "Don't tell me you have nothing to do with it." He speaks over Mei Li, ignoring her as he rants. "Four of my clubs have been closed this month alone. How am I supposed to make a living with you absconding with my property and relentlessly persecuting me?"

"The closing of your establishments and the removal of Aidan are two separate issues." Mei Li's demeanor remains coolly resilient as her head tilts to the side, her hands clasped lightly in front of her.

"Listen, I don't care about what kind of drivel you are spewing. I purchased Aidan fairly and I am out a valuable commodity. Now my business is suffering and what are you going to do about it?" Calder snaps, spittle frothing at the corners of his mouth. Calder is a man used to getting his way, regardless of the consequences.

"The fey had no right to take Aidan in the first place, nor did they have the right to sell him to you," Emma interrupts sharply, her own anger rising to match his. "It is not our concern if you are compensated financially. Your dispute should be with the fey, not us. And as for your clubs having been shut down, it has come to light that several under your employ are humans and not there of their own free will. If I were you, I would consider myself lucky that all we have done is to shut them down." Emma allows the fierce anger to edge into her tone.

"You know, at one point and time the Fury were to be only whispered about for fear of being heard." Calder scoffs as he steps forward, a palpable wrath flowing off of him. Emma moves, blocking his path to the dais and Mei Li, meeting his cold stare as he stands before her, his onyx eyes staring callously back at her. "It is clear to me that you are weak, pathetic reproductions of what you once were," Calder mocks.

Emma pulls on the energy wafting around them. Her eyes shift from hazel to a fluid copper as the temperature in the room drops. The group stands stone-still as their breaths plume in frosted clouds.

The two bodyguards leap forward, surging at Emma. Sidestepping the first blow, she brings an elbow up, smashing it into the first lackey's throat. With short sucking gasps, he clutches his throat as he goes down. From behind, a thick, meaty hand wrenches at Emma's hair. She turns into the hold and locks onto the man's hand. With a tiny amount of pressure, she twists his hand outward in an unnatural way until she receives the pleasant popping sound of the joints giving way. Dropping to his knees, the man bellows in pain and his mangled hand falls uselessly to his side.

"No, Calder, that is where you are wrong," Mei Li replies frostily as she gestures toward the doors. "We are stronger than ever. Have a good day."

Calder lasers them with his pointed gaze for several seconds, and his face blooms into a deep shade of red before he turns to leave. Each of his men receives a swift kick as he passes them. The two injured men stagger to their feet as they woefully depart.

Chapter 6

David sits cross-legged on a tightly woven Oriental rug that spans most of Mei Li's personal quarters. Everything within the space seems unchanged since the last time he was here. Warm colors of gold and burgundy ease some of the tension riddling his back and shoulders, but there is a lingering stiffness that won't dissipate. He rolls his neck from side to side, trying to get a crack to relieve a growing knot, but no luck.

Since being turned into a vampire, his body doesn't completely feel like his own. It's like putting on an old jacket that someone else has been wearing for a while. Will he always feel as though he is waging a constant battle against himself? While the transition has left him with heightened senses and increased strength, he still can't stomach drinking fresh blood. His body craves the blood, but he doesn't want to crave it. It is a necessity, that's all; for now, animal blood from a local butcher shop seems to slake his thirst.

Through some trial and error, he's found a decent way to warm it and keep it down.

A delicate movement and sound bring his attention back to the room. David's gaze is drawn to the small child lying on a thickly padded blanket before him. The baby's gentle brown eyes watch him curiously as his tiny legs wriggle and kick outward as he lies on his belly. His chubby, miniature body strains under the pale-blue jumper he is wearing, which is dotted with fluffy teddy bears. David must admit that all things considered, the baby is adorable.

He mentally checks off all the baby's requirements. The infant has been fed, part of which he promptly burped up on David's shirt, and he's gotten a bath and a brand-new diaper. Mei Li has apparently decided that she will be in charge of watching the child and has had a crib moved into her quarters. To be honest, David was really shocked when she asked him to watch the baby while she attended to her duties. Not too many people would be alright with a vampire babysitting, but it's not like he is terrified of kids. He chuckles to himself as he fondly remembers helping his mother tend his younger brother. It had been so long ago, but it all came very naturally to him.

As a human he never had given much thought to having children of his own. He'd often waver back and forth between the idea that it'd never happen and a hope that there was still time. It isn't clear if Gyges can even father children and a vampire can have them but there is a lot involved in the process. But now, even if he wanted kids, would Emma want them too? If they were both human, he'd ask Emma to marry him and maybe they'd start a family.

"Well, what do you think, kiddo? Do you think Emma would marry me if I asked?" David poses to the newborn. "It's alright, I can take the truth. I need you to be bluntly honest with me. You're a good man." The baby squeals, bouncing faster in response. David nods with a grin. "I guess you are right. We'll just have to wait and see." He and Emma aren't humans anymore so maybe it is just a waste of energy thinking about things like that.

Shaking his head, he studies the child, whose tiny arms and legs leap wildly. Large chocolate-colored eyes stare back at him with a powerful intensity. Reaching out, David picks up a plush elephant and lightly wobbles the rattle inside.

"You know what, little man, you are going to need a name pretty soon," David whispers. Tiny arms reach upward to the suspended rattle, fingers opening and closing. With his gaze locked on the desired toy, the infant pushes his body upward onto his hand and knees. After a brief wobble, he sits, flopping down onto a well-cushioned behind. David can't help but laugh as he hands the rattle over. The baby squeals with an open-mouthed, toothless smile in response. Clutching his prize tightly, the baby fights to stay awake, his blinks lagging and his eyes becoming slower to reopen. "Are you getting sleepy, little man?" David asks with a tilt of his head.

Moving quietly, he gently scoops up the little child and walks toward the crib. Even this far away from the surface level, David can sense the ebbing of the day. His body seems to be well tuned to the rise and setting of the sun. The baby nestles into David's arms as he paces in front of the crib. The warmth of his tiny form seeps into David's chest, heating his cold body.

From down the hall David detects the sound of someone approaching. Without any other indication he instinctively knows that it's Emma. Her light footsteps make barely a sound over the stone floor. She approaches cautiously and stands backlit in the doorway, watching him as her presence fills the small room. Tiny wisps of her hair have loosened from her bun and glow with a fantastic warmth as they catch the light. An aura of calmness flows from her as she leans a shoulder against the doorframe. When he is with her and her peacefulness envelops him, the night doesn't feel as cold. He'd bet anything that if his heart could beat, it would be flapping out of his chest.

"You look quite handsome with a baby in your arms," Emma jokes, a wispy smile touching her lips. She studies them with her soft hazel eyes.

"I have a little experience with babies, mostly helping my mother," he stammers, coloring with a nervous energy.

"Well, it looks like Mei Li has left him in good hands." Emma crosses the threshold into the room. The baby's head perks up and he smiles at her approach.

"Has anyone figured out a name for him yet? It feels off just calling him 'the baby,' David asks with a shrug.

"Mei Li has suggested that I name him. I guess because I'm the one that found him." Emma's brows furrow as she studies the child. "What would you name him?" Her intense gaze meets his under the waning light.

David inhales deeply as he contemplates all the possible names. How do you go about naming a baby? He mulls to himself. People usually name their kids after their parents or grandparents. But this isn't their child. "I guess I've always liked the name Aaron; it was my father's middle name."

"Aaron," Emma repeats as she digests the name. "Aaron is a fine name," Emma decides with a small nod. "What do you think? Isn't Aaron a good name?" She whispers to the baby and is greeted with eager laughter. "I think he likes it." Emma lifts an eyebrow at David.

"I think so too." David can feel himself smiling broadly as a warmth sweeps through his chest and the soothing calm settles through him. Young Aaron yawns widely as Emma takes him from David's arms.

"We'd better get you to bed," she murmurs. David watches her as she places Aaron in the crib and covers him with a blanket. For a moment she lingers beside him, softly rubbing his back as he drifts off to sleep.

"Do you miss it? Having kids, I mean," he asks with a small amount of tension in his voice.

"I miss my children every day, and I miss Sara. But the past can't be undone." A subtle melancholy is evident in her eyes as her form seems smaller than before, but she attempts a frail smile anyway.

"Sorry. That was a weird thing to ask."
David's voice is hoarse as he clears his throat.
"I didn't mean to bring up any bad
memories."

"It'll be alright." Emma waves it off. "My
children aren't bad memories and it's not the
weirdest thing to happen in the last few days."
She laughs at the confused look on his face.
"Every day lately has been an ever-growing
level of weirdness, and on top of that we have
our mysterious bundle over there." She
motions to the contentedly sleeping Aaron.
"For some unknown reason I've been getting
summoned to judge or aid someone, whether
I want to or not, and it's been happening
more and more often." Her body stills as she
makes the confession, attempting to downplay
her fear over it.

"You are compelled to go?" he asks,
processing the notion. "Well, are you forced
to judge?"

"I don't think so. It just seems that I'm
required to answer the call—that's all I can
really say at this point. But who knows? I'm
worried, though; what if it comes to the point
that I can't choose?" She shrugs softly as she

inhales, the dim light dancing on her hair. Emma rubs her hairline, nervously scratching the skin. "Before now, even on an assignment, I've always had a choice. What if I lost that? To just become a mindless zombie, doing things I don't want to."

"I don't think that's likely to happen. But I know even if it did, you would do the right thing," he reassures her. The deep crease in her brow lets him know it isn't working very well. "Okay, let's say, for example, that I turned into a raving lunatic killer. I would expect that you would judge me as needed–right?" He tries to keep the brewing emotion from his tone, trying to stow away his own fears of what he may become.

"I guess, if that is what needed to be done," she replies in a whisper, her gaze nervously darting around the room. He drapes his arms around her, holding her close in the moment of silence.

"I realize this isn't fun to talk about and I hope the situation never comes up. But my points still stand–in the end you'll do what's right and fair; that's all I or anyone can ask for. I assume you've talked to Mei Li about it. Is there something she can do?"

"Yes, I've talked to her about it. She says she's working on a way to diminish the potency of the calling. The problem is that Aidan has been spilling the beans to everyone about how to summon us. Our choices to resolve the issue are to either kill everyone who knows, or find a suitable work-around," Emma answers.

"We will figure it out. I know it's frustrating right now." David hugs her tighter to him and kisses her temple lightly, wishing he had answers for her.

"I'm so tired of fighting to be heard by them." Her shoulders sag against him. "I just want to feel as though I matter–that I'm not some old workhorse who's still just useful enough to not be put out to pasture. I always feel like I'm one step behind them. I've been alone for so long and I don't want to feel that way anymore." An agitated energy flows off of Emma as she struggles to maintain control of her emotions. "What if Thanatos was right? Maybe I will never be a welcomed equal to either one of them." Her eyes glisten with unshed tears. She needs to hold on to hope, and he prays that he can come up with the right words.

"No, he is not right." David turns her, clasping her shoulders. "He only said that because he knew it would bother you. You said yourself that this is unknown territory for all of us. Mei Li and Olivia don't know how any of this is supposed to go and we are all just fumbling around in the dark, but we will figure this out. Just give it a little more time." His stomach clenches at the sight of her, knowing she is troubled and not being to do anything about it. "You are very important to Mei Li and Olivia and to me." David gently strokes her arms, wishing he could ease her pain.

"I have learned over the years that people can care greatly for you yet have no respect for you as a person." Her expression is resolute as a solitary tear trails down her cheek. David wipes away the errant moisture with his thumb. He is drawn to her warmth, feeling it pulse into his flesh as he cups her cheek.

"People should respect people. All we can do is hope one day the world will see that." David sighs deeply. "And if they don't, we'll

just beat the crap out of them all," he says
with a toothy smile.

"All of them, huh?" Emma replies as an old
shimmer lights her eyes.

"Yep. All of them," he teases and she laughs
in response. She wraps her arms around him,
hugging him closely as she feathers his lips
with a kiss.

"Any idea yet what our little Aaron is?" David
asks, looking down at the sleeping babe.

"No. It's like he is a blank slate. I pick up his
human side, but there's something else there
and it's almost familiar, but I just don't
know." Emma's mouth crinkles to the side as
she searches for the right words.

"His other half could be a lot of different
things. At the end of the day, it may not even
matter. We'll just make sure he is raised right."
Emma snakes her arm around him, hugging
his side. She rests her head against his chest,
and he is submerged in the rich scent of her.
The fragrance of shampoo and body wash
tickles at his nose. Her soft form presses
delicately into his and the sensation of her full

breasts pushed up against his side makes his cock twitch.

"Ahem." Olivia coughs from the open doorway. Her short platinum-blond hair reflects the hallway light starkly and is nearly blinding to look at. "Is the baby sleeping?" she asks with a soft voice. Emma and David walk toward the door quietly before answering.

"He has just fallen asleep," Emma answers.

"Oh, pooh. I was hoping to spend some time before he went down for the night." Olivia pouts slightly before quickly returning to her stern expression and looking toward David. "Bastian asked that I let you know he is leaving."

"Does he need me to go with him?" David poses, secretly hoping she'll say no.

"He didn't say whether or not you should follow him and, as you know, he is painfully ambiguous sometimes," she says with a smirk. As his eyes adjust to the brightness of the hallway a ruby choker around Olivia's neck gleams and catches the light. Emma studies it briefly as well yet says nothing. "Anyway, I also wanted to let you know I won't be much help with the big vampire meeting." She makes quote signs as she speaks. "I have to babysit that pain in the ass Bray while also trying to find Moss–so much fun."

"Bray's not a bad fellow. Maybe a bit stubborn and emotional, but all in all he has a good soul," Emma reminds her calmly.

"I know. There's just something about him that sets me on edge. Moss has always been a dangerous type, and he has no qualms about the collateral damage to innocent bystanders. I don't want to have any needless distractions from Bray." Uncertainty flashes through Olivia's eyes.

"While he may be an inconvenience, I don't think Bray could be that distracting. Plus, as you said, Moss can be unpredictable; having some backup may not be a bad idea," David points out.

"Perhaps–perhaps not," Olivia counters, still looking troubled.

"I really wouldn't worry about it too much," Emma interjects. "It's not like you are in lov—" Emma's knees hit the floor with a jarring force.

David and Olivia rush forward, clasping onto Emma to keep her head from smacking the floor. Her eyes lift, reflecting a fluid sheen of liquid copper. They both stare on in horror as the tremors wobble Emma's body.

"Emma, what is it?" David fights back the near frantic rise of panic. His gut clenches and senses heighten as he scans their surroundings, searching for the impending attack.

"Someone's calling me," Emma grunts through clenched teeth. "I have to get up." David lifts her, carrying most of her weight as she steadies her tottering legs.

"What do you need me to do?" He shifts his arm around her waist. "Where do we need to go?"

"I won't know until I get there. You need to go with Bastian." Emma inhales sharply; another wave washes over her, and the color drains from her face. Olivia lightly grasps Emma's arm.

"No. I'm going with you," David replies inflexibly. While it was no longer his job to protect her, he'll be damned if he is going to abandon her.

"What time is it? The sun is still out, or it could be out wherever we appear," she blurts out frantically, pulling toward the door.

"The sun is set. It'll be fine." Emma searches his face, probably trying to come up with a valid reason for him to remain. But he would follow her no matter what she said.

"I need to open a doorway, I need to go." She groans as she stares at the wall in the hallway. Her desperate gasps for air echo around them. Each of them nods in response as they make their way out of the room.

"Are they always this bad?" David asks, turning her so they can all fit through the doorway.

"They all kind of sneak up on me, but this one's the worst so far." David feels Emma's body still at once, as all of the manic energy is shunted. Her gaze settles on Olivia as she stands in the corridor. "Why are you not affected? Can't you feel it?" Emma's voice shakes under the strain. With a fluttered motion Olivia's hand barely grazes the ruby in her necklace.

"I see." Emma's tone is frigidly cold as all the emotion seems to drain from her. Olivia looks on anxiously in silence. Stepping forward, Emma slaps the wall with a solid force, opening a portal. Emma quickly steps through and is swallowed by the inky blackness and David follows.

Chapter 7

As they step out of the portal they are engulfed by the crisp chill in the nighttime air. Billions of stars shimmer over the banner of sky. A thickly grown tree line surrounds them on all edges save for the side of the garage where they emerged. Trees and brush dance softly under the influence of an unseen breeze. In the far distance, small neighboring houses are sparsely illuminated by moonlight. Despite the lateness of the hour, David can make out small buds developing across much of the undergrowth. In spite of their eagerness for spring, the buds twinkle with a thin covering of frost. Even the coldest of winters will eventually end, he muses. The buildings are barely lit by the tiny floodlights that turn on as soon as they move. Even with exceptional night vision David's eyes still strain against the morbid darkness that lingers just beyond the lamplight.

A simple colonial house is attached to the other side of the garage. The downstairs windows stream light outward into the night.

In contrast to the evident calm of the night, they can hear heated voices carrying from within the house. At least one female and male voice rise and fall in an apparent argument. An unnerving tension radiates from the residence; a wave of uneasiness dances down his spine that has little to do with the outside temperature.

Walking up, he stands beside Emma, drawn instinctually to her heat. Small wisps of steam rise from her skin, and she shivers noticeably as she studies the building. If he didn't know her, the unearthly aura that emanates from her might send him running. It's at moments like this that she gives off a terrifying level of suppressed emotion, a tightly coiled spring that threatens to snap. Ever since the battle with Thanatos she's had to fight more and more to control herself. Her power has become a dark enigma that can be startling, but he knows Emma and has seen the light within her.

"What was that all about–between you and Olivia?" he asks, trying to examine her features under the dim light.

"For some reason she isn't being called the same way I am," Emma sighs in frustration as a feeble plume of vapor escapes her mouth.

"Maybe they only called you? Can it be that specific?" David moves closer to her, trying to lend body heat he doesn't have.

"I don't know. In the past when a Fury was summoned, all of them came. But that is probably something to think on for another day." Emma rubs her forehead. Her fatigue is more apparent, so he understands that for now it's best to change the subject.

"Do you know why we are here?" David asks in a gruff whisper. He touches her arm tentatively as he pushes away his own growing irritation, hating that they are walking into the unknown.

"Whoever is calling me is in that house." Emma's gaze never stirs from the house as she moves forward guardedly.

While approaching the front steps David quickly scans the area; he strains his ears to detect anything beyond the boisterous screaming from inside. Crashing glass echoes from within and the distinct sounds of a scuffle resonate from the small home.

As they step up to the landing the front door swings open and they are met with an ungodly blast of hot air. His skin prickles and sweat starts to collect on David's forehead. The two elements wage war on his skin as the cold outside attempts to freeze each sweat droplet. As much as he wants to wipe away the errant moisture, he forces his hands down, unmoving before the man who answers the door.

The young man standing before them is lean and well-built throughout his arms and shoulders. He is about David's height but clearly takes up all of the available space in the doorframe. Thick black hair and pale olive skin shines under the light reflected from the interior of the house. His hazel-green eyes study them stoically, strange eyes with the elliptical pupil of a snake. His white Armani button-down shirt is speckled with red flecks of blood, and he weighs them with his gaze, measuring them both equally before he breaks the growing silence.

"Erinyes," he notes with a nod to Emma. "I am Sanjay; we've been waiting for you. Please come in," he welcomes them curtly. There is an ancient quality to his accent as if he were more accustomed to speaking a much older tongue. Only the oldest of species referred to the Fury by their original Greek name.

Emma's eyes meet David's briefly before she steps over the threshold. Once they are inside, the front door closes behind them with a soft click. From within the foyer the rest of the house is deathly quiet. It is the silence that forebodes an event of great violence. The temperature in the house is oppressive with the heaters along the walls continuously hissing as they belt out moist warmth. The sweltering heat only fuels his agitation and a stagnant claustrophobia bears down on him. He inhales deeply, trying to get some much-needed fresh, cool air–no luck.

Entering the living room, David is instantly taken aback. Opulent seems to understate the area. Gold accents gleam from an errant light that cascades in from an adjoining room. Lamps and even baubles are set with precious stones, which catch the light, and the softest fur-lined rug runs the length of the room. Cream and grey wood offsets the gold highlights of the room, giving a clean look. The décor didn't appear as gaudy as everything might seem, working well together. Through a small doorway David can see what appears to be the kitchen, which is occupied by several individuals.

He shadows Emma closely as he steels his edgy nerves. At a moment's notice he'd flip that switch, shutting everything off, because he may need to kill everything in this house. It was a well-honed skill he had needed in the service and, so far, it had saved his ass quite a few times. Preparing a mental mindset steadies his nerves, calming him. Midway to the kitchen, Sanjay stops, turning toward them.

"Before we go in there you must know this—I support my brother in all things; unfortunately, we all knew this marriage would be troublesome," he states hesitantly as he shifts tensely from side to side.

"Why is that?" David asks as he scrutinizes the man for any signs of deceit.

"Manu is an honorable man and he doesn't take his vows lightly. We always felt this match was ill-suited for both of them." Sanjay seems to struggle for the right words. "Both of them have committed themselves to another who is quite the opposite."

"They say opposites attract," David counters, the stifling heat eating on his nerves.

"In some cases, yes. I only ask that you take all of the information into account when making your judgment. Aidan said we could trust you."

"Did he now?" Emma asks with a lift of her brow. David breathes cautiously; he's seen that look in her eye before–and she's pissed.

"Yes. He understands that these charges are taken very seriously by our people. Karlee said she reached out to him to avoid any unwanted shame. We would like the issue resolved with as much discretion as possible." His reptilian eyes shifting under the light, they glow as the smoldering emotions burn just below the surface.

Emma nods to him as a trickle of sweat slips down her neck. Even from this distance he can discern the fast beat of her heart, and how she is breathing heavier as she chews on the inside of her cheek.

Several recessed lights illuminate the open space of the kitchen. The color scheme flows from the living room into this area, but the gold is replaced with silver and stainless steel. David squints against the drastic change in light level. The kitchen has all of the latest and greatest gadgets and appliances for cooking—more space-age than contemporary.

Three individuals are huddled together in the small breakfast nook against the far wall. A lone man is seated at the table, his hands balled into fists as they rest in his lap. From this angle all David can distinguish is that the man has the same color hair as Sanjay—so probably his brother. A large, crescent-shaped welt outlines his visible eye.

A woman stands across the table from him, her arms bracing herself on the table as she leans forward. David notes that despite her angry scowl, she is exceptionally striking, an ethereal beauty that keeps drawing his eye to her. Thick waves of azure and olive hair flow down around her waist and her emerald-green eyes watch them with an undeniable intensity. The light sundress, which fits her form snugly, exposes arms and an upper torso covered with barely visible scales. With each subtle movement her skin shimmers with silver and green hues, which seem to illuminate the air around her.

Behind her stands two men, both of whom can only be described as strangely beautiful. Each of them has a deep blue and green pallor to their skin and vividly colored matching hair. Their semblance calls to mind images of nature or an untouched mountain stream. There is no way they could pass for human.

"Ah, the Fury has finally arrived." The woman addresses them with a lift of her chin. "I'm Karlee." She turns slightly, gesturing to the two men behind her. "This is my brother, Ford, and his friend Kai." Ford shares a striking resemblance to his sister, though his hair and skin are speckled with darker shades of browns and greens. Kai's teal-green skin is more opalescent than his companion's—his vibrant aqua marine hair is dappled with flecks of pink and yellow like that of a tropical fish. The spattering of color dances along his forearms and upward under the sleeves of his t-shirt.

"Water nymphs?" David asks warily. His experience has taught him to be vigilant around the more feral beings. These creatures are akin to mermaids and could kill indiscriminately.

"Yes, we are water nymphs." The glint in her eyes as she studies them raises the hair on his arms. The nearly palpable tension that surrounds them has a crushing weight in the confines of the kitchen. With bated breath, everyone seems to be carefully weighing and formulating their next move.

"So why exactly would water nymphs have need of a Fury?" David queries as he struggles to exude an outward appearance of nonchalance. Stepping slowly, he walks over, standing next to Emma but making no move to touch her. A minute tremor shakes her hands as she examines everyone. A subtle torrent of power flows from her and she strains against the force. As much as he wanted to, if he offered her physical reassurances, it would appear as if she were weak. In the midst of such company that could be dangerous.

"I want you to judge my husband and if necessary, to kill him," Karlee says.

David nearly chokes on his breath. Her demeanor is completely relaxed, an unsettling calm, as if she were asking them to run a quick errand. David catches the slight upturn of her lips as her delicate hands move softly in front of her. Sanjay skirts the edge of the kitchen, stopping to lean against the sink. He is near his brother, but enough of a distance away to be nonthreatening. His thick brows furrow with concern as his gaze darts about the room; his whole form radiates an unmistakable defiance. His movement only draws their attention for a brief moment before each turns back toward the center of the room.

"I think you need to give me a little more information than that. Explain why you have summoned me here," Emma asks carefully as her voice cracks and her gaze flicks from one individual to the next.

"Manu and I married several years ago. He saved me from a fisherman's net on the eastern banks of my stream." Her eyes drift down to the man seated in front of her. "I was as instantly drawn to him as he was to me. He promised to love me, to honor me, and give me children." Softness touches her eyes as she looks at her husband. "I thought nothing in the world would make me happier. But after all these years he has broken his vows. He has been unfaithful, and I still have no offspring." Karlee finishes coldly as any look of gentleness is swept away.

"So, you have asked me here is see if your husband is cheating on you?" Emma asks in a clipped tone, her lips pressed in a thin line. "I am not a marriage counselor."

"Yes, but he promised to be faithful. Are the Fury not the upholders of oaths?" Karlee snaps. The strength of her fervor pushes against them, seeming to rattle the room around them. "He swore to me before all of the Gods that he would love me, honor me. Do I not deserve the justice of your hand?" Her hands thrash about as she jabs at her husband.

"I have never betrayed you." Manu cries as he beseeches his wife; his voice is nearly hoarse with tension. Ford steps toward him aggressively but is halted by Emma's upraised hand.

"No one touches him in my presence." Her voice is a low and stern warning as she eyes the two men. Ford returns her solemn stare but stays his ground; his nostrils flare slightly as he glowers at them.

"Why would a nymph care that much about fidelity?" Emma asks. "Prudishness isn't a common species characteristic, and most of the nymphs I know are very content with open relationships."

"A promise is sacred, and I will not be tethered to an oath-breaker." Karlee's words ooze venom; her eyes narrow as they land on Manu.

"Why do you believe he has been unfaithful?" Emma asks as she approaches Manu. Her unyielding expression seems to unsettle the nymph, and Karlee steps back. For a moment Karlee stammers and David nearly laughs out loud as her mouth moves wordlessly and she composes her thoughts.

"Our marriage has turned cold. He is always away." Karlee fists her hands.

"You know that I have my duties. I would stay more if I could." Manu's voice breaks under the strain and he inhales raggedly, his whole body shaking.

"He has children from other women," Karlee spits with a fiery malice as her words slice through the air.

Emma breathes in and out slowly, her eyes giving nothing away. "Why is that relevant?" A heady silence grows as Emma continues to scrutinize Karlee. "Were these other children conceived during your marriage?"

"No. But he has chosen to give these other women children but not me. He wasted all of his seed on them when I am the one that deserves a child. When he returns home there is nothing left for our baby." Karlee's voice rises and cracks as her eyes widen, fretfully scanning the room. It's almost like watching a spooked animal about to bolt for safety.

"You will not let me near you anymore. How can we have children if you can't stand me touching you?" Manu barks, shifting uncomfortably in his chair as he blows out an exasperated puff of air.

"Have you seen a doctor about this?" Emma asks, her face softening for a second. "You know, a shaman, healer, seer, or a fertility doctor?" she explains at Karlee's confused expression. "Is it possible that you are the one who can't have children?" David's heart aches, seeing the barely perceptible empathy lingering in Emma's eyes.

"It's not me!" Karlee bites as she slaps her arms over her chest.

"Very well, I will speak with Manu now," Emma states coldly, all emotion slipping from her voice. He has glimpsed this side of her more times than he cared to. No matter what she was feeling she could completely detach from it, leaving behind only this pure, unhampered judge. The mere thought of those perfect hazel eyes staring at him with such cold judgment sends a shiver through him.

141

Emma turns, facing Manu where he is seated. Her head dips slightly from side to side as she studies him. She offers a hand to him and Manu jumps slightly at the movement.

"To know one's heart is to know thy soul. Your heart and therefore your soul are being questioned." Standing tall under the soft kitchen lighting, she appears otherworldly, as beautiful as she is frightening. "You are here under the accusation of breaking the matrimonial oath. Are you prepared?" She asks, her tone formal yet somehow gentle. Manu's gaze is transfixed to Emma and his eyes never leave hers as he lifts an unsteady hand, clasping hers.

Emma's eyes brighten and shift as the liquid copper color swallows their natural hazel hue. A chill floods into the room, wicking away the oppressive heat as she lays a delicate hand on Manu's cheek. Everyone's breaths begin to materialize as puffs of wispy vapor. Karlee hugs herself, warming her arms. David shakes off the small shivers that twitch within his muscles; he watches Emma warily as the seconds stretch into minutes.

The amount of time it can take to judge someone varies greatly depending on what is being looked for and the age of the individual. David's skin itches as the anxious energy builds around them. With his senses alert, he keeps a keen eye on everyone. Both Ford and Sanjay stand stone-still as they mirror each other. Thick arms folded tightly across their chests, their own stern glances survey the room. A small nerve ticks feverishly in Sanjay's cheek as he observes his brother. David allows his gaze to shift back and forth between Sanjay and Ford, comparing the two in stature and stance. He isn't surprised that they both radiate a fiercely protective quality– they are here to stand by their kin.

Kai nearly paces as if he's some caged animal, but he is fighting to hold his ground. Small ticks in his muscles give away his tightly controlled emotion. Although his age may vastly outnumber that of humans, David can see he is still fairly young for a nymph, still wet behind the ears and impulsive.

Karlee surveys everything with a starkly contrasting countenance. Her soft brows are knit closely together into an almost seamless line. She shifts ever so slightly on the balls of her feet. With the others he senses a potent readiness for violence, something brewing on the outer edge that raises the hairs of his arms. Yet he doesn't feel the same kind of emotions emanating from Karlee. He searches her face as he tries to grasp what it is that makes her so off–fear. A well-cloaked emotion, but fear nonetheless.

David's eyes shift back to Emma as her hands fall away from Manu. In a smooth motion she turns facing Karlee and the others, her eyes still flashing a fluid copper, catching the light as she turns. Karlee's hands flutter in front of her and she clasps them tightly, but David glimpses the tremor racing through her. Her pulse quickens and breathing becomes shallow. David realizes that this bird's going to flush. Karlee is barely keeping the panic at bay as Emma rounds on her.

"He has been judged. Now it is your turn," Emma announces, extending her hand to Karlee, who immediately retreats. She shifts backward, standing beside her brother and Kai. Both of them cloister around her as protection.

"What do you mean?" Karlee asks in a croaky whisper.

"Surely you understood the cost?" Emma's tone is foreign and icy-cold once again. Karlee extends her hand, pinching a small coin as she offers it. A slightly sinister smile spreads over Emma's cheeks and she shakes her head. "You asked that I judge someone on your behalf, so now you, yourself, must be judged to prove your merit." Her smile slips away and David's own tension begins to rise; it is in moments such as these that you understand the need to fight or die. More than likely they aren't getting out of here without someone getting their ass beat.

"You will not touch my sister," Ford commands, his voice nearly a deep growl as he steps forward, standing in front of Karlee. "Tell me. What did you see?"

"I saw a husband who has never been unfaithful to his wife." Emma's gaze is dark as she focuses on Karlee. Her head cocks slightly to the side as she lasers Karlee and advances forward. The space around them feels claustrophobic, with Emma nestled between the table and the wall to her right, Karlee and the two men mere feet from her.

"You're lying. You didn't see it; you didn't look hard enough." Karlee shakes her head frantically—her own feet betray her as she tries to get farther away.

Kai leaps forward, the obsidian blade in his hand flashing under the fluorescent lights. Moving faster than even he thought possible, David closes the distance between them, blocking Kai mid-strike. Shielding Emma with his body, he seizes Kai's arm with his right hand, redirecting and using his forward momentum to, grab the back of Kai's head, driving it into the wall next to them. The drywall shatters and Kai slumps to the floor, leaving behind a perfect head-shaped hole.

Ford bellows a savage war cry as he crosses the small area, lunging for David. With no time to react and so little room to move, Ford tackles David, sending them both to the ground. A dining chair skitters across the floor, knocked away by the force of their bodies. Though he is smaller than David, Ford's weight is unnaturally heavy as he rains down punches. David blocks the assault and grapples Ford's arms, grabbing his wrists as he wraps his legs around him. His muscles strain as he fights to gain leverage on his opponent. Calculating his movements, he knows he needs to contain the situation quickly.

A guttural scream echoes through the cramped kitchen. All eyes jerk around to follow the sound at the far end of the room. Quickly, David realizes that as he was distracted by Ford, Emma closed the distance between her and Karlee. Emma has the smaller woman pinned against the wall with a hand clamped around her throat. Karlee struggles violently as Emma stares at her with a focused intent.

Ford and David cautiously stand in unison. They are controlling one another with a fistful of shirt collar. As Emma's arm falls limply to her side Karlee staggers toward her brother. Ford releases David as he ushers his sister to safety. The young woman seems shaken but is otherwise unharmed.

"You drag me here in the middle of the night so you can lie to me, and all because you don't want to be married anymore." Emma's voice is an acid-drenched whisper; she turns to face them, and her irises swirl with fluid pools of copper and fire. In those depths, a molten hell storm is brewing.

"I didn't lie," Karlee stammers with a choked voice, her eyes glossed with tears and her appearance more sallow than it was earlier. "He has to be cheating." She shakes her head. "Aidan said you would help me; he said you would find out what he's been doing."

"Don't worry, I have seen the truth. You want a divorce but lack the guts to ask for one. So, you sought out Aidan, knowing that he has a kind heart and quite obviously a huge mouth. You hedged all your bets on a shot in the dark that he's been unfaithful." Emma seethes as she lasers Karlee with an unyielding stare.

"Did you ever love me?" Manu asks with a broken voice and his head hanging low, unwilling to look at his wife.

"I do love him," she answers to the room. "But I cannot be attached to one person for eternity. I need to be free to live and love whomever I want."

"It is your choice," Emma addresses Manu. "My advice is to let this one go, move on with your life, and find another who will help to make you whole." The kindness of words does not leak into her tone.

"I am not wrong in this. I've done what I had to do," Karlee shrieks as she tries and fails to pull away from Ford. Manu studies his wife, his face stricken and pale from the realization and pain.

"Did what you had to do?" Emma smirks as she scratches her head. "Tell me this? Did you have to fuck Kai over there?" She jabs a pointed finger toward the still-unconscious man lying on the floor. "Because you did that, didn't you?" Emma scoops up the silver coin that has rolled to her feet.

"But Aidan said…" Karlee whispers.

"Where is Aidan?" Emma demands. David steps forward but is halted. "Wait," she whispers softly and turns her gaze back toward Karlee.

"I think he's at work; he said he had a meeting–that's why he could not be here," Ford answers cautiously.

"Where is he?"

"His office is in Manchester–that's all I know."

Karlee's face drops into her hands as Emma slaps the nearest wall, opening a portal and stepping through. It closes before David can reach it.

"Damn it, Emma." He swears silently to himself as he pulls out a cell phone, scrolling through to find Olivia's number.

Chapter 8

Blood rushes through Emma's ears as she crunches through the dirty snow bank heaped between the road and sidewalk. Despite the icy air, her skin boils as it exerts to contain the bubbling rage that scorches her core, pushing her forward.

A rational mind would have asked for Aidan's work address, she chides herself. Unfortunately, she's not really of a rational mind at the moment. The uptick of her bizarre emotions seems so out of place to her. Fueled by the strong reaction, she only needs to think about Aidan and she is drawn in his direction. Not knowing the exact location of Aidan's office means she needed to search around a bit. Taking a random guess as to where to start, she's spent the last twenty minutes or so sweeping the area to narrow in on his position.

The wasted time does little to improve her mood. She pulls in a lungful of cold air, praying it will squelch the fire that rages there.

But the overwhelming weight of everything only seems to compress it, making it more potent. Why had Olivia and Mei Li not told her about their amulets? Were they going to tell her at all? Maybe she was simply foolish to think that their situation would be different after Thanatos. It appears as though they are content with the idea that Emma will shoulder the burden of acting as their hands. Is she still just an expendable implement that they wield as they please?

Loneliness has been a constant companion, an emotional state that she existed in yet shared with no one. After some time, you realize that solitude is survivable; spending centuries surrounded by others yet feeling utterly isolated became her way of life. The alienation feeds into other potentially dangerous emotions. Lately, there is a barely yoked anger that is alien to her. It is hers but not completely, as it seems to be lying in wait on the outer fringes of her mind. There is perhaps a part of her that has awoken to something to which she has no real connection. Being summoned for increasingly more mundane disputes is eating away at what little patience she has left. A deep-seated worry is that the next one may push everything over the edge, sending her to a place where there is no return.

She stares upward, inspecting the darkened office building. The seven-story structure stands out against the neighboring stores and offices. The angled walls of polished marble cut in on each other, creating a geometric shape that softly gleams under the ambient light. Closing her eyes, she pictures Aidan and knows he is inside. Emma's hands tremble against the urge to smash the glass of the front door. Aside from the intermittent car the road is empty at this time of night, so there is less concern about drawing unwanted attention.

At the main door she glances up and down the street once more to ensure there are no onlookers. She tests the handle to find the large glass paneled doors are securely bolted closed. Pulling at the energy around her, she focuses on the electronic locking mechanism. She pulses a stream of power through the door handle until the lock gives way. With a welcoming beep the door opens and she quickly enters, letting the door shut quietly behind her.

Thick shadows cloak much of the foyer with only the main receptionist desk and an elevator door visible. The highly reflective surface of the floor tile glistens under the moonlight. Her footsteps scuff loudly as she crosses the room. A green-lit arrow is displayed over the steel-paneled elevator; the number six shines brightly against the darkness. Emma presses the up button and after a few second the doors slide open, streaming fluorescent light into the foyer. The doors close and Emma jabs the button for the sixth floor. She nervously taps the handrail as the bubbling surge laps at the mental barriers she has in place. Blockades that will keep her in check. *I'm just going to talk to him*, she warns herself and inhales deeply, wishing she could blow out everything that was bad and broken inside her.

The muted *ding* pulls her from her thoughts as the doors slide open to reveal a simple waiting room. Alternating empty seats and end tables line the wall to the right. The soft hum of heating vents looms overhead. A partially silhouetted figure cranes his neck to spot her over a computer monitor. A thin man sitting behind a receptionist's desk puts his phone down at her approach and greets her with a tentative smile.

"Can I help you?" he murmurs fretfully. He is a lanky fellow with a shaggy mop of blond hair. Even under the dimmed lights of the foyer, Emma can discern the cerulean blue of his eyes and the remarkable gentleness of his face. A thick beam of moonlight illuminates a path directly in front of the receptionist desk and all that is behind it is in relatively obscured darkness.

"I'm here to speak with Aidan," Emma answers calmly as she crosses over a thickly padded rug. She can only see the man but there is something off, setting her nerves on edge.

"He's in a meeting." The clerk stands abruptly as Emma nears, but she doesn't slow her pace, heading straight for a set of oaken doors on the other side of the desk. "You can't go in there," he whispers with saucer-round eyes. Dipping around his outstretched hand, she rounds the desk and crosses the darkened path to the door.

When she steps into one of the few shafts of light, a low growl stops her in her tracks and a hand jerks toward her from the shadows. Her heart leaps violently as she becomes aware of another presence. How had she not sensed them before?

Her mind sprints and she barely spins out of its grasp when the mangled claw cuts through the air. Before her feet come to a stop, another hand arcs out of the darkness. Each time her feet settle, multiple clawed arms chase her and one manages to clip her, drawing blood, a hooked nail has caught on her armband before it is plucked away. Ignoring the blood soaking through her shirt, Emma peers into the depths, knowing that there is only one entity there. Her breath comes in heavy pants, and she scans the darkness for the next attack.

Spilling out of the inky shadows a massive form emerges on double-jointed legs, seeming to absorb all of the meager light. Emma steadies herself against the dense tendrils of fear coiling around her neck, threatening to steal her air. The hulking body is nearly ten feet tall with a fine layer of white fur covering its purplish-black skin. Two sets of arms flex methodically, each hand sporting jagged claws. The lower set of appendages seems tiny compared to their upper counterparts, but still well-built enough to easily rip someone in half. Blood-red eyes sneer at her from a ragged, doglike face as it huffs plumes of sulfur-drenched air toward her. Piecing the image together, Emma's mind churns to place the origin of her new opponent. Her stomach knots at the recognition of what this is, though her mind prays she is wrong.

The draegloth are a subset species within the drow—dark elves. They are vile creatures with an unending bloodlust for death and carnage, and though they are more intelligent than trolls, they are more savage as well. Some are magic users, cloaking themselves in shadows before they strike. But why is one here in Aidan's office?

Moving with a terrifying speed it closes the distance, slashing at her. Emma shifts back on her heels, sliding sideways to barely escape the strike. A second set of claws careen toward her—she evades them and has to roll away across the floor, skittering and dodging again and again as the beast's arms swarm her. Unyielding, straight-razor pincers arc downward and slam through the carpet mere inches from her, biting into the subfloor. Chips of wood and carpet fibers spray through the air as it wrenches its digits free.

The draegloth circles Emma as she staggers to her feet. It continually seeks to close the space between them. Her breathing slows as she starts to pull at the power around her, knowing she is physically outmatched by this behemoth. The cool copper of her armbands warms as the temperature around them plummets.

Moving lightly on her toes, Emma endeavors to move them closer to the door leading to Aidan's office. Yet the beast seems determined to keep her near the elevator. For each advance she makes, she is quickly pushed back; her frustration builds, fueling her rage. Seething inside, she is ready to scream yet stops as she is forced to sidestep the vinyl-covered chair flying at her head. The heavy piece of furniture explodes as it hits the wall behind her. Emma spins away, covering her head from the flying debris. The creature rasps and coughs and Emma swiftly comprehends that it is a coarse laughter.

The raging draegloth stalks toward her, swiping a razor-sharp claw midstep. She pushes off on her legs, lunging forward and under its swinging arm. Through the small open spaces around his form, she can see the door—that is her focus.

Emma raises her hands, planting them on the draegloth's chest as her feet come to a stop. His smaller secondary hands clasp around her wrists, securing her within melee range. As it glares down at her, a croaking noise rumbles from its throat, which Emma can only assume is its abysmal language.

Its talons stream downward toward her as she releases her stores of energy. Hot air floods the room as the electric current discharges from her hands into the draegloth, sending him careening backward. His hulking form hits the door and the polished wood surrenders under the immense weight. His body skitters over the floor, coming to rest only when it hits the resistance of an area rug.

Her blood feels as if it is boiling against her skin as it oozes from the closing wounds. Inhaling wild breaths of air, Emma tries to steady the unruly race of her heart. She stalks into the office, throwing her senses outward to detect any other threats as she crosses the threshold. Aidan sits, eyeing her nervously as she enters the room. His gaze flickers from the unconscious draegloth to a shadowed form seated across the desk from him.

"Emma, this really isn't a good time," Aidan states in an oddly formal tone.

"Shut it," Emma snaps; even she is slightly alarmed by the sharpness in her voice. "I only asked you one thing—to keep one secret to yourself. But instead you go and tell everyone. You fail to realize that I am not your servant, Aidan, nor am I anyone else's," she seethes through clamped teeth, forcefully jabbing a finger at him. Aidan watches her stoically, his forearms resting on the edge of his desk. "Tell one more person and I promise you this. If you force the issue and I have to visit you again, you will implore every god that is under the heavens for death."

"They needed your help," he answers
defensively. His eyes soften, although tension
remains and the muscle deep in his cheek
pulses. "I knew that you wouldn't leave them
helpless or hopeless." Pangs of guilt gnaw at
Emma's insides, but she maintains her
focused stare at Aidan. Emma's hands quake
as she fists them painfully at her sides. The
tears glossing her eyes only serve to fuel the
cauldron of stewing emotions. *Don't cry in front
of them.*

The shadowed form remains motionless, a
cloak of black hair obscuring his features. A
mild sensation of death lingers about the man.

"Did it ever occur to you to just ask me?"
Emma asks as her throat tightens. Her own
body is conspiring against her to constrict her
words, squelching their release. "I am not a
monster and I would have helped you. But
you never thought to ask me–instead, you
forced my hand, taking away what free will I
have left." Her voice trembles and she angrily
swipes away a rogue tear as it races down her
cheek.

Aidan studies her wordlessly for several
seconds. His gaze flickers to some movement

from behind her. From her peripherals and sensing it, Emma recognizes the feel of the portal opening. The auras are so familiar to her that she doesn't need to turn around to tell who it is. Her body becomes rigid as Mei Li steps through the gateway.

"Emma. What are you doing here?" There is a peculiar carefulness in her tone that is rarely heard in the confident mother.

"I am just having a friendly chat with Aidan." Emma turns to glance over her shoulder. Mei Li is flanked by Olivia, Bray, and Bastian. Bastian's keen stare locks on the seated figure and his impossibly white skin grows paler. Olivia stands beside Bray; she shifts nervously in the background–her gaze sweeps the room and she seems to assess the damage. A prickly energy dances along Emma's skin. She watches the apparent tension lingering about everyone.

"I am sure Aidan understands the point you are trying to make. Perhaps it is time to head home now. It is obvious that we have much to discuss." Mei Li turns her head to Aidan, addressing him in a deliberately formal tone. "I apologize for the unfortunate intrusion. It

is important that we remember that we are
emotionally driven beings, and that on
occasion we are in error by overstepping our
bounds." Mei Li's gaze flashes back to Emma
for the last part.

"The Fury have helped me in my greatest
need, so they will always be welcome," Aidan
adds tensely as he stands. "And I apologize
for any misunderstanding on my part. Emma
has given me much to think on."

"You honor us. You have an important guest,
so we shall let you return to your business,"
Mei Li states with a small nod. Every eye is
drawn to the rousing draegloth as he wakens.
With a shake of his head he uses all four
appendages to push himself up. The beast
glares at Emma, taking an expansive step
toward her.

"Ryl. Stop." Aidan's guest stands, turning
slowly to face the group. His voice is a low
baritone that thrums throughout the room,
with a touch of something Latin to his
tongue. This man is a looming mountain of
solid muscle with a nearly stifling presence.
Emma struggles to find adequate breath as the
sheer force of his aura fills the space around

them, crushing her. Bastian drops to a knee, his gaze plastered to the floor. The unease in Emma grows as she fights the urge to turn and run.

His lustrous black hair flows down the length of his back, ending at his waist. His vampiric black eyes study them with an unnerving calm. His nose is long and sculptured, equally balancing the straight lines of his chin and jaw. A sleeve of tattoos runs down the length of both of his arms. Emma can distinguish a pyramid, a sun, and an eagle flying through a field of jaguar pattern.

"Ryl lives for a good bloody battle. Once he sets his eyes on destroying someone, it is difficult to stop him. We are not here to kill the Fury and I would prefer not losing my bodyguard tonight." His head cocks to the side and he peers at Bastian, who is still kneeling. The giant of a man approaches Bastian, helping him stand with a firm slap of his shoulders.

"Guillermo, I wasn't expecting you until tomorrow evening." Bastian smiles anxiously; his gaze flutters about the room as the men embrace.

"There were a few things I needed to discuss with Aidan first, so it seemed better to come a night earlier. I hope that isn't a problem." Guillermo tilts his head to the side toward Bastian, who appears the smaller man in comparison.

"No, of course not. All is prepared–my home is yours for as long as you have need of it."

"Very good, my friend," he says with a wink and smirk; the white of his fangs gleam against his dark olive complexion.

"Guillermo is our king," Bastian explains. "Please allow me to make the introductions. Guillermo, this is Mother Mei Li, Olivia, Bray, and Emma." Bastian gestures to each one, and Mei Li and Olivia nod formally.

"Mother Mei Li, up until now our correspondences have been over a great distance. Even separated by the great ocean, I have heard much about the Fury and I am honored to finally meet you."

"I must admit that I am curious as to what your need of the Fury is, but perhaps it is best discussed later. I look forward to our meeting tomorrow." Mei Li turns to face Bastian. "Bastian, would you be so kind as to escort Emma home? Olivia and Bray have a pressing matter to see to and I want to make sure she gets home safely."

"I am very capable of seeing myself home." Emma bites her tongue at Mei Li's direct stare and she tries to keep her tone level, feeling the icy chill of her own words. "Very well, Mother."

Mei Li steps toward Emma, her voice softer despite the harshness of her words. "We will have a further discussion about your actions tonight."

Mei Li and Olivia open two separate portals. Olivia steps through one followed by Bray as Mei Li departs on her own. Bastian bows deeply before Guillermo and turns to face Emma.

"I can call for a ride if you don't mind a wait." Bastian smiles coyly.

"I can open a gate." Emma's shoulders slump as she shakes her head and touches the nearby wall. With a sweeping arm, Bastian gestures

for her to proceed, then he follows right
behind.

Chapter 9

Olivia taps her foot, trying to burn off anxious energy as she waits for Bray to finish talking with Isaac. Initially, she had argued against his insistence on stopping. Moss is still out there, and they need to find him. But that is only a portion of what is pushing her to complete this task as quickly as possible. To be honest, she realizes that her impatience has more to do with being stuck escorting Bray around. Admittedly, Emma seems to be correct in her assessment that Bray isn't a bad guy. Unless he is really good at hiding his true nature.

Even though the Fury are supposed to be able determine the character of an individual, she has been wrong before. Since their meeting where they defeated Thanatos, the thought of this man has plagued her. Sadly, this is not something that she can confide to anyone else. The Fury aren't allowed to feel confused or uncertain when dealing with people. To rationalize it, the obvious answer is that he is simply easy on the eyes, yet she knows that's not completely it. There have been several men within the Hallow and in her former life that one could consider attractive, so looks alone can't really explain it. His demeanor seems to distress her in a way that defies logic. The solution is to find Moss and get him back to Erebus with little delay, she silently huffs, trying to refocus her thoughts.

After the failed rebellion, Thanatos, Moss, and other Gyges were locked away in Erebus. Something tells her he will stay close, but what if she's wrong? For all she knows he could be on the other side of the planet by now. She didn't really think he would go back to his residence, but it was worth a look, so they had searched his apartment and found the place empty. None of the neighbors had remembered who he was, much less seen him.

Delay after delay is infuriating but at the very least it provides her with some time to think about their best options for locating Moss. Finding him will allow her some breathing room to move onto other, more pressing issues. She has enough to handle with Emma and Mei Li, so the last thing she needs is some werewolf making this worse.

Olivia and Mei Li were well aware that Emma would have to bear the brunt of any summoning until they could procure another amulet. But as much as she tries to put the matter out of her mind the outcome still doesn't sit well with her. She reminds herself that Emma is a capable woman, one who can handle most every situation that comes her way—yet Olivia can't completely ignore the pangs of guilt nipping at her guts. Perhaps they were wrong in assuming that there would be some respite for the Fury or that it is acceptable to let Emma shoulder this alone. If Emma's actions with Aidan are any indicator, they will need to find another solution and fast. Oddly enough she had been on her way to speak with Mei Li when Bray showed up this evening.

Olivia glances up from her thoughts as Bray clasps Isaac's shoulder, shaking his hand. From their mannerisms, she can tell that both men have a great deal of respect for each other. She really didn't know much about any of the wolves, but they seem to be a closely bonded group. Each of them seems willing to do almost anything to ensure the safety of the pack. Bray runs a hand through his blond hair after he hugs his friend and turns toward her. He approaches with a set purpose to his stride, seeming focused on the task at hand.

"Is everything ready now?" Olivia asks as Bray nears. His aqua-blue eyes eerily catch the stray light, momentarily distracting her pent-up frustration. The strange sensation dances along her skin, making a hiccup of breath snag in her throat. Perhaps it is from the remarkable aura of strength that emanates from him. After the experience of meeting Guillermo, the knowledge that powerful beings radiate a potent force is firmly evident.

"Yes. I always try to make it a point to let everyone know where I am going. Plus, I still need to keep my family safe. Though it seems some of the other packs in the area have been getting rowdy," he states with a brief shrug.

"Rowdy—how so?" Olivia asks, keeping her tone very smooth.

"In light of recent events, some feel that there is less of an importance to maintaining our laws."

"So, they believe the Fury are weaker and they can do whatever?"

"The Fury are the last line when it comes to preserving peace. A good leader will address potential problems before they become a larger issue. While finding Moss is vital, I still need to keep the peace among my people as well." Bray's expression gives nothing away as they both watch the wolves leave the Hallow through one of its many access points. "So any thoughts on where we can keep looking? His apartment turned up nothing."

"We should search Moss's quarters in Erebus. Perhaps we can find something useful–an address or correspondence." Olivia shifts tensely as the heaviness of the air presses down on her. She turns, heading down one of the long corridors that lead to the lower levels.

"Do you really think we'll find anything there?" Bray inquires as he takes several long strides, keeping pace with her. His soft footfalls quickly sync up with hers.

"It may be the best option right now. I'm not really thrilled about consuming a good deal of power and time, but perhaps we can find a hint that will speed up this whole process. Unfortunately, I doubt Moss will surrender willingly, so the element of surprise is a must.”

“Whether he surrenders or not is of very little importance. I hope you are aware that I need to see to it that Moss dies.” A cold determination resonates in Bray’s tone as his eyes darken and, in that moment, Olivia gains an appreciation for the pure, feral nature of his kind.

“The acceptance of what you want or need has yet to be determined,” Olivia answers stoically as they descend a set of stone stairs. A heavy iron door sits at the bottom of the stairwell, shrouded in pale torchlight.

“He killed my father. I owe it to his memory to seek justice.” Bray nearly growls, his teeth reflecting the ambient light and his nostrils flaring with tightly leashed emotion. The cumbersome door squeals in protest as she pushes a shoulder into the cold metal and coaxes movement from it.

"I am well aware of what he has done. It doesn't change the fact that his fate has not yet been decided. If the cord of his life is to be cut, then it may very well be you who is meant to sever it." She fervently claps the dust from her hands as they step into an even dimmer passageway; meager sconces dot the stone corridor ahead of them. The putrid air wafts around them as a stagnant cloud kicks up, tickling Olivia's nose. The overpowering odor incites dark imagery of death and decay, which is a prime reason she has avoided coming down here.

"Would you try and stop me from killing him?" Bray asks. His voice sounds intentionally apathetic, but Olivia notes the small nerve that ticks at the corner of his eye.

"If it is determined that he should die, then no, I wouldn't stop you." She matches his tone, yet she can easily sense his tension.

"Who makes that decision?" He turns to face her.

"It all depends. Our goals are seeing justice done while also maintaining harmony. Before a verdict is made all available information will be taken into account." Olivia stops outside a steel-barred door to Moss's last residence. She pulls a key from her pocket; metal scrapes against metal as Olivia fights with the stubborn, rust-laden lock.

"So is that how you come to all of your judgments? Because it would appear to me that Emma has at least a mild problem with one of your decisions." He smirks with a lift of an eyebrow. Olivia freezes mid jingle of the key to stare up at Bray's all too self-satisfied expression. It's never good when an outsider becomes aware of the internal conflict within the Fury; that's always been the general rule. It's bad enough that nearly everyone seemed to know about Thanatos immediately after it happened. The speed at which news travels can be amazing.

"I imagine that even you are capable of understanding that a cohesive team can still face some snags." Ripping the door off of the hinges after it's just been replaced would be bad, but it would make her feel so much better. Olivia sighs heavily as the stubborn lock finally gives way and the cell door swings open.

"I understand snags. I also know that those baubles you and Mei Li wear shield you somehow." He motions to her necklace. "I even managed to piece together that it was decided Emma wouldn't get one too," he explains while tapping his temple. "Isn't it amazing that someone like me could figure that out." He inhales sharply, placing a hand on his chest. His feigned shock added only to mock her further.

"I am impressed by your apparent mental prowess and I don't need to answer to you but just so you know, she will get one." Olivia's hand flutters up to her neck. "The stones are rare, and they must be purified in a laborious ritual. We were only able to obtain two at first." Her hands fist tightly as she forces her gaze from him, examining the space around them. She is still more than capable of killing him right here if she wanted, but she doesn't want to. Aside from being a serious pain in the butt, why is his presence so troublesome to her?

The cell is fairly small, dimly illuminated by a hanging drop light. A disheveled cot sits against the far wall. The sink and toilet are crusted with grime, as one would imagine they haven't seen a good cleaning for some time. A simple foot locker and table are the only other bits of furnishing in the quarters.

"So, Emma's amulet is on backorder?" He smiles with obvious derision.

"Something like that, yeah," she responds curtly. She allows her tone to be clipped in a futile attempt to convey her growing irritation.

"I can see why she would be a little pissed." Bray casually pushes a few items around on a nearby table. Olivia studies the lines of his profile. He is completely different in appearance from Eugene, her ex-fiancé—each man is attractive in contradictory ways, with very dissimilar souls.

"Well, it's not really something to concern yourself over." Olivia tries for a bored tone. "I've known Emma for quite some time, and I'm sure that once we can talk to her, she'll understand." She decides to avoid the bed, instead squatting to open the foot locker. "Just let it rest, Bray. This really isn't any of your business."

"Okay. I'm just saying is all." Bray shrugs his shoulders. He looks over to the dingy bed and grimaces. "You really want to search this whole place?"

"If you want to find him quicker, then yes." Olivia pulls out a small plastic doll. Its large blue eyes are faded and the once-radiant blond hair is caked with dirt and old blood. Why would such a man keep something like this? Olivia wonders. She gently wipes the filth from the doll's face as Bray steps up beside her.

"What exactly do you know about Moss?" Bray asks, with a minute shiver as his stare takes in the toy.

"Not much, really. He was the Gyges for Celia, another Fury." Setting down the doll, Olivia finds some old photos, faded black and white photos with thick cracks bisecting the sturdy paper backing. The grainy images stare back at her, and Olivia squints to read the barely legible writing on the back. One photo in particular draws Olivia's attention; it is a simple family portrait yet the image sends chills across her skin. The solemn faces of the adults are emulated by the two small children.

The patriarch of the family stares forward through thick-rimmed glasses—with the same black eyes of Moss. The fact that he is wearing a policeman's uniform does little to lessen the cruelty in his demeanor. The mother figure is a plump woman with her black hair pulled up as if in a hurry—her visage is a flesh-like death mask, cold and alien.

The small, raven-haired boy, who is no more than five years old in the picture, mirrors his father's soulless eyes. As Olivia flips through the stack of photos she notices that only the parents and young Moss remain constant. With each photo, Moss and his parents age progressively. Yet the second child never seems to age. With every photo the brother or sister of Moss changes, becoming someone new, and one of the small names written on the back of the photo is scratched out.

"The red-head that helped him kill my father. Was he close with her?" Bray's voice is strained as he inspects the pictures over her shoulder. Even he seems unnerved by the hidden collection.

"Yes." Olivia jumps somewhat at his question and inhales deeply as she shoves the pictures back into the foot locker. "Although I don't think he was ever really close with anyone." Her voice catches as she withdraws several yellowed newspaper clippings. *Local police officer and family killed in tragic fire.* Olivia swiftly scans the article, realizing that it is the report of Moss's parents' death. It is unclear as to how the fire started but the two-story home was quickly engulfed and the only survivor was the couple's fifteen-year-old son.

"So he wasn't friendly with anyone?" Bray asks, but he instantly shrugs at Olivia's exasperated glance. She sighs, trying to pull in calming air.

"This is not a place for friendships. As far as I know, Moss spent his time with Celia or by himself. And he wasn't a person to draw others to him." The brass badge she pulls out next glints under the meager lights and Olivia has to tilt it to read the numbers.

"Well, Celia is dead." With a long arm, Bray cautiously lifts some of the sheet from the bed, holding the offensive linens as far away as possible. "So where would he go?" he asks with a look of pure disgust twisting his features.

"That's what we are here to find out." Olivia shrugs her shoulders, her irritation growing as it becomes clear that nothing here is going to be useful. If they can't find anything to help them at the very least go in the right direction, then she may have to resort to using her powers. While it is an option, she would prefer to save what energy she has for a potential fight.

"You can search that rat hole all night but you'll never find anything." A disembodied voice fills the small space. Olivia's body snaps to a rigid alertness and she scans the immediate area. There is an eerie familiarity to the voice as a tremor of unease rumbles through her and her eyes dart to the cell across the empty hallway.

The darkened cell flickers with light. Thanatos appears as illumination floods his confined space, his left arm extended out as he clicks the knob of the standing lamp next to him. Even from the safe distance, separated by iron bars, Thanatos is an imposing figure. He lounges almost lazily in the plush reading chair as he studies them nonchalantly, his dark-brown eyes shadowed against the light.

The god of death, he had pretended to be a simple Gyges in order to try and seize control over the judgment of man.

"Do you make it a habit of just sitting in the darkness like a creep?" Olivia allows the venom to carry in her tone.

"Not particularly. The light was on before you came down, and I was reading. But when I heard you both coming, I turned it off." Thanatos's chin lifts as if listening for something, his gaze shifting to the edges of the hall.

"So you decided to hide from us?" Bray asks from over her shoulder. Olivia feels the savage apprehension rolling from him. It is clear that he has enough sense to fear death.

"Not hiding–just trying to determine if I wanted to interact with you," he answers calmly.

"Why would you think that I'd be interested in even interacting with you?"

"You're interacting with me right now, so what does that say?" Thanatos mocks with a lift of his brow. Even when Thanatos or

Ambrose, as he was known to her, was her Gyges he had managed to grate her nerves at every turn.

"Well our chat has been enlightening, but if you don't mind, we have more important matters to attend to." Olivia turns back to the already-searched foot locker, praying Thanatos will take the hint.

"You won't find anything of use in there. The only personal effects Moss had are in that box." His head dips toward the foot locker. "Moss is the quintessential minimalist, very few belongings, little to no companions. I can guarantee that you won't find love letters or an address book of friends in there. But if you want to waste valuable time and energy, by all means be my guest. Perhaps the dog can sniff a dirty pair of his underwear and track him down." His eyes light as a condescending smile spreads over his face.

"Well, what would you suggest, smartass?" Bray snaps, his hands balling into tight fists as he inhales a lungful of air.

"Don't feed into his need for attention," Olivia warns Bray. "We won't get anything from him that is worth it." She senses a battle of wills playing out between the two men. It is fairly unlikely that anything between them will come to blows, but their pissing contest is just irritating.

"I beg to differ." Thanatos leans forward in his seat; his forearms rest softly on his knees. "There are two people who have had close contact with Moss for a period of time, Celia and me—and Celia, as you know, is dead."

"Why would you help us?" Bray poses, his body stiff with a strained energy that threatens to overflow.

"Regardless of what you may think of me, my desire has always been towards maintaining a balance within the universe. While you may not agree with my methods, they are sane and work toward a greater good. Moss is a necessary evil, but without a controlling force he will run amok." His smile returns at Olivia's apparent confusion. "You see, to exact change one must understand that there will be losses. They are a natural part of the process, but doing so often involves less-than-savory acts. Moss could carry out those dealings without the distasteful burden of conscience."

"So he's a psychopath just like you. That is nothing I didn't already know." She huffs, trying to hurry him up.

"Not necessarily like me. As a god, I am not obstructed by your set of moral codes. To accomplish my goal is what gives me pleasure—not the action needed to get there. Moss relishes in the pain and fear inflicted, yet even he has limits to what he will and will not do. To find him you will need to think as he does. I was able to control him by providing him an outlet for his sadistic needs. While he is fleeing from you, he will still be drawn to what makes him feel alive." A frigid chill crackles along Olivia's spine as the true extent of his words bleed into her understanding.

"What kind of place could that be?" Olivia's voice trembles despite her best efforts.

"Look for a place that fosters violence—gladiatorial arenas, or clubs that cater to a bloodier and less-than-gentle clientele. I am sure there are enough out there for you to find him."

"Going from one to the next will be hit or miss at best," she sighs, feeling like she is starting all over again.

"But both you and I know that there is a more efficient way to locate him. Why don't you summon your snakes to find him?" Thanatos smirks with a faint perk to his lips.

Olivia's guts curdle under his knowing gaze. Her new set of skills aren't something that she has shared with anyone else. If she's to be completely honest the extent of her powers still scares her. So how is it that he seems to know?

"What is he talking about?" Bray asks uneasily.

"It will expend too much energy." Olivia's gaze stays locked on Thanatos.

"If you are always concerned about the risks you may as well step down. The Furies would hazard all to catch their prey and you must do so as well. You cannot know the extent of your power unless you push yourself; it is one of the reasons why I wanted to lead you—to see your potential develop."

"You will never lead us, I can promise you that." Olivia seethes at him. Thanatos responds with a hearty laugh, a booming sound that fills the cramped space.

"We'll agree to disagree." His features melt into a somber mask of focused energy. He studies her with an eerie determination that sets her nerves firing. "Don't you think we have wasted enough time? You have your prey to hunt."

Olivia makes no effort to hide her loathing of the man. But she inhales deeply, forcing any thoughts of him out of her mind. The temperature of the room drops and she draws on the currents of energy that surround her. The pressure builds within her and she envisions Moss, framing his face in her mind. The sensation crescendos and Olivia knows that the emerald mist has begun to seep and spiral from her skin and hair, rising from her in delicate tendrils. The wisps of vapor thicken, becoming more solid. Three of the main stacks develop into a serpentine form, their ghastly tongues flicking at the air. Kneeling, Olivia stretches an arm to the ground as the snakes curl their way to the floor. They slither over the dirt, darting outward as they speed toward different walls, each passing through the stone barrier without pause.

Olivia makes the briefest eye contact with Bray as she touches the nearest wall, opening a portal, and stepping through she follows her reptilian bloodhounds.

Chapter 10

Silence permeates the long-darkened space that lies between the two apartment buildings. Emma opens the portal in an abandoned alley on the side of her building. From years of surveying the area, she finds that it is the least populated spot around. Although it is still several hours until dawn, there is way too much risk having a portal open in the hallway outside her apartment. If someone were out, coming or going, it'd be difficult to explain if they were seen.

The chilled air of the alley washes around them as the gateway quickly snaps shut, transforming into the solid brick exterior of the neighboring apartment building. Emma takes several steps away from the wall as she studies the length of the alley; it is empty, and even the sounds of passing traffic seem far away. Bastian stumbles after her, his legs apparently still wobbly from the travel. She hides her mischievous smile as he must steady himself against a nearby dumpster. Pulling in a deep lungful of air, he's trying to dissuade the rising nausea that is common with traveling via portal.

"That is awful," Bastian rasps as he bends over, clutching the sturdy rim of the receptacle.

"After a while you barely notice it," Emma chides, not bothering to hide her amusement. She chuckles but understands the discomfort all too well.

"I think I'll limit my exposure to such things." He straightens up, smoothing his suit jacket with his hands as he tries to regain his composure.

"I can't say that I blame you. But it was your choice to see me home," Emma points out as they start walking towards the street. With a few long strides Bastian matches her pace, walking alongside her.

"Mei Li asked that I escort you safely home," he responds dryly but Emma can sense some underlying indignation in his tone.

Emma bites her tongue versus saying something she'd regret later. As of late she's found herself struggling to toe the line. The overt swings of emotion are startling and worrisome. Elements of her personality that had been so easy to control before are now clawing their way to the surface. *What had she been thinking, going over to Aidan's office?* She never before believed herself to be an impulsive person, yet now she feels an added pressure to guard even her words.

"David is making good progress," he stammers, as if nervously trying to change the subject. His icy-blue eyes shift anxiously to the scenery around them.

"I've known David for a long time–he is a fighter and adapts well to change." Emma's heart tightens at recalling the sight of David lying cold and bloodied on the dirt floor in Erebus. Mother Tatiana had tried to kill him, and Bastian was forced to turn him in order to save his life. It is a truly terrifying thought to realize how close she had been to losing him. She can't seem to settle the tremor in her hand as she dials in the code to the main door, and after a muted beep the glass door clicks open. Passing a long wall of metal mailbox slots, they enter a dimly lit foyer. A small amount of her agitation slips away as she sees that the space is empty, with no one else in sight.

"David is a good man. I have no regrets about saving his life, but I do wish it could have been done differently." Bastian's tone frays with emotion as he readjusts his jacket with a restless energy. "No one should be turned against their will. It has been an essential rule I have stressed to all of my children."

"Regret will smother you as ruthlessly as a constrictor if you let it." Emma meets his gaze. She doubts he is a man quick to tear up but the dark torrent of emotions swells behind his crystal-blue eyes. "While I also wish there had been another outcome, I am grateful for what you did for him. The world is a much darker place without people like David–and you."

Bastian nods, and there is a small hint of bewilderment that lights his eyes. They walk towards the elevator and Emma's soft footfalls seem offensively loud compared to Bastian's.

"It seems you pride yourself on instilling a strong code of ethics in your children." Emma dares a glance over toward Bastian.

"Of course. I have a great responsibility to them." Once more he regards her with a quizzical expression.

"I mean no offense, but that isn't all that common among most vampires, at least not the ones I have encountered," Emma explains.

"Age affords me a level of experience I can hopefully pass on to them. My goal is to help them avoid the more damaging mistakes I have made in my time."

"But one could say that despite your mistakes you have still managed a degree of success. It seems likely that it is your mistakes that help to drive your success." Emma presses the call button for the elevator.

"Perhaps. But there is a difference between hurdles in life and a bad decision that can either end or irrevocably alter your existence." Emma processes his words silently for a few seconds.

"So, Guillermo is your king?" Emma watches the descending numbers of the panel above the stainless-steel doors. "I've never had the opportunity to meet him, and the Mothers have always just referred to him as 'the king,' but it seems you have a lot of respect for him."

"He is the royal." There is intensity in his pitch. "I've known Guillermo for a very long time and for a period of years we both served under the late king, Killian."

"You are old friends?" she asks with a smirk, trying to image a much younger version of Bastian.

"Old acquaintances would be more accurate. Though truth be told, I have never figured out why he never had me killed once he became king."

"Why would he do that?" she pries tentatively. With a soft chime the double doors of the elevator slide open and they step in.

"Because I tried to kill him," he answers so calmly that Emma isn't certain if she heard him correctly.

"Come again?" She tries to hide her shocked expression.

"When Guillermo made his intentions for the throne known, Killian commanded that I find and kill him." Bastian stares forward; the shiny steel panel that surrounds them reflects only her image.

"He asked you to kill Guillermo?" Emma reiterates as the elevator door slides closed.

"At some point and time, we all came to realize that Killian had gone quite mad." A cold pulse skitters down Emma's spine at his calm tone. "We were under the service to Killian out of fear of his power versus any kind of respect for him. I, myself, was taken as a gift of conquest when he defeated and executed my father, and as his sworn servant, I was bound by honor to obey him."

"I imagine that was difficult for you—to serve the man who killed your father." Emma watches his features carefully. She finds herself feeling empathy for a young Bastian living through that experience.

"It pained me immensely, losing my father, but he had instilled in me the importance of principle."

"One would think that you would have been happy to see someone trying to unseat Killian?" Her voice is soft as she speaks.

"Perhaps secretly I hoped for Guillermo's victory. But when I met him face to face, I genuinely intended to end his existence."

"How is it that you both survived?" she asked, knowing that Bastian is more than capable of handling himself.

"Guillermo defeated me quite soundly and he could have killed me–he was well within his right to –but he spared me." Bastian shrugs slightly as he meets her gaze.

Emma silently studies him as the elevator sounds and the door slides open. Stepping out into the hallway, an instant chill clutches Emma's center. The air around seems to hang with an ominous potency as if she were watching a vase falling to the floor yet being too far away to stop it. A nearly imperceptible terror seems to echo down the length of the hall. The corridor is cloaked in the thick veil of darkness, with only the sporadic flicker of a failing light down toward the end. A shambled mass lies in the distance, nearly indistinguishable amid the debris and soaked in partial gloom. Bastian stands frozen as his friendly demeanor slips away, revealing an icy frigidity. He apparently senses the shift in mood; his predatory nature seems to be preparing for an upcoming battle.

From her vantage point by the elevator, Emma can see that her apartment door is ajar but the inside is completely dark. Slipping along the wall, she struggles against the strong desire to run away. Her breath catches sharply in her chest as she pushes forward. Closing the distance seems to take longer than it would normally, a strong feeling that seems dead set against her reaching the end.

As they near her apartment, the mysterious mass viewed from down the hall comes into focus and Emma studies the torn brown paper bag, its contents strewn across the hall and a large orange sitting just outside her door. Passing her neighbor's door, Emma's heart seizes as the familiar scent of blood permeates the space.

Inching forward, she sees the shaft of light spearing into her darkened apartment. The painful thrum of her heartbeat threatens to silence all other sound. Showcased within the thin band of light are the fingertips of a delicate hand.

Moving quickly, Emma squats and pushes her door farther open. Mrs. Van Buren, her elderly neighbor, stares out blankly from dead eyes. A tacky pool of stagnant blood has already jelled underneath her, seeping into the carpet. Despite the low light level, Emma can detect several mangled gashes that score the woman's torso and throat. Reaching out to her neighbor with her senses, she is only met with a resounding silence. The poor woman has been gone for too long to help.

"Your apartment isn't safe. We should leave here at once," Bastian murmurs. He kneels beside her as his eyes dart up and down the length of the corridor. But Emma's body refuses to move as her mind swirls from all of the sensory information flooding her system. "Emma, you can't help her. We need to leave now." He stares for a split second before gently touching her shoulder. The contact pulls her attention back and she lifts her gaze to meet his. "The police may already be on their way, we need to go and not come back." With a hand at her elbow, Bastian helps her stand.

"Wait. I need something from inside." She places her hand on his, stopping his movement as her eyes are drawn to the emptiness of her home.

"There is nothing in there that isn't replaceable," he states sternly, softly tugging on her arm.

"This isn't replaceable. You can leave if you need to, but I can't." She slips her arm from his grasp and carefully steps over the threshold.

"Damn it, Emma," he rasps through clenched teeth but follows her watchfully.

Emma quickly steps over the corpse, searching the darkness as she softly pads down her carpeted hallway. Wayward sounds seep in through the windows from the street below but aside from that, the apartment is deathly quiet. Reaching out with her power, Emma can feel a lingering echo of influence. There is a faint ripple through the air, yet she cannot tell the source. It seems so alien that a place that has been her home for years now feels wrong.

Ignoring the prickling along her skin, Emma sneaks to her bedroom door. The door now feels eerily foreign as her clammy palm slips on the plated metal before it finally turns.

The space is suddenly claustrophobic as the weight of the environment crushes down on her. She is only vaguely aware of Bastian's presence behind her as her eyes scrutinize the room. Everything seems to be as she had left it, yet she can't disregard the feeling that someone is here. Emma steps quickly to the side of her bed, where she withdraws a small shoe box from underneath. She nearly screams as her fingers fumble with the stubborn cardboard lid. The damn thing seems hell-bent on fighting her to open. With an audible pop the top finally gives and Emma removes a small cloth doll. Most of the fabric has fallen away, with a few patched areas, and it is covered in centuries of dirt, but Emma gently places it in the pocket of her sweat jacket. Heading back to the door, Bastian tilts his head at her, perplexed.

"I'll explain later," she mouths as she passes him. Emma focuses her thoughts on getting out of there, but she's halted in her tracks at the sight of a strange man standing in her living room. Half of his face is obscured in deep surrounding shadows while the other is dimly lit by the light that trickles from the streetlights outside. He appears reasonably young, and his jet-black hair is pulled tightly into a knot at the back of his head. Though she knows that she has never met him before, his eyes remind her of Mei Li's, but they differ in that his are filled with a callous cruelty. The leather of his jacket swishes as he folds his arms over his chest, and he almost seems to be casually waiting for her—or someone.

"Who are you?" Emma asks, despite the tightness in her throat as she tries to get a sense of what he is. Mentally, she checks off each species that she can determine—which he isn't. The vertical slit of his iris would lead her to think he could be naga, yet the type of power flowing from him is significantly different than the ones she met earlier. His power echoes with a very reptilian nature and an undercurrent of ancient magic.

"My name is Chen." There is a subtle dip to his head as he introduces himself.

"What are you doing here?" The question emerges as more of a croak than Emma intends. Her skin itches as the anticipation hangs thick in the air around them. Instincts scream for her to avoid this man and to run as quickly as she can from him. There is an inescapable darkness that shrouds his heart.

"I am here to see that you die." There is a glint of something in his eyes that almost appears to be excitement as he speaks.

A flicker of movement draws Emma's attention from Chen, and her insides immediately roll. A skittering shadow lurks over the corpse of Mrs. Van Buren. Its serrated talons gouge at the cold flesh as its eyeless face stares up at them. Its obsidian skin drawn taunt over a hulking skeletal form, it swallows the surrounding light as if it were a black hole. It is a visage that constantly fluctuates in and out of focus, continuously shifting between realities. The embodiment of a nightmare meant to terrify even the Fury. The distinct chittering and vocal clicks instantly identify the faceless. It stands, filling the corridor as coagulated blood and bits of meat drip from its elongated dagger-like fingers.

Her heart pounds against her ribs and goose bumps raise on her arms. From behind, Emma hears the distinct click of a gun's hammer being drawn back. The seconds slow down as each movement seems painfully drawn out. To Emma, minutes take up the time between every one of her frenzied heartbeats. When the faceless clips forward in a jarring gesture, Emma is propelled into motion. She clutches Bastian's sleeve and drops to her knees just as Bastian lifts his gun. With a muted thump she slaps her palm on the carpet, opening a portal in the floor. She jerks him into the hole as the shot explodes over her head. Hearing the shot, Chen dives toward the shelter of the coffee table. The sudden jolt on Bastian causes a misalignment of his aim yet the bullet still impacts Chen midflight. The flesh of his shoulder tears away as the bullet travels through him, embedding in the far wall.

They are swallowed up by the portal, falling at an incredible speed as a pitch-black vortex pulses around them. Emma desperately clings to Bastian as she struggles to orient them within the wormhole. Her pulse races as the clicking of the faceless seems to grow louder behind them. Risking a backward glance, Emma can see glimpses of the massive form falling toward them. Its shape cuts through the darkness as it gains ground, steel claws slicing the air at their backs. Emma spurs them on faster as the desperate need to escape grows.

They are halted for a split second, frozen in the pulse of a heartbeat as they pass through the barrier on the other side. Journeying through the sludge of space, they emerge, sliding several feet across the stone floor of the great hall. Emma's body only stops when it collides with a pew, pushing the flimsy furniture several inches.

The beast's body breaks the plane of the portal as it starts to close. The doorway snaps into a solid state while the beast's upper torso is still traversing through. For a second it hovers, suspended from the wall as an outstretched arm reaches for them. Then as if a cord is cut, the shape falls with a thick, wet splat to the floor.

"Emma," Mei Li cries as she rushes across the hall, her long, black gown swooshing around her. "What is going on?" She stops abruptly as she spies the mangled half of a faceless.

"It attacked us in my apartment." Emma's legs shake as she tries to stand but fails. Rubbing her hands together she resigns herself to leaning against the pushed-over pew. A broken leg of the bench stabs her lower back, but she doesn't care. Her eyes are continuously drawn to the dead monstrosity. Its large, barreled chest is cut just below the ribcage while the lower section of its left arm didn't make it through the portal. The force of the closing portal has cleaved in a clean line from the forearm down.

"We will need to get someone to clean this up." Mei Li's brow furrows as she watches the monster for a brief second before turning to rush out of the room. Bastian pulls himself up onto weakened legs as he staggers over to Emma.

"Are you alright?" he asks as he brushes dirt from his pants.

"I'll live. You?" A shiver hums through her as she struggles to steady her ragged breathing.

"I'm undead so I'll be just fine," he says with a smirk.

Emma is trying to think of a snarky comeback when the words stick in her throat. The faceless is changing; its skin, which is impossibly dark, seems lighter.

"Does it look different to you?" she inquires, pointing to the corpse. Her body grows cold with the unsettling realization.

Bastian cocks his head as he examines the thing. "Perhaps. Maybe it is just the lighting in here," he offers.

"No. It's changing." Her pulse quickens as they watch the ongoing metamorphosis.

With each passing moment, the form grows lighter and more supple. Featureless plated skin dissolves away, revealing the cold white flesh of a human. Emma slowly takes in the emerging features, but her heart nearly stops when her eyes reach the man's saved arm. A normal-enough-looking appendage but his hand has six bloody fingers. Emma drags herself up, walking over to have a closer look. The older man's grey hair is covered in a sticky sheen of a milky fluid that flattens the hair to his skull yet reveals the face. Her insides curdle at the sight before her, and with careening thoughts Emma stares into the cold, lifeless eyes of her previous Gyges, Alec.

Chapter 11

The vipers intertwine and they dance along the quiet street. Their tongues flicker wildly while they taste the air, searching for their prey. A green mist trails the vaporous beasts. Her snakes are all but imperceptible to humans–unless they are the one being hunted. It is truly an oddity to Olivia, but it is just one of the changes in her power that has manifested after their awakening. *When life gives you lemons, you get vaporous snakes to hunt people down with.* She chuckles quietly, prompting a suspicious glance from Bray.

The adders move forward with a determined pace. They don't stop to rest, nor do they seem to realize that Olivia can't simply walk through buildings as they do. Frustration builds every time she has to run or scurry around obstacles and try to locate them once more. But even at the quickened pace, Bray keeps up with little issue as the patter of their footfalls echo between the buildings.

Following their guides, they turn off of the side street and onto the main road, where several buildings tower around them. The area is surprisingly bright compared to the adjoining neighborhoods, and a gentle breeze blows around them. A large ornate archway spans the entrance into Chinatown as two white pillars support the intricately designed structure with a tiered green pagoda-style roof. Bright-gold characters shimmer under the glowing streetlights as stone lions stand lonely sentry against dangers.

The snakes slither unhindered through the entrance, which has limited foot traffic. Olivia and Bray step to the side of the alley as a green and yellow dump truck turns down the road. The bulky vehicle deftly navigates the narrow street, although it nearly clips a parked car.

Olivia's vipers dash under the wheels of the truck, darting down a slender side street. The space is drastically darker and it takes several seconds for Olivia's eyes to adjust. A layer of gooseflesh rises on her arms as the air weighs heavily around them. They stop at the mouth of a long alley as the snakes circle around a side-access door, their movements restless. A lone doorman stands vigil; his form is shrouded in darkness, and Olivia seems to sense his presence more than see him.

"Wait," Bray rasps as he holds up a hand. They step closer to a nearby wall and stop. The sentry doesn't seem to have noticed them as they hunker down among several trash cans.

"What?" she mouths back; her skin prickles, adding to her growing unease.

"This isn't a place we want to go into." There is an unsettling knowledge in his tone. Olivia watches him carefully, trying to read his face.

"It's a fight club," he answers plainly, his gaze flicking to the door.

"Moss is in there, so that is where we need to go," she answers back as she continues to observe the side entrance.

"This is a fight club for paranormal beings." His tone is dark, prompting her to turn back to look at him.

"Yes, I gathered that," she counters, confused by his sudden cryptic nature.

"Their fights are to the death, and they don't always ask the gladiators to volunteer. A pack member was killed here." There is a glint of anger touching his eyes.

"Well, we aren't here to fight," she tries to assure him, though she has no idea what to expect.

"To go in there, we either need to volunteer or pay the cover charge." He studies the building, the muscles in his cheek ticking feverishly.

"How much is that?"

"Depending on the place, it can be anywhere from two to ten thousand dollars."

Olivia nearly chokes at the answer.

"I don't usually carry that kind of cash on me. Maybe we can sneak in." she suggests as she checks again to make sure the guard still hasn't seen them. The slender guard peeks at his phone before pocketing it and resuming his watch.

Olivia surveys the building's exterior; all of the ground-level lights are off, as well as the ones on the upper floors. A glimmer of hope shines as Olivia spies a low light coming from a small basement window nestled behind a stack of cardboard boxes. Without a word she motions to the porthole, and they crouch as they make their way through the debris. Every sound seems to resonate loudly and Olivia's gut clenches as she measures each step.

"I don't think I'm going to fit," Bray whispers, sounding doubtful. Olivia leans back slightly as she estimates his dimensions.

"It'll be tight but you'll fit," she teases.

"I don't know." A look of genuine concern etches his features.

"You can always stay here and I can go."

"No," he huffs defiantly with a sour look on his face. Olivia works at the hinge quietly until the old latch gives way and the glass pane opens outward.

"Okay. Then we sneak in and find Moss." Silently, Olivia prays it'll be that simple.

"What do we do when we find him?"

"I haven't worked that out yet." She shrugs.

"Alright, but let me go through first. We don't know what's down there." He studies the darkness warily, but there is a determined set to his jaw.

Olivia props the window open as Bray shimmies through the opening; his feet disappear as he slides into the darkness. With a silent thought the vipers slip through the passage after him. The ground is cold as she lowers herself down onto her stomach. The space inside is eerily dark and she can barely see anything. Some muted shapes linger within, but nothing is clear. Pushing forward, she climbs through the window and braces as her feet softly make contact with the dirt floor. She turns, scanning the gloom and taking in her surroundings.

A knot forms in her throat as she stares down the double barrel of a shotgun. Olivia's eyes flash to Bray, who is kneeling on the ground, a second gun pointed at his head as a bead of blood trickles down his cheek.

Two individuals stand before them, pressing in on them with the force of their presence as they scowl with disdain. The woman, who stands at least a good six inches taller than Olivia, hovers closely. Her thickly muscular arms flex as she crosses them over her chest, and her blond hair is braided into a thick rope. The man rubs his goateed chin and chuckles softly as he studies them. He is a massive hulk of flesh, with a large belly that denotes his love of food yet perhaps also belies latent strength. There is a slight curl to his hair, which is pulled back in a taut ponytail. Despite his smile his eyes are cold and deadly. Olivia weighs the potential threat of the warrior and his female companion; this isn't the most hostile situation she has found herself in, but she's learned the need to never underestimate anyone.

"See, Ben, I told you we'd find some rats down here." The Amazon nods her head to the man beside her.

"What should we do with them?" Ben asks. "Maybe we could throw them in the pit—or we could just kill them and be done with it."

"We'll let Samuel decide." Her gaze never strays from them. There is an underlying hardness to the woman that isn't completely due to her toned body. She emanates the same danger as her companion. Olivia studies them carefully as her mind runs through the possible scenarios. Despite their underlying desire for violence, they don't seem in a real hurry to start something. Looking over, Olivia can see a small nerve ticking in Bray's cheek. Thankfully, he seems smart enough to avoid adding fuel to the fire. Her heart thrashes hard against her ribs as she pulls in calming breaths. A lingering mustiness clings to her skin. Each step going forward must be carefully planned. The air is flooded with an impending threat of violence.

"I don't want to be here all night. Give me like five minutes, they're dead, and we're back to the show." Impatiently, Ben starts forward, lifting the barrel of the gun toward Bray, and Olivia's stomach vaults. Every nerve within her instantly screams for her to move. Ben shoulders the shotgun and as his finger touches the trigger his motion is stopped by the woman's hand grasping the weapon.

"Don't touch them," a voice commands from somewhere behind them.

The colossal mass that is Ben–shuffles aside as a second man comes forward, emerging from the darkness with an uncanny ease. Olivia's breath catches in her throat, and she is taken aback by his stunning appearance. His skin is flawless, a warm taupe color that appears to glow under the dim light, and his eyes are piercing as he studies her. There is an unseen force to his presence–it tugs at her, making it impossible to look away. Olivia realizes his overwhelming draw isn't simply a matter of his good looks. There is a singular confidence, a swagger of someone who is comfortable in their own abilities. He brushes past the two guards, his hands smoothing his finely pressed suit which accentuates his well-built frame.

"Do you two know the reason I'm as successful as I am–why I've survived in a business that kills so many?" he asks his lackeys.

"You're a fucking badass. Someone comes at you, you bury them." Ben glows with an obvious pride in his employer.

"What about you, Rose?" He faces the woman. Even under the weak lighting Olivia spots the flick of his eyebrow.

"It's because you're smarter than the others." She inhales with an elated energy as she meets his gaze, and for a moment there is a softening of her features.

"That's right." He taps his temple. "In the pits, you can defeat anyone if you know who you are up against. You may be stronger, faster, but a desperate man can out-muscle you; he can outrun you. Take these two, for example." He motions to Olivia and Bray. "I can tell you this. If you decided to take them on, we'd be finding whatever is left of you in the morning." Ben's gaze flicks between Bray and Olivia, without a doubt confused. "Well, Benjamin, today is the day you have finally met a Fury." Ben's features drop but he doesn't seem frightened; Olivia silently gives him credit for that.

"My name is Samuel. This is my club." He addresses them, exuding a calm poise.

"We are hunting a person who is here at your event tonight. All we want is him," Olivia states, opting for the direct route.

"In my younger years, I had the unfortunate luck of dealing with the first Furies. From that day on, I swore to never make that mistake again. Cause no disruption and we will allow you to search for your man." His voice vibrates along her skin, despite his solemn tone.

"Your cooperation is appreciated," Olivia replies coolly. Samuel nods his head, but there is a minute trace of apprehension in his eyes.

"Benjamin will take you to the pits. Find your man and collect him when he leaves. I don't want any of my guests knowing who and what you are," he warns as he directs them to Ben.

Samuel and Rose turn, heading down a passage to their left. Bray stands cautiously, wiping away the blood from his face with the back of his hand. His blond hair is a little mussed up but aside from that he seems unharmed. The sense of relief is mildly unsettling—why should Olivia honestly care, she muses.

Benjamin sighs deeply, his thick arms crossed over his chest. "Follow me," he barks gruffly.

He nods at them slowly and turns to navigate a long corridor shrouded in faint light. Numerous crates line the walls, adding to a claustrophobic feeling that hangs in the air. Rows of ceiling lights flicker down the length as they make their way in silence.

On the edge of her perception Olivia hears the faint sounds of what could be a crowd. The noise grows more intense as they near a steel door at the end of the tunnel. Her pulse quickens and a trickle of sweat drips down the small of her back. This isn't the first time she's seen a fighting pit, but each can be different, with its own set of horrors.

Benjamin reaches out with a beefy arm and cranks down on the lever securing the door. "Stay close to me; Samuel has some reserved seats he holds for special guests. We'll make our way through–see if we can find your man. But cause trouble and I'll chuck your asses outta here myself," he warns, jabbing a pointed finger at them. Olivia manages to bite her tongue as he opens the door. Her better judgment wins out, although she really wants to tell him where he can shove that finger.

The swing of the door is silenced against the uproar of the crowd. The area is congested with onlookers pressed shoulder to shoulder. Despite the fact that everyone's attention is riveted on the oval enclosure sectioned off by a chain-link fence, the push of flesh is nearly overwhelming. High-intensity lights illuminate the central fighting pit. Three tiers of seating have been carved into the granite bedrock, though no one is sitting.

Shifting through the group, Olivia jumps reflexively as a stranger bumps her, making her skin crawl with an unnerving twitch. Benjamin is unfazed as he pushes his way through, ignoring a screaming man whose face contorts fiercely, his fisted hand striking the air. Some step aside while others are jostled out of the way. Olivia's heart beats painfully in her throat, and even breathing hurts. Every part of her wants to flee—to be anywhere besides drowning in a sea of people. She tries to focus on Benjamin, but his movement seems painfully slow and every motion around her grates against her nerves.

A subtle amount of relief trickles in when she spots the two empty seats and Benjamin turns sideways to pass another onlooker. The air is still stifling but the chairs are a much-needed oasis to abate the rising surge of panic.

They shuffle past the last few people as Benjamin unlatches a rope that sections off the seating. There are three feet of open space in front of them, pushing back the crowd. From the relative distance the throng feels less imposing. Olivia's breathing becomes easier as she surveys the mob.

Starting at one point her vision sweeps the crowd, cataloguing each face and discarding those that are obviously not Moss.

"There." She barely hears Bray's voice over the deafening sound. As she follows his gaze her eyes are drawn to the pit. Olivia squints sharply, looking past the crowd, the glaring lights, and the fence to confirm that it is him. Moss towers fiercely as he stands off with his opponent. Despite the distance Olivia can see the sweat and blood that glistens from his shirtless torso. A large club hangs at his side, bits of flesh and blood dripping from the weapon.

Another man stands across the area from him. His shaved head is illustrated with intricate tattoos. His left eye sits destroyed, a busted hole of mush where the orb used to sit. He sways slightly, but he still clutches a battered battleax. The metal glints under the harsh light. Several bodies lay motionless on the ground –those who have already fallen. Blood soaks the muddied earth that both competitors trod on. A rusty, eight-foot chain fence surrounds the arena and numerous chains hang from the walls and ceiling, each tipped with jagged hooks. A subterranean entrance looms at one end. The large wooden doors are black from centuries of splattered blood and viscera.

The men circle each other, their fatigue apparent by the lungsful of air they are pulling in. Moss leaps forward, swinging the club with an unnerving ease as his opponent backs away, blocking each attack. The bald man kicks upward, landing a solid shot to Moss's midsection. With an audible harrumph, Moss staggers, and his foe hauls the ax around and down, arcing toward his head. Moss barely raises the club in time but manages to deflect the strike. The worn wood of the club splinters as the weapon breaks in half.

A hint of a smile touches the bald man's lips, but it vanishes when Moss rushes forward. The force of the tackle knocks him to his back, with Moss on top. The bigger man's mass presses down on his rival, though he struggles to gain a footing–the weight advantage is too much to overcome as Moss rains down strikes. With every hit the downed man's head bounces off of the dirt floor. As his opponent's body goes limp, Moss staggers to his feet. His arms sag heavily as he bends to hoist up the man's cumbersome ax. With the stance of a lumberjack, Moss hefts the weapon up and brings it down as the sharp steel cleaves the other man's head off.

The crowd erupts in an earsplitting riot and the innermost rows push forward, pressing against the fence. A frenzied energy ripples through the mob, nearly choking the air.

"It's time for the final bout. He has to face the champion," Benjamin shouts over the howling mob, and a wide grin creases his face.

The lights dim and several crew members scurry about the arena, lighting oil braziers. Their nearly frantic nature isn't lost on Olivia. One young man stumbles over a corpse but is left behind by the others. He scrambles to his feet as the large wooden doors start to swing open. The energy of the crowd is stifled as all eyes turn to the opening entryway.

Icy fingers grasp at Olivia's throat as she gazes into what can only be described as the depths of hell. The monstrosity that emerges is in no way human, nor has it ever been. Even from this distance Olivia can tell that the beast is almost two feet taller than Moss. The solid beat of his heavy steps echo through the awed silence. The devil plods into the open space, trailing two long chains, each ending in serrated hooks. Its arms, legs, and even its lower face are also wrapped in multiple strands of shackles. His yellow eyes glow malevolently, an extreme contrast against the burnt-orange hue of his skin.

Moss seems unmoved by his new opponent as he watches the beast with his own dead eyes. The two fighters study each other and the solid doors close them into the space. Moss lifts the bloodied ax of his previous foe, gauging the balance in his hands. The chain devil rolls his neck, flexing the muscles in his shoulders. Moss bounds forward but must quickly change his direction and roll to the side to avoid a long segment of chain that flies from the devil's hand. The hooked missile embeds itself in the dirt, sending bits of debris pluming into the air.

The chains hanging from the ceiling and wall shake briefly before they simultaneously launch toward Moss. He skitters and dodges the majority, but a few make their way through, carving at his flesh as they pass. A primordial scream rips from Moss as he bats away the nuisance cables and charges for the chain devil once again.

The coiled metal appendages entwine Moss as he grabs hold of the larger man. With two hands full of chains, Moss yanks the demon forward, trying to unsettle its footing. They grapple for several seconds, each vying for the upper hand. Moss's oversized frame strains as he pulls the devil forward. He falls to his back bringing his opponent with him, then kicks upward, both feet sending the man flying through the air. He crashes through the fence and the metal gives way under his great weight.

The small mass of people push backward and away from the threat. Chaos erupts as the spectators scream and start fleeing in all directions. Through the commotion, Olivia spots Moss hauling himself up and staggering toward the door of the cell. She pushes forward, trying to make her way through the press of people. Bray darts ahead, opening a space between the escaping bodies.

They arrive at the breach in the fence as Rose calmly approaches the chain devil. Astonishingly, the larger woman gently soothes the demon as she touches his hands.

Ducking into the hole they quickly cross the gory battlegrounds, following Moss's trail through the mangled doors.

Chapter 12

The chilled porcelain leeches the heat from Nina's trembling hands. The gentle rocking of her body soothes her as she focuses her view on the tiled wall, reflected the mirror. The rush of water filling the basin covers the sounds of her labored breathing. Her eyes burn as they try to produce tears that haven't fallen in years. Weeping is a luxury she has never been able to afford. It's at times like this that she wishes she could just stay hidden away in the bathroom forever.

Letting the cold water run over her hands, she wills the icy flow to wick away everything. She pats dry her hands and carefully adjusts the hand towel until it is perfect. From a compartment below the sink, she pulls out a pill bottle. The sharp pellets jostle around in the container as she shifts two out, into her hand. Swallowing the pills dry, she quickly hides them again. If Chen found them, he would realize her weakness and demand that she throw them out.

She had been lucky enough to find a doctor to provide her medicine without insurance. She met him while seeking out the healer for some medicinal herbs for Chen. Nina had never met anyone like that before. So strange. When the old woman smiled it actually touched her eyes. Despite her incessant need to talk to Nina and ask her questions, the woman seemed good-natured. As if she could see the dark shroud that Nina carried within her, she was the first person to name it. So, she takes the pills to keep the sorrow at bay, but Chen wouldn't understand. Flipping the light off she walks into the kitchen to resume her tasks.

The hot steam wafts around Nina as she fills the small ceramic bowl. With a delicate methodology she folds and refolds a gauze bandage, making certain the edges align perfectly. Loose tendrils of her auburn hair cling to her cheeks and tickle the skin. Ignoring the irritation, she pushes the stimulus out of the bounds of her perception.

Unfurling a paper packet of medicinal herbs, she pours the contents into the liquid. As she stirs the mixture, a rich, aromatic plume hints in the air as the water turns a mild green hue.

Nina sets down the spoon on another folded napkin and clasps the bowl of near-boiling water. She glides silently down the hallway; her well-trained steps cause not even a ripple to form in the bubbling water.

She navigates the walkway to Chen's room as Logan swishes around her ankles. His soothing chirps echo through the space as his miniature legs carry him out in front of her. The little kitten's health has improved with the benefit of food and shelter. Although he spends most of the time in her quarters, he will on occasion venture out to explore the rest of the residence. Logan trots over to stand by the door and sits, his round belly full of food. Staring up at her, his piercing eyes seem to communicate vast years of knowledge.

The rented apartment is smaller than those they are accustomed to, but it is by far better than some places she has lived. Her life before Chen was cruel and broken, and she was nothing before meeting him. Her fingers are bright red and they tingle, but she ignores the discomfort as she sets down the bowl to open the door with a soft knock. Reclaiming the bowl, she pads softly into the room, which is dimly lit, with few furnishings.

"Why is that thing still here?" Chen lazily lifts an eye at Logan's presence. The undersized orange cat peeks sideways into the room, never daring to cross the threshold into the same room as Nina's master. Chen's bare chest is wrapped tightly in bandages with only the faintest hints of pink blood seeping through the fabric.

"He is still too weak to be on his own," Nina answers meekly; her gaze remains locked on the job before her. The familiar cold intensity of his presence flows around her.

"When we finish here you will get rid of it." His tone is resolute and unwavering. "There's no point in wasting energy on such things."

"Yes, I understand," she replies as she sets the bowl down on the end table next to Chen. She busies her hands, praying he won't see their tremor. She drops several pieces of bandage into the steaming water. His wound is healing quickly but it still needs care.

Her gaze flickers to the doorway as Logan continues to watch them. For a moment she is mesmerized by the pure green of his eyes, but quickly turns away, pushing away the discomfort in her stomach. She focuses her mind to her purpose as if nothing else mattered.

As a half dragon, Chen is the strongest being she has ever met, yet even he isn't invulnerable. He groans loudly as he sits up in the bed. Nina unwraps and cleans the wound, which is little more than a weeping scab. If the bullet hadn't passed straight through it would have meant some digging in order to get it out.

"One more day perhaps, and you will be completely whole." He leans forward as she rewraps his chest and shoulder. His back and shoulders are littered with long lengths of old scar tissue. The cross-hatched design speaks to an extended period of whippings that are ages old. Nina has never asked him about their origins, and he has never offered to tell her.

"It's taking too damn long," he scowls. The agitation rolls off of him as anger flashes in his eyes.

"My apologies, master." Nina scoops up the dirty dressings and cloth and places them in a wicker basket.

"It doesn't matter. The delay changes nothing." He waves it away, testing his shoulder and the fitting of the dressing. "Once the Fury are decimated and I have my vengeance then we will return home. I will reclaim my land." His voice lifts with an almost amused quality.

"What will we do then?" She battles the urge to fidget, instead clasping her hands tightly in front of her.

"I'll burn it to the ground and there will be nothing left but ashes." He meets her gaze with a callous resolve.

"And then what?" Her voice shudders as she dares the question.

"It doesn't matter after that." His black eyes laser her as all emotion seeps from him, leaving the undaunted shell that she has grown accustomed to.

"Is there anything else you need?" she asks, hastily picking up the basket of dirty linens.

"No, I have no need of you." The painful emptiness within her grows at his words. She should be used to it by now but despite all the years, the truth still pains her. "Have you been doing your practices?" he asks before she reaches the door.

"Not yet," she admits with shame, chancing a brief glance his way.

"Make sure you do. The tasks ahead are going to be difficult and you need to be ready," he warns.

"Yes, Chen." Since their first meeting, Chen realized her potential but insists that she constantly hone and improve her skills. Above all things she must be ready should he need her.

A firm knock can be heard from the front door. Logan's furred paws skitter along the wood floor as he makes a dash for the safety of her room. Their eyes lock as they listen to the sound resonating down the hall. An almost ominous silence follows as a prickling sensation flutters across Nina's skin.

"It's Calder and the woman." Nina senses the force of their presence flooding the air of the apartment. With clammy palms she wipes away the gooseflesh rising on her arms.

"Go and answer it," Chen orders, easing himself back down on the bed with a strained scowl.

Nina enters the hall and sets the basket in the bathroom. Several sharper bangs rattle the door as Nina pulls it open.

"Calder, Alba." She nods to each of them. "How can I help you?"

"Chen—where is he?" Calder snaps as he adjusts his glasses. His ruthless eyes peer straight through her as if she were invisible.

"It is late, and my master is resting." She keeps her tone calm and formal. Her gaze never shifts from him, meeting his stare without flinching.

"I don't give a rat's ass what time it is. Let me in." His voice strains despite his attempt to maintain a low volume. The simmering agitation within him tests the boundaries of his control, and a slight tremor skitters throughout his form. Clearly, this is not a man to be trusted. As a wolf in sheep's clothing, there is a monster subtly disguised behind his fancy tailored suit.

Without a word Nina opens the door and steps aside to allow them in. The two cross over the threshold, and Alba pauses briefly to measure Nina with a glacial intensity. Yellow irises rimmed with black radiate a pure malevolence. Nina shivers at the unnatural quality of the genie. Alba exudes a primal wickedness that has probably cowed many a brave man. She flicks her long blood-red tresses over her shoulder as she passes. The deep-burgundy hue of her skin appears nearly purple against the tightly fitted black leather of her top and pants. Her heeled boots click softly along the floor as she walks.

Nina shuts the door and follows them without a sound. Inhaling softly, she focuses on the two of them, ignoring the solid drum of the blood pulsing through her veins. The kitchen and hallway are stifling as Nina leads, making her way to Chen's door. She quells the urge to jump as a raspy hiss echoes from her room as they pass. Logan's back arches sharply as he spits at them and his fur stands on end.

"Dirty beast," Alba growls at the kitten; her heeled foot stomps the ground as Logan retreats inside. A flutter of panic clogs Nina's throat as she steps to block the doorway.

"He'll do you no harm," Nina soothes as she shuts her bedroom door.

"I have no fear of such a creature." Alba's tone oozes an arrogant derision.

With Logan safely closed away in her bedroom, Nina's breath eases. She never looks back to them, yet she is keenly aware of their movements. The two of them are dangerous, Alba more so than Calder. Hopefully Chen is right; as soon as he achieves his revenge, they can leave this place and Calder far behind.

She knocks softly before opening the door to show them in. Chen leans back against the headboard and as they enter, he makes no move to rise.

"Well, I'm glad to see you are resting comfortably," Calder mocks. His eyebrows rise above the rim of his glasses as he asks, "Are the accommodations, which I pay for, up to your standard? I'd hate to see you are uncomfortable after getting your ass handed to you."

"The Fury was supposed to be alone and she wasn't." Chen answers with a cold indifference.

"Was she there with an army? If you can't handle one vampire and a Fury, then why am I paying you?" Calder paces, his arms jerking about as he talks.

"The delay will not be a problem." The dragon's eyes follow the imp with a lethal determination.

"Not a problem? Because of your ineptitude we still have all three to contend with. And as we speak, the short-haired bitch and her pet dog are closing in on Moss. That moron is leading them into the caves." Calder's face turns a deep red as he spits at them.

"Even if they are, they won't find anything of use. Your sanctuary has been purged, all of your little secrets neatly hidden away. The only things they'll find down there are rats and an ill-tempered genie, and I doubt Dagan will show them any congeniality, much less the way out." Alba's demeanor tenses as her gaze flashes to Calder.

"Dagan?" Alba asks.

"Not now, woman," he growls at her before turning his attention back to Chen. "Do not forget that I am your benefactor. Without me, there's no money. You'd still be peddling your services out of a mud hut somewhere. You may be a good assassin, but you aren't the best." Chen's eye twitches slightly yet he remains silent. "We both serve the same master. Fail again, and I will have you buried so deep no one will find you," Calder warns as he plants his fists on his hips.

"Your master is not mine. I do this for my own reasons and will not be threatened by you, imp," Chen barks back.

"You are to do as you are told. You are easily replaced, and I will not have you ruining everything." Calder steps forward, jabbing a stiff finger toward Chen. Nina moves without thought, blocking his path. Calder is shocked for a moment as he stares agape at her for a second.

"Get out of my way, whelp." Calder spits in her face. A thick vein protrudes from his brow as he tries to puff himself up, appearing larger than he really is.

"Perhaps it is best to finish this discussion later. My master needs to rest, and you have outstayed your welcome." Nina catches his hand as it reaches to strike her. She twists his wrist, forcing him to hunch over with the pressure.

"Release me," Calder screeches. If he wasn't so disgusting, she may have laughed at his discomfort. Her eyes lift to Chen, who is watching in silence. With a faint nod from Chen, Nina frees her hold and Calder stumbles away.

"You'd better not fail me again." Calder is red-faced as he rubs his bruised shoulder.

"Nina," Chen calls, his gaze locked on the imp. "Go to the cave; secure Moss. If you come across the Fury and her companion, kill them." He lifts an eyebrow derisively to Calder.

Calder glares at them fiercely for a moment before storming out of the room.

"Dagan is in the caves?" Alba asks. There is a coarseness of her tone that scratches at their skin, a tingling irritation not easily soothed. Chen nods and she turns, following Calder out.

"Go to the caves," Chen repeats his orders quietly as he readjusts the blankets around him. "Kill the Fury and her companion and get Moss."

"Yes, Chen." A familiar numbness washes through Nina as she turns with a nod, heading out of the room.

Chapter 13

Bray and Olivia hunch over as they snake their way through the slender crevasse. Despite chasing Moss through the open door of the arena, they quickly lost his trail amid the quagmire of looping and dead-end tunnels. Bray had offered to lead the way, but his suggestion was shot down. Even with enhanced night vision he squints to navigate the dismal labyrinth. Olivia's serpents radiate a steady glow of green light, which helps to diminish some of the darkness.

The air is thick with the stagnant musk of decomposition. The scent of dirt, mold, and algae mingle, tickling at Bray's nose. Moisture oozes from the granite rock face, collecting in a small stream that runs along the length of their path.

Up to this point, traveling in the underground space has been manageable, but as the breadth between the walls narrows, a long-buried fear within Bray begins to stir. *As long as I'm standing it's fine—I can still move.* Bray inhales a ragged breath each time the rock face to either side of him grazes his shoulders. Damp moisture from the walls leaches through his shirt, raising gooseflesh on his arms, and his pulse quickens.

Sporadically, Olivia turns to glance his way. Despite the low light he can see the watchful concern in her eyes. For the most part she has chosen to remain silent, refocusing her gaze back to the path ahead after a few seconds.

"Nervous?" Olivia's tone lifts with a forced cheeriness. The green glow halos her face, bringing the image of an ethereal spirit to his mind.

"I'm not a fan of tight spaces." He shrugs softly and clears his throat, trying to work moisture back into his arid mouth.

"There seems to be a wider area up ahead. We can rest there for a few minutes."

"We should keep going," Bray urges. "He's probably gaining some ground on us."

"Moss is twice the size of you and me put together. He'll have more trouble in here than we will."

Rounding a narrow bend in the cave system, the walls slip away, forming a hollow space. The flowing water collects in a shallow pool. Olivia's serpents coil about one another, throwing off an added glow. The immeasurable depths of the water reflect back the eerie green light. Olivia's face lifts as she studies the area around them. The aura of light gently accents the smooth contours of her cheeks and the fullness of her lips.

With a heavy exhale of air, she leans against a fairly dry stretch of wall. Bray's breath becomes shallow as Olivia turns her mystifying gaze toward him.

"You don't like tight spaces, do you?" The calming purr of her tone floats through the air, yet it does little to ease the clenching in his gut.

Bray finds that his voice is stuck in his throat as he stammers, "No, I don't care for them."

"How long have you been claustrophobic?" She seems to be inspecting him, and while it doesn't necessarily make him nervous, his pulse speeds up just the same.

Bray instantly quashes the indignation welling inside him. For years he has survived by refusing to accept this vulnerability.

"Ever since I was a kid," he answers, forcing himself to meet her gaze. "Just a bad experience, but it left me with this to deal with."

"No worries. In my experience most people are afraid or unsettled by one thing or another." Bray studies her, his arms instinctually folding over his chest. "Don't worry. I'm not going to be running out to the local paper to blab. Like I said, everyone has something they are afraid of."

He wanted to argue with her that it wasn't fear, and that there was some other reason why he felt like ripping off all of his skin to get out of here. "What are you afraid of?" His voice is a rough whisper. The hammer of his heart is nearly deafening as a peculiar energy runs through him.

"I don't like heights," she admits with a low sigh as she rubs her shoulders and rolls her head to the side.

"Hmm," he smirks as he pulls his gaze away from her slender neck.

"What? A lot of people are afraid of heights." Her tone perks up as she hesitantly meets his stare.

"I just never would have guessed it would be heights. I imagine me taking you to a carnival and going on the Ferris wheel is out of the question." He sighs despondently.

"I used to love the Ferris wheel." She glances away, not looking at him as a subtle gloominess clouds her eyes. "Well, we should probably keep moving. Are you still up for this?"

Bray huffs deeply as he stands, brushing dirt from his hands. "I'll be fine, but it would be easier if we had better light."

The snakes press forward, circling around them, their iridescent glow lighting the walls. Specks of light reflect off of the quartz that is suspended within the stone, giving the natural corridor an otherworldly appearance. He pulls in a ragged breath and his peripheral vision blurs. Walking along, he reaches out his arm to steady himself against the wall. The cool stone provides him with something to concentrate on; the granite scrapes along the flesh of his palm. Olivia scuffs her foot across the ground, pushing the loose soil and rocks aside.

"Find anything interesting?" Bray strains his vision, focusing on the abysmal darkness shrouding her feet.

"Well, there are some dried-out roots here; they won't burn for long, but if we can find something else, we could make a torch."

"Hold on a second. Have you got a lighter?" Bray closes the distance between them as Olivia nods. A thick root system is interwoven through cracks in the stone and soft dirt. Digging his fingers into the soil he grips the largest root he can find and yanks it from the ground with a loud grunt. Bray passes her the root as he strips his shirt off. He nearly laughs aloud as he catches her sharp inhale and how her gaze flutters away from his naked torso.

After shredding the material, he secures it around the root and Olivia lights it. The warm light dances down the passage and Bray's nerves relax faintly. The walls, which he can at least see now, still feel as though they are squeezing in, but the biting panic ebbs to a controllable state.

His attention is centered as his boots crunch over a fine layer of rubble. The ground beneath them has several cracks that run the length of the passage. They have to navigate around larger fragments of stone that have broken away from the walls and ceiling. Bray's muscles tense as the pressure around them changes, the air seems drier than before, and a thin cloud of particulate dust hangs around them. Rocks have broken away from the walls, creating small mounds that run up and down the length of the passage.

Olivia stills as she listens down the path, her eyes sweeping from right to left. The flame of their torch crackles and pops as it greedily burns with a low roar. She steps forward, and a small patch of stone gives way under her and she starts to fall. Time slows as Olivia begins to descend into the gaping sinkhole and the torch hangs motionless while her hand falls away. Bray shoves forward on legs that seem to move painfully slow. His heart throttles his ribs as Olivia turns, her eyes wide with a panicked terror. His chest slides across the coarse ground as he clamors to grab at her. Stretching into the darkness, his grip closes on the softness of her forearm and he draws in a haggard breath. Despite the near void of light, his heart stammers at the sheer terror reflecting in her eyes.

"Bray," she screams, tears flowing over her temples and into her damp hair. The serpents wriggle around him as if urging him silently to pull Olivia up. Settling his feet under him, he drags her safely from the hole.

The small space clamors with the erratic pants of her breathing. Her open mouth is desperately gasping for air while her chest jerks violently. She is nearly consumed by the raging panic attack. The urgency and helplessness cascade through him. While he knows she isn't one to be touched, there is this indelible need to help her.

Bray silently curses to himself as he rolls over toward her. Following instinct alone he lifts her into his arms, holding her close yet gently.

"It'll be alright, Olivia. Oh God, I'm sorry. Please, it'll be okay," he soothes over and over. He breathes a silent prayer that she'll be alright. Perhaps he should just take her out of here back to the surface, where there are open skies and a solid ground beneath them. As her respiration slows to a normal tempo, he realizes she is holding onto him just as fiercely as he is to her. Olivia's face is buried in his chest, and he basks in her fragrance. He realizes it is the scent of a summer rainstorm.

Olivia leans back, and her long neck stretches as her unbelievably blue eyes stare directly into his. Bray's breath catches in his throat as he appreciates that in this moment, she is at her most genuine, her truest self. She peers back at him with no illusions, no armor of strength to hide behind. His gaze is drawn to her lips as she swallows roughly, trying to regain her composure.

"We should go," she whispers.

After helping each other stand, they search for the torch, but it is gone, either having rolled away or fallen into the sinkhole. Olivia closes her eyes, breathing softly as her vipers reform and collect around her. A loud clatter snaps both of their gazes to the corridor.

They advance slowly, listening amid the darkness for any sounds. The snakes swoop wildly from side to side and they seem hurried to move faster. Again, a thunderous clang resonates and Bray can detect a muffled voice. Several feet from them a muted light filters in from an adjoining tunnel. Stooping down, they enter the corridor, which is lit sparsely by two torches mounted to the walls.

Ahead of them, Moss hammers at a padlock with a sizeable stone. With each strike, he barks profanities at the inanimate object.

"Open, you fucking twat," he seethes. His exposed arms and chest are coated in a thick layer of sweat and dirt. Dull torchlight flickers as he jerks at the stubborn handle.

His fevered movements halt as he senses their approach. Gazing up at the ceiling, he laughs and turns.

"Congratulations." Moss throws his arms out, fingertips grazing the walls at his side. "You caught me. Now what do you plan on doing?"

"I'm going to kill you, that's what I'm going to do." Bray's hands are balled painfully tight as he glares down the length of the passage at his opponent.

"I don't think so, boy." Moss stares down his nose at them apathetically as though they are nothing to him.

"You killed my father and, guess what, you're not leaving here alive." Bray pushes back the urge to blindly rush Moss; he knows he must never underestimate his enemy.

"Don't do anything stupid," Olivia warns.

"Listen to her, scrappy. Test me, and I'll beat you to death with your own fucking femur. But hey, if you wanna see if you're fucking man enough, bring it, pussy. You'll die just like your dad, a screaming little bitch," Moss taunts, his lips curling in a sadistic smile.

A low growl rumbles deep within Bray as he bounds forward, closing the gap. Skin and cloth tear as his wolf erupts and his clothes fall away, revealing a lush coat of blond fur. Moss is undaunted as Bray's hands unfurl into daggered claws. Extended teeth fill his mouth as his jaw grows, elongating into a muzzle. Bray subtly notes that there is no hint of fear coming from Moss, just a fissure of darkness where nothing human lives.

Moss dips as he tries to evade the wolf's savage attack. Razor-sharp claws skitter along the stone wall and bits of rock are flung, but Bray continues to stalk forward, snarling as spittle drips from his jowls. Moss attempts to out-step his opponent, but Bray adjusts the angle of his strike at the last moment, raking his claws across Moss's mid-section. He is greeted by the wonderful aroma of the man's blood as it plumes the air. The scent of rich blood and bowel mingle, hinting that Bray's strike has hit vital organs.

Each man rushes the other as they collide in the claustrophobic space. For a moment they are deadlocked as each tries to gain the advantage. Bray is only vaguely aware of Olivia's shouts to him. The thrum of Moss's quickened heartbeat urges him forward. This isn't solely about a need to hunt, killing in order to feed. Bray resolves that this broken piece of garbage will never hurt anyone again.

Fueled by righteous vengeance, his strength
prevails and he forces Moss backward into the
wall with a jarring thud. Bits of debris and
rock crumble around them from the impact.
A fissure forms in the brittle rock and
crumbles away, revealing a small hole. Bray
yanks Moss's chin up with a clawed hand,
exposing his neck for a killing bite.

Moss's concealed blade plunges deeply into
Bray, inches above his collarbone. The knife
redirects off the bone, but pierces a lung. Bray
howls and reels back as the searing pain cuts
through him. The blade is not silver, but his
lung convulses as it tries to mend the gaping
wound. The thick smell of his own blood fills
the enclosed space and Moss, seizing on the
opportunity, withdraws the blade and stabs
again.

Using his weight, Moss pushes back, and Bray
scrambles for room to move. Moss wades
forward, giving no space for adjustment as his
blade is already moving. Clutching the
bloodied dagger in one hand, Moss flings a
clump of dirt into Bray's face, and while he is
able to deflect the majority of it, some gets
into his eyes, blinding him. The knife embeds

in Bray's shoulder with a wet sound and more blood gushes from the wound. Moss's hand slips on the hilt but he plucks it out, twisting the handle, wrenching a pained yelp from Bray.

As Moss steadies his aim for another strike, he freezes. His stoic, cold eyes widen and his arms fall limply to his side. An impressive green python coils up his torso, emanating a vaporous smoke. The skin of the snake ripples as it tightens its grasp, paralyzing Moss.

Olivia hurries over to them; a deep frown creases her brow as she scowls at both of them and checks Bray's wounds.

"Well, that was just the stupidest thing I've seen. What the hell is wrong with you?" Her features soften for a brief second as she meets his gaze. "Are you alright?" Bray simply nods in response. "Let's get him back to the Hallow. We'll figure out what to do with him once we are there," she adds.

Bray shifts back to his human form. Fur recedes as his body shrinks and reforms.

Olivia glances at him briefly and at once turns a flattering shade of red.

"Oh God, you're naked," she chokes out.

"Of course I am. My clothes don't survive the shift." He tries to hide his own amusement at her discomfort.

"Mei Li is going to have a cow if she sees you prancing around buck naked. We should have some clothes that'll fit you." Her gaze remains locked on Moss or the floor or the ceiling.

"Being nude is a very natural state," he chuckles with a toothy grin.

Olivia reaches out to grab Moss when a cold wave of power smashes into them. There is a sensation of millions of bullet ants scurrying across his skin as they are submerged in the flow. A flash of movement pulls their eyes toward the hole in the tunnel wall. A burgundy fox slinks from the inky darkness. It scans the room with intense reddish-brown eyes, and the light sets its coat alight in a fiery luster. Plumes of thick tails sprout from the animal's rear and they flick wildly, scraping against the opening as it crosses the threshold.

Bray's heart rate careens as his body is seized by an invisible force. The paralysis locks his muscles in a rigid grip, and his lungs burn against the rising horror. An insurmountable weight bears down on him as if he's being crushed by the space around him. With a concerted effort, his gaze slides to Olivia, whose eyes widen as she gulps for air.

The small fox gambols toward them with an unparalleled grace and ease. As the fox's narrow snout tests the air, Bray's gaze is drawn to a spot of muted purple light that softly pulses from the undercoat of its furry chest. As it approaches Moss, its form starts to morph, growing larger as the dense coat of fur recedes under a layer of delicate skin. The plumage of bright scarlet tails merges together, forming into the folds of a swooshing, wine-colored coat. Long tresses of auburn hair fall to the waist of the young woman who stands before them. While she is small in stature, there is no doubt that the thrum of power originates from her.

"You are quite lucky, Moss. If I'd been any later these two would have taken you." The strange girl addresses Moss with a tilt of her chin. Bray struggles against his invisible bonds, and his voice locks in his throat. Pitiful croaks are all he can manage as the girl's eyes flick back and forth between them. She studies them as a bird of prey watches a field mouse. There is a beautiful nature about her power, but something terrifying as well, and the hairs on Bray's neck rise at her approach.

"Yeah, yeah, just hurry up and kill them," Moss rumbles as Olivia's constrictor falls weakly to the ground. He walks up to them as well, clasping the ragged wound at his side. Dark-red blood still flows from the wound as globs of red, splatter to the ground.

"Your injury is grave and requires immediate care if you are to survive." She inspects the wound without touching Moss.

"It'll be fine." Moss stares down at the small woman with a mixture of disdain and apprehension.

"The wolf's claw has caught your liver and intestine. If we do not leave now you will die," she explains plainly. Her tone is sterile, giving away no hint of emotion. "My magic will only hold their power for a short time."

Moss glares toward Bray; his chest expands and he pulls in fatigued breaths. He winces against the effort, and his gaze flickers between Bray and his rescuer.

"This is not where you are meant to die," she warns with a startling sharpness to her tone.

The muscle in Moss's cheek clicks as he stares them down. Bray knows his own seething anger is mirrored back. "Very well, Nina," Moss finally huffs at her.

With a motion of her graceful hand, Nina traces a symbol on the wall. In the absolute silence, Bray can detect the abrasive sound of her flesh rubbing against the stone. A deep rumble resonates from behind them, followed by the jarring chaos as the tunnels they had come from collapse.

The result of the pinpoint cave-in sends minute dust particles rushing into the tunnel. As the air clears, Bray strains his vision to see through the cloud of dirt. Nina slices through the solid stone with the tips of her fingers and the granite bulges, peeling away. The rock groans as the opening widens to a brightly lit passageway. Nina glances back at them only briefly before she and Moss step through and the wall reconfigures behind them.

Instantly, the deathly grip on Bray releases and he nearly falls, but manages to lean against the wall as his lungs pull in deep gulps of air. Olivia mirrors him, resting her arms on her knees.

"What the hell was that?" Olivia asks in between breaths.

"Kitsune," Bray answers against the cold chill shaking his bones. Olivia's brow furrows, her perplexed gaze meeting his.

"A nine-tailed fox." Bray continues to shiver as he studies the solid rock used by Moss to escape. "We have to follow them. Can you open a portal?"

"No." A gut-wrenching void strangles her voice. "My powers are gone."

Chapter 14

Emma curses under her breath as she rounds the corner into yet another long corridor. After about twenty minutes of searching for Mei Li she is fairly certain the woman is nowhere to be found in the Hallow. The halls are desperately silent as a heavy aura swallows all of the ambient sound. Even the scuff of her sneakers scraping along the stone floor seems out of place. The musty air clings to her skin as she descends stone steps that are carved into the solid rock. Relying more or less on instinct, she follows the slight tug as she navigates the complex layout of intersecting paths. One could become easily disoriented in the tangled webs of interlacing trails.

She passes the library, which is sealed with a large oak-carved door that resembles Cerberus. The visage of the three-headed guardian dog of Hades stares ominously back at her with its lifeless eyes. Emma's nerves bristle as a vague object on the rough stone floor catches her eye. The details of its form meld into the haze of shadows and she strains her eyes to decipher what it could be. As Emma approaches, colors and lines sharpen, and she tentatively bends to pick up the red rose. To her amazement the flower is still supple as if it were cut that day; the rich fragrance wafts to her nose, and the pliable petals retain some of the moisture from the morning dew.

A small sound tickles her ears seconds before the library door swings open, birthing a shadowed figure. Emma recognizes Megaera instantly as she steps out into the torchlight. The familiar tightness in her chest grows, bleeding into a tangible fear. The primordial goddess numbly wipes some errant dust from her hands as her intense gaze finds Emma. The satin of her sheer red gown rustles as she closes the door behind her.

"What are you doing here?" The unexpected shiver clamps down on Emma's throat, producing a weak sound.

"For millennia this was my home." Megaera studies the carved door, running a delicate hand over the rough features.

"That still doesn't answer my question." Emma retreats several steps as Megaera drifts effortlessly toward her. She curses herself, torn between the fear of showing weakness and a healthy respect for a dangerous opponent.

"I come here as I am able to." Megaera exudes a cold confidence. Emma highly doubts that the goddess fears anything.

"Why here?" Emma's gaze drifts to the library door, feeling the need to break the eye contact.

"This was not always a library; here was not always what you call the Hallow." Megaera's long finger gestures toward the ground around them. "Once, eons ago, this was the underworld, a place of perfect stillness and repose. It was a paradise, untouched by the world above. So, I come here to reminisce." She lifts somber eyes to Emma.

"What do you come to remember?" The hairs on Emma's arms rise as her stomach vaults with an unexpected nausea. An alien sensation flashes at the edges of Emma's awareness.

"I remember a time when I had a purpose," she answers harshly.

A shrill electricity jolts Emma's spine, nearly buckling her knees. Megaera watches her apathetically as a clouded image swallows Emma's vision. The sense of the corridor and Megaera melts away into a swirling void of grey. Despite the miasma, shapes start to contort and sharpen; the vision pulls at her with a familiarity but there is something out of place.

A mass of colored floral textile obscures her field of vision. Short fibers of a rug tickle her nose and a warm wetness is thick against her skin. The overwhelming odor of blood assails her, but she can't move. Struggling against the paralysis, her limbs refuse to budge and no amount of force will lift her from her prone position. Panic surges as her lungs battle to pull in the stifled air. Without the aid of being able to see, her mind focuses on the sounds around her. Screaming and bloodcurdling cries ring out in a cacophony of mass chaos. Frantic footfalls thunder around her, echoing through the floor. Panicked voices are wild yet muddled and impossible to distinguish.

Emma bellows into the ornate carpet, cursing her frozen limbs. She senses a presence looming above her and her heart nearly stops. A deep growl rumbles over her and a hot, putrid breath flows over her neck and shoulders. Her vision blurs, and she is absorbed into the deafening thrum of her own terrified heartbeat. All sounds slip away and reality flows back to Emma's awareness with such a tidal force that she sags to her knees. An intense exhaustion weighs on her, but she manages to lift her gaze. Megaera is statue-still as she stoically watches Emma.

"What was that?" Emma wheezes and her lungs burn as they struggle to work again.

"It seems you have retained Agnes's gift." Megaera's head tilts to the side as she studies Emma. "How interesting."

"What gift?" Emma straightens but her legs shake uncontrollably. She leans a hand against the near wall to steady herself, pulling in long, labored breaths.

"Foresight. Quite a blessing, really, and it can be a useful tool." A subtle smile lifts her lips.

"How is that useful? I couldn't see anything." Emma rubs her cheek, expecting her hand to come away bloodied but finding nothing.

"Fate chooses when the visions come and how they are presented to you. Your task will be to find a way to use them." Megaera's icy tone slithers through Emma's core. The ruthless aspects of her personality are a distinct reminder that she is a being not to be trusted.

A distant pattering echoes from one of the adjoining hallways. Emma's nerves bristle as the footfalls prickle her ears. As much as her instincts scream at her to keep an eye on Megaera, she feels the compulsion to see the origin of the coming noise.

Mei Li's gown flares around her as she trots with a purpose down the length of corridor, her hands clutching bunches of cloth to hold them off of the ground. Wisps of her black hair fly around, haloing her face. Emma's eyes flash back to the voided space where Megaera was just standing. She scans the area quickly as Mei Li nears but she is alone.

"Emma, I've been looking for you." Mei Li sighs deeply as she halts.

"I was…" Emma tries to clear the fog of her mind. "I was looking for you as well."

"Are you alright?" Mei Li's brows furrow with worry as she watches Emma.

"Yes. Have you heard anything from Olivia?" Emma asks, attempting a weak smile.

"She was supposed to check in this morning, but I haven't heard anything yet. I didn't know if you had." Mei Li wrings her hands as her gaze flicks about the hall.

"I'm sure she'll return shortly." A nervous energy nibbles at Emma's insides. "I wanted to talk to you about the faceless from last night." Mei Li's face snaps to her.

"I'm not really sure why a faceless would be outside the Hallow, much less under the instruction of someone else. I'm looking into it but I'm certain it was simply a fluke event." Mei Li shifts with a minute agitation in her stance. "If you hear from Olivia, please have her come see me as soon as possible." She turns to walk away without as much as a nod.

"Were you ever going to tell me about Alec?" Mei Li freezes at the question, and Emma focuses her gaze on the ancient Mother.

"What about Alec?" Mei Li addresses her slowly as a calm irritation flows from her.

"The faceless that attacked us was Alec; how is that possible?"

"There's no reason to believe it was him," Mei Li explains.

"Well, it had six fingers and it turned into Alec when it died." Emma's brows lift incredulously.

"We really don't have time for this." Mei Li waves a hand at Emma, trying unsuccessfully to urge her on. Emma remains still, and the action forces Mei Li to stop as well.

"How old am I?" Emma asks with a raised brow. Tremors of anger roll through her as she struggles to keep her tone indifferent. "How old are you?" Mei Li stares, dumbfounded, for a brief second. "All we have is time."

"What is that supposed to mean?" Mei Li whispers, folding her arms defensively over her chest.

"I am not a child. Between the three of us I am the second-eldest." Emma shivers uncontrollably as she endeavors to remain calm. "I need to feel that I am part of us and not just a fledgling."

"So, you want to make decisions, is that it?" Mei Li's lips purse in annoyance.

"I just want to be part of them and not in the dark, the last one to know. I want to feel like I have a say in all this." Unwanted tears gloss Emma's eyes as she balls her hands tightly, feeling as though the bones may break. She hates showing her weakness to Mei Li, but she forces her gaze, not daring to look away. "I have to feel like I have some control over my life, my happiness, and nothing has changed since Thanatos except there are only three of us. If I'm still nothing more than a paltry instrument for you, then tell me now."

"We are all tools to one extent or another in this world. We all have a purpose and a place, both you and I; there is nothing I can do about that." A somber resentment flows from Mei Li. "There is no guarantee for happiness, and you must find it where you can."

"How can I find it when you block me from it?" Both of them still as the words roll from Emma's lips. The urge to wipe her sweaty palms is overwhelming; her pulse thrums in her ears as fear and excitement skitter through her. How long she had waited to say those words? How long had she restrained herself for the dread that they would destroy her? A bell once tolled can never be unrung.

Mei Li watches her silently for several seconds before exhaling her long-held breath. A tightly controlled tension uncoils from her as her shoulders droop with an alien exhaustion.

"I have known for quite some time your feelings for David and his for you, though I had hoped it was a fleeting emotion and would not need addressing." Her voice is low and tired. "The Fury, more than other creatures, are fueled by their emotions and we both know how easily a trickle of water can quickly become an uncontrolled river."

"Others before me have found love and their actions didn't cause the world to collapse. Love is but one emotion that feeds us." Mei Li, interlacing her long fingers, presses her knuckles to her lips as she listens. "For so long I've been alone; all I ask for is a chance at something of a normal life a life, that can allow for some semblance of hope."

Mei Li's hands drop to her sides as she sighs deeply. "Perhaps you are right. I will try to include you more when issues arise. As far as the situation with David, we will need to discuss it."

"You've said that multiple times," Emma argues, but holds her tongue at Mei Li's raised hand.

"You have asked for equal say, did you not? It would not be right to have this discussion without Olivia. So, the next time all three of us are together we will talk about this at length. Does that sound fair?"

"Yes." Emma allows herself a small grin which almost feels alien to her, but it falls away quickly as she catches a flash of color from down the hall.

Jillian's blue and grey hair swirls around her as she runs the length of the hall toward them. Her frantic footfalls echo off of the stone, mirroring the rampant upswing of Emma's heart.

"Emma. Have you seen Aaron?" she pants as she approaches.

"No. Who was watching him?" Emma's own fear grows in response.

"I was but he wandered off." Jillian's gaze flickers wildly up and down the hallway.

"Wait, what?" Emma stares back, perplexed. "What do you mean he wandered off? How does an infant wander off?"

"He's not a baby anymore." Mei Li finally looks at Emma, seeing her confusion. "He is aging much faster than a typical human, so I'd guess his age at about two years now. We need to find him; can you please help?"

"Yes, of course." Emma nods as they turn down an adjoining hall. "So, is he just going to continue to age? At this rate he'll be an old man in a week or two." Emma's insides knot with the unpleasant thought of little Aaron

dying of old age. What kind of life is that—
when your existence is measured in weeks,
perhaps months, and not in years?

"I don't really know." Mei Li's pace quickens
as they descend another flight of stairs.
Reaching out with her senses, Emma tries to
find a direction to follow. Through the murky
haze of the Hallow everything seems
diminished, yet Aaron's faint presence flickers
subtly from somewhere below them. Her
breath hitches as they stand before the solid
door leading to the entrance to Erebus.

"He's down there?" Mei Li's voice trembles as
she studies the door.

"Someone may have taken him down there. I
should go first." Emma clenches her hands
against an unwanted shiver.

"Maybe we should get the others? We don't
know what we could come across," Jillian's
voice chimes from behind Mei Li.

"No. We may not have that much time. Plus,
we have a pretty good idea already of what's
down there." Emma doesn't bother hiding the
bitterness as it wells to the surface.

Steeling herself, Emma meets Jillian's gaze
with a nod as she slides aside the cobweb-
covered bar securing the door. Swinging the
door open, she feels a flutter of dread at the
musty air that envelops them. She coughs as a
stifling fear squeezes at her lungs, yet she
pushes forward tentatively, stepping into the
darkened void. Faint torchlight breaks the
darkness as they edge their way along the
muted hall, and the cells that have been
vacant for millennia lie in darkness to either
side of them.

She must find Aaron and get him to safety,
the urgency spurring her feet to move.
Emma's silent prayer, urging her onward, is
that she won't fail him as she had Sarah.

"Aaron is down the next hall." Emma's throat
closes tightly as the guilt and shame wash over
her. *Stupid woman, focus.* She edges her way
down the hall. Mei Li follows so closely that
she nearly collides with Emma when they stop
just outside a hallway lined with even more
cells.

Emma releases a shaky breath and peers down
the length of corridor. Every solid thrum of
her heart seems to pulse at a deafening pitch,

echoing through the cramped space. A small boy sits in the center of the hallway. A mop of walnut colored hair gleams against the torch light. From this distance Emma can hear his soft, mumbled voice as he plays with a tiny red car. Running the toy across the ground he lifts it into the air, displaying it for an unseen person. Aaron's gentle brown eyes light as he giggles, and it's a cheery sound so in contrast with his surroundings. She steps lightly, struggling to calm her coarse nerves, but her lungs stutter with a constricting ache.

"Emma, it's so nice to see you again." Her insides curdle as she meets Thanatos's cold gaze. His long legs stretch out before him as he sits nonchalantly against the wall, and his arm rests on the bars of his cell. Despite his confinement he still exudes a terrifying predatory aura.

"I can't really say the same." Maintaining her gaze, Emma edges her way toward Aaron. Although the bars should hold him, Emma's senses heighten at being this close to Thanatos. She chances a glance downward, and Aaron cranes his head, seeking her eyes with his. His short arms reach upward as his hands open and close, beckoning her. In a smooth motion Emma bends, scooping the small child into her arms.

"I can see that you are still angry with me." A smirk graces his lips as he examines her with stoic eyes.

"Well, you tried to kill me, so yeah." Emma senses Mei Li and Jillian as they cautiously approach.

"Perhaps I acted rashly, but the goal was for the betterment of all." He manages a sheepish shrug.

"Is that what you choose to tell yourself? That it was all for the greater good?" Mei Li's tone is aghast as she glares at him.

"In hindsight there may have been some selfish aspirations, but yes, it would have been for the better," he admits.

"You're unbelievable." Emma frowns, not bothering to hide her contempt.

"Do you honestly think I am the worst thing out there? I hold no malice, no hatred towards man or beast. I gain no pleasure from the taking of life or destruction. In fact, my duty has always been to maintain balance between the living and the dead. As a soul leaves the earthly plane they become my ward and I am honor bound to care for them. Unfortunately, death and therefore life have become inconsequential. So, if I need to become a monster to restore stability, then so be it."

"What do you want with Aaron?" She tightens her grasp on the small boy reflexively.

"Nothing."

"Then why is he here?" she asks skeptically.

"I have no clue." Thanatos cranes his head to study Aaron. "He just found his way down here."

"What do you know about him?" Mei Li walks up to Emma's side. There is something unsettling in Thanatos's stare.

"It's difficult to say. I get the impression that I know the child, but truth be told I have no recollection of meeting him before."

"Why should we believe anything you say?" Anger inhibits Emma's airway.

"I can tell you this. Despite all the things I have done, I have never lied to you," Thanatos states smoothly, with a familiar confidence to his tone. Unsettled by his words, Emma turns, leaving the cell behind.

Chapter 15

A steady drop of water patters the ground next to Olivia in a melodic tenor. The cold stone floor bites numbly into her flesh as she sits, resting her head against the granite wall. Her initial panic over losing her contact with her power has subsided, but has left her feeling exhausted. After nearly an hour her powers are still greatly muted but its meager presence is returning, yet at a far slower pace than she would like. Somewhere through the miasma of Nina's magic her own begins to stir, and she can sense it distantly.

"How are you feeling?" Bray whispers. His wounds have completely healed with only a few bright-red marks etching his torso as evidence. If he weren't a werewolf the injuries would have surely killed him. A loss of life is always distressing. How close had Bray been to dying? Her strengths have never included healing so even with her powers at full the best she could have done would be to stabilize him until they got help.

Though truth be told, she isn't completely certain if they both would have survived a full-on altercation with Nina. The ripples of residual fear echo through her as she recalls the overwhelming energy that had emanated from the nine-tailed fox. On very few occasions over the decades has Olivia ever encountered someone with that much strength. With no doubt, the petite being could have easily ended them, so perhaps she should count her blessings that Nina chose to leave versus killing them.

"A little better." Her own voice sounds distracted and distant.

"Do you want to try again?" He motions to the wall, but she doesn't really want to. The last five times she's tried to open a doorway it failed miserably, and she really doesn't want to fail again. But the alternative of staying trapped down here isn't an option either.

Olivia groans as she pulls herself up, glaring at the spiteful wall. Shaking the pins and needles from her hands, she ekes out a few more seconds of peace. The source is still too far away and she knows the attempt will fail, but the rational part of her mind repeats that she has to try.

Centering her thoughts, she pulls at the frailest tendrils of her power. The wisps of energy flicker about, dancing in an unseen breeze as they evade each of her attempts to seize them. A thin line of sweat trickles down her neck as she strains, a scream of frustration bellowing up in her throat. With a feeble hold on the thin filament, her palm skims along the rough stone. The material fluctuates, shifting weakly between a solid mass and a pseudo-mushy chaos, but is still too firm to traverse. Even if they could break the surface, only a fool would chance it staying fluid enough for both of them to cross through. As if prompted by the thought, the stone's movement slows and reforms into its solid state. Closing her eyes, Olivia lets go of a faded breath.

"What about the door?" Bray asks as he rests casually against the wall. The dismal torch light highlights the sheen of sweat that coats his skin, emphasizing the swell of muscles along his chest and arms. He seems completely at ease in his naked state, but

Olivia finds it irritating and highly distracting. It's probably the reason she can't focus completely on reclaiming her power, she fumes to herself.

"The lock appears pretty sturdy, but if I could pull enough power, I can try to pop it." The simple mechanism sways subtly from Bray's earlier strikes. Old and rusted, the stubborn device refuses to open.

"Well, do you have enough?" The teal of his aquamarine eyes is fierce amid the errant glow of flame light. Perhaps under his façade of calm he is just as eager to get out of here as she is.

"I have no clue." Olivia's shoulders drop as she rubs the stiff muscles of her neck, the fatigue from the night weighing on her. "What about you–can you shift yet?"

"Not completely, not enough to break through the door." Despite the few strands that are coated in sweat his hair flops softly as he shakes his head.

Olivia blows out a lengthy breath, her gaze locked on the door that seems determined to stymie them. Maybe she should throw her body at the door until either it or the door gives way.

"You don't happen to have a knife or something sharp hidden on you somewhere?" Olivia taps her lower lip as her mind works.

Bray pats his chest and hips. "I left it in my other pants." He grins slyly at her as he stands.

"You don't need to be a smartass. I'm trying to get us out of here and you're cracking jokes," she chides, but realizes her tone is snippier than she intended.

"I don't know about you, but I really don't want to die of old age in here. Why, what are you thinking?" He stands with an unnerving grace as he seems to ignore her harsh words.

"I can possibly use some blood to amplify my power. The issue is I have to bleed first."

"I thought Fury could make weapons."

"We can. Problem is, it takes energy to do that and I can't pull enough. See the conundrum?"

"Do you trust me?" An odd earnestness rolls off of him. The constant underlying playful banter is gone and the weight of his words seems to carry a greater importance than before.

"What is that supposed to mean?" There is an involuntary shiver in her voice.

"I have an idea, but I need to know that if we try it you won't freak out and try to kill me."

"I trust you more than anyone else around." She eyes him suspiciously.

"That's not very encouraging."

"Well, you are being ambiguous." Goosebumps rise on her arms under the direct scrutiny of his stare. "Fine. Yes. I trust you." She just wants out of this place– or perhaps the thinness of the air is affecting her.

"My fangs are sharper than my claws. I bite you and we can get the needed blood." His gaze never falters as he stands stoically before her.

"What about lycanthropy?" Her voice a mere whisper as she concentrates on her labored breath. She's never been bitten before by anyone.

"Most beings aside from human are immune."

"Very well, if it will help us get out of here."

"Don't be nervous. I will try not to hurt you." His lips lift as that reliably confident grin returns.

"I'm not nervous," she blurts out, trying to steady the tremor in her treacherous legs.

"Your heart is racing; I can hear it." His voice is warm as it washes over her ragged nerves.

Bray extends a tentative hand toward her and for the briefest moment she glimpses the genuine worry in his eyes. Olivia offers her hand and his fleeting distress fades and he takes her hand in his. Everything seems to fall away; her mind is flushed with the sensation of his warm skin on hers. The steady tempo of his breath fills her ears and he gradually raises her hand to his lips. The ocean-blue of his eyes turns icy as his gaze remains locked on hers.

When the heat of his mouth grazes her flesh, Olivia releases a forgotten breath. The pain is sharp but short-lived, and as Bray lets go of her hand the blood begins to pool in her palm from a tiny puncture hole.

Holding her hand steady Olivia walks over to the door and manages to pour much of the blood into the rusted lock. Trying to waste no time, she closes her eyes and pulls at her power once again. The lock warms in her hands as she funnels the meager yet present force into the device. Sweat glistens from her brow, but the lock finally gives way with a heavy click.

"We did it," Olivia smiles.

"Good. Let's get the hell out of here." Both of them exhale in relief.

The door creaks and groans as they lean into the wood but it slowly opens. An unyielding darkness engulfs the corridor ahead of them. Olivia retrieves two torches from the passageway behind them and hands one to Bray. Stepping out into the next hall, the torchlight endeavors to push back the impending shadows. The humid air clings to

Olivia's skin and the temperature is noticeably warmer here. This place gives off a sense of the earth being alive around them as if they are in the belly of some gigantic beast. Similarly, the Hallow's power is embedded in the rocks that surround it; both are fueled by a primordial magic.

Olivia measures her steps as they wind through the eroded caverns. A slick layer of slime and algae coat the surrounding rock. The organic stench hugs her nose and she pushes down the rise of bile. She manages to stay centered along the path, not wanting to get anywhere near the oozing walls. Bray walks slowly as he leads and every so often, he turns, glancing back at her.

"Are you alright?" he asks from over his shoulder.

"I'm fine." She coughs into her hand.

"Are you going to puke?" Bray stops, turning to study her.

"No," she clips, looking dismayed. "The smell's just a little pungent is all."

"You are an odd one," he chuckles.

"What do you mean by that?" Olivia's eyebrow lifts as she crosses her arms over her chest.

"It's not meant as an insult. You are just a lot more complicated than I had first thought and there are two very different sides to you. One's that's a calm badass, unafraid, and the other side that is grossed out by mold." He shrugs and his tone is light, but his gaze is unwavering.

"First of all, mold is gross and second, being a badass is highly overrated. Being a badass means you get to trudge through muck and god knows what else. It also means being alone for years." Olivia catches herself before saying more. For some reason she didn't want him to know about Fury's imposed solitude and celibacy.

"Well, if you weren't being a badass, what would you want to be doing?"

"Right now? Eating junk food and taking a bath." Olivia's laugh echoes down the corridor. Bray's gaze flitters over her body before settling back on her eyes.

"No, I mean what would you be doing if you weren't a Fury?"

"Oh." Caught off guard by the question. "I don't know, really," she answers with a shrug. "What about you? What do you want to be when you grow up?" she asks in a light-hearted attempt to shift the focus from her.

"I'd be with my family," he states without hesitation.

"Emma said you all are really close. That must be nice. Perhaps one day I can meet them."

"I'm sure they would like that. Though I should warn you, wolves tend to be very touchy." He shifts from one foot to another, anxious energy bristling him.

"Touchy, how?"

"Physical contact is important for forming and maintaining bonds."

"Okay. Why would that be an issue?"

"Well." He pauses briefly as if collecting his thoughts. "I was informed that you have a touch phobia and I don't want there to be a problem for you, or them."

"I don't have a touch phobia. I'm just not always comfortable being touched by people I don't know. I have no problem having contact with someone I trust."

"My apologies." Bray's eyes drift into the darkness ahead.

"It's alright. Let's keep moving." She lightly touches his arm as they move forward.

The narrow tunnel snakes on for several minutes and they step out into an open cavern. The natural flow of groundwater has eroded the rock, creating a vast open area. Their torches meekly battle against the deep shadows that overpower the space. The span is flooded with eerie deep water that mirrors the darkness. Across the expanse, a raised platform is dimly lit from the soft glow of a brazier that is set into the stone. Its weak light gently flickers, sending blackened shapes along the gnarled wood of the door below it.

"How do we get across this?" Olivia squints against the darkness, her gaze searching for another path.

"Unless you can fly, it looks like we may have to swim." Bray leans over the edge, probing the murky water. "It doesn't look all that deep."

Olivia's nose crinkles as she follows his gaze. While the water is pitch black it appears clear and she is able to spot small rocks only a few feet below the surface. "I'd really rather not get in there."

"Me neither, but it's either cross here or go back and I don't think there is any way back the way we came. If it makes you feel better, I'll go first."

Olivia can only manage a weak nod as Bray eases himself into the black water. Shallow ripples pulse outward from him, but otherwise the surface remains eerily still.

"It's not too bad," he whispers. "The temperature is pretty warm and as long as there isn't a drop-off in the middle, we should be able to wade across." His calming tone does very little to settle the jittery irritation that claws at her senses. Olivia pulls in a deep breath, pushing the tension outward as she exhales and slides into the water as well. Despite Bray's observation she is shocked by the warmth of the water. The rich saline odor reminds her of the ocean, but they were too deep for salt water to have leeched its way down here. Though in a place such as this, you can travel mere feet down here and end up miles from where you started on the surface.

With measured steps they begin the arduous trek across the oval cavern, every noise jarring brashly. Her shallow breaths echo against the harsh silence that seems to envelop them. A hint of movement against one of the side walls draws her eye, but as she turns to look, she only catches the soft undulation in the water as its reflection bounces off of the surrounding rocks. Despite the temperature of the balmy water, chills prompt a soft shiver over her flesh. She studies the space, trying to reassure her nervous mind that she isn't being watched. After a few seconds she surmises that it was perhaps a pebble falling into the water below.

Bray reaches the ledge, resting his hand on the stone as he watches her slow approach. A flash of color and movement erupts from the placid water before a gasp can escape Olivia's lips. An amorphous mass of white with blue rings coils around Bray. Thick tentacles drag him under the surface, and Olivia's heart races as she pushes her way through the water. The exasperating fluid seems hell-bent on slowing her pace and as she reaches the ledge, her hands dive into the dark water, frantically searching for some sign of Bray. As the seconds tick by, she dips under the surface, reaching farther. Her eyes detect nothing, only the malevolent shroud of darkness and the small particulates that swirl about as her movement pulls long-settled silt up from the cave floor. For what feels like an eternity she continues to search the waters, moving forward, breaking the surface for a quick lungful of air, then plunging under again.

A sudden jerk on her leg pulls her backward through the water. Olivia manages to turn, staring through the murky gloom at her attacker. A hairless, grey-skinned man clasps her ankle with an outstretched arm; a set of flailing tentacles swooshes through the water from the base of his torso. Thick blue rings pulse along the cecaelia's skin, and he fiercely tugs at her, trying to keep her under.

Tentacle arms dart forward, entwining her limbs as Olivia struggles against their hold. Her lungs burn for air and she pries away a length of suckers, only to be trapped by another set. Kicking away from the floor she nearly crests the surface but is quickly yanked down again. The octopus hybrid pulls her closer, its beak-like mouth agape. Olivia's heart hammers and her vision blurs as she weakly pulls at her power, willing some kind of blade.

The hilt of the dagger nearly slips from her grip as it materializes. Her movements are hampered by the water as she pushes the blade into the creature's side, and its black eyes widen. The water clouds with a plume of blood, and she sends a lethal pulse of force into its body. As its hold on her slackens, she pushes away, breaking the surface and drawing in gasps of air.

Olivia's legs shake but her vision slowly clears. She spots Bray leaning against the far wall. Bray smiles weakly but his relief when he spots her is apparent. With bounding steps, she meets him at the ledge and pulls herself up onto the solid surface. Bray plants his palms on the rock landing and winces sharply when he lifts himself.

"Are you okay?" Olivia asks as she checks him for damage.

"Yeah, the thing bit me though." Bray lifts his arm, revealing a small set of puncture marks on the side of his stomach. The wound appears superficial and it has already stopped bleeding.

"How are you feeling?" Her tone is tense with concern as she tries to think past the thud of her own heart. Bray's skin is ashen, and although he is trying to hide it, she can see the slight tremor shaking his hands.

She grabs his arm as his knees buckle. Olivia pulls him away from the water's edge, and she helps him lie down.

"The little bugger must be venomous. We might need to wait for it to pass or else I'll be useless to you." Newly formed sweat sheens on his heated brow.

"These were cecaelia, not just normal octopus' venom. Will your body metabolize the poison?" Her mind whirls while his breaths become more ragged.

"I'm not sure, but I think so." He feigns confidence, but a small hint of fear lights his eyes. His weight sags against her, his chest rising and falling with greater effort.

Knowing that she needs to get him out of here fast, Olivia eases his head down as she scurries over to the nearest wall. Palm pressed against the cool stone she wills a portal to open, but the stubborn material refuses to comply. She can only guess the strength of the wards that surround this place, but they can block her at full power.

"What the hell?" She screeches and slaps the wall.

Her heart sinks as her stare remains transfixed on the rock for a brief second, before she returns to Bray's side. Her hands shudder as she tentatively clasps his. Screaming frustration rolls through her, watching Bray struggle for each breath. His body battles the potent toxin with each choking gasp.

Someone is whispering that it'll be okay, and Olivia barely realizes it is her. Biting down hard on her lip, she tries to keep the tears from falling that are weighing heavily on her lids.

Bray's grasp goes limp and a long sigh escapes him. Olivia's own lungs stop, she waits for him to inhale. Nothing. Her insides burn with a searing pain and she wills his chest to rise. Nothing. Pushing away the sheer terror eating at her mind, Olivia releases his hand. Tilting his head back she touches her lips to his and blows her breath into him.

With a single-minded determination, she continues, alternating breathing with chest compressions, not even certain she's doing it correctly. *I'm better at killing than at healing,* she fumes.

She's so focused on the task at hand she doesn't notice the hand resting on the side of her face. She doesn't notice anything until the soft yet firm tongue slips into her mouth. Shock and something she hasn't felt for a very long time flood her senses. His strong mouth explores hers as it nips and sucks. Perhaps she should pull away, but she doesn't want to.

Her hands rest on his chest as she greedily returns his kiss. As they finally separate, their breath coming in arduous pants, Olivia opens her eyes, meeting the intensity of his gaze.

"Are you okay?" Her voice is raw and shuddering; her breath mingles with his.

"I'm much better now." A wicked smile lifts his lips and a normal color returns to his skin. His face falls when he spots something over her shoulder. "When did you open the door?"

Chapter 16

Bastian's flittering fingers tap the arm of his leather chair with an uncommon agitation. From his own seat, David has spent the last half hour studying his new mentor as Bastian settles his late-evening affairs. With each passing minute he catches more of Bastian's subtle body language that lets his nervousness seep through.

After a steady stream of outside petitioners, his kin come in with their pointless prattling of business details. From his demeanor, David knows Bastian finds it as boring as he does, yet he sits patiently listening and doling out advice and orders as needed. On several occasions Bastian stifles an errant yawn in between requesters. David's job is a simple one, look mean and keep everyone in line. It's grunt work but it's better than sitting in his room all night.

The wooden double doors close with a muted click as the last supplicant leaves them in silence. Bastian leans back, rolling his shoulders with an audible crack, and it is on these rare times that one can see the heavy toll his position has on him. No doubt the recent added stresses are probably not helping the situation at all. No one has been able to answer why a faceless would have attacked Bastian and Emma, which is highly frustrating. Now add onto that the unexpected visit from Guillermo. David can only wager a random guess regarding the unusual relationship between the two of them. Knowing that they had both tried to kill one another in the past is a little disconcerting, to say the least.

"You think I'm foolish for trusting Guillermo?" Bastian's cold eyes peer curiously back under arched brows. David has learned to trust him but he isn't stupid enough to believe him tame.

"I never took you for a mind reader and I don't think you are a fool. But truth be told it is a weird situation." He stifles the urge to move in his seat, commanding his body into a statuesque pose. Bastian's soft laugh jostles his form, the sharp peaks of his fangs barely showing.

"When you've been around as long as I have, you will realize that what was once weird becomes normal. Always remember that Guillermo is a man not to be trifled with and he's hard, but he is just. Ryl, on the other hand, is not to be trusted."

"Why is he here?" David asks. "He has never visited the States before. Why now?"

"Guillermo does things in his own time and for his own reasons. I only found out about his intended visit a week ago, so it is really anyone's guess."

"Does it have something to do with Thanatos and the Fury?" David leans forward in his chair, releasing his white-knuckled grasp on the wood rails.

"Possibly. Under Guillermo's reign the vampires have tried to maintain the fragile alliance with the judgment."

"The judgment?" David peaks his brow.

"Under Killian's control there was no peace with the Fury. He believed that no other species should dictate our existence. For centuries there was constant warring, and our numbers were decimated. Those who survived started referring to the Fury as the judgment."

"That's why he was overthrown?"

"It was one of the reasons, yes. Most of us just wanted the slaughter to end."

"And Guillermo was one of them?" Bastian nods in silence. "So, you think he's just here for a social call?"

"No. My best guess would be that there has been some restructuring, like when someone dies, is replaced or will be. It is possible that he is here to ask my counsel on adequate candidates."

"Interesting. He is looking for new staff?"

"Why? Are you seeking a new job?" Bastian feigns a lightness that doesn't reach his dark-hooded eyes.

"Not really. But considering I have no job here, I'd like to keep my options open."

"You are still very green." He presses his hands together in front of him. "I want to make sure all that I sire have plenty of time to adjust."

"And what will you have me do after this adjustment period?" David returns the intensity of Bastian's gaze.

"You are not bound to me, but staying here is always an option and it would be foolish not to utilize a man with your skill set. You can have a very comfortable life under my employ and I just happen to have need of another lieutenant. You would only answer to Poe and myself."

"What about Emma and the Fury?"

"What about them? The vampires and Fury are not intrinsically linked. While I consider them allies, they will continue on their paths, as will we."

"Perhaps I could act as a liaison between you and the Fury? I know them, and it could help to maintain peace," David offers tentatively.

Bastian sighs heavily as he rises from his plush chair. Strolling over to a table that showcases antiques and relics, he slowly spins a globe, seemingly lost within his own thoughts for a moment. "I don't think that is a good idea."

"Why?" David shoots up from his own chair, pushing it across the carpeted floor.

"I understand your anger, but perhaps patience and a cool head is the better course of action." Bastian's gaze flicks to the door, then finds David again.

"Why, just tell me why," David spits, his voice booming through the small space.

"It's not that simple, David."

"Bullshit. You've kept me held up in here, running simple errands and being a guard dog. I want to know why." His blood boils as the rage courses through his body. Anger and frustration are barely leashed, biting at the bit to be released.

"Keep your voice down," Bastian barks through clenched teeth. "Guillermo will be here shortly, and we can discuss this when his business here is done."

"No, tell me now or I'm walking." Jerking a thumb toward the door, the cold resolve echoes in his voice.

"I'm trying to save you the pain of losing Emma," Bastian blurts out, his carefully concealed desperation seeping through, instantly quenching David's smoldering rage.

"What do you mean?"

"These are dangerous times." Bastian's voice trembles slightly.

"No." David shakes his head.

"What will you do if you pursue a relationship with Emma and Mei Li denies it?"

"Things are different now and Emma is her own person."

"No," Bastian parrots back. "She is a Fury, one of the three. If Mei Li forbids it for fear it will destroy them, then you may very well be forcing her hand."

"Mei Li wouldn't harm Emma." David's chest tightens at the thought.

"Unless she feels she has no choice. For Mei Li the greater good will always win over personal gains. And if you chose to defy her, I will be forced to take sides, putting my children at risk." Bastian's shoulders slump as he rubs the back of his neck.

"How?" David's voice is hollow as words and thoughts spiral into a place of darkness.

"You are now my child." Bastian's raised hand halts any argument stirring in David. "If conflict breaks out between you and Mei Li, I will take your side. But we will have no aid from any other vampires, not even Guillermo. Mei Li cannot show restraint or mercy, and we will die and you will lose Emma. I'm only advising you to just give it time and, gods willing Mei Li's nerves can be set at ease and you will have eternity with her."

A subtle knock draws their eyes to the door. "Yes," Bastian answers, though his gaze remains locked on David.

Poe juts his head through the double door, and he eyes the toppled chair warily.

"Is everything alright?" Poe's alarmed tone asks more than his words.

"Yes, we are fine," Bastian answers.

"Guillermo has arrived; do you want me to ask him to wait?" His stare shifts nervously between both of them. Apparently, he, along with everyone else, has overheard their conversation.

"No, please show him in."

"I'll see you tonight then." David turns, making his way cautiously to the open door.

"I'd prefer you to stay."

"Do you foresee an issue with the king?" David rounds back to Bastian.

"No, but as one of my lieutenants, your place is at my side."

David grumbles silently to himself and rights his overturned chair as the doors swing open again. The monstrous draegloth, Ryl, has to duck as it steps into the room. Its beady, blood-red eyes squint; this creature is more at home in the darkest shadows. David's senses are alerted at its arrival as he remembers Bastian's warning about him. Ryl seems to have a terror-inducing aura that fills the space around him and David has to steel himself against the urge to shake it off.

Guillermo follows a few paces behind; although not nearly as tall as Ryl, he still seems to dwarf the small room. The thick mane of onyx hair is woven into a single braid that lands below his back, and both sleeve tattoos are shown prominently against the black of his t-shirt. He doesn't appear overtly menacing yet there is a potent intensity about him.

"Guillermo, it is an honor to welcome you into my home. I am at your service should you have need of me. I wasn't certain as to how long you'll be staying so I have prepared one of my finest rooms for you." Bastian gestures to one of the seats in front of his desk.

"As always you woo me with your flowery words and pretty mouth." Guillermo's lip lifts in a sideways smirk. "I thank you, but have already made arrangements for this day and provided I can finish my business quickly, my stay should be short." His gaze shifts to David, scrutinizing him from top to bottom. Guillermo steps toward David with the confidence of a seasoned hunter. Fighting every urge to take a swing at the man or run, David strong-arms his body deathly still as he stares blankly forward.

"This is David, he's my newest lieutenant."

"Odd. He seems like a new blood, but there is something much older about him."

"It is a complicated story," Bastian's voice warbles as he tries to brush off the comment. "I don't mean to rush you, but the sun will be rising soon."

"Do you trust him?" Guillermo asks, ignoring Bastian. David focuses on the rigidity of his body, showing no fear or hesitation. Ryl's throaty growl rumbles through the air. He eyes them suspiciously, spittle gleaming from his jagged fangs.

"More than I trust you." Bastian answers coolly.

The king's cold stare lasers Bastian as his callous eyes are cloaked under thick brows and the breath of a few seconds seems to drag into an eternity. Guillermo's head shoots back and his form shakes as the vigorous laughter rolls from him. "You've always been a good judge of character, despite your incessant need for honesty."

"The older I get the less fond I am of needlessly fluffing one's ego." Bastian shrugs as he strides to a liquor cabinet, pouring several snifters of brandy. The warm fluid sloshes into the crystal glasses refracting the light along the walls.

"I admire that about you. If I'm being an ass, you'll find a courteous way of telling me. That's why I knew you'd be perfect." Guillermo takes the offered glass but doesn't lift it to drink.

"I'm sorry? Perfect for what, exactly?" Bastian asks, his brow creasing with uncertainty.

"A prominent position has just opened up in my council."

"The last time I was in your court, half of your council wanted to take my head. What makes you think I'd be suicidal enough to head into that lion's den?" Bastian's lips lift with a semiserious smirk as he passes a glass to David.

"Ryan is dead." Guillermo shifts uncomfortably as he plants a hand on his hip.

"What happened?" Bastian stops, his glass half raised to his lips.

"Short story, he went mad and died." Guillermo's braid sways across the length of his back as he shakes his head. Without any great skill at reading people David knows Guillermo is hiding something. The fractional shift in his stance and how his focus drifts from Bastian to the room around them are telltale signs of his discomfort.

"What is happening, Guillermo? Give me the long version," Bastian presses firmly.

Guillermo takes several long strides over to a large bay window. He scratches at the scruff of his chin while staring out into the waning darkness. A few times he lifts the glass to his lips yet lowers it without drinking.

"Guillermo," Bastian repeats.

"Someone is trying to unseat me." Guillermo sighs loudly, his shoulders falling minutely as he turns to face them again.

"You've faced challengers before. Why should this be any different, and what does that have to do with Ryan?"

"He's not challenging me as other contenders would. Instead of coming directly at me he's removing those who support me. Ryan has always been one of my most powerful supporters."

"When they were screaming for my head, Ryan kept them at bay," Bastian admits solemnly.

"He was the most rational of all of us back then, still was, even the last time I spoke with him. It is that very reason I doubted his sudden break with reality. I sent out my men to find out what really happened."

"And you found what?"

"Someone or something drove him insane." Guillermo flops down in a nearby chair and the wood groans under his weight. "As the sun sets one night, he is perfectly normal but then before the sun crests his entire clan is dead. Whatever sickness ailed him lifted with the rising sun, and so engrossing was his guilt that he leapt from a high window to meet the morning light."

"How do you know he wasn't attacked? Someone could have made it appear like madness," David asks, and three sets of eyes turn to study him, making his skin itch.

"One servant managed to escape. She was hiding amid a pile of corpses when we found her. The poor wretch was in such a catatonic state that it took nearly two days to get her to talk, and when she could, she confirmed our suspicions."

"Do you know who this challenger is?" Bastian pours more brandy into his glass.

"He's an old blood by the name of Victor."

"I have never heard of him. Are you certain that he is an old blood?"

"What's an old blood?" David interrupts.

"A vampire sired prior to colonization," Guillermo answers with a sideways glance.

"At first I thought he must be a hybrid anomaly as everything about him seems out of the norm. As appalling as it is, I actually went to mother to ask for her help." Guillermo's eyes narrow slightly as his head dips to the side.

"You went to go see your mother, Siv? How did that turn out?" Bastian grins slyly as if there is an unspoken story there.

"Well, she's as wicked and foul-natured as always, so the fact that I didn't wring her frail neck is a miracle." Guillermo tips his head toward them and is met with another deep growl from Ryl.

"Calm yourself, Ryl." Guillermo glares at his companion.

"Did she at least give you some information?" Bastian's question pulls Guillermo's attention back to them.

"Victor is millennia old but was inconsequential for most of his existence. According to Siv, he was the joke of his clan. The youngest of all of his siblings, he wasn't strong enough to survive their standards and was considered a mistake more than anything else."

"So, what happened?"

"Don't know. About six hundred years ago his power started to increase exponentially. No real reason why."

"That's pretty uncommon, unless it's through black magic or a frenzied mass feeding."

"Either is a good possibility. His clan was a bunch of treacherous swine, more so than even my own. The fact that they would dabble in the black arts wouldn't surprise me."

"Was?" David asks as a cold chill works its way down his spine.

"As Victor's power grew, he seized control of his clan and butchered them all. Aside from his own children, none of his family survived."

"So, what does this have to do with your visit here and now?" David inquires, trying to piece it all together.

"I need to show my strength in the face of this challenge. Solidarity of force is needed at this time, and with Ryan gone, I need Bastian to step up and take his place."

"Why me?" Bastian asks with wide eyes.

"You are well respected within the inner circles as well as honorable and loyal to those you serve. I do not have the luxury of instilling in anyone my complete trust as it is a fool's dream, but I have need of people who are dependable enough."

"While I am honored by your offer, I have many responsibilities here that require much of my time."

"I am certain that you would be able to delegate some, if not all of the responsibilities. Perhaps it is best that you take a few nights to think on it."

Guillermo rises, placing his untouched glass on the edge of Bastian's desk. Walking to the door, he is followed closely by Ryl, who eyes them with primal loathing. Poe stands rigidly as he holds open the door, offering a brief nod as the king exits.

"Poe," Bastian beckons the man. "See Guillermo off safely. When he has left, I want you to secure the house, then take the basement passage. I will need word sent to all of the head of the houses. They are to meet with me here in three night's time."

"What's going on?" David asks.

"Guillermo isn't the only one with a council. I need to speak with those under me, as a decision like this shouldn't be made rashly." Poe nods in response and leaves the room, closing the door behind him.

"Are you going to accept Guillermo's offer?"

"I don't think I really have a choice." Bastian stares hard at the closed door.

Chapter 17

The subtle click of the deadbolt echoes through the foyer. Poe shifts the curtain aside as he checks the locks of the window. Staring out, he studies the yard, which is deathly calm, with barely a leaf stirring save the occasional movement as a steady beat of rain falls around them. Along with some modern security features, rune stones are embedded into the exterior of the house and are activated by the cresting sun. They act as an additional barrier from any paranormal beings that may try to enter the building during the daylight hours. Despite the skyline being dark he can feel the draw of the dawn. The weight of his limbs feels heavier and slogging through the house to secure all of the entry points is becoming decidedly more difficult as his body slows, wanting to enter a deep slumber for the day.

Sleep won't come anytime soon for him, though. He must protect this house before he can leave to contact the other houses. A simple-enough task, as once he traverses the underground tunnel system, he can leave word with one of the sentries for Nikos Di Angelo. If all goes well the cascade effect will mean all of the houses should be notified before the meeting date.

He descends the stairs leading into the basement; a single halogen light flickers, sending limited light into the dim area. The heavy clop of his boots echoes off of the damp cement walls. Much of the subterranean space below the house is held for crypts and living quarters. This area remains empty and unused, as it must be unoccupied in case of an attack, leaving them a clear path should they need to evacuate.

The soft earthen floor gives under his weight as he steps off the concrete slab. From a small cubbyhole Poe fishes out the key for the door that leads to the tunnels. Shifting from side to side, he tries to find a spot to stand that will allow enough light to shine through to aid him a clear view of the keyhole. Even with the help of exceptional night vision he must strain to see, and it takes several exasperating seconds for the key to slide into the old lock worn from decades of use. His stomach

clenches for a split second as the key demands
to turn the wrong way.

"Damn it," Poe mutters under his breath, and
he silently curses at the last person who used
this door and forgot to secure it again
afterward. Pushing the thought away he
unlocks the door and swings it open.
Obviously, the lax judgment with the door
will have to be addressed later. There is a soft
bed and a good day's rest waiting for him to
complete his task.

The light shines through the doorway,
illuminating only a few feet into the stone-
carved passageway. Without aid of some
additional light it will take twice as long to get
there and back. Poe grabs an electric lamp
sitting on one of the small tables and switches
it on, its artificial light fanning out across the
floor.

Poe squints against the bright light as his
insides drop. The dirt around the door is
disturbed in a peculiar way. Angling the light,
he can see his own footprints making their
way toward the door. But several prints of
varying sizes are headed away from the
threshold. Looking back toward the stairs,

Poe inspects the concrete, finding the nearly faded markings of wet shoeprints.

The hair on the back of his neck springs up as the first guttural scream resonates from upstairs. Breaking his frozen stance, Poe leaps forward, dropping the lamp as he careens up the steps.

Pushing the upstairs door open, he chances a glimpse out into the kitchen. A weighty aura seems to hang thick in the air. It's almost as if he has stepped into an invisible miasma that sends a pointed shiver down the length of his spine. A strangely familiar scent tickles at his nose, an odor he keenly recognizes from somewhere in his past. He crouches as he scans the open kitchen and his ears pick up an errant bumping upstairs, but no other sound.

Poe edges forward, cautiously moving to the foyer. With each step the air tightens around him, blurring into a thick fog. The smoky vapor obscures his vision as features of the kitchen are enveloped, leaving him frozen in the dense cloud. The floor beneath his feet transitions into spongy wooden planks that slowly shift from left to right. A faint knocking is timed perfectly with the sideways rock of his body as the nearly imperceptible sound of water can be heard. The smell is haunting as his mind snaps with a realization of its source, black powder.

In the face of all logic telling him that the hallucination can't be real, every sensation is fueling the delirium. His mind works frantically against the unnatural thrum of his heartbeat. Where the refrigerator should be stands the broad wood of a mast, with massive cords of rigging rope swaying softly. A bone-chilling shiver jostles him in spite of the warm ocean air wafting around his body.

"There you are, you dirty bilge rat," a gruff voice shouts.

Poe locks eyes with his long-dead captain. The dingy peacock feather flares limply from his tri-cornered hat. Numerous thin braids on his head and beard fall atop the soot-covered velvet of his doublet, which at one time had been a deep burgundy. The black of his breeches and thigh-high boots appears to meld into the obscuring fog that swells around them.

"What? Got nothing to say to yer ole captain Eli?" He smiles wickedly through grime-caked teeth.

"You're dead," Poe says, more to himself than the specter as ant-like chills scurry along his skin.

"Aye, I'm dead and you let them kill me." The soft soles of his boots scuff the wood as he advances several meandering steps. His cool, black eyes are lifeless as they scrutinize him.

"I had no part in the mutiny." Keeping his voice steady, Poe struggles to maintain his senses.

"You did, though." Eli's skin picks up a slick, rubbery sheen. It wrinkles as rivulets of water begin to stream down his head, quickly soaking his hair and coat. "You, who swore an oath to protect me, to be my blade. But you stood idly by while they threw me into the dark waters."

"I was a child of nine. What would you have me do?" Poe barks back, surprised by the sudden surge of startling emotion.

"I was your captain. You should've followed me into hell and back." A small crab peeks from the open folds of Eli's billowing shirt. In one smooth motion he unsheathes the cutlass from his side. The girth of metal and the deadly point glint under an unnatural light. Eli weighs Poe with an elated anticipation.

"The men hated you and I hated you," Poe says. "You were my captain, but now you are centuries–old fish shit at the bottom of the ocean."

The Eli specter lunges forward, swinging the blade in an overhead arc. Instinctually, Poe dips to the side to avoid the strike but is halted by an invisible barrier that collides with his hip bone. Pain pulses down his leg and the mirage around him flickers; the shimmering sight of the kitchen flashes briefly into existence. Poe gropes the countertop island, trying to find a weapon before it vanishes again, and his eyes catch the broad handle of a kitchen knife. As he is drawn back into the hallucination, he forces his mind to focus on the sensation of the grained wood in his hand.

The deck of the ship reemerges from the fog just as the cutlass blade crests his line of sight, swiping at him. Ducking under the blade, Poe darts to where the kitchen door should be. Terror clamps down on his innards, judging the distance to the door, he'll have to leap over the bow of the ship and either he's hitting the door or landing in the black water.

Poe plants a foot on the slick wooden side and propels himself over the rail and out into the night. The humid ocean air washes over him, and he starts to second-guess his gamble. Thankfully and painfully the solid kitchen door splinters as he crashes into it. Wood shatters, and small fragments scrap and cut his skin—not enough damage to cause concern but enough to dissolve the illusion. Rolling across the floor Poe comes to a halt as he hits the far wall of the foyer. Glancing back, he sees that the kitchen is eerily quiet, no ship or captain to be seen, only the destroyed door.

He pulls himself up, listening to the uncomfortable silence that surrounds him. His senses are ablaze, picking up the distant sound of shouting and screams. The sporadic timing of the shouting makes it painfully difficult to follow as it is differing voices coming from separate areas of the house.

Grasping the hilt of his knife, Poe follows the sounds, heading through the house at what seems like a snail's pace.

The fireplace is mere embers as he sneaks into the living room. A rasping scream shreds the air and Poe whips around, seeking the source. Scanning the murky darkness, he finds David's form hunkered down behind a couch that barely conceals him. His face is deathly pale as his eyes focus on something that is not at all in the room. David barely peeks over the rim of the cushioned back of the sofa, his stark eyes scanning something in the distance. He clutches something to his chest that is invisible as his whole body is wracked with a convulsive shiver. Poe can only imagine what kind of illusion David is trapped in, and his mind works on how to rouse him.

"Collins, McEnroe, stop gawking and get in those fucking holes!" David barks an order as his head shoots up, staring at the ceiling. His eyes are wide as they scan above him. "Incoming—get in your hole, get down, take cover!"

A rising panic builds in Poe as he realizes how far David's voice carries. Whatever is causing this may still be here, roaming the floors. Beyond the yelling he can hear a distinct thumping from down the hall.

"David," Poe rasps as he shakes his shoulders, knowing that he needs to wake him up and quickly. As the sense of urgency plumes, he studies David's movements; he needs to time his strike before David can react. Jumping forward, Poe grabs hold of David's smallest finger, wrenching until he hears a defined crack. David roars in pain and his eyes blink feverishly before finding Poe.

"What the hell?" David hisses through clenched teeth, clasping his broken digit. His wide eyes flick around the room as his senses return. "Why am I here?" A clear confusion resonates in his tone.

"I think everyone in the house is being influenced by some sort of dark magic, hallucinations. What is the last thing you remember?"

David stares at the dying fire. "I was in my room, getting ready for rest, and then I was in the woods."

"We need to find Bastian and the others before it's too late to get out of the house." Poe claps him on the shoulder as he helps him stand.

Climbing two steps at a time they vault up the stairs. The hallways are shrouded in a bleak darkness.

"Something doesn't feel right," Poe whispers as he glances down the hall. A prickled anxiety brushes across his skin, raising the hairs of his neck.

"It feels like the house is underwater, like I'm walking through soup," David muses, his features grim.

The doorknob to the first bedroom they encounter feels strangely cold. The door swings open easily and the room within is cloaked in darkness. The shades, which block any errant sunlight, are drawn and secured and only the paltry light trickling in from the hall illuminates the space. Their gaze sweeps across the room quickly as they search for any movement. Poe stops as his eyes fall on a small area rug at the foot of the bed and an unusual mound of dirt. Every muscle in him tightens as David creeps over to the heap. Thin tendrils of light draw attention to the arched brow of the skull. David gently pushes aside the soft ashes and his hand comes away with a small pendant buried within the debris. The brushed gold of the pendant flickers in the light, and Poe's heart sinks as he recognizes it.

"It's Laurel's." Poe pushes back his brewing panic and dread. Laurel had been part of the clan for a long time, even longer than he. She was trustworthy and not one to easily fall victim to assassins. A deep woman's shriek rips their gaze from the mound of ash.

The house is oppressively dark and quiet as they slowly make their way down the long corridor. Wayward beams of light skitter down the walls from pre-dawn traffic. There were only two occupied rooms down this hall; one belongs to David and the other is Jillian's. Each man takes a position on either side of the closed door. Their superior hearing strains as they try to distinguish any sound. A wretched sobbing resonates from the other side of the door and Poe warily pushes it open. Jillian huddles in the small space between the bed and her closet. Hugging her knees to her chest, her red-rimmed eyes stare distantly as she rocks.

"Dad." Her voice is a haunting whisper as she exhales. "Why did you go? Why did you just give up?" She seems to be listening to a voice that no one else can hear. Jillian closes her eyes as tears wet her cheeks. "I know you were sick, but I need you. Why couldn't you stay with me?" She hides her face in her knees as she weeps mournfully; it's a harsh sound that carves at Poe's insides.

"How do we wake her?" David asks, his brow etched with concern.

"I'm not sure," Poe responds.

"How did you wake me?"

"I broke your finger."

"Well, I am not breaking her finger and I am not letting you do it either," David barks firmly.

"I'm not suggesting we do that, but pain seems to break this thing." After a few seconds, Poe steps toward Jillian but David's hand on his arm and fierce glare stops him.

"What are you going to do?"

"I'm going to pinch her," Poe answers and is met with another scowl from David. "Or I could smack her with a pillow. What would you suggest?" His gruff whisper carries across the space.

"I don't like this." David's eyes scan the area once again.

"Neither do I, but we have to wake her."

Poe approaches Jillian with a startling amount of unease. Her shoulders heave as she sobs into her lap. Reaching out he gently shakes her arm, wanting to soothe her pain and not give her more. "Jillian," he murmurs. She doesn't move, nor does she respond. Poe settles his nerves as he reaches out again, grabbing a finger full of the soft skin under her arm and pinching. Jillian's head shoots up as she cries out and her gaze meets his a second before she strikes his face with an open palm. Shocked and disoriented, Poe reels backward, landing firmly on his ass.

"What the hell are you doing?" she growls, fangs lengthened by her anger.

"I was trying to wake you up." Ashamed and embarrassed, Poe palms the tender flesh of his cheek.

"You could have just… why am I on the floor?" Her gaze flickers about the room, taking in David then finally resting back on Poe.

"I can't explain right now, but we have to gather the others and leave." Jillian's gaze swoops between them again before she nods and allows Poe to help her stand.

"What are ye doing? What's going on here?" All of their eyes turn to take in Liam as he stands in the doorway. His long scarlet hair is disheveled, falling around his face, and a large bruise on his forehead is nearly faded. He studies them critically as his emerald eyes dart about.

"We are under attack. Where is Bastian?" Poe takes hold of Jillian's arm, leading her toward the door.

"I have not seen anyone. I woke up from a nightmare when I ran into a wall." Liam still seems to be sloughing off the effects of the magic as he shakes his head. "We need to go," he parrots back from a befuddled state.

Liam lurches forward as he braces his hands against the doorframe. His face contorts into a hollow mask as bloody spittle sprays from his mouth; his skin shifts from alabaster to an ashen grey. Slumping forward with a weighty thud, light glints off of the dagger hilt sticking from his back. Bastian glares down at the dead vampire with callous, lifeless eyes.

"Bastian?" David asks tightly.

"Do you think I would let this stand?" Bastian's voice is cold, an alien imitation of the man they know.

"Bastian, you need to wake up." Poe keeps his tone smooth, trying to cloak his rising alarm. This man he has known for several centuries now eyes him as a stranger. More than a stranger. Bastian's eyes narrow as the bloodlust consumes him.

"Bathing in the blood of your kin has not slaked my hunger. My vengeance will only be complete when you are utterly erased. For what you have done to my children, my son and Grace, you will die by my hand." Bastian walks into the room with a terrifying ease. In a smooth movement he withdraws a machete from a sheath at his side.

Poe's eyes flick to David a second before they both rush forward, tackling Bastian. If not for their combined weight he would have remained standing but together they pull him to the ground. David grapples Bastian's arm holding the blade and manages to knock it away. Pinning Bastian down with his face in the carpet does very little to control his bloodlust. He bucks and nearly escapes Poe's grasp. Glaring up at them Bastian's face is unrecognizable, coated in Liam's blood, which has soaked the floral carpet.

"Jillian, cut him!" Poe orders. She wavers for a second before retrieving the machete from the floor. Drawing the blade across the back of Bastian's hand produces a thick stream of blood and a brutal roar. His eyes rapidly blink as the recognition flows back into them.

"Bastian?" Poe murmurs, still holding fast.

"What's going on?" An unchecked emotion rolls off of Bastian as his voice trembles.

Poe and David release Bastian, allowing him to right himself. Poe kneels to the side and David rolls to his back, breathing heavily.

"Where are the others? Is everyone alright?" Bastian's gaze falls onto Liam, and he freezes. Panic surges in Poe as he quickly realizes he can't move and as much as he screams for his muscles to engage, they refuse. Using his peripheral vision, he sees that everyone else is petrified as well.

A shadowed figure moves into the doorway. Wisps of pale-red hair are haloed from the light. The young woman who glides into the room doesn't appear all that powerful, but the energy floating off of her is crushing. From behind her another man and woman enter, and the already-oppressive air pounds Poe into the ground. If he weren't locked in his position he would've collapsed. The man's hair is slicked back into a tight bun and his brown eyes narrow as he surveys the area. The second woman is straight out of a nightmare, with blood-red skin and wild garnet hair flowing down her back.

The leather of the man's jacket squeaks as he saunters in, his hands clasped in front of him. His ginger-haired companion walks over to Bastian, and Poe's throat burns from the roar that is lodged there. Bastian's eyes widen minutely as her fingers gently graze the skin of his lips; his jaw cranes open and a fierce howl bellows from him. All of their mutual rage is funneled into that one guttural cry. Bastian's body, along with everyone else's, remains locked in place, yet his mouth seems free to move.

"Who are you? What is the meaning of this?" Bastian seethes, spittle flying from his mouth.

"I will ask the questions. You will answer, and you will do as I say," the strange man states stoically.

"You will burn for this."

The man strides over to Bastian and hammers a fist into the side of his head. The blow whips Bastian's head to the side but his body remains frozen. "You're a fool if you think a dragon can burn—I'm fireproof." The man's eyes shift to a serpentine-yellow with distinctive, slit irises.

"This is boring, Chen," the red-skinned woman moans. She exudes an unfettered evil as she lasers them with loathing. Looking at her curdles Poe's insides with a deep-set terror. "We should just kill them and be gone."

"Not yet," Chen bites back, giving her a sideways glance. "You." He points a thick finger at Poe. "You will go to the Hallow and bring the Fury back here—all three of them. You will do this quickly, and if you don't, I will kill each one of your kin." Chen gestures to the other three, emphasizing his threat.

"We aren't helping you." Bastian glares at Chen.

"Perhaps we should give you some incentive to be more compliant." In a swift movement, Chen unsheathes a dagger and buries it to the hilt in David's chest. Bright blood pulses from the wound, staining his shirt. Bastian bellows and Poe's stomach seizes as he recognizes the knife—the blade of St. Michael. David will remain alive, in great pain, as long as the blade is buried in his flesh but remove it and he will die.

"If you will, Nina." Chen smirks wickedly as the smaller woman strides over to Poe. She touches his shoulder lightly and his body drops. Her dainty hand rests on his arm as if lending support as his limbs quake. "Maybe the Fury magic can save your friend, maybe it can't. Go now, go quickly."

"Go, Poe," Bastian orders.

Pushing himself to his feet, Poe staggers around the trio and out the door. The world moves by at a blinding speed and within seconds he is back in the basement. Opening the wooden door, he bursts into the darkness of the tunnel.

Chapter 18

Olivia stares fretfully at the simple door. It wasn't open when they pulled themselves out of the water, but there it stood, ominously gaping back at them. The warm glow of candlelight wraps around the rim of wood, making the cavern they are in feel colder. For a reason she can't really know she is equally drawn to and repulsed by whatever lies beyond that door. From within the depths of the room a muted ruckus spills out as a distinct clinking pours from the enclosed space.

"Do you really want to go in there?" Bray asks, hoisting himself up. The bites marks that riddled his flesh have faded, leaving behind flawless skin. With a haggard breath he rubs the nape of his neck—it has been a long night for both of them.

"I don't think we have much choice." Olivia gazes back toward the tunnels they came from and knows the way back would be blocked. How long had they already been here, a couple hours or days? Going back could be a waste of even more time.

Bray swallows a deep breath as he strides toward the partially open door. Following at a close distance Olivia strains her ears to listen. A minute tremor shakes Bray's hand as it pushes against the smooth wood and a yawning creak echoes as the door moves.

Squeezing by the door, Bray halts. He stands stone-still, his brows creased as his eyes focus on something in the room.

"What is it?" Olivia breathes as she leans into him. His gaze flicks to her briefly before he shifts, moving farther into the room. Her heart beats at a harried pace as she steps around the door.

Candles burn low in sconces that are carved in the stone as a cinder light splashes against the walls. The fire within a cobbled fireplace along the far wall is burnt down so only the dull red embers glow faintly. The form of a man stands with his back to them as he studies something on a table that stretches the length of the tiny room. The charcoal-black skin of his wide back is intricately etched with symbols that Olivia has never seen before. A wild mane of black hair falls to the center of his back. She quickly assesses that his overall appearance, while alien, isn't what is making her skin itch with an irrational fervor. There is a sickening darkness that seeps from his aura, causing the bile to rise up in Olivia's throat. An otherworldly force flows from this being that has no connection to anything human.

"I'm more than a little surprised that you made it past the cecaelia," the stranger states, not bothering to turn around. "Though truth be told, you are only the third group that has made it as far as the cavern." His tone is indifferent as if he is completely unimpressed by their presence.

"What happen to them?" Olivia's voice cracks, despite trying to keep it level. A weakness wracks her knees, yet she refuses to go down, instead opting to clasp the open door. The solid wood helps her center her thoughts. Moving with a measured pace, he turns, facing them. The etch marks that score his back continue onto his naked chest. Blood-red eyes burn at them as he scrutinizes their appearance. Olivia pushes back at the irrational fear that bubbles up in her guts.

"Both of them died facing the monsters out there, one group on the way in and the other on the way out," he states with the faintest of smirks. Olivia catches a glimpse of a small chest on the table and the stranger quickly sidesteps to block it from their view.

"What are you?" Bray asks as he smells the space and his nostrils flare. His body is rigid against the overwhelming tension that chokes the air.

"I am Dagon," he answers with a clipped, almost indignant tone. A prolonged silence confirms Olivia's suspicion that he won't be forthcoming with much helpful information.

"How do we get out of here?" Olivia asks pointedly as a compelling desire to leave washes through her.

"You have to release me." Dagon's lips lift in an eerie grin.

"And how exactly do we do that?"

"You just need to claim what is in this box." He sidesteps, gesturing to the chest.

"What's in there?" Olivia allows her gaze to flick over to the table. Vaporous shadows, cast by the light, dance along the surface of the box.

"It is an ancient relic."

"What does it do?" Bray asks.

"That, I do not know. I am bound to this place until the owner of this relic returns to collect it."

"How do you know we are the owners?"

"You are here, aren't you? This tunnel system is dimensionally locked." He must have detected their confusion as he continues. "Once you entered the waters of the cavern you are bound to the place as I am and only the relic will allow us to leave."

"Why didn't the two other groups just take it and leave?" Olivia asks, knowing that he is lying about something but unable to determine what it is.

"I've already explained that." Another stillness spans between them and Olivia wonders if he'll tell them. Dagon glares for several seconds before breaking the silence. "The first two were devoured by the cecaelia before they ever made it to the door. The second group decided they did not want the relic and left. By then the cecaelia had returned."

"Why should we help you?" Bray glares at Dagon, obviously feeling as uneasy being around him as she does.

"You are not helping me," Dagon bites back, anger and offense surging off of him. "You take the relic and the cave allows us to leave– that simple. Or you can walk out of here and see if you can escape the guards outside. Even if you do, you'll wander lost in the caves for millennia before you die here."

"What will that thing do to us?" Bray motions to the chest.

"It won't do anything to you," Dagon answers unblinkingly.

"So, we just take the artifact and walk out?" Olivia asks.

"Inside the box are a glass bottle and the relic;
break the vial, and you can take the object and
leave."

"What's in the bottle?"

"Nothing—it is simply a charm that summons
the cecaelia and smashing it will stop them
from being drawn back to this place. Good
can come from our meeting. You can take the
relic and protect it from the evil that wishes to
possess it, and you can save yourself as well,"
he urges.

"Fine." Olivia answers after some thought.
She doesn't believe him, yet she can't think of
another way out. Dagon steps away from the
table, providing a clear path to the chest.
Flipping up the bronze eye-hook latch, she
feels a small shiver as Dagon's intense gaze
pins her. The lid lifts open to reveal a velvet-
lined space which holds a simple ceramic
bottle and a second, much smaller container.
No larger than a ring box, it has a small script
etched into all four sides.

Olivia grabs both items and turns to see
Dagon watching her, an intense force lighting

his fiery eyes. "Now break the bottle and you can go."

Olivia fights the urge to rescue it as the vial slips from her hand. It spirals end over end before crashing into the stone floor. Wisps of vapor rise up from the broken shards, swirling toward Dagon as he inhales the fumes deeply. He locks his gaze on Olivia, a flick of a smile gracing his face before his body is engulfed in flames. She shields her eyes against the glare of light but realizes that the flame throws no heat and, as it dims, she sees that Dagon has vanished.

Somewhat befuddled, she finds Bray standing there equally dumbstruck. With shaking legs, she walks to the nearest wall. The chill of the stone seeps into her hand as she tenderly grazes the surface. Pulling at her energy, she is nearly buckled by the strength of it. Whatever power that muted hers is now gone and the stone shimmers into the swirling pool that she has come to know. Her connection to the portal is solid, remaining stable as a warm relief eases her breath and they step through.

The familiar atmosphere of the Hallow envelops her as her foot plants on the cool earth. Bray staggers through, bracing on the far wall as he endeavors to steady himself and his hair haphazardly halos his face. She watches him orient himself and a heat flushes Olivia's cheek. He's surprisingly unashamed, and she can't help but admire the lines of his nude body. The muscles of his broad back flex as he inhales, and her eyes are instinctively drawn toward his mouth. She savors the brief memory of his lips on hers— the taste of him still lingers there. It's not like it's the first time she's been kissed, but surely no one has ever kissed her with such a need. Although she enjoys the sight of his body, she is less thrilled about letting the others see him this way.

After rummaging through several of the unoccupied quarters they find some ill-fitting clothes for Bray. Guarding the door, Olivia keeps a lookout while he dresses. The t-shirt is too snug and the jeans are only slightly better, as they hang off his hips. Yet it is better than having Bray walk around completely naked, giving Mei Li a stroke. A tiny smile touches her lips, and Bray responds with a quizzical raised brow.

"I'm just imagining Mei Li's reaction to you tromping around in your birthday suit." She tries to wave it off, but her cheeks burn red.

"So, you are thinking about me being naked?" Her insides wriggle at the focused intent in his eyes.

Enclosed in such a small space she is acutely aware of Bray's presence; his energy and aroma wash over her in an intoxicating union.

"Perhaps." Her voice emerges breathier than she intended as she tries to swallow moisture into her parched throat.

Bray steps over to her slowly, the light dancing in his eyes. There is an ease to his gait that sends her pulse skyrocketing. A wicked smile graces his lips. He must be able to sense her reaction.

"Quite an interesting night, wouldn't you say? Not too bad for a first date." The corner of his mouth lifts as he moves closer.

"You consider that a first date?" Her pulse is careening now as she forces her eyes to meet his, blood flushing under her blistering skin.

"No, not really, but it's a start." His fingers lightly glide across the soft skin of her neck, just below the ear. The undemanding contact sends waves of goose bumps rolling across her flesh. Pushing up on the balls of her feet, she finds his mouth with hers. Wrapping his arms around her Bray pulls her into him as he returns the kiss, mirroring her desire. Olivia can feel him all around her, his chest pressed tightly against her as her hands explore his thick hair and shoulders.

After an exquisite eternity they break apart, each heaving breathlessly. Olivia's lips are deliciously swollen, and her heart hammers against her ribs.

"We should find the others." she moans, not attempting to hide the growing disappointment. Bray nods slowly, composing himself as well. Backing out into the hall, Olivia bumps into the doorframe as her legs learn to move again.

They detect the low hum of Mei Li's voice through the door as they approach. Without looking at the time Olivia can sense that dawn is near. Turning the latch, Olivia swings the door open.

Mei Li stands close to Emma down near the far end of the hall, and they appear to be having an intense conversation. Though their voices are low their mouths move at a hurried pace. With the sound of the opening door, their eyes swing over, finding Olivia and Bray.

"Olivia, where have you been?" Mei Li calls out as she rushes over to them, her long gown clutched in her hands. She studies them closely and her eyes widen as she takes in Bray's state of dress.

"We followed Moss into a cave system and were trapped there for a while," Olivia explains.

"I take it he got away?" Mei Li's troubled brows wrinkle, and she rubs her hands together briskly.

"He has a potent accomplice." Olivia's insides harden as she recalls the tiny woman who could have easily killed them. "She was able to spirit him away." Mei Li frowns at them as she continues to wring her hands.

"She was a kitsune, a nine-tailed fox that–" Bray states.

"I am aware of what a kitsune is," Mei Li interrupts. Her gaze flickers between them as Emma strides up. "It seems Moss has established an outside benefactor. It is important to determine the source of this."

"We did find this." Olivia pulls the small box from her pocket and hands it to Mei Li. The mother takes the artifact gingerly in her hands.

"Any idea what it is?" she asks as she runs her fingers over the delicately carved surface.

"Not really," Olivia answers with a shrug. "Best I can tell is it's a relic of some sort, but it had substantial security for it."

"And you found it where?"

"A cavern in the caves, guarded by cecaelia and something else."

"We'll keep it isolated until we can determine its nature." Mei Li walks to a wall and opens a small portal. She places the box inside and as her hand leaves the space it closes. "But that may have to wait as we have some larger issues to address."

"What's going on?" Olivia is taken aback by the underlying anxiety that both Mei Li and Emma are trying to hide.

"Some of the faceless have gone rogue. So, until further notice, if you come across one, treat it as a hostile." Mei Li continues to fidget, showing she's uncomfortable admitting that they seem to have lost control of their minions. Olivia's stomach plummets, as she's faced several of the faceless and lost. Going head to head with more of them is less than ideal.

"Perhaps you should tell us about the faceless now," Emma says stoically. Olivia examines both of them, confused as to what is really going on. Why does she feel like she's the only one not in on a joke?

"What happened?" Olivia tries to arrest the rise of emotion in her voice.

"Emma was attacked in her home by a faceless controlled by someone else." Mei Li's raised hand stifles Olivia's stream of questions.

"And?" Emma asks.

"And what? That is all we know right now." Mei Li feigns and fails at a look of ignorance.

"Why did it turn into Alec?" Emma retorts, and Olivia's jaw nearly hits the floor. They stare in silence at Mei Li, waiting for her to answer.

"You can't keep us in the dark on this." Emma directs her sternly.

"Very well." Mei Li sighs deeply, not willing to look at either one of them. "As you know, back when the first Mothers awoke, they tried, through varies methods, to increase the potency of the Fury. But very few know that their experimentation was not solely directed toward their own. They branched out, seeing if they could augment the power of the Gyges as well. The faceless are an unfortunate side effect of that research." Heaviness chokes the air and Olivia concentrates on her own breathing as she processes the admission.

"So, the faceless used to be Gyges?" Emma asks, her voice low. Mei Li manages a small nod in response.

"What changes a Gyges into a faceless?" Olivia's voice wobbles as she glares at Mei Li.

"Death." The single word from Mei Li resonates through the room.

"What do you mean?" Emma asks.

"We quickly realized that when a partnered Gyges dies their mind slips away and they become…" Mei Li's voice fades off.

The door at the far end of the hall bursts open and Poe rushes in. His eyes are frantically large, scanning the room. Sweat gleams from his skin and his long legs carry him across the space. Olivia eyes flash to the space behind him, because his reaction leads her to think that something may be chasing him.

"Emma," he pants heavily. "It's David, he's hurt, you have to come now." Emma's face drops, turning an ashen white, and she steps toward him.

"I'll go with you," Olivia offers with no hesitation.

"You all have to come." Poe's eyes shift between all of them.

"Why all of us?" Olivia pauses, apprehension rising in her.

"They said all of you had to come. If you don't, they'll kill the others," Poe pleads.

"What about Aaron?" The corners of Mei Li's eyes tense as she looks to them. "He's still too young to be left alone."

"I'll stay," Bray chimes in.

"Are you sure?" Olivia asks against the rising fear.

"Yes. I've watched many children within the pack before." Mei Li nods at his response, seemingly satisfied.

"Let's go." Mei Li adds. Olivia's palms tremble as she slaps the nearest wall, opening a gateway to Bastian's home. Olivia looks back to see Bray watching as the four of them enter the portal and an overwhelming dread rises.

Chapter 19

A cold tremor racks Emma's body as they step out of the portal. The tunnel, which runs under Bastian's house, is swept with a frigid draft that wicks the heat from her. A fog of silence permeates the caves and any incidental sound prompts an involuntary flinch from Emma. The wards on the house are still active so they had to enter through the caves just outside. Poe opens the door that leads into a basement area; crossing the threshold, his gaze sweeps the room before he gestures for them to follow. A low light fills the barren room, the musty air clings to their skin, and a palpable weight seems to hang around them.

"How many are there?" Olivia asks.

"Three that I know—I didn't see any others," Poe answers. His countenance is haggard, hair disheveled, and cheeks hollow. By now the sun has fully risen, which is adding to his fatigue. A nervous energy rolls along Emma's skin but she endeavors to stay calm and breathe. A horde of insects skitter just under her flesh as all of her muscles constrict. She feels as though she is walking through sludge and her movements are painfully slow. Exhaling a breath that feels more like acid than air, Emma pushes forward and the urgent need to find David overwhelms her senses.

"Emma, where are you going?" Mei Li looks at her incredulously.

"I need to find David." She looks back briefly.

"We don't have a plan yet."

"I'm going to find David and if I see anyone up there whom I don't know, I'm going to kill them."

"Don't be stupid," Mei Li snaps.

"David is in there." Emma stops, rounding to glare at Mei Li, her lungs seizing with churning emotions. She clenches her hands into tight fists, battling against the wash of fear and rage that cascades through her. The edge of her vision blurs with a well of cold tears that rim her eyes and she fights for a breath. "He is either dead or dying. Bastian, who has risked so much for us, could be dead or dying." Emma doesn't register the plummeting temperature in the room until she catches on that their breaths are coming out in clouds of vapor. In the midst of the torrid emotions a singular voice whispers to her, enticing her to let go of her control– everything will be fine if only she does what she has been designed to do. Mei Li's face drops yet she stands motionless as she weighs Emma. "Come with me or not. I'm going."

Not waiting for a response Emma climbs the stairs, the slick wood frosting under her feet. The soft pad of steps echo from behind her as she cracks open the door and peeks into the kitchen.

Muted lights filter into the empty space upstairs. Pushing out her power Emma strains to sense what is in the house. The area seems to pulse with a heady undercurrent of energy that comes from no direction in particular.

From one of the adjacent rooms, Emma detects the soft sounds of shuffling items. The sound of clinking and jumbling of paper is deafening against the stark silence of the rest of the house. Her pulse quickens with a resounding thud against her ribs despite the odd numbness that creeps through her.

Emma's eyes catch Poe's as he scans the area cautiously, flanking Mei Li. Meeting Olivia's gaze they both tread nearer to the source of the noise. Craning her neck around the doorframe, Emma spies a tall woman riffling through some items on a small writing desk. Thick tresses of maroon hair fall about her slender waist and the eerie light gleams from the slick leather of her pants, highlighting the rich plum color of her skin. A jitter hits Emma's stomach as the stranger's aura plumes outward, washing over them. She quickly realizes that this woman isn't undead but she's not alive either—or at least not in a way she's ever come across before.

Olivia steps forward, carefully measuring each foot placement, one in front of the other. The crass whine of the creaking wood draws their eyes to the floor and the woman spins around. Their gazes dart up, spying the subtle grin that lifts her red lips before she lunges at Olivia with a primal scream, catching her off guard. The two women fall to the floor as Emma jumps into the room. Time slows with Olivia landing on her back and the woman pinning her. The red woman howls, her clawed fingers straining for Olivia's throat, each of them battling for leverage.

Emma rears back her leg, landing a kick to their attacker's face, causing her red hair to flare wildly as she tumbles across the floor. Olivia leaps up and vaults to catch up before her foe can come to a halt. Rolling onto her back she glares up at them with scorching eyes, and they can feel the subtle pulse of power bloom about them as a cloud of vapor wisps up through the floorboards. A roiling terror crashes into Emma's mind, staggering her. Olivia battles against the effects of the magic as she pushes through the cloud of impression and yanks the red woman by her hair. Bringing her arm down, Olivia strikes her several times with hammering fists until she stops moving. As soon as the woman is unconscious the mist subsides, pulling with it the scourge of her enchantment.

Finding some ties for the curtains, Poe secures the woman and they drag her into the kitchen pantry. The red woman moans softly as they close the door. They'll most certainly have to deal with her later, if they survive.

"You should just come upstairs now." The sound of Bastian's voice rings out through the darkened halls.

Emma's legs clang as she mounts the stairs. Steeling her nerves, she tamps down all of the emotions that cannot serve her right now. Olivia and Poe are just behind her, their soft steps echoing her own. Poe motions down the corridor toward an open door, and Emma's eyes are drawn to the tips of two feet that peek out into the hall. A steady numbness that has been percolating within Emma aid to wash away her fear, leaving just the void filled by rage and a righteous purpose. The last instance she recalls feeling this way was when she judged Celia. The steady momentum of her legs is the only connection she has to this world.

A murmur of sound spills from the room and Emma steps up to the threshold. Poe brushes past her, where he strides over to kneel by Bastian and Jillian. Their faces are more ashen than normal and their wide eyes flick toward her. A small amount of dried blood lines the side of Bastian's face. Emma's heart stalls as her gaze falls on David's body, the intricately carved hilt still protruding from his chest. Wrenching her eyes away, she clenches her fists and scans the rest of the room.

The small form of a woman catches her eye and Emma recognizes her from the alleyway, where she'd fed the cat. For a moment her mind frantically works as she searches for the woman's name. *Nina, that's what it is—but why is she here?* Nina's eyes focus on her, giving no recognition away, but Emma notes the tremble of her hands and a sharp fatigue that tracks the lines of her eyes.

Her growing confusion rockets as she sees the man standing next to Nina. The man who had attacked her in her own home is leaning casually against the far wall. His cold stare takes them in as Emma manages a few tender steps into the room, followed by Olivia and Mei Li.

"Hello, Mother." With a shallow dip of his head, his cold gaze brushes past Emma and focuses on Mei Li. "It is so generous of you to come at my request." There is a well-disciplined rage that spirals off of him as a

muscle ticks at the corners of his eye. Emma
is determined to keep her eyes locked on him,
but she can feel the stifling tension that
clamps hold of Mei Li.

"We are here, Chen. Now you can release the
others." Mei Li's tone is smooth, yet rigid.
Poe rises to his feet, ready to get the others
out.

"No. No one will leave this room alive." He
pins them with a frigid stare. "Nina, hold
them all," Chen barks. Poe struggles against
her hold and his muscles strain, but he can
only manage to lift Jillian to her feet. The
fatigue shows on his face as he clings to her.

"I cannot, master." Nina's voice wavers as she
chances a glance toward him. "Locking them
for this long is overextending my powers."

"Never tell me that you cannot; I have no
time for your excuses." He sneers at her with
a sideways glance. "Perhaps we should finish
off the wounded one first?" He finally meets
Emma's gaze, lifting a thick brow at her.
"What do you say, Nina?" His demeanor
shifts rapidly between extremes.

"The wounded one poses the least threat. It would make more sense to destroy the strongest ones first, but I will do as you command of me," Nina answers stoically.

"True, but killing him first will hurt them all– won't it?" He seems to be asking them versus Nina. His dark-brown eyes shift to a golden tone as his iris elongates. Emma's mind whirls, quickly calculating her limited options even as the thrum of her rampant anger builds. Her concentration battles to maintain control against the eagerness crawling along her skin, urging her toward violence.

Chen holds her with a stare as he saunters over to David's fallen form, and her feet move on their own. Emma releases a deliberate breath as Nina turns, rushing towards her in response. Emma dodges the flurry of strikes that come at an astounding speed, but a well-timed kick connects with her stomach and the air catches in her lungs. Still gasping for air, Emma pushes forward, driving her shoulder into Nina's midsection and lifting her over her body. Nina stumbles, yet lands on her feet, only to be met by Olivia and Mei Li. Nina's movements blur as she strikes and defends the oncoming assaults. Emma turns her attention back to Chen while the three women circle each other behind her.

Emma pitches up both arms to block a sweeping kick aimed for her head, and pain missiles through her hands and they fall limply to the side. Chen dives at Emma, pinning her arms as he wraps her in his. With an unearthly strength he squeezes, pressing the air from her lungs causing her vision to falter. With a renewed urgency she rears her head back and smashes it into his face, staggering him and forcing him to releases his hold.

Wiping errant drips of blood from his nose, he lasers her with a fierce stare. "Your boy is already dead– nothing you can do will save him." His words cut as he bends down and wrenches the blade from David's chest.

A feral scream tears from Emma as her tenuous self-control ruptures with a devastating potency, and with several quick strides she collides into Chen. Her mind and body fall into the muscle memory of centuries of practiced exercise. Each strike, each dodge comes as second nature. Their pace revs up and she pulls more energy in, allowing the power to flow through her unabated. A crystalline sheen of ice forms across every surface, and her breath comes out in thick puffs as frost glitters in the air. Channeling the power into her movements, her vision tunnels as anguish cements her determination to kill him. A straight kick to his chest flings him across the room, his back slamming into the post of the bed. Pushing aside the broken shaft of wood, Chen bellows, his face a mask of vehemence and blood. The skin of his hands peels away, reforming into raptor claws, and the steely talons gleam as they taper to a razor's edge.

Chen launches toward her, forcing her to backpedal several steps. She dodges many of his furious attacks, yet one connects with her shoulder. The flesh tears easily and the hot blood flows down the length of her arm. A sideswipe kick lands squarely on his knee and a distinct crack sounds as the bone breaks. Chen sags to one knee and Emma seizes on the opportunity, striking with a quick jab to the soft flesh of his throat. He spins backward, rolling to the ground. As his ragged gasps echo in her ears, he tries to stand but the destroyed joint refuses to support his weight.

All else in the world falls away save for Chen's labored breathing and the steady plop of her blood as it pools below her. It's time to end this. Her body thrums, but as she moves to step, her foot is locked in place.

The vacuum of power loss nearly buckles her legs and an empty void echoes back as she calls on her energy– but it's gone.

Searching for the source her gaze finds Mei Li stretched out on her stomach, clutching Emma's ankle. Her cheeks are stained with blood and tears as she looks up pleading with solemn eyes.

"Don't kill my son." Mei Li's words shatter Emma's focus. All of her residual strength drains away, and she weakly fights the hold as Nina scurries to Chen. She helps him stand and rush out the door past a befuddled Olivia.

"Mei Li, let me go." Emma struggles to release her leg, squelching the urge to kick at her. "David," she cries, her own tortured pleas finally persuading Mei Li to free her.

She races over to David as he lay in a puddle of blood, and his cheeks are hollow. Sweat glistens on his pale skin, collecting on the lashes of his closed lids, and a minute shudder wracks his body.

"David." Her voice is a coarse sandpaper, shearing away at her throat. David's eyelids move bit by bit before they snap open as pain contorts his features, his clenched teeth arresting the bellowing scream. The ragged wound pumps copious amounts of blood, recoating the floor.

"Why is he not healing?" Emma's gaze sweeps to Poe.

"The blade of St. Michael was created to destroy vampires." Tears drape the rims of Poe's eyes as he lowers his gaze. Emma shakes her head, denying the unwanted reality. Her heart thuds with a tenacity as she rests her palms on David's chest pulling at all of the energy she can. She locates the source of his damage, trying to rebuild the flesh. She funnels more and more power into that spot, but it has no effect and David cries out. A small whimper escapes her as she studies the wound that remains unchanged. "It's a death that no magic, no amount of blood, can heal," Poe echoes to her somberly.

"Will my blood save him?" Her voice cracks as her eyes flick about, searching for the blade. Her heart sinks when Poe shakes his head at her. "He'll become a faceless?" she asks, her gaze beseeching Mei Li, and the thick sheen of unshed tears answers her question.

Emma's vision blurs, and acidic blood courses through her veins. Her lungs burn as thick tears flow freely, pattering onto David's chest. Her eyes clench tightly against the choking air that won't come as she gasps in vain.

The lightest of touches pulls her gaze up as David's knuckles brush softly against her cheek. "Don't cry," his hoarse breath feathers her skin and through the agony his eyes are serene. There is a calmness there in opposition to the misery thundering inside her.

"Stay with me." Her voice is strangled as if she has swallowed broken glass. "Stay with me and we'll leave here together, right now. We'll steal away and take off into the night.

You and me, we'll start over and they'll never find us." Her words roll out in a growing frenzy as a sad smile touches his lips and he shakes his head.

"I know you and you know me—that's all that matters." Blood trickles from the corner of his mouth as he coughs violently and groans. "I've always loved you, Emma, and I'll love you forever. Promise me you'll remember that." A tear streaks from his warm brown eyes and across his temple.

"No, no, no." Emma's asthmatic pants wring through her constricted chest. She shakes her head against the blistering pain that hollows out her insides. She looks up blindly at the others, seeking some sign of hope in their gaze, only to be met by their despondent stare. *There has to be someone to help him, anyone.* Her limbs shake unconsciously as she gropes at the cloth of his shirt, eyes studying every line of his face, trying to etch the memory of him into her mind. David's chest rises and falls in an overly exaggerated movement as his skin grays. Through the haze of tears, she meets his gaze, touching her lips to his frigid fingers.

A crackle in the air pulls her eyes open, seeking out the newest danger. Everyone huddles closely as the lights dim unnaturally and an emerald vapor floods the room. A clawing fear inches along Emma's spine as she peers into the darkness. Her eyes follow the ever-shifting movement within its depths and instinctively she lowers her body, trying to shield David.

Three translucent forms crest the darkness as the vapor falls away behind them. Emma recognizes them as they step forward, taking on the appearance of a physical form. Mei Li steps forward to address them but is halted by a look from them. The soft green fabric of Tisiphone's dress brushes the floor as she approaches with Megaera and Alecto trailing just behind her.

"Why are you here?" Emma's voice is surprisingly calm in the face of the three primordial goddesses. Emma follows Tisiphone's gaze as it falls to David. "You are not taking him," Emma growls.

"We are not here to take the vampire. We are here because you have called us." An odd look flashes across Alecto's face as she studies them. If she were human, Emma might have guessed it as sympathy, but it seems unlikely, as the Furies are not known for such things.

"I didn't call you." Emma swallows hard, trying to work saliva back into her mouth.

"But you did." Tisiphone focuses her stare on Emma. "A shattered heart cries out the loudest, reaching even the darkness of the void in which we reside."

"So, what will you do? Will you find those that have killed David? Will you seek justice for him?" Emma asks, her tone overflowing with spite. "Or will you simply appear at an inopportune moment and offer cryptic advice?" She lasers each woman with a condemning glare.

"You would be wise to watch your words," Alecto snaps.

"Our reach is limited in this state." Megaera motions to their bodies.

"Then what good are you here?" Emma's eyes find David's as his grasp on her hand slackens. The tendrils of his life force are slipping away.

"Our fates are woven well before we are but a glimmer. All that has been done has led us to this moment, and it is here that you must decide."

"Decide what?" Emma chokes on her own words.

"Will you let him live or die?" Alecto peers at her sideways.

"What?"

"We can peel back the hands of time for him, before the dagger and tonight—before he became undead. But there is a price to pay." Alecto's eyes shimmer.

"What price?" Her heart pounds against her fragile ribs.

"He will be returned to his state before he was bonded to you, in body and mind." Megaera approaches; her intense stare bores into Emma, and she fights the urge to whither.

"He will forget about me?" The hard realization slaps her.

"Yes, and if he is reminded of your bond or of you then he will return to this state as he is right now and he will die." Megaera kneels by David, her eyes flicking to him then back. "Decide quickly as the life has left him. Within moments it will be too late." As she chances a look down, Emma reels as a vacant loss claws at her throat. David's hollow eyes stare blankly outward as bits of skin turn to ash and begin to fall away.

"Your answer!"

"Yes, do it." Searing pain envelops her and weighty tears fall as Megaera places a single palm on David's bloody chest and the part that her palm touches glows with a blinding light. The odor of burning flesh rises in the air as David's eyes snap open and he roars; every muscle in his body seizes as he screams wordlessly. As Megaera's hand lifts, David slumps to the floor, a deep slumber overtakes him, and he breathes softly.

"Remember your word," Megaera warns as she rises.

Emma manages a numb nod as her gaze remains transfixed on the rise and fall of

David's ribs. Leaning over him, she gently traces the line of his cheek before kissing him. She doesn't struggle against the hands that lift her; she doesn't want to risk waking him. Emma memorizes his features as it is the last time she'll ever see him.

Chapter 20

The slow walk back to the Hallow is fragmented in Emma's mind with only the most pronounced stimulus seeming to fracture her detached thoughts. The haze of muted words and footsteps echo around her, but none of it is able to break through the barrenness of her feelings. This disconnected sensation separates her from her body as she shuffles along the corridor, barely registering the weight of her feet on the ground. On the edge of her perception, Emma realizes that the others have broken off, going their own directions. Only Poe remains by her side, his steady presence both soothing and a painful irritation. His steady pace matches hers as they walk in silence.

Though she has spent centuries walking these pathways, the air settles on her skin with an alien and inhospitable chill. Without any direct realization or forethought her feet stop on their own just outside the door of her temporary quarters. Her eyes seem to focus intensely on the subtle defects of the wood and how dust has collected in the corner of the frame. A rolling emotion claws its way up through her center, gutting her from the inside out. If she looks at anyone right now, she'll break and she knows it. With heavy limbs, she reaches for the door handle and her quivering hand halts as she catches sight of the dried blood that coats her arm. The thick layer clings to her hands, up her forearms, to each of her elbows. Her lungs seize, squeezing out a choked gasp.

"Go inside, clean up, and get some rest. I'll come and check on you in a bit." Poe steps forward but doesn't attempt to touch her. His voice is so distant through the impenetrable fog that swathes Emma that she turns to see if he is not as close as she thought. He hovers just outside arm's reach before he dips his head and turns to leave.

"Poe." Her voice is a weak murmur as she forces the words. "Wait here for a moment." He stills as Emma opens the door and enters her room. Sliding down onto her stomach, she retrieves the soiled doll from under the bed and hurries back to Poe. The well-worn fabric feels scratchy on her skin as she rubs the material knotted into a human form. "I want to ask a favor of you–well, actually two."

"What is it?" he asks patiently, waiting for her reply. Emma swallows hard as he watches her with an unbearable kindness in his eyes.

"Keep David safe." She works moisture back into her mouth as a tear runs down her cheek, landing on the puppet. "Secondly, I want you to give this to him. Don't tell him who it is from."

"What is it?" He eyes the mass of braided cloth.

"I made this for my daughter the summer before she died. After she was gone it was all I had left of her, and it became my most treasured possession." Her voice quivers as she inhales sharply. The image of sun-kissed brown hair flashes in her mind. "This became the last link to my humanity, a connection to my heart and now I want David to have it; I want him to have my heart. Even if he doesn't remember me and doesn't want it anymore."

Poe nods softly as he takes the doll. "I'll make sure he gets it." Poe steps backward, hesitating. For a moment she's not sure if he'll say anything. His dark eyes study her silently for moment before he turns and leaves.

The look of pity radiating from his eyes is nearly Emma's undoing. Her legs shake and through sheer willpower only, she locks them in place until Poe is out of sight. Reentering her room, Emma closes the door as she gasps for a breath that won't come. A cold sweat trickles down her back as she staggers to the small sink and turns on the faucet. Soon, a steady veil of steam clouds the mirror, and her white-knuckled hands clamp the rim of the basin as she tries to steady herself. Grabbing a bar of soap Emma submerges her hands into the scalding water, scrubbing away the dried blood. With skin a bright shade of red, she dabs them dry, vainly wishing the discomfort will be enough to clear her mind.

Time and time again she tries to push away all of the thoughts in her mind, but each time she closes her eyes she sees David's face; his smell seems to overpower the floral-scented soap, and his voice echoes in her ears. She wobbles into the center of the room and her head spins as a rush of panic overtakes her.

The frantic pulse of her heart resonates throughout as if it is trying to burst from her chest.

The world around her churns, and the hollow ache in her chest blooms into crippling sorrow. Her lungs seize as a wordless scream rips through her. Her defective lungs struggle, only pulling in half gasps, and there is a momentary thought that she may pass out. Turbulent sobs roll through her as her legs give out, sending her spiraling to the floor. Curling into a ball, letting the tears soak the fabric covering her knees, she gives in to the anguish. A weeping bawl pours from her as she wishes for death– longs for the earth to open up and swallow her into the darkness.

Emma lies shivering on the floor for what could have been minutes or hours. The focus and meaning of time are of no importance. As her sobs lessen, she stares blankly at the stone ceiling, wishing for its collapse. Her staggered breath levels out as a small knock sounds at the door. Perhaps if she ignores it, whoever it is will go away.

As if prompted by her thought, another knock sounds. The metal of the door handle clicks softly as it turns. Any urge to look up is sapped away by the overwhelming weakness that has settled in her limbs.

"Emma?" the small voice calls out. For a brief moment, Emma doesn't recognize the speaker and her head lolls to the side as she blinks against the light from the hall. Aaron's short frame stands encased in the doorframe. His wide eyes study her as his tiny hands clasp a steaming mug. "Why are you on the floor?"

"I'm just tired." Emma calms her tone, fighting to keep the shudder out of her words.

"I brought you some tea." He shuffles into the room, carefully balancing the cup in his hands. The light bounces off of his light-brown hair; the overgrown mop will need to be trimmed again. There is an exuberance of life that pulses from the apparent six-year-old that only fuels Emma's feeling of melancholy. For a moment, she wishes she could save him from any upcoming heartache, but in truth she knows it is a futile hope. Not bothering to stifle her groan, Emma lifts herself up and hobbles over to sit on the edge of her bed. As the emotional riptide breaks, her physical injuries come to the forefront of her mind.

"That's very nice of you." She musters a weak smile as she gingerly takes the hot mug. His lips lift in an awkward, toothy grin, revealing a prominent gap where a tooth is missing. Emma sips the tea and its warmth rushes through her, pushing a small amount of the chill away. Aaron approaches carefully and eases himself down next to her. They study each other wordlessly for a moment. "Aaron, did someone ask you to bring me tea?" She blows across the rim of the cup.

"Mei Li said you were sad and that tea would cheer you up." Emma keeps her demeanor light as she processes his statement. There was no need to blast this poor kid because Mei Li is still trying to control them. *Of course, she would send the child*, Emma fumes. A nervous apprehension rolls off of him.

"Are you afraid of me?" A low tremor coils in her gut. "There's no need," she reassures him.

"I'm not scared of you, but I don't like it that you're sad."

"Everyone gets a little sad sometimes." Again, she forces another smile, knowing that it isn't very convincing.

"Emma, what can you tell me about my mom?" he asks, his large brown eyes watching her as she stills mid-sip and looks up from her thoughts.

"I didn't really know her."

"Mei Li said she died having me. Was she pretty?" he asks as he fidgets with the hem of his shirt.

"Yes, hon, she was pretty." Without knowing how much Mei Li told him, Emma decides it's best to say as little as possible. He leans over into her and she drapes her arm around him.

"What about my dad? Did you know him?" he asks after a few moments of silence.

"I'm sorry, no."

"Sometimes I think about my mom and dad and get sad. Is that why you are sad, or did you lose something?"

"Yeah, sweetie. I lost something." Emma closes her eyes against the tears that resurface in her vision. The purity of his concern and the vacant throbbing in her chest are nearly too much.

"I can help you look for it."

"Sure." A shiver runs through her as she meets his gaze.

"Could you find him?" Aaron asks and her brows furrow in confusion.

"Who?"

"My dad."

"I don't think…" Emma pauses at the discouraged look on his face. "It won't be easy, but we'll see."

"If you can't find him, do you think David can be my dad?" His russet eyes light as he asks.

"David will be very busy and I'm not sure how much he'll be around. We'll see." She looks away, unable to meet his gaze, feeling horrible for lying to him but unable to tell him the truth.

"Okay." The young boy nods as he takes the mug from Emma. She detects a slight rumble coming from Aaron's stomach.

"Have you eaten?" Aaron shakes his head with an almost embarrassed look. Emma sighs as she clasps his small hand in hers. "Come on, let's get you some food."

You are all alone now. The unwanted words flood her mind as she bites her trembling lip and pushes them away.

Emma's attention is drawn back to the doorway as Mei Li approaches. Aaron rushes over to Mei Li, showing her the empty cup. "Mother Mei Li, Emma and I are going to get some food. Do you want some?"

"That sounds excellent." Mei Li smiles as she clasps a well-worn book.

"Why don't you go and find Olivia and see if she is hungry too?" Emma suggests. Aaron nods but is stopped by Mei Li.

"I would prefer if Aaron stays close while we talk." She offers the book to Aaron and motions him to the bed, and Emma tilts her head sideways toward Mei Li, wondering her intent. Until recently she has always held an unwavering trust in Mei Li's motives, yet right now she stands before her as a complete stranger. Aaron takes the book and flops onto the bed, opening it to a dog-eared page.

"Talk? Do you think having the boy close will stop me from speaking my mind?" Her anger brews, flicking at Emma's insides as she glares back at Mei Li.

"I am doing no such thing," Mei Li balks.

"Please don't lie to me." Emma's voice quakes as she closes her eyes with a shake of her head.

Mei Li clasps her hands in front, her back held arrow-straight. "I understand that you are upset."

"I'm a little more than upset," Emma interrupts, folding her trembling arms over her chest.

"Be that as it may, you know as well as I do that there was nothing that could have been done for him. The outcome was already decided before we arrived."

"And yet you opted for your own personal reasons to forestall my judgment," Emma bites back.

"It's not that simple."

"Well, actually it is. You chose to stop me from doing what needed to be done. For all your talk of duty, you chose Chen over everything else." Mei Li's gaze nervously flicks over to Aaron.

"Aaron, if you find Olivia, I'm sure she can make you some food," she calls, summoning him forward.

"Are you coming?" He peers up at them, his eyes questioning as he strides over to them.

"In a bit. Emma and I just need to have a talk." Mei Li's tone leaves little room for argument. Aaron nods as he glances between them tentatively and leaves, heading down one the of long lengths of hall. Emma studies Mei Li wordlessly as the Mother waits for Aaron to disappear from sight.

"You didn't tell him about David?" Mei Li stares back at her with an almost quizzical look.

"No, why would I? Plus, there's no point causing him more pain than is necessary." Mei Li nods at her response.

"Perhaps that is best for at least now." The Mother crosses the room, working her hands as she glides. "I imagine you have some questions about what happened at Bastian's."

"Not really," Emma interrupts and Mei Li stops, meeting her gaze.

"What do you mean?"

"I mean there is no point, as I'm leaving here. You will give me that amulet and no one can summon me like a dog again. And neither you nor Olivia will try to contact me." Emma struggles to keep her tone cold. Her emotions are a void, but her innards are strangled.

"You can't just leave." Mei Li's eyes widen for a second before schooling her features into a refined mask.

"Yes, I can."

"You are Fury. We all have a duty, and you can't just ignore that."

"I was Fury, and you stopped me from completing my duty," Emma responds coolly.

"David was going to die no matter what we did, and killing my son wouldn't have changed that."

"Your son is a monster. He has murdered the innocence and attacking us as often as he can, on multiple occasions. And this only what we know that he has done. Are you so blinded that you honestly believe there is hope for him?"

"That's not fair. If it was your child you would still hold out hope," Mei Li argues.

"My children are dead, and right now, hope seems to be a fool's errand."

"How would you suggest we fix this?"

"I really don't know if there is a way to fix this. That's why I'm going."

"Don't be ridiculous! You and Olivia and I can sit down and work this out." Mei Li reaches out to her.

"No, we can't." Emma shakes her head. "We can't work this out because at some point, I'll try to kill Chen again, you'll try to stop me again, and one of us will die. We can't work this out because you and Olivia lied to me about the amulets. How long would you have allowed me to be tortured? Answering the call every time so you both can remain untouched." Emma sighs as she angrily wipes a wet tear away.

"So, you are just giving up?"

"No, I am accepting the inevitability of it." Emma pushes the feelings away and meets Mei Li's stare.

"I understand that losing David is traumatic, but you can't allow this to destroy you–to destroy us. This is the reason I feared allowing personal attachments."

"You don't understand. This isn't just about my personal attachment to David," Emma barks, her tone rich with spite.

"What is it then?" Mei Li studies her with such a stern intensity that Emma is momentarily at a loss for words.

"For all this time, I have had to carve out the majority of who I am to do my duty. The part of me that longed for compassion and sympathy had to be ignored for fear of being weak in your eyes. So, I hid away all the broken parts of myself so I could survive here. I became someone I didn't want to be." Emma spreads her arms to the room around them. "And despite all of that, I squirreled away that one bit of myself that I refused to lose to this place or to you. It was hope–the hope that I could somehow one day regain my life, with some sense of peace."

"We all have lost a part of ourselves here and we have all lost heart." Mei Li's own voice was as cold as Emma's.

"I don't want to lose heart," Emma bellows. "I wanted to believe. And you took that from me today; all the days before were just chipping away at that dream." She studies her hands briefly before looking up at Mei Li again. "I think you should go now. You probably have much to attend to and I have a few things to do before nightfall." Emma pulls at a slight amount of power, just enough to flood her eyes with a copper sheen.

"I'll let you rest for now and we'll continue this conversation later." Mei Li backs away to the doorframe.

"No, we won't." Her answer is a scarce whisper. Mei Li seems to mull over the idea of arguing some more but then simply nods, leaving an empty doorway behind her.

Chapter 21

Aaron rocks back and forth in his seat, and his sticky fingers glisten with syrup as he clasps a square of waffle. Olivia washes her hands in the stainless-steel sink as she finishes the dishes from their breakfast. The kitchen doesn't see a lot of use these days so she should count herself lucky that there was some kind of food in here. Not having a secondary residence outside of the Hallow, Olivia has taken it upon herself to keep a fairly stocked cupboard, and she was actually putting supplies away when Aaron came along.

The little boy has a decent appetite so keeping him sated seems to be a full-time job. She can't hide her smile as he greedily noshes on his breakfast. Despite his unknown origins, he's a good-natured child and he seems to be a normal kid, running around doing normal kid things. Hopefully, they'll be able to decern who his parents were and what happened to them, but that will probably have to wait. Though Olivia would prefer to keep him sheltered from that unpleasantness for as long as possible.

"Mei Li, Livia made me waffles." Aaron squeals and waves the last bit of food as she enters the kitchen. Mei Li smiles softly at Aaron as she walks up to him, stroking his brunet hair.

"That was very nice of her. Finish eating and wash your hands. Aidan will be here to pick you up shortly." Olivia tilts her head at Mei Li quizzically. "Aidan has agreed to take him a few mornings throughout the week. His clan has several children that he can learn and play with," Mei Li explains.

"Hmm, that makes sense. I guess keeping his upbringing normal will be difficult as it is, and God knows we are going to be an unusual influence on him."

"We have to figure out what will be the best course of action for him." They watch Aaron as he lifts his plate into the sink and washes his hands. Standing on his tiptoes he stretches to reach the faucet handle, a look of determination creasing his brow.

A small knock sounds from the door as Aidan steps into the room. He smiles tentatively as he spies them. "Hello, I know I'm a little early." He shrugs as Aaron scurries over to him, bounding with excitement.

"Aidan, are we going to see Mia?" Aaron asks as he grabs a plastic dinosaur from the table.

"Yes, we are." He gleams a wide smile down to the small child. He lifts Aaron up into his arms and his probing gaze turns back to them. "What's going on?"

"It's nothing to be concerned about right now." Mei Li quickly brushes the comment aside.

"Are you sure–you look like someone's died…" He stills at their glares.

"We'll discuss it later," Mei Li cuts him off as her eyes flick to Aaron and back. Aidan nods with a furrowed brow. His eyes shadow with worry, but they won't tell him what happened–not with Aaron within earshot. "Keep a close eye on him until we come by to collect him, and under no circumstances are you to let anyone take him except if it's Olivia, Emma, or me is that understood?"

"Yes." He nods deliberately.

"I'll explain when I can." Mei Li's tone softens slightly, and Aidan seems mildly mollified as he turns, still carrying Aaron, but lags when Mei Li addresses him again. "Aidan. Thank you for your help." He watches them thoughtfully for a brief moment before simply dipping his head and leaving. Aaron grins as he waves with a keen enthusiasm. Olivia's ears strain as she listens to the fading sound of Aidan's footfalls.

"How is Emma?" Olivia asks when she is certain there is no one within earshot, the weight of the morning's event suddenly hanging heavy on her. She rolls her neck as she tries to work out the built-up tension that lies there.

"She's obviously upset." Mei Li sighs deeply as she clutches her hands. With as much as Mei Li works her hands, Olivia is surprised she hasn't rubbed them off.

"Well, she's heartbroken."

"I know. I had hoped that separating them would give us more time to figure out the potential risks. This is exactly what we wanted to avoid and why personal attachments were forbidden."

"'Personal attachments'– you mean love? You also know that the distance between them would not lessen their feelings." Olivia lifts her brow as her head tilts. "The problem is that you seem to want to forget that while we are Fury, we are also human. We will never be the same as the original three; it is a blessing as well as a curse. And as of late I have been thinking that perhaps we were wrong to hide from our human nature."

"All we could go by was what it did to the original three, and they allowed love to destroy them."

"Perhaps love wasn't the issue? These goddesses had always simply been fueled by rage and to seek vengeance. Maybe it's that they had no experience with love and that was their undoing? Such an alien emotion could very well be what drove Alecto mad. Honestly, think about it—we never had any rules forbidding the act of sex because it was apparent that the three were familiar with it. We understand what it is to love as well as what it is to be without it, and that's one of the vast differences between us."

"I know that." Mei Li's forehead creases as she obsessively scours her hands together. "We've all lost so much, I was trying to save them the heartache. But in the end, perhaps now David will have a chance at a somewhat normal existence." She looks to Olivia, perhaps hoping that she will provide her some encouragement.

"He's a Gyges with no connection to the Fury– how can that lead to anything normal?" She loathed feeling that she's crushing Mei Li's hope, but she won't lie to her or sugarcoat anything.

"Bastian and the others will keep him safe."

"If he doesn't remember any of them, why would he stay there? Oh God, what if he comes back here–what will we do?" A flush of panic rises in her stomach.

"He won't come back here." Mei Li nods perceptively, yet Olivia doesn't bother trying to hide her doubt. "I left him with very clear orders to stay there and aid Bastian until further notice and that I'll come to relieve him. Besides, he won't be the first Gyges to remain outside the fold," Mei Li counters as her chin lifts stubbornly.

"Yeah, and we still have to hunt down Moss and he's anything but normal," Olivia reminds her.

"Finding Moss will remain a priority. He's a danger to us as well as many others. But I'm more concerned about Emma at this moment—that she'll make a rash decision."

"You mean like hurting herself?" Chills slither down Olivia's spine as her gaze snaps to Mei Li.

"No, maybe, I don't know." Mei Li frets as she pulls out a chair and sits gingerly with a groan. "She's talking about leaving us."

"Do you think she'll actually leave? There was no way we could have helped David, and her running off won't change that." A rush of dread constricts her lungs. Losing David is hard enough, but to lose Emma as well is a whole new level of chaos she doesn't want to think about.

"She's really hurt and angry, and those emotions often lead people to make foolish decisions."

"Truth be told, I don't necessarily blame her. It's a tough call–I can see your side as well as hers."

"I couldn't stand there and let her kill my son." Mei Li rests her chin in her hand, and her tortured gaze drifts off.

"Why is he doing this? What is he? You have been a Fury for millennia so there's no way he is human."

"His father was a dragon."

"Excuse me? You mean like knights and dragons and hoards of gold in the side of a mountain?"

"No. Not all dragons are of the European nature." Mei Li eyes her curtly.

"How does one end up married to a dragon anyway?" Olivia folds her arms over her chest.

Her interest is piqued as she realizes how little she knows about Mei Li. For a moment she's convinced that the mother will refuse to tell her. Yet she seems to concede as she exhales a long breath.

"I grew up on the outskirts of a small farming village by the Yangtze River. Our livelihood depended on the rain and the land. One year we had a great drought and each day we struggled to collect enough water for the crops. Despite the difficult times our taxes were still paid, and we had adequate food to eat. Then one evening a traveler knocked at our door. I did not know the man but my father seemed to recognize him because he greeted him as Jiang Long and invited him in. We shared our food with him and offered him shelter for the night. As the sun rose in the morning he was gone and I was told by my mother that he was to be my husband."

"It was an arranged marriage?"

"Yes, at the time it was quite a normal process," Mei Li explains. "It was after we were wed that I discovered his true nature and we traveled to his family's home in the southern mountains. Being separated from my parents was difficult, yet I tried to do all that I could to be a good wife and daughter to my husband's family. After a time, we grew to love each other and I gave birth to our child, Chen." A sad smile graces Mei Li's lips.

Olivia's throat is dry as she works up enough saliva to speak. "What happened?"

"I was collecting water at the river when I was grasped by a Shi Gui and pulled under the surface. My companions could only watch as I disappeared under the waves." Olivia cocks her head at Mei Li as she tries to place the strange name. "A drowned spirit," Mei Li clarifies. "But the Shi Gui could not inhabit my body as my death awakened the Fury within me. When I pulled myself from the water, I managed to make my way back home. I was stopped before I could enter the house by Jiang's mother; she said that I had become an evil spirit and couldn't rejoin them. I spent a cold night in the forest and by the following morning the Fury found me."

"Why didn't you seek out your husband?"

"It was not my place to question my mother-in-law's wishes," she states matter of factly.

"Perhaps I could go and talk to your husband–he might be able to answer some questions."

"No, he has passed." Mei Li shakes her head.

"Oh, I'm sorry. I didn't mean to…"

"Don't worry. As I understand it, he died quite some time ago." Her tone is stoic yet a solemn emotion flickers in her eyes.

"Well, it seems that Chen is determined to get revenge and his sights are set on all of us."

"A man who sets out seeking revenge should dig two graves, one for his victim and the other for himself."

"Well, I don't think Chen is too concerned about how many graves he has to dig."

Their eyes shift to the doorway at Bray's approach. He seems to have found better-fitting clothes as the dark-blue fabric of his shirt clings to his chest. A jittering energy rolls through Olivia and she fights the strong urge to look away. Mei Li rises with another heavy sigh.

"I'm going to try and get some rest. Will you keep an eye on Emma? And if she tries to leave, come and get me as soon as possible." Her voice trembles slightly as she dips her head to them before seeing herself out.

In their solitude, the air seems thinner and Olivia's pulse quickens. Her awareness of her body is heightened as he nears. With a nearly infuriating ease he leans against the counter, plucking an apple from a fruit bowl and biting into it. Olivia swallows hard; her mouth is parched again, and her mind races as she watches a stream of juice run down his chin.

"How are things with the pack?" she asks, trying to ignore the quiver in her voice.

"They are well. Isaac is very capable, and he'll keep everyone safe while I'm away."

"You have a lot of faith in him?"

"Of course, why wouldn't I? He's smart, loyal, and one of my most-trusted friends."

"Trust is important; it can make your bonds stronger."

"I know that if anything ever happened to me, he would do what's right for us and he'll make an exceptional leader, should he choose to take it on."

"In many ways the Fury are different from your pack." She pushes aside the uncomfortable loneliness that crawls through her chest.

"It seems to me that you are all pretty close." Bray takes another bite before throwing the core into the sink.

"It's an awkward closeness, like going to a family reunion where there are too many secrets."

"I can see that. Perhaps it will improve over time."

"Perhaps, perhaps not. As of late I've come to believe that if you want something, then you have to take a chance and work for it." Bray blinks at her quizzically with a tilt of his head.

"I wanted to ask you a question." A tingling sensation dashes up her spine and her pulse thrums, fueled by her nervousness. She struggles to calm her breathing as she meets his intense blue eyes.

"Okay." He eyes her cautiously.

"Do you find me attractive?" Her voice is barely a breath, and his back straightens with a fractional movement.

"Yes." Bray answers quickly as his eyes light with a penetrating hue.

"Good, because I'd like to have sex with you." The words tumble out, rich with an urgent need.

"Here?" His eyes flick about the room. "Don't take this the wrong way, but why?"

"I just need to feel something. I don't want to wait for opportunities, and I don't want to wake up one morning knowing that everything has slipped from my fingers." There is still a minute sign of hesitation in him. "I'm not saying that we're getting married or anything," she adds.

"Is this some kind of test?" His tone is measured as if she were a potential threat.

"No test, just let me know if this isn't what you want." He watches her silently in response and she nervously crosses the distance between them. "In there." She nods toward a supply closet. Clasping his hand with her own shivering ones she pulls him up, urging him to the closed door. Her breath comes quicker as she opens the space and flicks on the small overhead light.

The cramped space is often used to store dry goods and other kitchen supplies. Old canned goods are coated with a thick layer of dust, and a flimsy white tablecloth is draped over some unused furniture. Olivia inhales deeply, pulling in Bray's scent. Sliding her hand around the back of his neck she pulls at him until his mouth meets hers. He returns her kiss with a greedy need, and a heated ache builds in her core. The signature taste of Bray mingles with the fresh apple across her tongue. His hands knead her arms, her back, and the fleshy meat of her ass, seemingly everywhere all at once. Breathlessly, their mouths part, his lips feather the soft skin of her neck, and her body shivers in response.

Bray nibbles and licks her neck as she guides them farther into the room. Cold air rushes between them as she breaks from him, yanking the cloth away from a piece of furniture. She eyes the wooden chair, which is old but should be sturdy enough. His eyes are ablaze as she urges him down into the seat. Her legs quiver as she stands before him and lifts the hem of her shirt to unbutton her pants. For several seconds the stubborn clasp refuses to budge but when it finally relents, goosebumps rise on her legs as she slides the material down. Olivia steps out of her discarded jeans and pulls her shirt off in one motion. A quake rolls through her as she meets Bray's heady gaze again. The pulse of his aura flows around her as the solid tempo of his breath fills the tight quarters. With an unabashed confidence her eyes drop to the thickened bulge that strains against the fabric of his jeans.

The soft skin of her breasts aches as her nipples tighten under the thin material of her bra as she strides toward him. "Do you still want this?" she asks, trying to settle the jumbled nerves of excitement in her belly.

"Yes." He nods as he extends a hand to her.

His skin warms her hands as she swings each of her legs over his, straddling his lap. The heat of his body seeps into her and she melts into the solid warmth of his chest. Her hands run across the span of his rib cage savoring the firm muscles that lie beneath. Bray strokes the length of her back as her lips capture his. A soft groan escapes him as she nips the sensitive flesh of his lower lip. Holding his face in her hands she uses the rise and fall of his response to gauge her pace as she grinds deliciously against him.

"Do you want me to fuck you, Bray?" Her heated breath mixes with his.

"Yes," he nearly growls.

Her hands work feverishly at the zipper of his jeans. The solid extent of his cock frees from the confines of his briefs and she glides her hands down the length. Bray pulls her forward and the exquisite friction of him against her slick center arches her back. His fingers part her supple lips as he explores the tender folds of flesh. Olivia clings to him as her legs shudder with an unbearable need.

"I need you now," Olivia groans, her mouth hovering a breath away from his, and he urges her forward with a subtle nod. Lifting her up, Bray shifts her panties to the side, and his hot breath fans over her breasts. Olivia eases him inside of her and their eyes remain locked as she slides down. When she is nested against him, she relishes the sense of fullness. Their breath intermingles as she rocks forward, feeling his length moving inside as his body rubs her most tender parts. She grinds against him as the friction and exquisite tension starts to build. Soon, the rise and fall of her body syncs with her labored breath and as the orgasm hits her, she hears Bray's throaty growl. She slumps forward, resting against Bray as their breathing calms. He strokes her hair and softly kisses her face and forehead. Her eyes close and tension slips away as their scents intermingle and she is lulled by the strong thrum of his heartbeat.

Chapter 22

The cold is impossible to shut out—no matter what you do, you are always frozen. Wrapping around you, it clings to you as a second skin. David's fingers burn through the material of his winter gloves as he vainly tries to warm them with a puff of breath into his cupped hands. The Ardennes Forest may be beautiful during the summer, during peacetime, or some time other than now. But during the starkly cold winter the woods are simply a grey hell. Immersed in a world of varying shades of a monochromatic nightmare, the only vivid colors created from death and destruction—red blood awash on the snow. The lucid dream is familiar to him, a recurring memory that revisits almost every night. The realization does little to dissuade the creeping terror or the bitter cold that numbs his core.

He's hunkered down in his foxhole as the prevailing blackness of night presses down on him from all sides, even as the morning sun struggles against the darkness. The frigid chill seeps in from every point of contact, which includes the freezing cold of the barrel of his rifle as it rests against him. A murky haze of fog flows around the trees, blanketing the forest floor and muffling any stray moonlight. Mist-cloaked ghosts rise from the snow-covered earth, beckoning the living to join them.

Snowflakes flitter in the air with the morning sun breaking the horizon. A few of his men scurry from hole to hole and they shift out from patrol, as fresh snowfall coats the land with a deafening white noise. The eerie silence is broken only by the faint crunch of snow under their boots. Each man tries to sleep as he can but there is no rest for them—not until they can go home.

His eyes dart upward as a faint boom sounds in the distance. The familiar whistle signals the approach of artillery and his guts clutch. "Incoming," several voices call out, seconds before the first artillery round strikes. David lurches forward in his cramped foxhole and grabs his rifle. His breath comes in haggard rasps as he scans the line of trees for movement. Men clamber into holes as the forest floor explodes around them. Dirt and shrapnel shatter into plumes of debris, and adrenaline scours his system. A tree explodes; the top half topples to the ground and barely misses an occupied hole. Palmer, the gunner inside the foxhole, racks the bolt of his machine gun and readies to return fire. Anxious shrieks of soldiers ring out, adding to the cacophony of sound erupting around them, and two men dash along the tree line, clutching their rifles as they run.

"Collins, McEnroe—stop gawking and get in those fucking holes!" Collins slides feet-first into a foxhole, McEnroe following a second behind him. McEnroe's body whips around as a sniper round tears through his chest. "Medic," David bellows as he jumps from the cover and rushes to the fallen man. McEnroe coughs up frothy blood and is trying to pull himself up as David skids over to him.

"I gotta move," he wails as his ashen face contorts in desperation. His words stream outward in a spill of anguish, and he makes a pitiful attempt to pull himself up.

"You're going to be fine McEnroe, just hang on. I need a medic!" David screams as he compresses the wound with his hands, trying to ebb the stream of hot blood that flows through his fingers, soaking his hands. The field medic scrambles over to them, already ripping open the package of cotton gauze.

"We have to get him off the line," David orders, but halts mid-motion as an eerie stillness falls around him. Snowflakes hang suspended in the air, reflecting the morning light, gleaming as crystals from a chandelier.

Time crawls at a somber pace as his eyes fall toward McEnroe; the man's chest rises and falls drastically yet his look is focused. "He is coming for us," McEnroe chokes as red spittle seeps past his lips.

"We'll hold 'em back, don't you worry," David assures him as his eyes flick to the wood line once more, yet all is stillness.

"You have to save us—you have to save us all. Heed the unseen in the cave. If you allow your heart to be swayed by the husk of innocence, then your ruin will spring from the deepest of caverns. It will rise up and devour all that is light." A stark frost races through him at the realization that the man's voice isn't his own and that he isn't talking about the Germans.

He staggers on shaky legs and calls over another soldier to help them. The extra men clasp McEnroe under his arms and haul him away from the front line. The ominous fog thins as David wrenches his gaze away from the fallen soldier and picks up his weapon, darting back to the line.

His breathing calms despite the solid thud of his heartbeat, and he surveys the grey calamity at play before him. The low rumble of tank units echoes through the trees, and the heavy smell of ammunition, fire, and death lingers. The realism of the memory that surrounds him helps to shake off the sensation, the warning, that he shouldn't be here. Men are shouting as they volley rounds at the enemy and the world is exploding all around them, tugging him further into the dream.

Another artillery round explodes fifty yards down the line and he crouches, hugging close to the trees while moving. A choir of whistles stream through the air, and the shockwave of an artillery hit flings David, unprepared, into the trunk of a broken tree. His shattered body shudders and wheezes for air as it locks up from the blinding pain. Warm fluid seeps into the cloth of his uniform and fountains of his life blood flow from the shrapnel wounds. The deepest, which is in his stomach, pumps out copious amounts of blood as the chill encroaches in on him. He resists the darkness as it eats away at the perimeter of his vision. Endeavoring to calm his racing pulse, his mind is flooded with a thought that something is missing, though he struggles to remember it. The medic hovers and his numb skin doesn't register the man's attempt to save his life. The medic's mouth moves with no sound as David is pulled into a murky gloom. As the last of his thoughts float into the darkness, a warm breeze brushes his skin and strands of soft brown hair blow mysteriously before him.

The fog of sleep clings to David as he tries to center himself. The pain from his wounds echo in his mind as a distant memory, but the dull ache pulsing in his chest seems all too real. The soft sheets, which are too nice to be his, cradle him atop the plush mattress. Keeping his eyes sealed, he senses only stillness surrounding him and there is an itching familiarity of scent as he breathes. While the smell and sounds of war still linger about him, the memory of it seems distant as if he is far removed. His addled mind works to separate himself from the clutches of his nightmare. The haunting words of McEnroe still resound in his ears, leaving him feeling rattled. Never before had something so peculiar happened during his wartime hallucinations.

Memories and thoughts come back as segmented flickers, fleeting tendrils that he can't grasp hold of. Adding to that is him being unsure of where he is, which only doubles his frustration. Cracking open his eyes, he tries to make sense of his surroundings. The small room is faintly lit, casting expansive shadows over most of the area. A large wardrobe and vanity sit against the far wall and are carved from similar dark wood. The bathroom is pitch black, with only the rim of the toilet visible in the murky darkness. Soft bedding attempts to restrain him snugly as he tries to lift himself to a seated position. A poignant ache sears his chest and glancing down, he finds a healing wound. The flesh over his heart is soft and tender as the pink skin mends itself together. His gaze zips over to the end table and the ragged doll that sits there. Torn and aged cloth has been knotted to resemble a macabre human form. Picking it up, he senses that it is quite old with an ample coating of centuries-old dirt and grime.

A sound draws his attention, pulling his gaze to the door. Lying back down, David settles and shuts his eyes as the handle of the door softly clicks. His nerves are alight as the door opens and closes. A barely perceptible rustle of cloth scratches at his ears, steeling his breathing as he waits for a sign of approach.

"How are you feeling, David?" He allows the silence to draw on, hoping they will believe him still asleep. "We know you are up; your heartbeat quickens its pace when you are awake. It's alright–you are safe here." The voice calls calmly to him.

His weak lids open and he winces against the light as his eyes try to adjust. The bedroom is much brighter as he takes in the two individuals that stand before him. The first, a young man with jet-black hair and eyes. The woman stands next him, her hair flowing freely in a vibrant mixture of blue and black shades. She holds a small tray in her hands as she watches him with oddly familiar violet eyes. There is no mistaking their cold confidence that is commonplace for vampires.

"Who are you?" Sandpaper coats his throat as he coughs out the dry words.

"My name is Jillian, and this is Poe." Her eye flicks to her partner anxiously as she gestures to the man standing next to her. "You don't remember us?" She offers the cup and lowers the tray, holding it in front of her. David can't stifle the groan as he pushes himself up. Leaning against the headboard, his stiff joints protest as he takes the glass and cool water sloshes onto his hand. As he brings the glass to his parched lips, he gulps down the much-needed liquid; his thirst is abnormally strong, as if it has been months since he last drank.

"No, should I?" David suppresses another cough.

"What is the last thing you remember?" Poe asks as he folds his arms over his chest.

"Being in the Hallow. I was leaving a training session and I was heading to speak with Mother Mei Li. Where is she? What happened?" Jillian and Poe exchange glances and she pulls a folded piece of paper from her pocket, offering it to David.

"Perhaps you should read that." Poe motions to the note.

He studies the waxen seal, displaying the three entwined serpents, the symbol of the Fury. He runs his finger over the raised design before he breaks the seal and unfolds the thick piece of parchment. David quickly scans the orders from Mei Li. Her elegant script details her desire for him to aid Bastian and his clan in their time of need. The handwriting seems as if it were rushed but he recognizes her lettering. The question of why she would send him versus a more seasoned Gyges troubles him.

"How long have I been here?" David ignores the pain in his chest as he readjusts in the bed.

"You've been asleep for almost a day," Poe answers.

"What happened to me?"

"We were attacked this morning and you were injured in the fight." Poe's words are cool, yet something flickers behind his eyes.

"Was anyone killed?"

"We lost two, aside from you and Bastian being injured."

"How badly is Bastian hurt?"

"They are superficial wounds, but I will be taking on his duties while he heals." The tiny muscle below Poe's eye twitches.

"So, you want me to stay here?" David surveys the room.

"You read Mei Li's request, and we have use of you at this time."

"Who attacked us?" With some concerted effort David untangles himself from the bed linens and gets his feet onto the floor.

"We aren't certain." David senses that Poe is being upfront about that.

"Why do I feel like I'm forgetting something–
like I lost something?"

"We had a healer take a look at you while you
were unconscious. They said you may have
some memory issues for a while."

"You mean amnesia? Did they say when it will
return?"

"They didn't."

"What's the date?"

"March fourth."

"Of what year?" His head snaps to Poe.

"2018."

"Last I remember it was early summer. I can't
remember the last eight months." A cold fear
scurries along his spine.

"Give it time, perhaps it will come back," Poe
offers before turning to Jillian. "I imagine
David is quite hungry. Would you please see if
there is something in the kitchen?" She
watches them for a moment before dipping
her head in a slight nod and leaving. David
notes the unusual silence between them.

"What's the story with the doll?" David asks.

"It's for luck."

"Are you serious? Who's it from?"

"My mother." Poe's eyes tick away fractionally before coming back to meet David's. "You don't need to carry it with you wherever you go. You were hurt and I figured you needed all the good luck you could get."

"Thanks." David answers, uncertain of what else to say.

"I understand this is quite confusing, but unfortunately we need to get you up and moving sooner rather than later," Poe adds as he turns back to face David.

"What's going on?" David resettles himself, fighting the overly plush comforter that threatens to suck him back in.

"I realize that you may not remember any of us, but I need your help. There are enemies at our gate and with Bastian out of commission for the time being, it has fallen to me to take the reins."

"I guess I need to catch up, so why don't you start from the beginning."

Chapter 23

Shrouded in darkness, Emma jolts from her sleep with a wounded gasp. Clawing her way back into reality from the deathly grip of the nightmare is stymied by the shadow-cloaked room. Her muddled mind works as she remembers her surroundings; she didn't recall falling asleep after Mei Li had left. An amnesic fog swirls through the pitch black of her room, trying to snatch away the remaining fragments of her dream, and her heart thunders as the last seconds of terror replay through her mind. She struggles, suspended between the waking world and the thorn-laden realm of sleep. Fear of closing her eyes pulses through her, as if she were to fall asleep again, she'd be yanked back down into that terror.

The cold stone of the cave floor leaches heat from her bones as she struggles to move, the hulking darkness itself seeming to bar her movement. She fruitlessly cries for David with a strangled voice; her screams are mere coarse squeaks against the roar of silence as the abyss surrounds her, swallowing everything. In her mind's eye, she witnesses herself with David, standing in her kitchen. She staggers against the remarkable gentleness in how he touches her cheek, yet as quickly as the scene appears, it is devoured by the tar-like gloom.

The paralysis locks her in place as another miniscule point of light blooms into a grisly scene. David lies prone, held by the same oppressive force. His bare chest heaves and shudders as a long, skeletal hand rakes across his flesh. Strips of his skin are pared away, exposing the meat and muscle underneath, and the blood flows freely. His tortured bellows boom through her core as she bucks against the unseen restraints of her claustrophobic cage. His pained eyes search hers as another silent scream rips from her throat. Emma inhales against the abrasive pain of her insides as she tries to push away the remains of her dream.

Rubbing the sharp ache that radiates in her chest, her hands quiver and her breath comes in short clips. After several seconds her pulse slows as Emma pushes down the waves of panic. She stares into the darkness that envelops her, understanding that it is the same as the emptiness that is nestled inside of her, wicking away any desire to move. Yet drawing in a haggard breath, she knows that she has to move. With a clouded mind Emma swings her legs off the bed and drags herself up.

She staggers towards the bathroom to wash her face and as the tepid water flows over her numb hands her gaze is transfixed by the rippling movement of the fluid. "Be like water," she whispers. "Drift at will, and even if you are trapped know that one day, you'll be free."

With no real personal effects, she gathers herself and leaves the room behind. Her melancholy feeling seems reflected against the gray walls of the corridor. How many times has she walked these halls with a purpose? Now it is a blank space with no real meaning for her, barely registering the sensation of her feet on the ground. Perhaps she should have left a long time ago, before Thanatos and the uprising—before she met David. At least then maybe she wouldn't be hurting so badly right now. A trembling breath escapes her constricted lungs and her legs wobble mid-stride, forcing her to brace herself against the wall. The cold stone is a poor support as it, much like everything, feels bogus. A fragile gasp escapes her lips as a wispy visage of David strides down the corridor toward her and her blood hammers through her veins. A single tear slips from her eyes as he smiles, the light dancing in his eyes. "I know you," his ghostly image whispers in that softest of voices that he saved for her alone. The ache in her chest nearly doubles her over, and she averts her gaze away from the mirage. Her muscles strain from the effort of holding herself up, and when she finally lifts her blurring eyes again, the hallway is barren.

She works her way along, making her way up to the common areas. The soft pad of her shoes echoes through the abandoned space, adding to the ominous nature. Oaken chairs are stacked atop one another, and a thin layer of dust coats the surfaces. The low sounds of talking tickle her ears. Soft voices, which are perhaps no more than whispers, are coming from the direction of the great hall. Emma's senses are alit as time slows with her approach; an uncertainty thrums through her, cautioning her movements.

The door leading into the great hall is open as flecks of dust float in the shaft of light that gleams through. Stopping just shy of the threshold, she glimpses Olivia crossing the length of the massive room. She seems not to have noticed Emma, and there is a graceful calm about her as she glides over to Bray, who is resting a hip against one of the tables. Their words are muffled, just a deep tone of sound that falls beyond Emma's hearing. Olivia passes him a piece of paper, and there is an oddness in how her hand lingers on his a little longer than it would normally. It is the simplest of gestures, but there is a certain weight to the act. Olivia's face confirms her growing suspicion. Olivia's eyes light with a soft intensity that she has rarely witnessed. People get that look when they glimpse something or someone that has become important to them.

Emma's cheeks burn as a sudden wash of shame and guilt flow through her. She turns, feeling like an unwelcome intruder, trying to make a swift exit. "Emma," Olivia's voice calls out to her, perhaps catching the flash of movement. Emma quickens her pace, but the thud of footfalls sounds from behind her.

"Emma, stop!" Olivia grabs her arm, trying to halt her. She wrenches her arm loose, yet stops and turns to face her.

"Where are you going?" Olivia asks with a deep sigh. Bray shadows her closely yet stands a few yards away, watching them carefully.

"I'm leaving." Emma struggles to keep her tone smooth, yet she can't seem to meet Olivia's gaze.

"You can't just leave."

"Yes, actually, I can." Emma folds her arms across her chest.

"Why don't you just wait until Mei Li comes back? We can all sit down and talk this out."

"I don't think there is really any point. I've already said everything I need to say to Mei Li."

"Come on Emma, don't be silly."

"Is that what you think of me? That I'm being silly?" Emma's anger spikes and consumes her already-frayed resolve.

"That's not what I meant and you know it."

"Oh really?" Emma bites back, and she inhales, attempting to pull in some soothing air. "It seems that everyone thinks I'm being a child, or acting foolishly."

"I didn't say that."

"Olivia, I'm tired." Speaking the words only seems to sap away her last remaining energy.

"You need to rest, then, not be running away. I know this is difficult now, but I promise you that it will get better with time." Olivia reaches for Emma's hand but Emma steps back, not wanting the comfort.

"I'm tired, but no amount of sleep will help me. I'm tired of feeling so lost and tired of trying so hard only to fail and have everything turn sideways. I'm always off, a day late, just missed out. Too late to save David or Sarah; I can't even save myself. But perhaps if my life is meant to be a miserable pile of shit, then I want my life to be my own, my fate will be determined by me, not you two."

"I've never tried to control your life." Olivia stiffens.

"Maybe I am a fool. Perhaps Thanatos was right–Mei Li and you will never see me as an equal." Emma's voice is gruff.

"That's not true."

"You think so? Let me ask you this. Why did Mei Li choose to give you that amulet? You are stronger than I and the most capable of the task of judgment. Or at the very least, we could have gone together and shared the burden. But that was not the decision, was it? Better yet, if you went to Mei Li to tell her of your new boyfriend, what do you think she would say?" Bray steps forward but is halted at Emma's look. "I like you, Bray, so please don't do anything stupid."

"It's not like that," Olivia stammers.

"Really? Do you think I'm blind? I know that look, and I can guarantee you that she'd allow it without batting an eye. She values you and your needs, not mine."

"What do you what me to do? I want David back as much as anyone, but I can't change what's happened. I can only try to do better for all of us. I'm sorry, Emma, but feeling this way won't help anyone."

As Emma opens her mouth to respond, a swath of cold wraps around her, clawing its way along her skin, and the vision clouds her mind. The feel of Olivia's hands clutching at her falls away as the waking dream steals all outside sensations. Enveloped in a vast darkness the syncopated sound of droplets of water splashing into a pool rings against her ears. Screams and howls resonate, bouncing off of walls. The darkness breaks, revealing a cavern oasis filled with dark blood. Dim torchlight illuminates the crimson pool, and the viscous liquid drips from the ceiling of the cave as it breaks the surface with colliding ripples.

Humid air clogs her lungs as she tries to breathe. Her heart shudders as she is surrounded by the sounds of torment and the flowing movement of fluid. The tempo of the spattering blood picks up, matching her own pounding heartbeat, and the walls seep copious amounts of life blood. Soon, rivers of red gore stream down the vertical rock. The warm blood laps at her feet and red rain falls

around her as it coats her skin and hair. A veil
of fog rolls in again, leaving only the
awareness of splatter on her flesh.

Lightning flashes, strobe-lighting a string of
terrifying images that play out before her.
Sharp fangs snarl inches from her face as a
putrid breath floods her lungs. Another spark
illuminates black, malicious eyes staring back
at her as another focus showcases a scene of
flesh being flayed from meat and bone. She
claws her way through the darkness, vainly
swinging at the unseen foes, and her breath is
exhausted as her strikes hit nothing.

A low growl pulls her gaze as a dragon's roar
shakes the walls around her, its slender body
writhing against a dying light. Golden eyes
glower as thick rivets of blood stream from its
talons, and it is bathed in a wall of flames. As
the inferno builds Emma shields her eyes
from the blinding light, the deafening roar
blocking out all other sounds.

The snap of silence forces her eyes open, and
she stands in front of Bastian's home as it sits
in stillness against the night sky. The chilled
spring air licks at her skin, raising goosebumps
along her arms. She notices the darkened

windows a second before they explode outward and the house is engulfed in flames. Screams call out into the emptiness of night as the home burns to the ground. She rushes toward the front door as a second explosion propels her backward and the trees speed past her. With lungs seizing and blood filling her mouth, the mirage melts away. The forest blends into stone walls as the floor shifts to the granite slabs of the great hall. Slumped against the wall Emma tries to stand as Olivia clutches at her arms, but her wobbly legs refuse to work.

Emma runs a finger along her gums but comes away with no sign of blood. Her gaze flicks rapidly around the room before settling on Olivia and Bray. Emma works to swallow saliva past her parched throat as her heart rate still thunders in her chest from the vision.

"Emma, are you okay?" Olivia frets as she examines her for injuries.

"I'm fine, I'm fine." She lightly slaps Olivia's hands away.

"How often are the visions coming? What did you see?" Olivia's brows furrow with worry.

"Death." Emma's voice trembles.

"What do you mean, death?" The blast from the shotgun echoes around them as the slug hits Bray in the chest. He staggers backward as he slams into the wall, blood pouring from the wound. Olivia screams as she leaps over to him, trying to shield him with her body. Bray's torso blooms as a mass of red, and for a brief second Emma is confused if this is real or another vision.

"I think she means us. If I'd had known the dog was going to be here, I'd have brought my silver shot," Moss shouts, shouldering the shotgun as he racks another round and levels the weapon at them. Chen, Nina, and the red demoness flank him on either side. Calder peers over the rim of his glasses, smugly grinning at them, his own bodyguards in tow.

"Olivia, get Bray out of here," Emma orders, her eyes staying locked on Chen.

"I won't leave you," Olivia barks as she tries to ebb the flow of Bray's bleeding. He gasps deeply as his face contorts in agony.

"We are outnumbered, and Bray is injured."
Emma chances a look toward Olivia. "The
shot isn't silver, but it will still slow him down.
Now you can stay and we can all get captured,
possibly worse, or you can get the hell out of
here so that at least we have a chance."

"They'll slaughter you." Her brow creases
with deep concern.

"Not before I kill that son of a bitch." Emma
narrows her eyes, glaring at Chen as her barely
fettered rage bubbles within. "I need you to
get out of here and find Mei Li."

"You're not going anywhere." Chen interrupts
coolly as he watches with a murderous scowl.

"You want to make a bet, dick?" Emma spits
as she swivels on her hip, stretching out as she
slaps the ground next to Bray. Before Olivia
can speak the floor rolls as the portal opens,
sucking Olivia and Bray into the swirling
vortex. As they clear the hole, the ground
solidifies, returning to hardened stone. Emma
hoists herself up gingerly as she tries to shake
the blood flow back into her limbs.

At the subtle nod from Calder, his two lackeys step forward, moving with a purpose toward Emma. The smaller of the two men flexes his grip on a metal baseball bat, veins bulging in his dense forearms, and his dead eyes glaze with a lethal intent. Emma rubs her fingers together, feeling the slickness of Bray's blood; even the floor around her is speckled with thick red globs. A frozen vacuum expels the heat from the great room with a near-audible sound as the copper hue overtakes Emma's eyes.

She pushes forward, and with a flick of her hands two kukri daggers materialize from the droplets of blood. Despite the pounding of her heart an eerie calmness settles over her and within several steps she is face to face with her opponents. They seem unfazed by her curved blades, and the larger of the two surges forward, his meaty fists aiming for her head. Ducking out of the way, Emma drops down and flips the blade over in her hand. The sharp weapon cuts easily as she pushes it forward and up, slicing from his groin through his abdomen in one single motion. The earthy smell of entrails plumes around her and his guts plop to the floor. She dips away; watching him fall face first.

A slight tick plays with the muscle in the second goon's cheek, registering his companion's death. He glares at her from hooded brows and his nostrils flare. The veins in his neck flex and a hoarse bellow rips from him. He rushes toward her with the bat arching over his head. His movements are substantially faster than the other man's and he lunges toward her, swinging the hefty bat. For several seconds, Emma is forced to stutter-step as she attempts to evade the avalanche of strikes and kicks. Each time she utilizes the kukri to deflect a blow, sharp pain shoots up her arm, and her swollen hand threatens to drop the weapon. One errant swing connects with her shoulder, sending her flailing back and she has to regains her footing.

Her breaths come in heated pants while the world spins around her. Timing her steps, she feigns her movements, hoping he'll over-commit somewhere. He barrels forward in a sharp overhead swing while she steadies her nerves. With a sweeping motion she slides under the bat swing, skimming the floor, and she turns on her knees. She draws the blade across the back of his legs, cutting meat and tendons. Emma barely registers the sound of his howl while she jumps over to his injured form. Bringing the weighty blade down it barely slows as it slices through the nape of his neck and a viscous pool of blood spans out over the floor and his head rolls to the side.

Rolling her neck, Emma turns her eye back to the group. Her limbs ache but she pushes the distraction aside, fixing her gaze on the goal before her, taking in her opponents as she settles her breathing, calming the biting urge to fly at them. Emma narrows her thoughts, focusing her mind on the sound of the blood dripping from her blade. Taking them on all at once would end very poorly for her. She is well aware that she probably won't survive this, but that doesn't matter now. She'll accept death as long as she takes Chen with her.

"Take her, Alba," Calder barks. A gleam of light obscures his eyes under the lens of his glasses, his twisted face sneering at her with a vile elation. Alba steps forward but is blocked by Chen. "What are you doing, Chen?" Calder's face melts into a petulant frown as he glares at the other man.

"Send in Alba if you wish to, but you'll lose her." His eyes never leave Emma as he speaks. "The only way she can hope to win is by thinning us out first."

"What do you suggest we do then? Stand here all day?" His eyebrows dart above his rims as he asks.

"Who do you call on when you need to catch a Fury? Nina, prepare yourself." Without missing a beat, he withdraws a small bronze talisman from his jacket as Nina levels her golden gaze on Emma. A prickling sensation flitters along her skin as cold sweat drips down her back. The light dances as it passes through the ruby, splashing shafts of red glow throughout the room as all the lights dim and flicker. The irregular flashes of light dip and rise against the darkening walls. Adrenaline courses through Emma's veins, followed by a fresh wave of terror as she finds her legs locked in place. Nina's intense stare remains steadfast on Emma as a frightening skitter of clicks echoes through the empty space. Emma battles with her useless limbs as her eyes dart fretfully around her. A gut-wrenching chill slides up her spine as a shadowed movement catches her eye.

The spindly limbs of the faceless move in an inhuman fashion as it materializes from the darkness; bones and joints bend and twist in ways they were never meant to. From opposing ends of the hall another two faceless creep along the edge of the light. They tick wildly, seeming to feed off of the terror they produce. A sandpaper scream scours at Emma's throat as she pulls at her power, groping at it with numb senses. A claustrophobic panic builds as she is trapped within her own body and lurking monsters are approaching. The slightest movement seems so far away, and she concentrates on the wooden handle of the kukri in her hand.

The jarring gait of the faceless is emphasized as they move closer. They step cautiously as if they are watchful about closing the gap. She studies her adversaries, taken aback by their near human qualities, and she wonders briefly as to their identities. Knowing that each of them at one point was a Gyges makes her uneasy about the coming battle. They may or may not have any conscious thoughts, and even if they did it wouldn't stop them from ripping her to shreds. Emma's lungs pull hard against the effects of the paralysis and the muted rise and fall of her chest fosters some frail hope of freedom.

The taller of the three steps forward and is within inches of her face as its putrid breath wafts over her. If it is talking through the random sets of clicks and hisses, she has no idea, but its tone is seething with unhinged rage. Beneath the scaly black sheen of skin, Emma can barely discern where its features should have been. The raised bump that is perhaps its nose seems misshapen as if it had been smashed, a broken mass of cartilage remaining even after his transformation into a monster.

Emma's eyes flick over to Chen as he looks on stoically, seeming unaffected by the events transpiring around him. Nina appears slightly the worse of the two as her face is pale and glistens from the strain. Nina's fatigue spurs Emma forward, and with a renewed vigor, she strains against her unseen bonds, nearly laughing out loud as her wrist limply twitches. The faceless lifts its hand as jagged copper claws emerge from the black flesh, the tip grazing Emma's eyelashes. Raging at her stubborn body as her heart thuds wildly against her ribcage, she yanks at a sporadically whipping tendril of power and as she secures it, she draws it closer. The shock of energy nearly staggers her, and the jolt sends her blade into her own leg, instantly drawing blood.

The smothering weight of Nina's magic lifts as the faceless slices at her, its talons cutting the air. Pushing backward, Emma falls, landing on her hip, but she scurries back to her feet. The two flanking faceless advance, instantly stalking around her. In a blur of movement, they flood toward her with a volley of fevered attacks. Blocking is near impossible and she finds she is just trying to avoid being hit. The strikes that do get through–shear through her clothes and rip into her flesh. Within a few seconds her breath is coming in pained gasps, and her vision hazes as the venom that coats their claws infects her blood. They circle around as if playing with her. Readjusting her grip of the blade, her power flickers and pulses as distant voices call to her mind saying *just let go*. Gruffly, she forces away any thoughts springing from the three.

Stumbling, Emma manages to duck out of the way of one attack and in a split-second decision she lunges toward one of the creatures, taking it by surprise. Her weight and momentum topple both of them, and she drives the kukri into its chest as they land. Even as she draws out the blade its skin begins to shift into an ashen grey.

Her muscles scream as she claws her way up to her knees. The numerous tears along her skin burn, and the potent toxin drains what little strength she has left. As much as she struggles against it a black veil slips across her eyes as she slides into the darkness. The fragility of her senses registers the muted rake of claws over her skin just as everything falls away.

Chapter 24

The conservatorium lies in a dormant silence, its stillness a vibrant pause of color against the cold grey of the early evening. The steady darkness of the encroaching night wicks away nearly all of the warmth of the day. The fresh scent of rose and lavender tickle David's nose. There is a soothing follow to the narrow cobbled path as it winds its way through patches of shrubbery and bushes. Despite the rush of heated air flowing into the room from the vents that run the length of the hothouse, he can't seem to shake the enduring chill that drapes his core. All of his efforts to warm himself seem fruitless, as if he's been cold for way too long. Nothing is the way it should be, and his brain works to form an understanding of why everything is off kilter.

This lingering feeling of disconnection tugs at him; it is as if a huge swath of himself has been carved away. His irritation peaks every time he attempts to wrangle these fragmented thoughts and form them into a concrete answer–it seems impossible. He is trying to build a sand castle, but all he has is dry sand. How it is possible that he's lost so much time? What really happened to him?

David recoils as the smoldering ember of cigarette singes his fingers. He's been so absorbed in his thoughts that it had burned down past the filter without him noticing. Muttering a curse, he strips the filter and stands as he crams it back into his pocket. Gruffly running a hand through his hair, he studies the area, his eyes drawn toward a rose bush. The bright-red blooms hang heavily on their stems and a brief memory lingers at the edge of his mind. *It doesn't matter though. In the end you will still lose her and she will lose you. The ribbons are woven and cannot be undone. Struggle as you might, you will be separated from one another.* The words resonate in his ears, sending a shiver down his spine. His gaze sweeps the room, fruitlessly trying to locate the source of the words, yet he sees no one. Why is he affected by this space?

Over the last day he's been inexplicably drawn back to this area, staring at the same rose bush. Maybe he's picked up a love of flowers somewhere in his gap of time that eludes him, or maybe it's because the vampires of the house rarely come out here. Not that they are a particularly bad bunch as far as vampires go. Most of them seem reasonably harmless as they scurry around trying their damnedest to avoid him. Bastian is still bedridden, and Guillermo is either with him or seeing to his own business, though he would be a fool to think that even they are truly tame. The draegloth, Ryl, is concerning more so than anyone else. While he hasn't done anything overtly shady, David has noticed the beast studying everyone as if they are his next potential meal. Yet, it is Jillian and Poe that worry him the most, when they keep acting as though he should know them. On occasion he's caught them watching him with what seems to be pity. Normally, he'd just reject it outright, but he can't shake this feeling that maybe he should know who they are.

Measuring his steps, he tries to move silently as he makes his way back into the main house. Every click of a doorknob or creak in the floor ratchets up his unreasonable unease. Several times he feels the need to linger in a doorway to avoid running into anyone. Mei Li's note told him to stay here until she came for him, but he really needs to find her. Maybe she can clear up his missing memories? Perhaps he is just grasping at straws, but he can't shake the unsettling feeling that something happened during the near yearlong void in his memory. What was it? He draws a deep breath as he attempts to settle his growing agitation. Waiting around isn't going to get him any more answers. With a quick nod of his head, he decides that come morning, he'll head out to find her. He should be able to get to the Hallow and back before anyone realizes he has gone. Hopefully, he can find the answers to at least most of his questions.

Climbing the stairs, he can overhear the muffled voices and movement as the occupants of the house begin to stir. Light-blocking curtains remain closed over the double-hung window that sits at the far end of the hall. Approaching the door to the room they've told him is his, he pauses as an icy chill drifts over his skin. He searches the darkened length of the corridor as he tries to sense any impending danger. Despite the distant sounds the space appears to be empty, yet his heart pounds in his throat. With a long exhale he dips into the room, shutting the door behind him with a soft click.

Engulfed by the heavy darkness, he fumbles for the light switch for several seconds and an alien sensation of panic clenches his lungs and the solid thump of his pulse roars over everything else. Terror seizes him and his heart threatens to explode painfully through his chest until his fingers graze the switch and the lights flicker on, flooding the room with light. Even though he can now see, he struggles to steady his ragged breath, trying to subdue the raging thrum of adrenaline flooding his body. *What the hell man, get your shit together*, he scolds. He thought he'd taken care of this, that enough time would free him from the weight of war. Yet it chases him like a bloodhound, even past the grave. For several seconds he closes his eyes and breathes deeply, coercing his body into a calmer state. Stress always seems to make it worse, but he has found that the breathing helps.

As the muscles in his back start to relax he chances a glance around the room. Crushed under the great weight of fatigue, he walks

over and sits on the edge of the bed. Some of
the clothes in the bureau are his, so that only
confirms that this is probably his room, but
very little in the chamber feels familiar to him.
His eyes settle on the bizarre doll Poe had
given him. Such an odd thing, yet Poe seemed
insistent that he take it. His first thought had
been to throw it out as soon as they'd left,
which he still might do. But the pressing sense
that it may be of use means that it has stayed
there untouched.

His breath slows as his ears detect the delicate
sound of one of the doors in the hall opening
and shutting, and eyes snap toward his closed
door. After the bizarre events of the morning,
he's seen a lot of traffic coming and going
from Bastian's room. He spied one fellow
heading in there with a mop and bucket, and
guess that someone had made a mess.
Fighting the urge to sneak a look out into the
hall he figures it is better if he lets them attend
to their own business without his intrusion.

The barely audible knock pulls his eyes back
to the door. A sharp pain throbs in his chest
as he stands and strides over to the door, and
with a heavy sigh he pulls it open. The blue in

Jillian's hair is a brilliant hue as it contrasts and melds into a solid black, and her deep-violet eyes study him with a peculiar interest.

"What can I help you with?" He clears his throat.

"I wanted to see how you were doing. Your wound." She gestures to his chest as her gaze flutters over him.

"It's healing fine," he answers coolly.

"Why don't I take a look at it."

"I don't think that's necessary." He argues, and his tone is a little terser than he'd like. He wages war against his scattered mental health as he tries to ease his vise-like grip on the door.

"And I also want to talk to you." She sighs deeply. "Why don't you humor me?"

Mulling over his options for a few seconds he finally steps aside, ushering her in.

"You're too high-strung," she winks as she slides into the room with a lithe energy.

"I think if our roles were reversed, you'd be cautious too."

"Fair point, but honestly, if I were going to attack you, I'd just wait until you were asleep," she smirks, flashing a small bit of fang at him. Before he can check his reaction, his face drops and a flustered groan ekes out. "Relax, okay?" She tries to calm him.

Ambling across the room she briefly studies the space before settling down on his bed. Despite her outward calm, David senses a slight nervous energy that barely touches her shadowy eyes.

"Now, let's have a look." She pats the comforter next to her, entreating him to sit. Moving deliberately, he slides a padded office chair over and sits. Jillian simply watches him for several seconds, patiently waiting for him to move. In an exasperated motion he yanks the t-shirt over his head and she scoots forward to the edge of the bed, peering at the thin, red scar that runs a few inches over his chest. Gooseflesh rises along his skin as the room seems cooler than it should be.

"It looks to be healing well." As she runs an icy finger over the tender flesh, he nearly jerks. His reaction catches him off guard. Why was he so uneasy? This isn't the first time he's been alone with a pretty woman.

"Is it still sore?" she asks in response to his jolt.

"A little bit." He forces a calming breath into his lungs.

"What is this one from?" She traces another scar that runs along his rib, prompting the hair on his arms to rise.

"Shrapnel."

"And this one?" Her finger glides lower down his stomach, and he gently captures her hand in his.

"Please don't." He attempts to keep his voice soft as his pulse thrums through his veins. She doesn't pull her hand away, opting to let him hold it.

"I know that everything is really confusing for you right now. Your memory may return, but maybe it won't." A softness touches her eyes.

"You shouldn't have to go through this alone. Let me help you." She rises up, her shins pressing into the chair as she stands between his legs.

Craning his neck, he looks up to meet her gaze. An incredible light dances in her eyes, and she touches his cheek tenderly as her soft mouth brushes his. He hesitantly returns her kiss, pushing back at the nagging feeling that churns in his guts. Shelving the unpleasant reality, he invites the spiced floral scent of her hair to wash over him as his tongue explores her ample lips and mouth. Her hands score the length of his chest, urging him on as the rampant thoughts of his mind hush and he simply clings to the solid feeling of her pressed against him. This is something he understands, and it doesn't need any complex thought. It's basic and real, and can silence the biting doubts and isolation that plague him. His fingers snake through her silken hair as she suckles his lower lip, a low moan escaping from her.

Jillian breaks from the kiss, leaning over him as a dark hunger glimmers in her eyes. David's heart stutters as her visage flickers and morphs into a hazy fog of a stranger. The face of the figure looming over him is obscured, but a halo of golden hair catches the ambient light. Its mouth and jaw move frantically as if screaming something at him. The mirage beats and claws its hands on his chest for mere seconds, before melding back into Jillian, and a crippling tremor rages through him.

"What's wrong?" Her brow creases as she searches his face.

"I don't know… I'm sorry, I can't do this," he stammers, barely able to meet her gaze.

Jillian steps back and he pulls himself up onto shaky legs when a howling shriek rips through the air. Their eyes snap to the empty corridor, and David is already moving out into the hall. The sounds of a scuffle and shattering glass ring from Bastian's room. Several vampires linger outside the chamber, their faces aghast as they peer in. He brushes past the onlookers to glimpse Poe and Guillermo struggling to hold Bastian down on his bed. They lay their full weight on his arms and shoulders while Bastian bucks wildly against them. Driven by instinct, David lurches forward but halts at the foot of the bed, spotting a fluid script that mars Bastian's skin. A dark, cryptic pattern of tribal runes rises and falls across the length of his visible flesh. The watery tattoo snakes its way along his skin, torturing the vampire, and he screeches against the pain.

"What's going on? What's happened to him?"

"Help us hold him down," Guillermo barks, and David steps forward to clasp Bastian's legs. The coiled strength of the vampire pulses beneath his fingers as he struggles to capture the spasming limb. Bastian's heels dig into the mattress, arching his back upward, and he bellows as David fights against the unnatural power. Wriggling and shifting, Bastian manages to get a foot loose and the quick up-kick catches David in the face. As his mouth fills with blood, he spits in anger and reclaims his grip on Bastian.

"Grace," Bastian cries as his head whips madly back and forth. "Where is Grace?"

"Be calm, friend. Grace is fine," Guillermo soothes. David notes the hurt and worry washing through Poe's eyes.

"I need to see Grace." Bastian's mouth moves wordlessly as the onyx symbols flutter under his pale skin.

"You will, but you need to rest first." Seemingly eased by Guillermo's reassurances, Bastian's body slackens, his breath shallow as a strange sleep overtakes him.

They watch him for several seconds, fearful of making any noise to wake him. His haggard form seems so frail in stark contrast to the two men standing beside him.

"What's happened?" David repeats.

"He's been poisoned," Poe answers, his eyes locked on Bastian. "When he tries to feed this happens to him." David's eyes flash to the smashed remnants of a blood-filled decanter as streaks of red stream down the ornate wallpaper.

"Not poison," Ryl argues. His speech is thick and guttural; the sound coming from him seems impossible with his mouth shaped as it is.

"If it's not poisoning, what is it?" Poe snaps as he fretfully rubs at his forehead. "I've never seen anything like this."

"I've seen it before–it's a curse," Ryl counters roughly. "He will waste away, unable to feed, and soon, when there is nothing left, he will die and turn to ash."

"How do we save him?" David asks, pulling the gaze of Poe and Guillermo.

"We need to figure out of the three that attacked us, which one wielded the curse." Guillermo scratches his chin as he thinks.

"Attacked us when?" David frowns as he looks around the room.

"The battle where you were injured," Poe explains.

"All three are very strong, but I'd say we should be looking for the Kitsune. Nine-tails are powerful and this one even more so than others." Ryl's eyes pulse with an eerie, possibly delighted, red glow.

"Ryl will go and find the nine-tailed fox and bring her here," Guillermo orders as his gaze falls back to Bastian.

"I don't think she will come along to remove the curse willingly, plus what if Victor is working with them? He could be walking into a trap," Poe snarks back.

"Ryl is quite capable of handling himself, and I would be very pleased if Victor is with them—two birds. If the Kitsune can't remove the curse or won't, then bring me her head." There is an almost enviable callousness in Guillermo's tone as he nods to Ryl.

"What about asking the Fury? They may know of something to help him. I could go and find out," David cautiously offers.

"No," Guillermo states coldly.

"It makes more sense to look at all the possibilities."

"Very well, but you will stay here." He lifts a hand before David can speak. "Ryl is a seasoned hunter. If there are issues getting the nine-tailed then he will go and seek aid from the Fury. If Bastian has another episode, we will need your help here."

"But I have more experience with them."

"True, but you can't remember most of it right now. Also, Ryl is a little too brutish; he might try to restrain Bastian and end up breaking his back. Oh, and if I need yet another reason, Ryl can use portal magic. Can you?" Guillermo arches a brow as he asks. Seems he isn't used to anyone arguing with him as the spike in his temper is apparent.

David swears under his breath as he catches a slight smirk gracing Ryl's misshapen lips. The large beast flashes a smug look at him as he turns and, with a clawed finger, etches symbols into the air. A large area begins to blacken as it pulls the light into itself. A sickening wind that pushes around them pulses with a potent darkness as this creature's magic prickles along David's skin. His emotions spike as he is assaulted by an irrational rage response. Tamping down the thoughts, he forces his hands to unclench. The swirling vortex measures from ceiling to floor by the time it's done, and Ryl is sucked into it, versus stepping in. As soon as he is through, the portal flakes away, dissolving back into the air. A steady feeling of unease builds in David as he studies the space where Ryl once stood. At this point, he can really only come to one determination–he doesn't care for the whole damn situation and he doesn't like Ryl much, either.

Chapter 25

Olivia and Bray fall through the weightless space connecting the portals and the fluid miasma of the void rushes around them. All sense of direction and motion are skewed with them being enveloped in a heavy shroud of darkness. Cold sweat coats her skin and a hammering heart beats at her chest. She clings to Bray, terrified to lose contact with him. Barely able to make out his features in the shallow light, she has to rely on her other senses to gauge his condition. His breathing is weaker than she would like, but it is there. His skin is flushed and warm as his body generates heat and heals the wounds from the shotgun.

Her free arm flails in a vain attempt to find some purchase, some way to slow their descent. She has no idea where they are going since Emma was the one to open the portal. Yet it is a waste of energy cursing her as they spiral out of control in an unforgiving land. How many before her have been claimed by the abysmal darkness? Perhaps they were just stories told to the young Fury to scare them into taking the dangerous passage seriously, but, truth be told, she's struggling to curb her own terror. Fear allows this place control over you, and your terror feeds it as it devours you. She's always been the one in charge within this realm as she is the master of her emotions, and it will bend to her will, not the other way around.

Inhaling deeply, she centers her thoughts as she pushes out the rush of stillness that surrounds her and focuses on calming the spike of fear until it is silent. When her nerves start to settle the sensation of dropping in her stomach ebbs and they seem to slow. She pushes outward once more with her senses, trying to find some indication of their direction or destination. Peering into the void, their bodies lag for a brief moment when they hit the opening portal gate. Her breath catches in her lungs as the current that generates the gateway courses through her body.

Olivia blinks against the disorientation and as she opens her eyes, the cold night air blasts her skin from a bristly wind whipping around them. Panic clenches her stomach as the ground rushes toward them; her mind works feverishly, with mere seconds to react. A darken car lies directly below, and she realizes there is no avoiding it, no way to redirect them. Time seems to slow and she clings to Bray as they collide with the unyielding metal. Glass shatters around them, and her mouth fills with blood as she bites into the flesh of her tongue. As they slide and collapse to the ground, Olivia wheezes for breath as her lungs battle to pull in air. Pain explodes throughout her body as she is paralyzed against any movement for what feels like an eternity.

Bray's jerky movements draw her attention; blood trickles from his ear and the veins in his neck bulge while he struggles to pull himself up. As she gingerly rises, a bolt of pain rockets through her, nearly knocking her back. A searing agony in her side snags with each breath and several ribs move unnaturally in her chest. Ignoring it, she hobbles toward Bray and tries to hold her fractured bones in place.

"Are you okay?" Her pulse quickens and she searches him for additional injuries.

"I'm hurting but I'll survive. You?" His voice wobbles and his skin has taken on a pasty sheen.

"I think my sternum is broken." His eyes widen and she quickly tries to calm him. "I'll be fine. Where are we?" she asks, glancing around the empty yard, trying to ignore the ache in her chest. A large cabin sits across an open area with a few vehicles that are shrouded in darkness along the side of the house. The edge of an extensive chicken coop peeks from the rear. Only a few lights glow from the curtained interior, but it seems far more welcoming than the cold forest that surrounds them.

"This is my home." A tiny smile graces his lips

"That's why Emma sent us here, because she knew you'd be safe." Olivia shudders as she loops an arm around Bray. "Come on, let's get you inside."

Grimacing, they use the damaged car to get to their feet. The air is crisp as it pulls the heat from their bodies. Walking the distance to the door is an arduous task; each step barely seems to cover any ground and every breath nearly seizes her lungs.

Olivia jerks with a start as a thunderous screech roars through the night air. Perhaps it is a train whistle, but it is eerily off and such a simple sound shouldn't cause the hairs on her neck to stand on end. Her gaze sweeps the length of the wood line, searching for any motion, yet all she can decern is the subtle sway of the trees as a light wind moves through them. The agitated clucking of chickens draws her gaze toward the back of the house.

A flash of shadowed movement from above sends her scurrying backward in an instinctive response to dodge the attack. Catching her heel on a rock she tumbles down, and a burst of agony wracks her body as they smack into the ground. The glint of metal reflects the moonlight and a hulking form lands heavily in the space between them and the front door. Olivia's mind works frantically as she tries to piece together the monstrosity standing before her.

Its reptilian body is balanced over four muscular limbs, each flexing with coiled energy. Breathing heavily, Olivia's insides pole-vault as she takes in the metallic beak that gleams from its terrible birdlike head; its jaws hang open as numerous tentacles writhe wildly. Viscous liquid drips from the wriggling appendages and they seem to be lurching forward, reaching out for them.

As the beast lunges forward a shotgun blast hits it center mass, sending bits of feathers and scales spraying into the air. A fierce bellow rings out and it unfurls its massive, scaled wings. The wind pushes around them and it lifts up into the night sky. It disappears into the darkness, and Olivia's eyes snap to the front porch to see Isaac unshouldering the gun. He observes them keenly for a second, the rich, warm light of the cabin silhouetting him for a moment before he hops down the stairs. Several other wolves vault after him as they hurry to Bray's side.

Bray stands with the aid of his family members. He assures them with a haggard voice that he is fine, and they guide him into the house. Their apprehensive gazes study her with a fair amount of suspicion. Only Isaac remains with Olivia as the others slip into the house.

"What the hell was that?" Olivia asks as she scans the blackened tree line, searching for any sign of movement.

"The snallygaster," he answers, as if this is somehow normal.

"So, it lurking around your house is a common occurrence?" She doesn't bother to hide the incredulous tone in her voice.

"Don't get me wrong, it's a pain in the ass, yes, and it took a few of our chickens last year. But this land is its, just as much as it is ours, and it has some benefits—it keeps nosy teenagers out of the woods." He shrugs. "It comes around so rarely, we usually pay it no attention."

"Interesting. Seems a nasty beast to be roaming the forest."

"Nay, just give it space and maybe a chicken or two." His head dips minutely as he studies her. "Are you harmed?" His demeanor softens.

"No, I'm good," she lies, not wanting any of them to know the extent of her wounds.

"What happened? Was it Moss?"

"Yes and no. There are some issues at the Hallow, so I need to get back. I just want to make sure Bray is safe beforehand."

"He'll be well guarded here." It is Isaac who now searches the depths of the woods. "Our strength lies within the pack as a whole and we are more resilient when we are together. That is why we can't offer any further help to you." His tone is solemn as he rests his hands on his hips and looks away, unable to meet her gaze. "The Fury have helped us, but they've also hurt us, and after losing Jackson we aren't ready to risk Bray."

"I understand and I wouldn't ask you to foolishly jeopardize Bray or anyone else. Do you mind if I check on him before I go?"

Isaac watches her with a cryptic gaze for a moment, his golden eyes flashing brilliantly under the soft light, before he nods and gestures her into the house. The worn wood of the stairs creaks as she climbs up onto the porch. A warm glow of light fans across the well-worn steps and, for at least the meantime, she escapes the darkness outside.

Stepping over the threshold, a welcoming cloak of toasty air envelops her. Isaac scans her and the rest of the room with his focused gaze as he shuts the door behind them. She enters the expansive living room as several wolves walk Bray up a flight of stairs. Those helping him focus on their task and never bother to take note of her intrusion. Everyone else is keenly aware of her presence, and they stiffen rigidly. As if responding to the potential danger, the room swirls with the surge of their energy, the weight of it threatening to freeze her in place. There is a thin line between diplomacy and dominance, she reminds herself. Could she really blame them for their distrust? Yet if she appears weak in front of this group, they will eat her alive—probably quite literally. Olivia lifts her chin a little higher as she meets each stare with her well-practiced stoicism.

She can feel the heft of their heated stares as she ascends each step, desperately fighting the urge to run. The tension eases as she crests a long corridor; her breath calms and muscles relax. The cluster of doors along the hall are closed save the one down at the end. The wafting fragrance of oak wood burning in the fireplace downstairs mingles with a scent she knows is distinctly Bray. Reaching the doorway, she hears a low, muffled conversation. Bray lies on the bed without his shirt; a young girl that bears a striking resemblance to him is holding his hand. His wounds have completely closed, leaving behind only deep-red marks that score his chest. With very few outward signs, Olivia knows they are aware of her presence. Bray's company stiffens, an action that is imperceptible to most unless you are really looking. In unison the pair turn their gaze and Olivia shifts nervously on her feet. The girl's wide aqua-blue eyes meet Olivia's with suspicion and a surprising amount of fierceness.

"Elizabeth, this is Olivia– she's the Fury who has been helping me."

"You mean the Fury that you have been helping and risking your life for?" Elizabeth interjects with a minute tremble as she battles the bitterness that reflects in her eyes.

"Finding Moss is important–he can't be allowed to walk after what he did to our father." There is the familiar stubborn set to his chin that Olivia has come to recognize.

"And what if you end up like him? Dead? What will that accomplish?" A hint of moisture gathers in her soft eyes.

"Death waits for us every day and while I do not embrace it as a lover, I will not run from it either. We can only try to leave this world in a better place and do what is right. This is my choice–to make this world safer for you and others."

"You are fine with this?" Elizabeth turns her glare, pinning Olivia with the question. Not waiting for an answer, she nods as she folds her arms over her chest. "Of course, you're alright with this. Your kind lives for vengeance–when it suits you." The scornful anguish in her tone is nearly too much and Olivia fights to maintain eye contact.

"Elizabeth," Bray scolds. "One day I will die but trust me, it will not be at the hands of a piece of shit like Moss." She starts to argue as Olivia steps forward.

"Listen." She struggles for the right words. "As I am sure you are aware, your brother, while extremely brave, is also a bit bullheaded. If we had forbade him from pursuing Moss, do you think he would have obeyed?"

Elizabeth's gaze fretfully shifts between them for a second before she shakes her head in response. "Believe me when I say that losing more innocent lives is never our goal." Olivia is uncertain if she has convinced or reassured her as Elizabeth's demeanor remains unchanged.

"I'll leave you two alone for a few minutes." She stands with a stiff spine and walks to the door. "I'll be just down stairs if you need me. We'll all be downstairs and you only need to call on us." Elizabeth's severe gaze falters for an instant before she disappears through the doorway. Olivia strains her ears as she tries to follow the sound of Elizabeth's soft footfalls descending the stairs.

"Give me a few minutes and I'll be ready to go." The bullet wounds may be healed, but his skin is still very pale and his movements have a forced ease to them.

"I think you should stay here."

"Wait, what do you mean?" His brows furrow and the tilt to his head highlights the sheen of perspiration that coats his skin.

"Going back into the Hallow to get Mei Li and Emma is going to be dangerous."

"Yes, and all the more reason for me to go with you."

"You have to understand the position that I am in. Even if we survive, if anything happens to you, your family will view us as treacherous enemies."

"My family is my responsibility, but I will do what I know is right. Some of them will understand that and some of them won't, but that's my issue to deal with, not yours."

"This is just asinine." She throws her hands up. "Do you realize how crazy you sound?"

"Perhaps." He shrugs softly with a knowing smile touching his lips. "But if you leave here without me, I'll just follow you to the Hallow anyway."

"Maybe you remember how to get in there, but I highly doubt that you will know how to get around. You'll be lost in five minutes with all of the caverns and dead ends." She smirks with a nod.

"Not true."

"How do you figure?"

"So far I've successfully snuck in there twice, and both times I got to exactly where I needed to be. Do you think that was just by dumb luck?"

"You know I was actually wondering how you managed to find your way in that night with Thanatos," she asks, folding her arms over her chest.

"Easy–Aidan. He's a smart guy with a big heart, so it didn't take any arm-twisting to get him to help."

"So, you felt it was okay to endanger him as well?"

"Not endanger," he parrots back. "He is quite capable of handling himself. And when he found out why we needed to go, there wasn't much that would stop him. We needed his assistance and he wanted to go."

"I'm not going to be able to make you see reason here, am I?" Olivia huffs, slapping her thighs.

"No."

"Okay, fine," she huffs, blowing out a breath of air, silently scolding herself for not leaving as soon as the wolves had brought him inside. "But just so we understand each other, you coming means that you are taking on the risk. If you are injured or worse, that is on you. I'm heading downstairs and hopefully won't end up as a chew toy. You have five minutes, then I'm leaving." Bray nods as she turns, walking out of the room.

Overlooking the living area below, most of the pack members have left, but she highly doubts that they are very far off. As she's about to reach the base of the stairs a large man steps in front of her, blocking the path.

"What is she still doing here?" His beer-touched breath tickles her skin yet his focus is aimed at Isaac. Artic-blue eyes that are nearly hidden under the tufts of his bushy brows glare down at her. The veiled image of a neck tattoo peeks out from the shaggy length of his beard, and his dirty-blond hair is pulled back tautly in a ponytail. Every detail of his appearance is tailored to incite either fear or respect.

"Ease up, Blake," Isaac warns as his golden eyes flash with a restrained feral energy.

"Her kind is nothing but trouble, and she endangers us all by being here."

"That may be the case, but she is our guest." Isaac's tone is clipped with an understated anger that is just below the surface.

"She's your and Bray's guest, not mine, and I don't want her here." Blake steps forward, his massive body nearly brushing up against her. Olivia tenses but never averts her gaze as she prepares for the impending conflict. This isn't the first time she's squared off against a werewolf, but experience will only get you so far and taking them lightly will get you killed.

"Blake, stand down," Isaac orders.

"No." The tall man argues but is cut off by the low growl that rolls through the room. Each of the wolves seem to shrink back as the warning touches on some primal instinct to beware. Even Olivia isn't immune to its effect, and she allows her eyes to flick over to Isaac as he strides to them.

"Test me again and you'll get a worse ass-beating than the last one." Standing nearly nose to nose with Blake, he is deathly serious as he lifts a brow, emphasizing his point. Blake stares back but seems to falter in his resolve, and after several seconds his eyes dart away as he retreats. The few wolves that linger about the room also look elsewhere as if they too are leery of making eye contact.

"I apologize for that. We all get a little more on edge around the full moon."

"I didn't think it was a full moon tonight." Instinctively Olivia turns her eyes to the nearest window.

"Four more days, but we'll feel its pull for a time beforehand."

"Sounds like I'm missing all the excitement," Bray announces from the top of the stairs. He smiles widely but it doesn't touch his eyes as he surveys the room. He has changed into a clean white t-shirt, and Olivia silently prays the shirt will be just as clean by the end of the night and they'll survive what's to come.

Chapter 26

"Emma, wake up," the vaguely recognizable voice squeaks with urgency. The hurried nature of its tone yanks her from the dreamless slumber. Musty linens press against her face, besetting her senses with a long-settled stench of stagnant death as she wrenches open her heavy eye lids. Shifting her position, she has only seconds to orient herself before the agony that beats her body hits with a full force and her eyes snap open. Gulping a lungful of stale air, she bites back the urge to groan. Her back is a scorched expanse of razor cuts that stretches its fingers down her arms and legs. Each breath only adds to the pain as she weakly tries to lift herself. Through the waves of nausea and uncontrollable tremors, she manages to swing her feet onto the earthen floor.

Her vision wavers, and darkness lines the edge of her peripheral vision as it threatens to pull her back under. As she clutches the edge of the flimsy cot Emma focuses on the tempo of her own breathing, trying to slow the

careening scene around her. When the vertigo
eases, she rolls her head to the side, gingerly
testing the waters of what her body will
tolerate. Ragged claw marks that score her
arms burn as the skin sutures itself closed.
The process is slow, and every movement
draws her attention with a keen awareness.
Prickling anxiety hums through her as she
realizes that her senses are inhibited, with
thoughts and actions slowed and even her
connection to the source weakened. In spite
of the haze she can tell that she is still
underground. A distant sound of flowing
water through the rocks leads her to believe
there may be a subterranean river nearby.

Letting her gaze roam, she spots the thick
iron bars that enclose her on three sides. She
is locked in a cell devoid of any furnishings
save for a cot and a single hanging light that is
carved into the stone ceiling. Two rows of
identical cells run the length of this faintly lit
corridor and an empty darkness swallows the
view to each end. Her breath jumps as her
eyes settle on Mei Li in the prison cell across
the hall. Mei Li's hair is disheveled and her
dress is muddy as she stares despondently at
Emma. Even against the scarce lighting, she

spies the dried blood that trails the length of
Mei Li's face. An icy chill zips along her skin
as she catches the flash of metal, and light
glints from the copper collar that encircles
Mei Li's neck. Her hand reflexively darts to
her own throat, finding the warm metal. The
copper tingles and stings as her fingertips
brush against the smooth surface. Before the
panic can set in, the small figure sharing the
confines of Mei Li's cage pulls her attention.
For a brief second Emma doesn't recognize
the young boy, but his soft brown hair and
eyes call to her. Astonishingly, Aaron has
continued to age even from this morning. He
was perhaps six or so the last time she had
seen him; now he is maybe a year or so older.

"Emma, are you okay?" Aaron asks as he
clutches the bars to his cage. Examining him
closely seems impossible, given the
predicament they are in. She notices the dirt
smudging his cheeks but other than that, he is
reasonably unharmed, and with a forced sigh
she allows the breath to leave her tightened
lungs.

"I'm alright." Emma muffles a cry as she
stands, limping over to the cell door. "What's

happened?" she grimaces as every movement
seems to test her pain tolerance and even her
clothes are a scratchy torture device. The pain
will subside–it usually does.

"They ambushed me after I went to get
Aaron." Mei Li's eyes flicker with a pained
expression before her normal stoicism
returns. "What about Olivia? Where is she?"

"Bray was injured, but they got away."

Mei Li nods her head weakly; her rigid form
slackens a bit as she reclines against the stone
wall. "At least one of us is still out there but
we shouldn't wait for her to find us. If we can,
we should find a way to secure an escape on
our own."

"Where are we, exactly?" Emma rests her
forehead against the cold bar, trying to block
out all other sensation aside from the cool
metal. Glancing through the bars, she
confirms that the pathways running right and
left, only allowing vision for ten feet or so
before the cloak of darkness engulfs them.

"We are somewhere in Erebus–that's all I
know. It's hard to say more than that as

everything seems so… muted." Mei Li scans the room with wide eyes and a subtle tremor shakes her hands. Perhaps this is the first time Mei Li has had to endure the copper chains.

"It's an unsettling process, but you'll be able to adjust to it." Emma nods as she tries her best to reassure Mei Li.

Her muscles tighten reflexively as she more or less feels the metal gate, buried within the murky gloom of the corridor, open before hearing it. Locking eyes with Mei Li, she strains her ears to detect the approach of sound. The swish of fabric echoes through the confines of the hall, ratcheting up Emma's heart rate. In a staggering feat to calm her nerves, she draws in a deep lungful of breath and encounters the fragrance of a field in the spring. A vaguely perceptible breeze brushes around them, churning along with it the understated scent of primrose and hyacinths.

Nina's pale-red hair flashes as she steps under the light. The potency of her aura bellows outward, pushing down the length of the corridor before her. There is a rare coolness that radiates from her being as she seems to glide effortlessly. Which is rather opposite to what rumbles through Emma, and she silently curses herself each time she jerks due to a wayward noise. The muted crinkle of a bag resonates as it sways along with each of her steps. Stopping in front of them, her head dips and angles as she surveys Emma for a scant moment. Her burnt-auburn eyes gleam with a well-trained intensity, a feral wisdom.

"I'm glad to see that you are all awake. I brought you something to eat." Nina's hands slip into the open bag, pulling out a crimson apple. "There was quite a bit of food upstairs but I wasn't sure if you had a preference, so I brought some fruit."

"If your plan is to kill us, why feed us?" Emma squeezes the bars, trying to still the quiver racing through her limbs.

"My intent was only to simply bring you food," Nina answers coolly as she offers the fruit to Aaron. His hungry eyes flitter between the apple and Emma. "I would suggest eating it quickly before someone comes down." A flash of apprehension touches her eyes, yet Emma can't decern if it is malice. With a subtle nod from Emma, Aaron reaches through the bars and gingerly takes the apple.

485

"Thank you," he whispers as he holds it up to his mouth. Emma takes an offered orange, holding it up to her own nose. The aromatic smell of citrus makes her mouth water, but she can't detect anything of note beyond that. How rarely are things what they appear to be, but perhaps an orange is just an orange.

"Where is Chen? I want to talk to my son," Mei Li asks as she takes a second apple from Aaron.

"My master is attending to some business but will be down shortly." Nina folds the bag with an unusual care before placing it in her pocket.

"Your master?" Emma asks, cocking her head as she studies the other woman keenly.

"Yes. As you have dedicated your life to the Fury, I have dedicated mine to serving Chen."

"That comparison is debatable and while I am part of the Fury, I have no love for them." Emma inhales sharply as she struggles to keep the venom from her tone. "Our place in this world is to see to the greater good, while Chen's purpose is only to destroy." Pangs of guilt gnaw at her insides, but thankfully she can train her gaze on Nina, avoiding meeting eyes with Mei Li.

"His goals are his own; mine are simply to see that his desires are achieved."

"That may be the case but you must still take responsibility for your choices and the lives you have ruined." Emma tamps down the sudden rush of emotion that sizzles her skin; it urges her to use her power and punishes her with it as well.

"I do regret the pain that the loss of your lover has caused you, but I will do as I must to bring my master success."

"You are a fool for loving him." Emma turns to her coldly.

"It goes much further than love. I owe him my life."

"And is this debt worth ending yourself? I've seen that you have a good heart, but seeing this through will only serve to destroy you."

"I was nothing before Chen. He has given me purpose and without that, I will return to the nothingness. As it is, I am not much longer for this world and while I can, I will not fail him."

"You are not just a tool for him to use." Emma presses against the iron bars as the words touch on a deeply buried wound.

"But I am." A sorrow touches her warm eyes. "When Chen found me, I was held captive, owned by a group of marauders. They were men with no honor who only saw value in the things they could steal and the lives they took. The thieves happened upon my den when I was a mere kit." The light seems to fade in her eyes as she stares off into the darkness. "They slaughtered my brothers and sisters before they realized what we were, thinking of us only as their next meal. Perhaps one of them was keen enough to see my true nature and as a magical child I became their pet, a means to increase their possessions and power. No amount of time will wash away the memories of villagers burning in their homes as I held them in place. Their cries haunt my dreams each night and it's a meager atonement for my failing them. But then fate brought Chen into my life; he became my gift and savior. So I will do all that is within my power to be of use to him, even if that means giving up what little life I have left."

"And that will be your ruin." Calder's voice rings out from the darkness, and Nina's posture stiffens as subdued footfalls pad toward them. The fae moves with an infuriating stealth, and a flash of white reflects from Calder's glasses as he steps out under the lights. "Has it occurred to you that even your paltry talent is wasted on the likes of him? I've seen Chen's type before; outside is a guise of stoicism but underneath he is controlled by his emotions. And I'll admit that he has lofty goals, thinking he will reclaim his home. The problem is that in the end he is simply weak. His arrogance will be his downfall and yours as well." Folding his arms over his chest, he leans against the bars of an empty cell.

"You know nothing about my master." Nina's tone is heated but her stare remains locked on an unseen point.

"Don't I? The world in which we live is built and maintained on the backs of his ilk. In the end we all serve a master; the difference is that when mine returns, I will stand by his side. Chen's place has always been to serve others stronger than he, but you are too foolhardy to realize that and he will, without difficulty, toss you aside when the time comes. Even a resource such as yourself is simply a bargaining chip and expendable in the end."

"What do you mean bargaining chip?" Mei Li asks, her white knuckles pressed into fists as she shifts to the end of the cot.

"It's quite simple." Calder turns, pushing up the rim of his glasses with a bony finger. "In exchange for funding and men, Chen has agreed to provide his particular skill set for this job. Additionally, I have garnered another trade that I believe will benefit us both."

"What is that?" Emma's mouth is parched, making her swallow hard, and thousands of frozen ants, scurry along her skin while an unsettling energy pulses through the air.

"A reasonably fair exchange, Alba for Nina," he answers so nonchalantly that for a brief moment Emma isn't sure if she heard him correctly. Nina's eyes snap to him. "Alba will serve him perfectly, providing the means for him to get all that he wants."

"Why?" Nina's voice wavers.

"Because I can. You dared to insult me and for that I will see you burn." Calder looms in the confined space, forcing Nina to step back.

"You are a repulsive piece of garbage." Emma clutches the bars as wisps of smoke rise from the bands around her neck and arms. "The lowest form of life, who kills for a perceived slight."

"No, not a perceived slight. I've worked too fucking hard to be disrespected by some mongrel beast." His voice hitches to a roaring level and his nostrils flare, but within a moment he pauses, breathing as he reins in his emotion. "Perhaps when we are done this little task here, I won't kill her." His tone is now flippant. "Maybe I'll send her to be one of the new pigs in my brothel. She'll fetch a good price—at least at first."

"Killing is just a task to you isn't it? A box to be checked off?" Emma sneers.

"Well, not necessarily a task per se, but in this case, it is certainly a pleasurable one. You've cost me a lot of money."

"Yet you only have two of us." Emma lets a smirk touch her lips. "Kill us and Olivia will come for you; there will be nowhere you can hide." A chill coats her skin as his lips turn in a sickening smile. He leans forward, staying out of arm's reach, searing her with his deadly, cold eyes.

"I'm counting on it, and I only need one of you bitches for this to work." Calder steps toward her and Emma's hands itch to reach out for his throat.

"For what?"

"Calder," Chen barks from behind, his staccato voice cutting through the silence. "They will be dead soon, so there's no point in telling them about events they'll never see. A word in private, if you please." Chen's gruff tone is barely veiled despite his formalities. For a few terrifying seconds Calder maintains his icy stare that lasers them before he turns, meeting Chen several yards down the hall.

"Emma, I wanted to ask you a favor?" Nina lowers her voice as she nears the cell.

"Are you seriously asking for a favor at this point?" Emma allows the bewilderment to ooze through her tone. Nina watches her with large, fragile eyes. "Requesting something from someone you are about to kill is a little absurd, but hey, why not? What is this favor?"

"You are broken and bound and the likelihood that you will survive this encounter is not very promising. Even if your third could make it here in time, she wouldn't be able to save you, and over the centuries, I have learned it is best to not leave important items to chance."

"If you were concerned about failing, then why wait to kill us? You could have easily killed me up in the great hall."

"Truth be told, I had advised Chen to do just that, but it was not his desire." Her gaze breaks from Emma, darting over to Chen and Calder, who are still in the midst of their conversation. "My concern is for Logan."

"Your cat? Why? What do you think I can do?"

"When this is over, I will not be able to care for him or take him with me. He will be alone again and in need of protection." Her auburn eyes glisten. "Please tell me that you know of someone who will take him and care for him." Nina clasps Emma's hands over the bars, and the violet jewel around her neck pulses faintly.

"Where is he now?"

"The apartment we are renting."

The overwhelming exhaustion and hollowness weighs on Emma and she can only manage a subdued nod.

"Find Aidan, tell him that I'm asking him to do this and that if he does this, I'll forgive his indiscretion. And tell him I'm sorry for how I treated him; he didn't deserve that." Emma blinks away a pained tear as Nina squeezes her hand lightly before backing away. Calder and Chen approach and the air hangs over them with a palpable weight.

"Give me a moment with my mother." Chen's stoic tone echoes as his dark stare penetrates the shadows that swathe Mei Li's cell. Without a word Nina and Calder retreat, letting the dark corners of the corridor obscure their forms. The darkness is impermeable, lending to the sense of isolation. Mei Li steps forward gingerly as she pulls Aaron away from the door, her hands holding firmly onto his shoulders.

"Well Mother, have you nothing to say?" His chin lifts as he stares down at her and his listless eyes are void of any emotion. "No sage advice? Are you not disappointed in the monster that I have become? The beast you made?"

"I hold no responsibility for your actions or decisions." Mei Li's voice is low yet there is the familiar poise in her tone.

"Is that what you tell yourself? That your actions hold no consequences? When you walked away, letting everyone believe that you were dead, you set into motion a chain of events that has led us to this moment."

"I did die," Mei Li balks.

"And yet here you stand, looking the same as the day you left."

"You have to know that I could not have taken you with me; your grandmother and father would have never allowed it."

"You are wrong—he is the one who sent me away." His voice breaks as he slams a fist into the bars. The grate shudders as bits of debris dust the air.

"No." Mei Li whispers with a shake of her head. "Why? How?" Light shines from the unshed tears that edge her eyes.

"Do you honestly believe he was the same after you died? He searched for you for years at a time, then he brought in an unending line of new mothers and concubines, each of them more insipid than the next and all of them failing to fill the hole in his black heart." Chen steps forward, nearly pressing against the bars. "And when replacing you didn't work, he decided to erase you. I was foolish enough to believe that I could help him, that I was still his son, but I realized that the mere sight of me caused him such great pain that I was only a wretched burden to him. Near the end, there would never be enough drunken beatings to stave off his grief, and that is when he sent me away."

"To where?"

"To a relative that wasn't there, in a village that never existed." The flush of emotion boiling within him seeps away, leaving the cold shell behind.

"I am sorry, Chen. If I had known…"

"Don't. Your meaningless apologies will not change the past nor will they alter the future. The Fury took everything I had and now I will erase every last trace of them."

"Chen, do not do this. I know I cannot make this right but let me try."

"There is no point." Chen turns to leave. "I want nothing from you, I need nothing from you."

"What will you do with Aaron? He is innocent in this," Mei Li pleads with a ragged breath, and her body shakes uncontrollably. Chen tilts his gaze toward her, watching for several seconds.

"The boy will be unharmed, but he will remain with Calder."

"You can't let him..."

"I'm done talking." Chen yanks the amulet from his pocket as the corridor echoes with the terrifying ring of clicks and chatter.

Chapter 27

The desiccated air hugs Olivia's skin as she and Bray snake their way through a twisting bend in the cavern. Soft shadows pulse along the surfaces, a wayward light meagerly cast off by twisted root sconces. The occasional scuff of their footsteps or an errant rock that skitters across the stone floor careen her nerves into overdrive. Traversing the darkened passageways under normal circumstances is daunting; now, the ominous aura is stifling.

Receiving a small pulse of power, her bloodhound snakes writhe and glow brightly as their tongues flick at the air. The fragile bond she has with Mei Li and Emma guides their direction, leading them dangerously lower into the depths of Erebus. Bray's hand clasps her arm, bringing her to a stop as he stiffens with a tense energy. Touching a finger to his lips, he turns his head as he listens to a sound that her own hearing can't register.

"What?" she mouths to him.

"Something's down that hall." His voice is a low whisper; he bristles as a muscle ticks in his cheek.

"What do you mean, something?"

"Not a human but not an animal." Bray inhales deeply as his nostrils flair, scenting the air. "Reminds me of a fae, but it's different–natural, but not."

An electric throb flutters along her skin, and her vision blurs. She scans the length of the hall, and everything along the periphery of the path obscures as it morphs into a pitch-black tunnel. A singular point of light wavers in the distance–the only tangible anchor in this incorporeal haze. The small beacon shines through a shrouded doorway; all else around it is indiscernible.

"I don't like this." Despite the murky darkness Olivia can detect the understated tremor that shakes Bray's form.

"Neither do I."

"Can we go back?" His head turns amid the unwavering darkness.

"Possibly, but this is the only way I know for certain."

"So, it's either go in there"–he nods down the hall before them– "or turn around and probably get lost."

"That pretty much sums it up." Olivia exhales the stagnant air that seems to permeate her core.

One of her snakes hisses a crass warning and she turns just as a huge, clawed arm sweeps toward her. Darting to the side, she barely escapes as jagged talons bite into the skin of her back. Her battered bones are mending yet they scream against the jarring movement. Warm blood seeps down her sides, soaking into the fabric of her shirt as Bray grabs her shoulders and pushes her down the path. Several arms branch out, cresting the darkness and swiping at them from the shadows. The disembodied limbs strike out from the gloom with a frantic urgency, narrowing their path. Olivia blinks back the tears of pain as her flesh works vigorously to mend itself.

High-pitched screeching surrounds them and the spark of metallic nails scraping against the walls propels them toward the end of the hall. Her heart pounds, and she knows that they are being corralled, yet there are no other options readily available–her mind races as the mud and stone walls fly by. As they reach the doorway, they are stopped by the jarring silence from behind them; the chaotic sounds of their pursuers cease. Olivia senses their presence in the abyss, standing outside of the fragile glow of light. Her skin itches as she scans this unseen, yet living, barrier across their path backward. Only their battered breaths echo against the ominous void as Bray risks a tentative step into the gloom. Before he can even crest the darkness, he leaps back, sidestepping the two clawed appendages that jut out toward him before slipping away.

"Any ideas?" Bray asks, watching the gloom and retreating to the door.

"Forward may be the only way to go."

Chancing a backward glance, Olivia studies the room as light from an unknown source flares, pulsing feeble illumination into the area. A single open archway lies across the circular chamber and long, carved-stone panels span from floor to ceiling as they rim

the walls of the decagonal space. There is
nothing in the room save for dust, yet the
ominous air rises a fear of moving forward.
The push of frenzied evil from behind licks at
their backs, pressing them farther into the
room.

"I really don't like this, but we have to move."
A trickle of blood flows from the fresh gash
on Bray's cheek as he lightly touches her arm.

With shoulders touching, they step over the
threshold. The crackle of energy flows
through the room, a subtle hum that saturates
every cell in their bodies. Her jelly legs move
slowly as they carry her over the square slabs
of the stone floor. Measuring each step, she
scans the area for any possible pitfall, but the
space seems too quiet –unnaturally so.
Running along the outer perimeter they reach
the midpoint of the circular room as a
frightening click breaks the silence. Hefty
stone slabs unlatch from a compartment
above each doorway, quickly falling to bar
their exit. Miniature plumes of dust swirl as
the barriers slam into place.

"Shit, shit, shit." Bray curses as he rushes to
the blocked door and searches fervently for

some kind of hold. For a brief moment they are surrounded by a hollow silence, each sound echoing back against them. The scrape of Bray's calloused hands against the smooth stone is unnerving, and Olivia steadies her breathing as she scours the room for any weak points. The segments of stone wall that surround them shimmer and fluctuate, thrumming with an unnatural flow of energy. The material shifts rapidly through varying hues of grey in an almost hypnotic pulse. As it finally settles the mineral has taken on a brilliant, mirrored sheen. In each panel Olivia spies a perfect reflection of themselves. Seven of the mirrors reflect back an impossible number of clones, each of them moving in sync with her own movements, save one.

Olivia flies back instinctively as a cloaked figure leaps from the still mirror.

The stranger's form seems veiled in smoke, yet despite the deceptive blur Olivia catches a glimpse of its grey skin and silver hair. The thing lunges at her, wielding a sharply curved dagger that cuts through the air inches from her. Before she can counter, it steps back, sliding behind the smooth surface of the mirror.

"Drow," Bray's throaty growl resonates against the walls and glass.

"Have you ever faced one before?" Olivia asks as she keeps her gaze focused on the assassin.

"Nope."

"Wonderful." Reaching up under the back of her shirt her fingers come away, still tacky with her own blood.

The hooded man's violet eyes are unyielding as he shifts effortlessly from one panel to the next, circling them. He prowls around with a heady power that beats along her skin. Unblinking, he tilts his head to the side and taps on his side of the mirror; "Bleed." The hoarse word is scarcely a whisper from his lips but all of the mirrors are set into motion as they shimmer into a semi-liquid state and dozens of fluid shards emerge from the glass surface. With seconds to react, Olivia flicks her wrist, drawing out a machete as hundreds of needle-sharp spears are loosed from the mirrors. Bray yanks them to the ground as the missiles collide and intersect over their heads. Lying prone, they dodge the mass of shattering glass, but the sharp pain in Olivia's legs and back lets her know that a few found their mark.

Bray is partially shifted before he leaps to his feet, a thick mat of golden fur ripping through his skin and strips of his white shirt fluttering to the ground. The pelt catches the light and he rears back with a feral roar. Olivia breathes heavily, pulling herself up as their attacker springs from the glass. Bray swings wildly with massive claws, but the assassin deftly evades each attack. Darting away with a striking agility, he spins and his slash catches Bray's ribs but he pivots, charging again.

The assassin dips, sidestepping around her, but she sees the movement and brings her weapon around. Relying on decades of training, she shifts her stance, mirroring his to keep their range as she slashes with her own blade. Metal bites into metal, and for a split second they stare each other down. With a firm push he skitters away and Bray comes barreling forward, teeth and claws bared yet he melts back into the reflection.

His cloak flares with an ethereal current and the surface of the mirrors shimmer yet again. Olivia strains her vision, forcing her eyes to remain focused on him as his reflection splits in two. The dual images step away from each other, crossing the panels in perfect sync. The spectral twins stand across from one another for a beat before leaping from the surface, each one attacking a different opponent. Olivia and Bray shift to the outside of the room, endeavoring to use the cramped space available.

Olivia's assassin leaps toward her, slicing with his dagger. With a flick of her wrist, she deflects the strike but is staggered as the kick that follows collides with her midsection. Her opponent advances, striking with an inhuman speed, and for each of her parries he seems to have another one on deck. Each staccato attack carries a surprising amount of punch and lends no opening for the counteroffensive. Sweat glides down her back, burning the fresh wounds, yet she tries to maintain even breaths.

For a fraction of a second, she senses a sudden tightness in him as Bray tosses his counterpart against a mirrored wall. The glass wobbles and flexes and it surely would have shattered if the hit hadn't landed firmly on the seam between two panels. Heartbeat sprinting at a furious tempo, she seizes on his momentary lapse and dashes forward, spearing the sharp edge of the machete through his abdomen. A haggard breath catches in her throat as the blade passes weightlessly through his torso as if it were air. Jumping away, Olivia briefly notes there is not a speck of blood on her weapon nor on him as he swarms her again.

The jarring clang of metal sings as their weapons skim off of each other. Her exasperated breath rushes out as she shakes herself, certain that her blade made contact with him. Yet there is no sign of blood; even against the black of his clothing there should be something. He lunges at her, closing the distance between them, pushing her so that her heel clips the mirror. With a palm against the glass, she guides herself to the side as he comes to a quick stop. His deadly gaze lasers her as his thin lips lift into a malicious smirk and he beckons her forward, taunting her. The hard wrapping of the machete's handle bites into her hand as she readjusts her grip, and her mind focuses on finding any kind of weakness. How to slay a monster that cannot be cut? Are they simply illusions?

She chances a peek toward Bray, only to find that he seems to be in a similar situation. Thick blood drips from the bristly fur on Bray's back as he relies on brute force to bypass his opponent's defenses. With dagger-sharp claws and teeth he fruitlessly swipes at the apparition, only to be on the receiving end of some very real punishment. If they don't do something quickly, neither she nor Bray will make it out of here alive.

Olivia's eyes narrow as they shift back to her own foe and her own problems. She catches the glint of the copper blade as he flashes in front of her, flicking faster than her vision can follow. Instinct takes over as the knife arcs toward her, dropping her weapon to secure his arm. She stops the momentum of his attack just as the tip of the blade breaks the skin below her collarbone. Her muscles clench as the hot blood trickles down her chest. With a height and weight advantage he captures one of her wrists as he pushes her back against the cool, mirrored surface.

As she struggles to hold the blade at bay, a thick growl draws her attention; Bray grasps his adversary with two meaty claws and tosses him haphazardly across the confined space. Movement slows and the illusory assassin flails his limbs as he tries to right himself midflight. Just as he makes contact with the glass, his form is seamlessly absorbed with a small ripple into the surface. The reflected image throws back its head and croaks as it laughs, fists planted on his hips, and the sound echoes around them. Bray throws out his arms as a ferocious growling howl erupts from him, and he bounds toward his foe. A fist strikes the mirror, sending shards of glass cascading down.

The grip on Olivia slackens and she looks up at the contorted face of the drow as a thin line of blood seeps from a slash across his cheek. Rage and fear light his violet eyes as she battles against his hold. Feeling a real sense of urgency, she uses the heel of her boot to kick backward, making solid contact with the panel. As the glass clatters and smashes to the ground the drow staggers, weakened legs shaking as a wide path of red blooms through the fabric of his shirt.

Scooping up the machete, she smashes the next panel and is met with a wretched bellow from her foe. "Bray, break the mirrors," Olivia orders as she clubs another section of looking glass. An oddly placed smile curls Bray's lips as he makes quick work of the panes around him. As each fragmented mirror falls away the drow reels, a fresh gash erupting across his flesh. The cacophony of shattered glass is accompanied by a shrill yelp as he falls to the ground, pulling the cloak over him as if to shield himself from the damage. With only one panel remaining, the drow's huddled form shrinks under his once-flowing mantle. Bray cautiously hovers over the shrinking form as uncertainty flashes in his eyes. She smashes the machete through the glass with all of the strength in her. An intoxicating relief washes over her as she watches the shriveled mass dissipate and the linen flattens out.

Light floods through the open doorway, and she must shield her eyes from the glare. The bolt of energy hits her with a blinding force, and her feet slip from under her and she is tossed into the room. She skims across the floor, rolling and skidding to a stop. Her seizing lungs struggle for breath through the bloom of pain. Her body screams at her but she weakly clambers to her feet. Clutching her chest, she watches the doorway while a robed figure enters. Olivia's eyes narrow on the wispy woman gliding forward, her feet dangling above the ground. A wild mane of white hair blusters about from a mysterious gale that touches nothing else. The stranger's fiery-crimson eyes glare at them with unbridled rage. An aura of magic swirls around her while tiny flicks of electricity arc between her splayed fingertips and dance light across her charcoal skin.

Bray's large, clawed hand snatches her by the throat and the sorceress' legs flail out in front of her. A croaking screech gurgles from her lips when talon-claws dig into the skin of her neck. Her small hands pull at the fur-laden clamp that locks her in place. The unseen force that holds her magically off of the floor slackens, and her full weight sinks into Bray's hand. A bloody gasp explodes from her open mouth as the tender flesh of her throat tears away. With a flick of Bray's wrist, a gush of viscous fluid surges from her neck and her lifeless body plops to the ground.

Dropping the chunk of ragged flesh the wolf lifts his focused eyes to Olivia's. Beneath the monstrous form Bray is there, staring back at her knowingly. He steps forward only to halt and cock his head to the side as he listens. Olivia strains her own ears as a barely audible sound drifts down the halls.

Chapter 28

The iron shackles bite into Emma's wrists and while it is a nagging irritant, it is the combination of the collar and her own armbands that leaves her weakened and scarcely able to lift her head. Focusing on the chill of the stone floor is the only thing that helps her to stay conscious. She shifts with a pained wince, from one cheek to the other as her legs and toes tingle with pins and needles. Each time, she has to work around her arms and the handcuffs that are strung through a hooped spike in the floor. Mei Li mirrors her stance as they rest against the wall, both choosing to remain silent since being hauled in.

As much as she tries to avoid it, her gaze keeps being drawn to the macabre devices that surround them: Tables with wooden gears strung tightly with rope and racks that are blackened from years of being awash with blood. Various tools for torture hang from the adjacent walls—clubs, pliers, and chains are tarnished as a flail shifts subtly in an unseen breeze. The rusted set of keys they used to secure their manacles taunts her from its far perch on one of the tables. She forces her attention toward Aaron, who sits apart from the others. The poor boy shifts nervously, his fretful eyes scanning the room as he clutches onto his seat. Emma wishes he were closer so she could offer some comfort but there is nothing she can do for him in this state.

"Aaron." Her voice is raspy, fighting past the aridness of her throat. "Aaron, look at me." She waits for him to combat his distress enough to meet her gaze. "If either Mei Li or I tell you to run, then just run and don't stop for anything."

"What about you?" His gentle eyes rim with moisture. Such a resilience in the boy, but there is no way he should be forced to watch them die. A coiled apprehension clamps down on her insides as she meets his kind eyes.

"No matter what happens to us, just remember that it will be okay. But if you can get away…"

The swift kick from Moss catches her thigh and jostles her with a start. "Wake up," his half bark and laugh grates her nerves. "You're gonna want to be awake for this. It's about to get interesting." There is a cold spark in his eyes as he stares down the length of his nose at her. Looking past Moss, she focuses on the group standing a distance away.

Ever since the chorus of screeches began echoing from the darkened corridor, everyone's attention has been glued on the doorway. Worse even has been the agonizing silence that followed. She can barely sense Olivia's presence at the outer fringes of her mind, but it's a frail line of hope, sparking as the connection grows stronger.

Chen stands between them and the door as he listens closely, his shadowed eyes surveying the room. There is a cold indifference that he casually exudes, an unflappable air about him. Nina shadows his movements as a morose expression touches her features. There is a stark contrast between Calder and his flock of men and Chen. With minimal effort Emma can detect their racing pulses and nervous energy as they pace about tensely. More than a dozen fae bodyguards prowl like a pack of hyenas waiting to steal a fresh kill. Despite their greater numbers, Calder and his men aren't the largest threat in the room. Her stomach drops each time she catches the jittery movement of the four faceless that dip in and out of the shadows. Their sporadic clicks echo off the walls of the open room. She jerks against her bonds as the sounds of shattering glass and the accompanying anguished wail reaches them.

"Get out there," Calder commands. "Kill the wolf and bring me the last Fury." A small group of men scurry out the door and Moss turns, following them out. "Where are you going?" Calder calls out, his face contorted in a flabbergasted expression.

Moss only pauses for a second as he turns back. He addresses Calder yet looks past him, peering directly at Emma as a grin lifts his lip. "I'm gonna kill a fucking wolf." There is a pure evil reflected back in his lifeless eyes as he walks, chuckling as he shuts the door.

The devastating silence hammers Emma's ears as she struggles to capture any hint of sound. Time seems to pass at an agonizing pace as the seconds spread into minutes, and her breath is labored. Her muscles wrench painfully as a large weight slams against the opposite side of the door and the old wood groans from the force. Grunts and yelling are stifled as they are hampered through the barrier. Seconds pass at an arduous pace as Emma's ears are flooded by the solid thump of her own heartbeat. Another hefty force hits the door, and despite the oak flexing, a massive crack appears, running its length. Flakes of wood fall away as the door is rapidly rammed from the outside. The fracture widens and gives as the door splits down the center and one-half slams to the floor with an ear-piercing thwack.

A hulking werewolf crests the threshold, obscured by the blizzard of dust that wafts through the air. Tiny particles of dust settle in the golden fur that is splattered with blood. Bray strides into the space with a clear purpose, his long-fingered claws clutching the face of the lifeless fae as he drags him into the room. The back of the guard's head is a shattered mess, with bits of bone and wood showing through the fractured skull.

Bray's throaty growl rolls through the air as viscera and spittle drip from his pointed fangs.

His dark feral eyes pin the individuals in the room and as he shifts to the side Emma spots Olivia stepping in. Olivia studies the group with an eerie calm as a slender ribbon of blood trickles from her brow line. The blade of her machete sheens with a red gore.

"If I'd known you were planning a shindig I would have put on my glad rags." Readjusting her grip on her blade, she weighs the group, locking eyes with each one.

With everyone's focus drawn, Emma motions to Aaron, beckoning him over. At first, he is tentative, but after collecting his courage he tiptoes over, silently crossing the distance. "I need you to help get these off of us," she whispers, holding up the shackles. "Then you need to run as fast as you can."

"Okay." He nods quickly, his eyes darting around the room. She feels the tremors shaking his form and her heart aches for him, wanting nothing more than to ease his fears— but there is no time for that right now.

"Go and grab that key on the table. Bring it here." Emma gestures as Aaron crouches, hugging the row of tables. He reaches the key just as Emma spots that Nina is watching him as well. Her breath breaks in her chest as Nina's sideways glance follows the boy for a second. She fights back the urge to scream, knowing that this is going to end badly. Yet Nina makes no move to warn the others as her gaze sweeps back to the fighting before her. A strangled breath escapes Emma as Aaron turns back to them.

"Kill the wolf," Calder shouts, jabbing a pointed finger at Bray. Five of his men break from the crowd, unsheathing long swords as they try to circle around a snarling Bray. Chen motions a hand in unison, and the faceless slide from the darkness to Olivia, who readies her stance at their approach.

"You idiot, we need one of them–just have her freeze them," Calder bellows, glaring at Chen as he gestures at Nina.

"She can't." Chen's fists are balled and his brows crease as he pins the fae with a hateful glare.

Aaron makes quick work of the shackles securing Mei Li and scurries over to Emma. He squats in front of her as he fights with the stubborn lock. His small hands work feverishly against the unyielding metal as tears rim his eyes and tiny grunts of exasperation escape him.

"You're doing great," Emma whispers, trying to calm his racing pulse.

Mei Li wrestles off the last cuff and it clinks against the ground just as a rare moment of silence prevails throughout the room. The errant sound draws Chen's attention with a snap as he and Nina whip around.

"Nina," Chen spits the word coldly, his gaze lasering his mother. "Bring me her head." Without hesitation she steps forward, unfurling two butterfly blades from her side as he vaults forward, rushing Emma.

Feeling the clasp give way, she frees her hands and pushes Aaron to the side. "Run," she urges, trying to get him away. Thankfully, he darts off to one of the darkened corners of the room and hides within its recesses.

The air stirs as the blade of Chen's dadao cuts the wind, the tarnished copper glinting the light as it moves. Acting on instinct alone,

Emma rolls to the side as the blade bites into an empty manacle and sparks flick into the air. Throwing steel at her, Chen strikes rapidly, and Emma stumbles, trying to keep the edge of the blade away from her. Her breath comes rapidly, and sweat prickles along her skin as she searches for some means to protect herself.

The chaos around them reaches a fevered pitch as the deafening sound of combat chokes the air. Calder bellows orders to his four remaining men as they stalk toward Mei Li. Blades drawn, they measure their movements and Calder urges them forward. Across the room, a guard is perched on Bray's back, fingers digging into his eyes as the two others slash at him. Olivia's arms are lined with streaks of blood as she hacks at her foes. One of the faceless swings weakly at her with a freshly severed limb, and its black blood splashes over the ground.

The long spikes of the morning star catch Emma's eye as it stands out among the scattered items on one of the long tables. She knows the weapon is too unwieldy to be effective, but it may still be of use as she pushes forward.

Rolling under one of Chen's broad slashes she edges along the length of the table, grabbing at the spike as she moves and allowing the sharp tip to score the flesh of her palm. The pain and fresh flow of blood washes away her instinct to run and the rush of anger fuels her. With a pulse of energy, she flicks her wrist, urging the katana into being. She weighs the weapon in her hand as they stare each other down. The cruelty reflecting in his eyes draws the image of David to her mind–smiling eyes, then eyes clouded with agony.

Her body itches to move; with trembling hands she readjusts her grip on the hilt. So strong is this desire to kill him that she nearly staggers from the overwhelming pull. Fortunately, her unspoken wish is granted as Chen roars and darts toward her.

Emma sweeps to the side, deflects the strike with her blade and, using her momentum, swings the katana to slash at him in return. Yet the edge cuts only the air as Chen dips out of the way. *Your opponents will never fight fair.*

You must always assume they lack honor and that they will use every weakness you have against you. Remember that. David's words ring in her ears as she tries to focus on the opponent before her. Pushing forward, she attacks violently as she searches for a weakness. The metal sings as the blades skim off of each other and Emma sweeps her leg low, making solid contact with both of his ankles. His back slaps the ground with a thwap as the air rushes from his lungs. Her arms burn and perspiration speckles her brow as Emma pivots her sword, stabbing downward, aiming for Chen's dark heart. He rolls away as he wheezes for breath and the katana bites into the earth and stone.

She curses silently as the misstep costs her dearly; his blade scores a long path across her back, slicing deeply into the flesh. Emma swallows the brewing scream, sucking in air as the pain nearly drops her to her knees. As Chen leaps at her again she manages to dislodge the blade and block the looming assault. Heavy overhead strikes batter her weakening arms, and fresh blood pumps from her wound. The bitter sting of sweat seeping into the gash keeps her senses focused.

As another arching attack comes at her, she drops to the side, dodging the slash, and brings her knee up into his stomach. He groans and swivels to create distance between them, but not fast enough as her sideward slash catches his midsection. His steps falter but he remains standing as he clutches his side and a red mass blooms across the fabric. His eyes darken with rage as he screams wordlessly at her.

Emma steps quickly, nearly tripping over the body of a guard dispatched by Mei Li. A deep gash runs the length of his torso; dead eyes stare out into the emptiness. Chen lunges at her and she jumps back to avoid the strike, her eyes tracking his movements. She collides with something solid and a searing pain explodes in her lower back. The scream bursts from her throat and her legs wobble as she stumbles–perhaps she struck the corner of a table, her mind works frantically. She turns to look for the source of her distress. Calder's form blocks her vision. She pieces everything together as her eyes lock on the bloody dagger in his hand. The weapon isn't copper so it shouldn't kill her, but her body bobbles just the same as her legs give way. She falls to her knees as the fringes of her vision blur.

"The manticore's venom has a paralyzing effect, though truth be told I wasn't certain it would work–but I'm glad I brought it." A vile smirk touches Calder's lips as he methodically cleans the blade and sheaths it. He glances to Chen, mouth opening to speak as his body lurches forward. Swirling around, Emma spies Aaron clutching the small club. His whole body quivers as he glares up at the much taller man.

"Aaron," Calder warns. "Go sit down."

"No." Aaron shouts as he squeezes the weapon tightly. "Stop hurting them."

"This is what needs to be done." Calder bends over, placing his hands on his knees as he speaks. Though his tone is a paltry attempt at soothing, his demeanor is oppressive. "One day you'll understand that I am doing this for you." Calder reaches for him, but Aaron slips away. "Go sit down, before you get hurt." Calder's voice cracks under the strain. Emma silently screams at her stubborn legs to work. Her heart thuds savagely against her ribs as her eyes locate Mei Li, who is held at bay by the three guards. Nina stands stone-still as she observes the scene, a fierce light gleaming under her mask of stoicism.

"No." Aaron lifts his chin as he returns a fierce glare.

"Do as I say," Calder roars as he lunges forward. Aaron swings wildly as he steps back, and a solid strike finds Calder's head, sending his glasses skimming across the floor. The fae clutches his face and screams in primal rage, his hand coming away wet with blood.

"You fucking little shit," Calder spits as he slaps the club from Aaron's hands, the blood staining the white streaks of his hair and running into his eyes. Hoisting Aaron up on his tiptoes by the collar of his shirt, Calder seethes, shaking him, and the open-palm slap crumples Aaron to the ground. Aaron's cheek turns a deep shade of red and his eyes are immediately rimmed with tears that he refuses to let loose. Calder pushes aside Aaron's hands as he grabs his clothes, yanking him off the ground as he rears his hand again.

The blur of Nina's form rushes toward him as she tackles Calder to the floor. A flash of light glints from her blade, and they battle to gain advantage. Nina's eyes glow as she stands guard over Aaron, paying no attention to the welling blood at her side.

"You will not touch him," she yells through clenched teeth. Her anger slips away and genuine fear flickers in her eyes as Calder starts to laugh. It is a putrid sound that turns Emma's stomach to jelly. A small purple stone dangles from his fingers, pulsing faintly as it sways. The mocking nature of his laughter dies off, and a steely glaze overtakes his eyes–Nina's hand feathers her naked neck and her eyes snap to Chen, who only looks on distantly.

"Stupid bitch. Do you think I didn't know your weakness–this is the last time you'll piss me off." The stone falls as the chain spirals behind it. Nina darts forward as it lands next to Calder's foot and before she can grab it, his foot moves, crushing the glass bead.

Nina stumbles with a haggard wheeze as her skin turns a horrifying shade of white. Her terror-filled eyes study the powered stone as a vaporous purple smoke swirls from the remnants before she collapses.

"I grow tired of this shit, Chen–finish it," Calder states coldly, seemingly indifferent as he turns his attention back to Mei Li.

"You let him kill her?" Emma cries. Everything within her shakes, and she finds it impossible to pull her eyes from Nina's lifeless form.

"What's done is done." Chen's tone is apathetic and mechanical. Emma tears her gaze from the corpse, looking up at him as his own eyes glaze over, settling on nothing. "In battle there are casualties; things are won and lost but I will continue forward." Emma stares agape for a moment, processing his words and battling waves of rage and sorrow.

"How can you be so callous about this?" the unrestrained quiver jars her words.

"It is the nature in which we live and die." His free hand clamps down on the bleeding wound at his side.

"Bullshit. You feel nothing over Nina's death?"

"The loss of her skill and talent is regrettable, but her death is of little consequence to me."

"You're disgusting. Nina loved you, she devoted her life to you, and you stand there and toss her away—a broken weapon that is of no more use." Her vision blurs with the falling tears yet her lame arms still refuse to wipe them away.

Calder grabs one of the men and pushes him toward Nina. "Take her. If we wait too long to harvest the organs, they'll be worthless to me." The guard squats tentatively, trying to lift the body, perhaps fearful of touching her. "There's no time to move her." He barks, slapping the man's head and offering him a blade. "Cut them out now and be quick about it."

"Do something," Emma pleads with Chen.

"You talk too much." His gaze drops to the floor as his hand works against the worn leather handle of his sword. "Nina's greatest flaw was her kind heart, a bright flame, a weakness that I thought I needed to extinguish. I tried to make her harder and she tried, but she was not built for this. A gentle plum blossom is most fragrant even in the coldest of winters. There have been many wrongs in my existence and atonement is impossible for me, but perhaps I am contented to know that this is how it all ends."

An aura of energy surges around him and a vapor of golden smoke swirls as his gaze locks on Calder. The palpable power washes the room, and Calder and his men turn quickly to find the source. "Chen, hurry up and kill that one." His face pales as he senses the difference in Chen's posture. "What the hell are you doing?"

"I'm nullifying our contract. You can't have Nina or anyone else." Chen flexes his sword arm as he steps toward the group.

"Fucking kill him." Calder's voice wavers as he barks at his men.

There is a slight wobble in Chen's gait just as he pushes forward, vaulting toward the men. Three guards charge to meet him, their blades drawn. Bringing up his foot, Chen kicks the first man in the stomach, who grabs his midsection and stumbles. Chen blocks the downward strike of another and spins to slash the staggered opponent. A mist of blood sprays through the air and the first guard falls. The two remaining men snarl as they circle, each of them carefully gauging Chen. Their long, sinewy limbs seem to move in a hypnotic dance.

They attack at once, hacking with a blinding speed, their eyes wide and teeth bared. Yet Chen moves with a practiced ease, countering each strike. One of them catches Chen's blade with his, trying to yank the weapon away from him. Chen flows with the movement, retaining his hold, but is met with a harsh kick to his bloodied side. He reels and his knee kisses the ground for a moment before spinning to slice at his attackers.

Emma's fingers twitch, yet her legs are still numb, flopping uselessly underneath her. As she lists to the side, she spots Olivia trying to free herself from the weight of a dead faceless. A pile of dead guards are strewn about Bray, but he is hobbled, kneeling on the ground.

Chen's bellow draws back her attention as one assassin drives a blade into Chen's back. His weapon is lodged in one of the men and as he yanks the sword out, he spins around, glaring at the last henchman. Both men pant and the fae act first, wading in with a volley of assaults. As the man overreaches, Chen steps to the side and brings down his dadao in a clean arc. The fae's head slips from his shoulders before his body can follow.

Teetering with heaving breaths, the rise and fall of his chest is noticeable as Chen struggles. He rounds on Calder and his eyes blaze with a painful hatred.

Calder smiles coolly as he pulls a revolver from his jacket pocket. Emma nearly laughs as that disgusting smile slips from his face and Chen rushes him. The muzzle flash is blinding as Calder rapid fires into Chen. Possessed by an unnatural force, Chen barely flinches as each round finds its mark. He collides into Calder, driving the blade straight through his stomach, and the blade emerges from his back. Calder's wide eyes are frantic as he coughs, blood splashing onto his glasses, and with a swift jerk, Chen pulls the blade out, letting him crash to the floor.

Chen's body gives out and he slumps to his knees before crumpling. Mei Li rushes to his side as he claws the ground, dragging himself toward Nina. She tentatively touches him, speaking soothing words in their archaic language. Pins and needles hammer Emma's limbs as she finally pulls herself up and tries walking on weak legs. Her back screams with every movement and blood still flows from her open wounds, soaking her shirt and jeans. The strong desire to see Chen punished beats heatedly at the fringe of her thoughts. Mentally tallying the wrongs done to Nina, to David, and to herself–how many of those sins can be laid at Chen's feet?

"You have to help him." Mei Li's grief-stricken voice breaks through her thoughts, her wide, tear-soaked eyes pleading. She kneels next to Chen's bloodied form, clutching his red-drenched hand in hers.

Emma wavers as the weight of it all seems to crush down on her. Her intense anger for Chen and Mei Li falters at seeing a mother's worry for her injured child.

"He's done so much to hurt others." Emma's tone is not as confident as she wanted and a tremble weakens her words.

"I know, but he has helped us too. We probably wouldn't have survived this if not for him." Her voice quavers as she waits for Emma's response. "Please, Emma."

"Very well." Emma nods feebly as she forces her legs to move. As she approaches, Chen's head is turned toward Nina and he whispers. He gently touches her cheek, leaving spots of blood as her form shifts, growing smaller as brilliant red fur sprouts from her skin. Emma watches silently until the tiny fox takes Nina's place, the numerous tails fanning out behind her.

"Please hurry," Mei Li urges.

"No." Chen's terse tone stops her mid-step. "I don't want her help."

"What are you saying? You are dying." Mei Li's countenance is aghast as they all try to digest his meaning.

"I have wasted my life, done much that I am not proud of. At least allow my death to salvage what little honor I have left."

"No." Mei Li shakes her head weakly as the tears flow freely, dropping into her open palms as they rest in her lap. Her bloodshot eyes lift as Chen touches her hand.

"Our red thread has always connected us; perhaps it has been tangled and frayed, but it has never broken." Chen squeezes his mother's hand as he gasps for breath and tears fall across his ashen skin.

"You are my good boy." She cups his cheek, brushing his tears with her thumb. Her expression drops as his hand slackens in hers, and his gaze slips away. "My boy." Her voice breaks and a crippling sob overtakes her. Emma wraps her arms around Mei Li, letting her weep on her shoulder. Her own heart breaks for Mei Li and an old, anguished longing for her own children.

As Mei Li's tears and breathing settle, Emma helps her stand and leads her over to Olivia. The copper singes her fingers as she unclasps the collar around Mei Li's neck. They are all bloodied and bruised but appear reasonably unharmed.

"Is she okay?" Olivia's brows crease with concern.

"Physically she will be fine, but she will need time to mourn." Guiding Mei Li forward, she lets Olivia take her arm. "Take her to her room and let her rest. I'll come back in the morning to check on her." Emma turns.

"Where are you going?" Olivia asks as she removes Emma's collar.

"There's something I need to do but I'll be back, I promise." Not up for arguing, Olivia simply nods and turns her attention to Mei Li. Emma kneels as she pulls Aaron into her arms and his simple warmth eases the frayed edges of her nerves.

"Are you alright?" she asks as she checks his swollen cheek.

"Fine." He nods.

"I'm glad. I know I should scold you for not running but I'm not going to. You're a brave child. Keep Mei Li safe and I'll see you in a bit." Aaron nods as she touches his head for a moment before walking from the room.

Chapter 29

Warm light streams into Emma's window as the sun dips below the tops of the surrounding buildings. Easing back on the couch she pulls the soft blanket around her legs, trying to push away the needling thoughts in her mind. Returning from her trip to the Hallow has left her worn thin and just wanting some peace and quiet. Her heart aches for Mei Li and what she is enduring, and whatever anger she felt toward her seems less significant in light of all that has happened. Mei Li's process will be long and hard, but she can't really decide if being there with her is doing more harm than good–for either of them. But as she had promised, she completed the few errands she had and went back to check on her. Not really knowing what to expect, she was a little relieved to find her sleeping in her room and Aaron, true to his nature, fast asleep in a chair beside her bed. Restful sleep can be so elusive, it seems cruel to wake her.

With a chirp, Logan hops up onto the cushion beside her, and his penetrating green eyes study her as he kneads the blanket strewn over her lap. Bending his front paws under his chest he settles, curling up next to her feet, and a solid purr rolls from his tiny body. The vibration travels through her legs, leeching away any pent-up tension. As she scrubs behind his ears, he tilts his head back, mouth open as he pushes into her palm. Her hand glides effortlessly through his silken orange and white fur as his coarse tongue flicks out, sporadically grazing her flesh. Thoroughly sated, he drifts off to sleep with drooping eyelids. Resting her head back, she sits in silence listening to the even patter of his breathing.

The kitten's head snaps up a second before the soft knock sounds from the door. Maybe if she ignores it, they will go away? Yet the rap comes again, this time a little louder, and Logan jumps up, vaulting into the bedroom.

"Emma. It's Aidan, open up." There is a veiled pitch to his voice that raises gooseflesh on her arms. Steadying her frazzled nerves, her exhausted muscles shriek as she drags herself from the couch. The quiet pad of her steps sound as she walks to the door. Stretching up on her toes, she peers out of the peephole to see Aidan fidgeting as his fingers drum rapidly against his thigh. She can sense his agitation through the door as well as the other presence with him.

"What can I help you and Ryl with today?" she asks through the wood.

"Can we come in?"

"I'm not really up for visitors right now."

"Bastian's dying," Ryl states curtly, his guttural tone harsh and grating.

"What?" Emma pulls the door open before thinking. She cranes her neck, taking in the impressive Draegloth, who chokes the hallway with his sheer mass.

"The fox cursed him, and we were hoping we could force her to remove it."

"Nina is dead," she answers.

"We know that and that is why we need you."

"You think I can help him?"

"Probably not, but I was commanded to come and get you." Ryl's obscure features twist as the crude words slip from his jagged mouth.

"Why is Aidan here?"

"He didn't know where to find you." Aidan jumps faintly at Ryl's growl. "Hey, this is your gig, but I'm not lying to her." He holds up his hands, shaking his head.

"Bastian's at home and I can't go there." Emma pins both of them with a steady gaze, folding her arms over her chest.

"Everyone has been made aware of the situation, and you are to be assured that you will not see anyone you don't want to." The words meant to assure her only deepen her dread. Never has she thought she would need to avoid seeing David, and the prospect is too much to think of right now. Bastian's helped them more times than they deserved, though and he shouldn't die because she wasn't willing to try.

"Okay," she nods, releasing a long breath as she shuts her door.

Ryl draws symbols in the air with a long-pointed finger and the portal rips violently open before her door. He motions for them to enter and she has to tamp down the overwhelming urge to run away. Crossing through the barrier, Emma detects the subtle contrast to the passages that they create for themselves. There is a darkness to this place that cannot be dissipated by any amount of light. The scratching hiss of thousands of whispering voices needles at her. Their words and meaning are lost but leave her with an unsettling chill, and she hugs her arms, picking up her pace.

Ryl's massive, clawed arm stops her and he once again motions in the space before them, opening another doorway. A low-lit hallway emerges into view as the slit in the air opens. Stepping out, her eyes are drawn to a painting that hangs on the wall. The sun shines brightly over a field of vibrantly colored flowers, and the faint shape of a woman can be discerned in the distance.

"He's in there with Guillermo." Ryl points to the door at the far end. "You'll have to stay outside," he adds to Aidan.

Her pulse quickens, racing painfully by the time she reaches for the handle. Guillermo and Poe are already looking her way as she swings the door open. Worry wears on their faces, heavily creasing their brows as they stand tentatively. Bastian writhes on the bed, his skeletal body riddled and emaciated as a dark script flickers across his filmy skin.

"How long has he been like this?" Emma asks, trying to find her voice.

"Too long." Poe's shoulders sag as he studies his father.

"I may not be able to help him." Her gaze is transfixed on the swirling text.

"Please try. Tell us what you need."

"I don't even know what we are dealing with." Her knees wobble as she strides over to Poe's side of the bed. A minute tremor rattles Bastian as sweat sheens on his forehead. Sitting on the edge she tentatively touches his hand as his face contorts into a mask of torment. The mysterious writing seems archaic, yet she can't say that she's ever seen anything like it. Why would Nina curse

Bastian specifically? Someone would have to hate him very much to do this to him.

Holding his hand, she pushes out with her energy, trying to find the source of his suffering. Her experience with curses is minimal at best, and removing them can be costly to the afflicted as well as herself. Hexes exude a strong magical signature and that can be used as a homing beacon. The key is finding the anchor point where the curse is attached, and from there you can try to carefully pry it loose. If it is not done with caution then the hex can transfer to you or even be shared between the two.

As soon as she begins her exploration, she can sense that this is very different than what she expected. There is no pulsing throb of magic and nothing to guide her. His body is flooded with a sickness that cannibalizes everything around it. A corrosive stream of toxins flow through his system and it is befuddling as it is, magical, yet not–natural, yet not.

She realizes that as she touches a point the illness recedes, flowing backward, perhaps toward the source. Controlling the movement of power, she scours the infected areas, driving it back. Winding through each network of veins, the affliction draws her to a small puncture wound at the nape of his neck. As she chars the entry point, she senses the endless shiver that has wrecked his body start to subside.

Breaking contact she stands and shifts his head to the side. There, almost too small to see are the healing remnants of a wound.

"Did you do it? Has the curse been removed?" Guillermo asks, a thin quiver touching his tone.

"He should be fine, but it seems to be a poisoning, not a hex. There is a puncture mark on his neck."

"Who would poison him?" Poe barks, his lips draw back, exposing his sharp fangs.

"I'm not sure. But that's something you'll probably want to figure out." She staggers and catches herself on the end table as the weight of her own body threatens to yank her down.

"Are you okay?" Poe reaches out to catch her.

"I'm fine. I just need to go home and rest."

"Thank you." He nods, and deep emotions touch his eyes as he clasps her by the elbow. "We'll find Ryl to get you home."

"Emma, for what you have done," Guillermo adds with a dip of his head. "Thank you."

She allows Poe to usher her to the door and out into the hall. With an addled mind and heavy limbs, she can think of nothing else except for being home. Perhaps a good night of sleep will help? Who knows?

They move from one hall to the next and Poe keeps a hand on her while scanning along each corridor.

"I'm not sure where he has gone." An agitated heave of air puffs his cheeks as they stand before the front door. Emma surveys the warm opulence of the parlor, searching for a smooth wall.

"I can open a portal."

"Are you sure? You don't look well. I could drive you home if you'd like."

"You know how to drive?" she asks, and he nods in response. "Perhaps that will be best."

"Stay here and I'll go and grab the keys." Poe trots away, leaving her alone. Muffled sounds echo from some deep recesses within the house. With the darkened skies outside, the residents of the house will emerge from their sheltered rooms and begin their nights. The movement of a small field mouse catches her eye. It shuffles on tiny legs, moving briskly as it hugs the wall before darting behind a bookshelf.

She detects the presence before her mind can form his name. Her eyes are drawn back into the room as a floorboard creaks under David's weight. He looms inside the hall and assesses her with an alien amount of distrust. *You are nothing to him, he doesn't know you,* she reminds herself as she chokes back the rise of emotion.

"Can I help you with something?" he asks, stepping into the room but maintaining a fair distance.

"I'm just waiting for Poe." She battles to keep her tone even.

"I'm looking for him as well." His head tilts with a critical gaze as he folds his arms over his chest. "You're a Fury. What business brings you here?"

"I've just concluded my business." Poe enters and hesitates for a brief second as his eyes flick between them. "Are you ready to leave?" She tries to focus her attention on Poe.

"Ah yes. Forgive the delay." The keys giggle in his hand, and he turns to David.

"I was told you were looking for me. Is everything okay?" David asks.

"Yes." A minute crease touches Poe's brow before it vanishes. "I just need to run a quick errand–I'll come and find you when I get back." He turns, walking to the door.

"Wait a second," David calls out. Emma screams silently for them to keep moving yet they halt, her feet refusing to move. A massive vise-like claw squeezes her lungs as she turns, looking back at him. "Something is bothering me, and I have to ask. Do I know you?" A familiar kindness touches his eyes, and she almost crumbles under the weight of the oppressive air. Unwanted moisture licks at the corners of her eyes, heralding her impending failure. Steeling her breath, she slaps away the treasonous feelings as they are of no use to her now. She meets his gaze, wanting nothing more than to lose herself in those rich brown depths.

"I'm sorry but we've never met before." She wonders if he can detect the anxious tremble in her tone, but she turns on bucking legs and yanks open the door, charging out into the night. She shivers against the chill of air that wicks away her body heat. At this moment she welcomes the cold as it numbs some of the pain rolling up in her chest. Hugging her arms tightly she ignores the frozen tears that streak her cheeks as she walks to the road.

The End.

Thank you for reading *Digging Two Graves*. If you enjoyed this book (or even if you didn't) please visit the site where you purchased it and write a brief review. Your feedback is important to me and will help other readers decide whether to read the book too.